THE BEAUTIFUL LIFE

Novels by EDWIN GILBERT

THE BEAUTIFUL LIFE
AMERICAN CHROME
THE NEW AMBASSADORS
THE HOURGLASS
SILVER SPOON
NATIVE STONE
THE HOT AND THE COOL
THE SQUIRREL CAGE

EDWIN GILBERT

The Beautiful Life

A NOVEL

G. P. PUTNAM'S SONS
NEW YORK

All the characters in this novel are products of the author's imagination, and bear no relation whatever to any person dead or alive.

—E.G.

"The strongest passions allow us some rest, but vanity keeps us perpetually in motion."

—SWIFT

"Without some tincture of snobbery, society is never found; and snobbery is more amusing than admirable."

—DIXON WECTER,
The Saga of American Society

1. 1027 Fifth Avenue

The people who live along this patrician thoroughfare, like those who dwell on nearby (but less elite) Park Avenue, are of a breed who particularly prize youth. But in their doormen they seem to find age a valued asset. Most of the residents of 1027, for example, prize Andrews because he is their eldest doorman: they treasure his hoary appearance, the veined mosaics of his cheeks above the wing collar, possibly even his artery-swollen legs. If he suggests the demeanor of an old family retainer, it is not only because he feels a certain paternal regard for many of the tenant-owners of this cooperative apartment building, but because he knows his air of solicitude is both pleasing and proper to their rank (or what they might wish their rank to be).

But, like the people who live in this gilded enclave of the 17th Congressional District, he takes pride in the neighborhood; though his pride, unlike that of the zone's residential proprietors, is purer, not being burdened by the handsome tax benefits, investment potential or profits which ownership confers.

It is a fine autumn afternoon in 1964, but being Sunday, Andrews is not at his best: you take your crowds, they're lookers, gawkers, rubbernecks from elsewhere, and they'd just as soon spit on your sidewalk as not. He casts his critical gaze upon the pavement, this highly assessed strip of New York real estate which is protected from sun, snow and rain by the canvas canopy of white and gold which hoods out to the curb: ah, there is someone—Mrs. Peysen, and he'd better hasten out to the car and see if she has any packages. No, not today, seldom on Sundays. He gives her his warmest (seniority) greeting— Alfreda Peysen has lived here for over forty-four years—and he shuts the door, nods to the chauffeur who moves on to drive around the block and return the old Rolls to its berth in the garage beneath the building. As Andrews accompanies Mrs. Peysen to the entrance foyer, he recognizes coming along the Avenue from the south, Mr. Dexter Knight.

With a young woman. Pretty, isn't she? Holding his arm, too. Not a usual sight, Mr. Knight with someone like that. He's an odd one. But Andrews is fond of him, and he regrets he cannot be on hand to open the doors for him and the young lady. But he always takes Mrs. Peysen all the way in to the elevator, which Dexter Knight will understand and no hard feelings. And when Christmas comes he will give Andrews the envelope with the money in it, plus some little extra like a bottle of whiskey or a gold pencil or a silver carafe; always so nice of him, and what difference does it make if Dexter Knight does pass on to him some of the holiday favors he has received from the finer hotels, clubs, restaurants, as well as thoughtful or ambitious hostesses, and others who want to wish him a merry yuletide —and isn't it just possible they might also win Mr. Knight's goodwill for the forthcoming social seasons?

For Dexter Knight, stout, sable-eyed, clad in topcoat of palest gray, with dark velvet collar and gray Homburg, the day was rather a novel one, rather a tonic—not merely lunching at Voisin, but being there with Rosemary Grovenour. And this autumnal stroll back now was a delicious reprieve from work, though he supposed everything he did was in one way or another a part of work, wasn't it? If Dexter Knight didn't make the definitive jottings of what some dear souls still liked to call New York society, who would know what really went on or who really mattered? (Let the newer scriveners be as irreverent as they chose, it was still Dexter Knight whose chronicling was the *dernier cri.*)

As he and Rosemary moved northward, he saw Alfreda Peysen being shepherded into 1027 by Andrews, and he was relieved Rosemary didn't ask him who she was, for though Alfreda Peysen was indeed one of the few remaining of the Rock-Ribbed, and one of the few Indestructibles of a world nearly vanished, and though she was indeed a charming and formidable woman, she sometimes made Dexter feel a shade sad: once as a young man he had trembled to meet her, once when he'd first moved to 1027 he'd conspired to wait for her at the corner, acting for all the world like the young Marcel Proust hoping to ambush Madame de Chevigné on her daily promenade. Now of course Mrs. Peysen was a good friend of his, and his youthful infatuation of twenty some long years ago had cooled. Decades! Was it any wonder he sometimes felt this *tristesse?* Yet it was gratifying to know the elderly woman was his good friend now, though if truth were told, he found himself a bit bored these days by even these splendid archetypal ladies who were indispensable to the warp and woof of society's fabric. However, some cruelty in his nature caused him to enjoy the deterioration of this same society, a threat which had been gaining such force since World War II. So that he could not always resist, in his weekly or monthly pieces, taunting the Old Guard while at the same time teasing the new, the arrivistes whose aspirations he found shoddy. He had become a kind of ultimate arbiter, respected by all; feared, fussed over by many, loved by few.

That was the agreeable part of being with Rosemary Grovenour. Though he had never known her well, he had known her for a long time; though he'd seen her seldom through the years, her presence in New York inspired him to compensate for his neglect. He felt properly paternal toward her. Also he could enjoy her ebullience, her attractiveness and her abiding confidence in him without having to be in the least suspicious that she might only be seeking his patronage. Yet even Dexter had to admit being surprised, if pleased, that she had netted a husband like Grove.

The poor suburban darling had been running her feet off for over a month looking for a cooperative apartment to buy. She and Grove had sold their Connecticut house and for the past weeks had been living in a hotel. When Dexter had heard about the penthouse on the fourteenth floor coming up for sale, he had immediately called the Grovenours, and yesterday she had come to see it, and again this afternoon, this time to meet Grove there.

He peered at her now. "Darling, you look suddenly *morte*."

"Do I?"

He surmised he should have had his car pick them up after lunch. Instead they'd taken this agreeable stroll. At least he had brought Rosemary what, for her, could be called a small touch of luck: for they'd passed the slender woman in the dark glasses who was Jacqueline Kennedy, and he'd greeted her and nodded to her entourage who, reading from Left to Right, were all the familiar faces of all the good Gentlemen-and-Ladies-in-Waiting. But for Rosemary it had been a charming little peep-show. (The last time he'd squired a visitor along Fifth Avenue, the only thing he'd been able to produce was a glimpse of Richard Nixon, stepping from a taxi and looking affluent, jowly and unmistakably or unwittingly Sacramento, despite the Manhattan milieu of his current life or his present domicile.)

Rosemary said, as they neared the white and gold awning, "I think I've walked more in this one month in New York than in the entire seven years we lived in Connecticut." She halted, shifted from one leg to the other.

"It's all those flat heels and tennis sneakers you girls wear in the country, ruins the tootsies forever, you know," he said.

"But I'm glad I've done all the trudging around, it makes this apartment seem even more marvelous. If only Grove feels the way I do about it."

"Let's hope he does, darling," he said, going on to suggest that she and Grove come down to his apartment for drinks when they were through.

She gripped his arm, a cozy, nestling gesture. "Dex, that was such a lovely lunch, though I felt like somebody's country cousin. I suppose I looked it, too."

"No. Not at all, of course not, darling." It would have been pointless to say her tweed dress with its rather bizarre cape, though original-looking and of excellent material, was really a curious mating midway between Design Research and Bloomingdale's, Stamford. Fortunately, however, she was attractive enough and slim enough and still young enough, being thirty-one, to get by.

"Anyway, as my neighbors used to say, it was funzies." Rosemary went on about the lunch and how diverting Dex had made it for her with his commentary about the traditional Sunday brunch where men or women of broken marriages fawned over the children with whom they were having visitation rights, and where the divorcées scouted the room for eligible divorced men and vice versa. "I must say it's been much too long since I've seen that many chic women in one small room." Rosemary paused. "I guess I must have taken my Envy Pills today."

"Darling," he said, "you've been earnest for seven years, and it's time Grove exposed you to a more frivolous existence."

"Can't you see it?" said Rosemary. Then: "It's hard enough just getting him to look at places in this part of town. Oh, I do hope he sees this the way I do. But you know Grove."

He nodded. Bayard Burton Grovenour, who grew up in "this part of town," was a sometimes unpredictable gent of thirty-five who battled anything or anyone who represented what he himself was—or had once been: Pure Establishment. Strangers, as well as his own clan, dubbed Grove too readily as being a shade eccentric. Dex, however, found him engaging.

Now as he and Rosemary moved to the building, as he held open one of the glass doors for her, he saw Andrews, the doorman, coming back across the marble-walled lobby, having safely deposited Alfreda Peysen into the guardianship of George, the operator of one of the two passenger elevators. That was Andrews, who sensibly enough placed Mrs. Peysen at the top of the pecking order.

"Hello, Andrews," he greeted the man whose rotund face was as ruddy as a seaman's. After decades of being exposed to the whip of wind which Fifth Avenue could unleash, the hide of the doorman looked impregnable, if not immortal. "Tell me—any emergencies, tragedies or other gambits of interest since I left this noon?"

The veteran doorman said, "I was just looking after Mrs. Peysen—"

"Yes, I know. Andrews, if there is one person around here who is more of a snob than I, it is you," said Dexter. Then: "We're expecting Mr. Grovenour. When he comes will you see that he's taken right up to 14 A."

In the elevator he removed his Homburg and kissed Rosemary. "Good luck," he said. "Bless you, darling."

He was let off at the eleventh floor. He went to his apartment and immediately called out "David," and waited in the foyer for the voice of his young secretary to respond. He waited, not stirring, until the sound came. It was a superstition, a fear, a rite.

2.   1027 Fifth Avenue

The woman from the real estate firm regards Rosemary Grove-nour. It is obvious today that Mrs. Grovenour is serious. This is the time for the agent's decisive judgment: her intuition about prospective buyers is seldom false. For the past sixteen years of her widowhood, Mrs. Katherine Reeves has worked for the realty company that manages this building, and others in the district, for the tenant-owners. In the field of selling luxury cooperatives she has made something of a record. She can be depended on to screen out any objectionable buyer. (Even here at 1027 or the other cooperatives nearby, those owners who, in her opinion, are not of the proper rank or character were not *her* sales, you can be sure!) When she recommends a prospective buyer to be interviewed by the building's Board of Directors—and this procedure must be observed before negotiations begin—you can be sure the Board relies on her judgment. The antenna of her perception is quick to detect the socially undesirable or the financially dubious or the politically suspect.

Ferreting out the inferiors of this world provides her with many delicious moments. She has identified herself with the

milieu of her business life; though she began as a simple demo-
cratic person of lower middle class family, she has slowly come
to elevate her outlook and even her station. She lives amidst
mahogany English furniture in a discreet apartment on a chic
street in the East 70's. She is now an active worker for the Re-
publican women's group in her neighborhood; she has in-
vested discreetly in blue-chip securities; she has become proud
of her conservative opinions; she is unashamed of her conservative views of all forms of modern art, and if her private life is
sterile, a spectrum of monotones—the only vicariously bold
aspect of it is her secret addition to Suzy Knickerbocker's
column—she does find simple satisfaction from passing judgment on the lowly and on the highly who come within the
precinct of her verdicts: Katherine Reeves, despite her oat-
meal façade, is one of the happiest of human beings.

(Happier, she suspects, than this little creature, Rosemary
Grovenour.)

But as a potential buyer, Mrs. Grovenour will present no
serious problem, though sometimes even a name as prominent
as hers can deceive you.

Mrs. Grovenour, however, does seem generally acceptable,
and also, since Mr. Grovenour is in real estate himself, he knows
that the price being asked for the apartment is firm, inflexible; the purchase of the shares in the building's corporation is
in cash, no payments. All to the good.

Yes, Mrs. Grovenour ought to be acceptable. A trace of out-
of-town in her speech, but very slight; she seems fresh,
enthusiastic, charmingly enthusiastic, and she *does* examine
the placement of electrical outlets. You can tell when people
are lookers or serious buyers: the lookers seldom bother with
such details. And Mrs. Grovenour herself is agreeable to look
at, slender and small-boned and her dark chestnut hair is

straight and simply done. Her clothes? Well, they can be called individualistic. She might be artistic from the looks of her—*but not, thank heavens, Bohemian!*

Too bad, though, that the entire afternoon is being used up. And now as she and Mrs. Grovenour are finishing their inspection of the master bedroom, the telephone rings. More delay: it is Mr. Grovenour and he wishes to speak to his wife.

As soon as Rosemary heard the telephone she knew it could not be anyone but Grove. She was right. So right. He was at Pennsylvania Station. He'd been there all day.

"But Grove—it's *already* late. Sweetie, I don't like to keep Mrs. Reeves here all day. You mean you're *still* picketing?"

Rosemary regretted saying it, for Mrs. Reeves, who was on her way out of the room, paused for a rigid second as if the ugly word had suddenly blocked her path. It was funny, and ordinarily Rosemary would have been amused, except that in her anxiety to have Grove here, having him approve of the apartment and end this living in limbo, she could not concentrate on anything else at this time.

Grove was saying: "A lot of architects have turned up. Philip Johnson is here and I want to talk to him and the others. I want to see if we can't keep the picketing up for a week instead of just for today."

"Oh, Grove—" She was relieved to see Mrs. Reeves close the door behind her. "Listen, Grove, I'm serious, you've simply got to get here. Mrs. Reeves has been very patient but I can't keep her all day—and wouldn't you know it, she just told me that someone else has made an appointment to see the place tomorrow. Wouldn't you just know it!"

"How was your lunch?"

"Dex took me to Voisin."

"I know. But how was the food? Was it worthy of the tongue, kind to the kidneys, good to your cuticles and your pretty frontage?"

"Listen, sweetie, this is no time for kidding," Rosemary said. "When can you get here? You've got to see it. And this building —it's one of those very grand old—"

"I know the building," Grove said. "Designed by John Russell Pope or Delano and Aldrich, American Classical Renaissance, very Beaux-Arts. It's just the crowd that lives in it that's not to my taste, most everybody there is heavily wadded and weighted. I used to have a cousin lived there. She left two and a half million dollars to the S.P.C.A. and several other worthy charities—and three thousand bucks to me."

"Oh Grove, of all times—"

"Well, you know how I feel, and it is a helluva wad to lay out for something strictly S and S," he said.

"But it isn't," she protested. "I mean it needn't be if we did it over—Grove, this is ridiculous, talking like this. When can you get here?"

"You're really all jazzed up, aren't you, Rosie? Dex has inspired you. I'll be there half-past three. Count on it."

Translated into Grove's terms that meant at least four o'clock. She rejoined Mrs. Reeves in the immense L-shaped living room: yes, she'd have to admit the owner's furnishings and décor were, as Grove had already anticipated, strictly Safe and Sound; Standard and Straight.

Grove would growl. She knew it. Just the sort of environment he was allergic to. But it didn't have to be, if she could do it over. Though why? Why did she have to do everything over? It seemed that almost everything she'd done in Connecticut, all those droopy minor projects of hers, always had to be done over. Was it going to be the same in New York? For once, Rosemary thought, why not let something be. This apartment, why not let it be what it was? Conventional. But gracious. In the spirit of the building itself. Though you could never say that to Grove. To him all this would merely represent what he disliked most about the entire Grovenour family—or "mob" as he called them. Even to this day he would blast out his old resentment: "I have the goddam signature," he would say, "and I get all the bull that goes with it, I get everything except that vulgar wad of green. I'm like a sharecropper who happens to have the Boss Man's name."

Exaggerated and extravagant.

But Grove enjoyed saying it: it was more pleasurable than saying he'd never been poor or that his particular gift for complex real estate operations in New York had already almost raised him to a financial level of the very family members he abhorred.

Well, she understood what he meant and she knew he had his good reasons.

Just as he had his good reasons for making the move back to New York. He was the City Boy. He'd been the one to push it. Not that she opposed it. After what had happened to him—to them—she was relieved to be away from Connecticut and that whole horrid circle that had closed in on them.

Better not to think of it.

She was afraid to.

She hastened back into the living room. To Mrs. Reeves she said, "My husband is going to be late," and adding apologetically in a manner she'd had many occasions to perfect, "he was on his way actually, but sometimes people insist on detaining him and he doesn't like to say no. You see, he's picketing the Pennsylvania Station today. It's a kind of hobby of his when—"

"Picketing?"

"No, that is, these projects which he gets himself involved in," Rosemary said. "A lot of people are picketing there today.

The building's going to be demolished, you know. And it's an important landmark in a special way."

"Yes, I daresay it is." Mrs. Reeves' tone was vague, dutiful. Then she said, "I understand you heard about this apartment through Dexter Knight—?"

"Yes." And noting the inquisitive look on the woman's face, Rosemary said, "I've known him for a long time."

"Really?" Mrs. Reeves' thin aquiline nose quivered discreetly. Everything about her seemed consciously discreet, from her oatmeal-colored Peck and Peck suit to the single strand of pearls to the modulated tone of her gray voice.

"Since I was a child, actually." Rosemary needn't have said it; she could have kept Mrs. Reeves wondering. But somehow she needed to tell her; somehow she felt she had to break down this air of complacence or superiority that the realty agent seemed to emanate. She therefore told her, briefly, how her mother, a widow, and Dexter Knight's mother, though very much older, had once been friends in Philadelphia, though this friendship never became serious until Mrs. Knight had been stricken with her fatal illness. By that time Rosemary and her mother were living in a distant suburb. Nevertheless they would drive two or three times a week to visit the ailing woman, to help comfort or divert her. (Though Rosemary's mother was undoubtedly sincere, she was also romantic and naïve, and began to believe she would receive some lavish bequest from Mrs. Knight's estate. She didn't.) It was during that period that Rosemary first met Dexter, who had returned from New York to be by his mother's side.

"Mr. Knight is a delightful person," said the realty agent, invoking a tone of tribute. Then reverting to the business at hand she took Rosemary down to the sub-street rooms where the maids could do one's private laundry, and she showed her the garage and the Chauffeurs' Waiting Room. When they returned to the fourteenth floor, she explained that maid service was available by the hour (minimum of three hours), the day or week, this service to be arranged through the housekeeper's office on the ground floor, rear. Maids, butlers, housemen, were all obtainable as was excellent catering for cocktail or dinner parties. She paused then, and in a brisk but polite manner glanced at her wristwatch again.

Rosemary said, "Mr. Grovenour ought to be here very soon." Excitement was getting the best of her, and as she looked around, once more yielding to the room's splendor, she heard herself confiding, "Oh, I'll have to work on him, I'll really have to."

The woman nodded in a way that suggested she'd heard other wives utter the same resolution.

But more than excitement, Rosemary was conscious of the spur of old aspirations, of that hope or ambition she'd lost but had once had in the years prior to her meeting Grove: this move —this leap in life, if she could measure up to all it implied, all Grove demanded, was something she'd make the most of.

She had to.

Any more failures would doom her.

Doom: how wrong, foolish; why, the very atmosphere of this apartment, of the city, inspired achievement, didn't it? Rebirth.

Oh, she had to take out her Optimism Pills.

Prepare for Grove.

The doorman, Andrews, finishes reparking a tenant's car near the corner. As he steps away he notices the man on the side street, the same one who turns out to be Mr. Grovenour.

Andrews squints, peers hard at the lanky figure: Almighty God, what he's doing there is he's stooping down by the syca-more tree and then he's pulling up all the weeds from the little circle in the sidewalk. Then this man looks around and then he goes to the corner to the litter can and dumps the handful of weeds.

But of course you take your New Yorkers, there are plenty of peculiar ones. Here is this man stopping to weed a tree on someone *else's* property.

And now it's the same lanky man at the door and saying he's expected at 14 A.

Yes, he is Mr. Grovenour.

The doorman studies him more closely (respectfully?) : in his thirties somewhere, hatless, no topcoat, the brown hair roughed up from the wind, blue eyes lively, on the go, a man who can tell a joke. Grovenour. That name. Which one? That suit has seen better days, those shoes look about ready for the Salvation

Army. The shirt is all right, a mustard color, custom-tailored. He could be rich enough to buy the whole building or he could just be skimming by. As Andrews is always trying to tell his wife, you take your rich, sometimes they go around looking like they could use a handout.

The only thing: *that stopping to weed somebody else's tree.*

Andrews steps into the vestibule now, goes to the recess in the marble wall and telephones apartment 14 A to announce to Mrs. Reeves that Mr. Grovenour is on his way up.

Grove said to the elderly elevator operator, "Did you know they are tearing down Pennsylvania Station?"

"Yes, sir. I knew that," said the man. "A shame it is."

"You think so, huh?" A grin bloomed on Grove's face. "Well, you think right. What's your name?"

"McMahon, sir."

"McMahon, you're a damn good man," Grove said. "Because there are very few good men left in this city, and it's a pleasure to meet one."

"Thank you, sir." The operator did not seem embarrassed by Grove's statement: he must have an ear for what is true and what is the old bacillus bullfosis.

The genteel buzz of the elevator telephone, and the operator answered the call: "Yes? No, I let the maid off at the sixth floor. She's still in 6 B. The rear service is off today."

As Grove witnessed this muted functioning of the security system (recently installed), he was grimly reminded of the cooperative downtown he and Rosemary had decided to buy almost a month ago and how two days after they'd decided to put down their deposit, one of the tenants, a woman of forty, had come to her Manhattan demise, having been robbed and beaten to death, her body found in the automatic elevator.

Since then they'd seen nothing that had seriously interested them: he didn't want to buy into one of those contemporary buildings on Park Avenue or points east, those façades of glazed white brick whose style was neo-Subway Toilet. He had given up Brooklyn Heights. He'd seen nothing suitable at the Dakota or other places along Central Park West.

(Apropos this migration to the West Side by certain people, Dexter Knight, in one of his pieces, had satirically observed: "Not since Hannibal and his elephants crossed the Alps, has there been anything as hazardous and courageous as the way some of the beautiful folk have daringly crossed Central Park, bravely forging westward toward chic Columbus Avenue, their historical pilgrimage accomplished stoically with nothing but their trust funds, their decorators, and the homage of *Vogue*.")

As a final try, Grove could always turn to the management listings controlled by Edwards and Osgood, the realty firm with which he was associated. But like other officers of the firm, he knew it was wiser to live in a building totally divorced from the business affairs of the company.

Grove had been with Edwards and Osgood since 1958, though he'd gone there by the somewhat circuitous route of a degree in City Planning from Harvard in 1952, and six years working for the City of New York as a City Planning Consultant. After those six backbreaking years, battling commissions, committees and building speculators, grappling with bureaucracy and interior politics, he'd bogged down, discouraged, exhausted. He quit.

"Your trouble, Grove," the Mayor of New York had affectionately teased him, "is that you don't care for this town enough."

With that dubious laurel, he'd gone to his vice-presidency at Edwards and Osgood where he'd mastered the acrobatics of realty *coups* while at the same time pursuing his prime passion or hobby in the fields of landmark preservation, urban renewal and city planning.

"Sorry to be late," he called as soon as he stepped into 14 A, moving on into the brilliant arena of sunlight of the penthouse living room, seeing Rosemary at once, recognizing at once the big presentation on the small face, that air of caged excitement which he hadn't noticed in some time. He kissed her, and then she introduced him to Mrs. Reeves, another of those ladies he knew so well and who had become invaluable in the field of luxury real estate in New York.

"I've asked Mrs. Reeves if I can show you around," said Rosemary.

"Please do, go right ahead," said the woman. She was glancing toward his shoes now: he stooped and hastily dislodged the spiked weed from his trouser cuff.

But they stood there talking about the apartment for a few minutes. He reached for his cigarettes; his pack was almost empty, and he noticed Rosemary's warning glance. He lit up: though he was impressed by the statistics linking smoking to cancer, he was more impressed by the resilience and longevity of his ancestors. (It was one of the few Grovenour characteristics which he chose to accept with grace.)

"Come on, Grove," Rosemary said presently, "I want to show you everything. I think we ought to start with the dining room." She led the way. "You will try to keep an open mind, won't you, sweetie?"

"Yes," he said. "But this is still an S and S establishment and I know it's not to my taste, inclination, disposition, style, manner and not to my eye, my mind or my gut."

"Grove"—she stopped, turned to him—"If you're going to be that way—"

"Open mind. I promise," he said. "At least I'll admit that in

one of these old dowager buildings you can't hear the john flush-
ing in the next apartment."

Soon the tour was under way, and with it the enthusiastic
presentation which always preceded or accompanied any project
Rosemary was excited about: she talked rapidly in that breathless way, as she led him on a "first overall feeling" tour
through the dining room, pantry, kitchen, the hallway and into
the master bedroom. "I'm not trying to pressure you, Grove,"
she said, "I mean, I didn't take my Selling Pills—but what I
love about this apartment is that it is so self-contained. Lots of
space yet it doesn't just ramble all over the place." Then: "Have
you ever seen such a bedroom? This is what I mean: it's large
enough to throw a small party in it, yet it's got this intimate,
gracious quality. Unfortunately, all this lovely French furniture doesn't go with it."

Gracious.

He smiled down at her: her use of the word seemed to be a
recent addition to the often changing flavor of her vocabulary.
The recurring use of one or two specific words usually heralded
some new phase of Rosemary's activities: until they'd had that
crisis, she had been the busy little hand of the cottage industries
in Connecticut, having during the past seven years gone from
one often abortive project to another, from easel painting to
illustrating children's books to ceramics to the Early American
decoration of toleware.

"It's gracious as hell, Rosie."

It was then that Mrs. Reeves appeared to give him the set of
plans which showed the previous layouts and present alterations
which had been made in the apartment. He studied them for a
moment. "This is the only bedroom?"

"The only one, Mr. Grovenour, except for that little one by
the service hall, the maid's room, or storage. This used to be
part of the duplex from just below. Of course, as Mrs. Grove-

nour said before, this does keep maintenance down to a minimum, and with only two in the family—"

Immediately Rosemary stirred. "Grove—I want you to see how this dressing room is laid out—"

"Yes."

The woman left. The tour resumed, though now Rosemary's presentation seemed to have lost some of its shine, just as Grove himself felt the chill of an old grievance.

When they inspected the maid's room again, he said, "Isn't this something new for you? Minimum maintenance?"

"What do you mean, Grove?"

"I mean I've never heard you sound off on efficiency."

"Oh—I just said that to her—she's such a starchy—"

"Because there's no point in buying one of these S and S barracks if there isn't enough room for—" He stopped; he saw the movement in her eyes, the summoning of defenses.

"Actually, Grove, don't think I haven't thought about it," she said.

"Oh?"

"I mean I've had one or two ideas, good ones, on how we could change the plan."

"For example?" He could not quite subdue the skepticism or challenge in his voice: the prospects for space expansion here seemed limited: no other noise in their life except their own two voices.

"Well, for example—Grove, I can't very well show you what I mean if you keep backing out of the door."

He'd been unaware of it. He stepped into the room again.

"I worked out one plan," Rosemary resumed with a determined air, "where we can take down this hall wall here, open this all up, so that you could get one large—well, fairly large—extra room, plus a small bath over there. In case."

No doubt of it. Rosemary was on the offensive; something

even more radical than the impending change in their lives was moving her to serious action or resolve. She was carried away: she was holding on to this chance with both hands.

He looked down at her and he smiled though he did not say anything. But he let himself feel, admit that a new communion between them was, or could be, possible.

More than possible.

He let himself venture: "Rosie—I take back all I said about these barracks. I think it's fine. I think it's for you."

"You *do?*"

"Yes," he said. "For us."

"Actually?"

"The point, Rosie, is that I can see how it adds up, it's all over your face. I didn't expect—"

"Expect what?"

"I didn't expect that look," he said. "But goddammit, Rosie, it's glorious to see."

"You've got a look on your face, too," said Rosemary.

"I have?" said Grove. Then: "As a matter of fact, I have a feeling all over me that everything we discussed has a chance to work out. I'm even in a mood to make up and hold hands with City Hall again."

"That couldn't mean politics?"

"Well, I suppose not." He hesitated. "But at least my metabolism doesn't kick up at the idea, at least not as of now. What I'm trying to say, I suppose, is that I feel now I can use all the potential of being here, living here. And so can you." Then: "If we don't—"

"Yes," Rosemary interposed hurriedly, as if to stress her awareness of this turn in their lives, of how determined she was to match his hopes.

Ah, Rosie. Hold on. Maybe our time is here.

His mood altered; it changed in a sweep. They returned to

the master bedroom, and after a while he said, "You know, now that I think of it, this is a pretty sexy room, has a nice dirty, elegant hotel-roomish kind of pollen in the air."

"Umm. Yes, it does," said Rosemary.

"Why don't we get rid of Madame and try it out?" said Grove, as though his earlier reflections had never been aroused. He contemplated the large twin beds with their quilted French toile headboards.

"Wouldn't it be nice if we could?" said Rosemary. And when they returned to the living room, she said, "I've saved the very best for the very last."

It would be the terrace, he knew.

And now Rosemary hastened to the west wall, the Fifth Avenue side, pushed back one of the high sliding glass panels which gave onto the penthouse terrace. Then she stood aside, the jacket of her thin tweed suit open, her small, supple hands firmly notched at her hips, that endearing gesture he knew well, which often embellished or consecrated some moment of her making.

Grove moved past her then, stepped out to the tile expanse of terrace, the most impressive he'd seen in a long time, L-shaped, formed by the front, or Fifth Avenue line, and turning the corner to parallel the side street. And there flowered inside him the purest exaltation as he absorbed the view which held in its great breadth, the lakes and hillocks and greenswards of Central Park and the myriad apartment towers bulking against the western sky.

And the plants. In floral flourish, set in the brick bed based along the entire parapet, the autumnal russets and vermilions and topazes.

"It isn't too bad, is it?" Rosemary's voice behind him then. "Naturally I know you'd do it all in a different way, but—"

Yes. He would. But it wasn't even the beauty or the prospects which this terrace held for him as an amateur horticulturist, but also the sheer exuberance Rosemary now radiated as she anticipated, shared the experience of his pleasure.

Possibly it might have been a peak, a summit of communication between them. When they went back inside again, however, he made no comment and no commitment, though he knew that despite his earlier reservations he would acquire this address: and with it the chance to enrich, expand the sphere of his activities in the city.

And the chance—ah, Rosie—for us.

4. *The Discothèque*

A slit in the wall is the aperture through which Roy Noonan sees, judges, activates his nighttime world. Roy is the disc jockey —or *disquaire,* as he is called at The Discothèque, which in turn is called Big D's by ordinary hard-core society as well as the livelier non-hard-core society. This sacrosanct dancery is situated on Park Avenue near enough to the Park-Regent Hotel so that ladies can walk there even in the most finely wrought Roger Vivier shoes.

Through the small oblong orifice behind the dance floor, Roy is mighty pleased to dig Dexter Knight at a table on the right side of the room, the right side being the preserve of royalty, local and international. Knight is there with his secretary and, according to Roy's always authentic info, Mr. and Mrs. Grovenour.

Roy likes to know details like this. He is not a common, anonymous *disquaire.* He is now a popular figure, a darling, Roy the Joy Man some debutantes call him, for he can be wild. Born in Amiable, Oklahoma, he has come a long way since he drifted around Europe as a postwar G.I., musician, dancer, jack of all nocturnal trades, and temporary resident in a few small jailhouses in a few of the better watering places. If people don't know much about his "colorful" past, it is only because they never get around to asking him. Nowadays, since becoming a figure in the social landscape and the subject of an occasional interview or article, his rank has risen. At home (six rooms in Queens) his wife, a passive, sallow and intelligent woman, keeps his scrapbook up to date.

Thanks to Mr. Dexter Knight, who was quick to detect his talents, he has lately expanded his activities: he is now an invited guest to many high-echelon parties where his hostesses have come to depend on him to jazz up their sagging soirées with his contagious manner of rousing young and old, leading them in all styles of twisting configurations known, in 1964, by such dainty names as the Frug and the Jerk, just as in 1968 there will be other dances with yet other names. But it is Roy's hope that he will still be making the scene for many years hence. He will be the first to admit he's not as indefatigable or gifted as someone like Killer Joe who, after all, is a professional dancer. Roy is primarily a *disquaire,* and primarily this is his true love. This is his trade, craft, special art. It is why the owner of The Discothèque pays him a mighty nice salary which his wife puts into their bank account in Queens quicker than one can say Baby Jane Holzer.

Roy stands now in his cubicle, in his shirt sleeves, his Western cowhide belt (it has come to be his trademark) riding low and snug on his narrow hips, his rivulets of copper hair moist from the heat, his big ginger moustache bold as a frontiersman's, Roy scarcely moves: within reach of his long arms are the tightly packed shelves of 45 rpm records (no tapes for him), the three turntables and the black control panel.

Watch him now: a record is playing on the first turntable; a second record is already silently spinning on the second turntable; a third is in place. As the first disc nears its rockrolling end, Roy deftly drops the arm onto the second platter so that one overlaps the other and he reaches to the control panel and juices up the volume so that the changeover is made with kinetic brilliance; and then he dials it down again and prepares the record to go next on turntable number three.

But this is not the artistry for which he is paid. Roy's gift lies in his ability to pace the dancers, and to anticipate their moods:

Is the Frug blasting too long?

Is the age group changing?

Is fatigue or boredom seeping in?

Are there too many dropouts?

Do the dancers look like they're drying up and need alcoholic refueling?

Has he caught the signal from the bar that business needs to be escalated?

Is it time to switch to Latin? An old Cha-cha or Samba or swinging beat?

Or does the black-tie crowd look like they need a jab more of the Stones or Hermits or chugging plantation harmonics by Singer Mick Jagger?

Roy knows how to keep this spastic mob of fickleskins turned on: he watches them through his slitted window, he knows many of them, they're mostly all here tonight, the old Crust and the young Crust, the Café Mafia, the Jets, the Pop people, and a few, a very few, Just Plain Money. Yes, they're mostly all here tonight, the pretty young Crusts, and the middle-aged Crusts. Who else? Over there smack center sits William Boggsen and his popular blond flash of a wife, Bobbsie-Ann Boggsen, who is wiggling her fingers trying to semaphore a greeting to Dexter Knight.

Nice to know all of them as long as you take them in stride. Never let them get under your hide. None of them. Except maybe one. But she's not here tonight.

Roy's whole nervous system is keyed, tensed to control, manipulate the dancers, even the watchers. He rarely falters. What was it that woman called him in last week's Sunday paper? A master puppeteer.

Yeah.

Go!

As Dexter Knight raised his eyes from the drink, he found himself trapped: Bobbsie-Ann Boggsen, jiggling fingers, wrinkling her nose to claim his attention. So that his smile, when he put it forth, was less gay than satanic.

And Rosemary Grovenour, beside him at the table, said, "I don't know her, but I have a feeling I'm supposed to. Why is that?"

"I have no idea, darling," he said. "Of course it might possibly be because despite all of Bill Boggsen's money, Bobbsie-Ann models for fashion magazines with an amateur zeal that verges on gluttony. Or it might just possibly be because she pays a little public relations person to keep her puss constantly before the multitude." He viewed the Boggsens' table as he fitted a fresh cigarette into his ebony holder. "I must confess that that swoop of blond hair is getting to look more and more like a gaudy Niagara Falls."

"What I like about you, Dex," said Rosemary, "is your sweet charitable nature."

"Bless you, darling, but you know if I loved everyone the way I do you, I wouldn't be able to scribble a single line—" He was about to reach over to pat Rosemary's arm when he noticed the slight drift of his secretary's attention: David, no mistake about it, looking leftward toward the center of the room. At that same person. "It must be remembered, darling," he said to Rosemary, though arrowing his words at David, "that in the cellar of my world there are more rats than wine."

The target, he noted, was properly struck: David with that faint shrug of indifference betrayed his petulance or anger.

Grove must have perceived the byplay, for he quickly said, "Dex, the dinner you laid on tonight had a lot of fine wine for a cellar like that. I tell you, it was good to my knuckles, my marrow, my whole epidermis."

"Why not?" said Dex. "It was something of an occasion, wasn't it?" The Grovenours had taken possession of their apartment at 1027 yesterday, the 2nd of November. After dinner he had decided to take them to Big D's to cap the evening with a fillip of frivolity. He knew Grove avoided this kind of hangout, but he also knew Rosemary would enjoy the spectacle which indeed she did. (And didn't she look quite *ravissante* tonight? He'd sent her to his Italian, Lorio, who'd desuburbanized her dark hair, reshaped it into an elaborate coiffure. And she was wearing the new black sleeveless dress from Martine, a Parisian friend of his whose flair for clothes and snobbery was establishing her boutique as a minor landmark of fashion. Dex was not displeased by the change he was helping to create in Rosemary; it was merely a beginning, of course, but at least she no longer looked like a refugee from the wilds of New Haven Railroad society.)

" 'Scuse me . . ." David murmured and rose. He moved around the dance floor, past the bar, to the foyer. The fit of his tuxedo was unquestionably splendid, the somber ensemble setting off the fine golden hair.

Dex had to look away, not wanting to let his apprehensions destroy this otherwise agreeable evening. But the secretary's precipitous departure for the john, the covert glances across the room, was too much to suffer, at least too much in view of the unpleasantness of this afternoon; a perfectly normal afternoon like so many others. Except that he'd made the mistake of walking into the library room where David was working, typing up the piece Dex had dictated earlier, and interrupting him to ask if he'd ordered the flowers for the dinner for the Grovenours. No, David had not forgotten, answering him in a voice a shade churlish. And when Dex had tried to probe for the reason, the younger man had been evasive, so that the exchange grew more heated until finally David had come out with it, blustering it out; and what David dared to say was that he would have greater incentive and much more security if he knew that someday this apartment would be deeded over to him.

Deeded over to him.

The sudden thrust, the shock, had completely undone Dex: the bitter irony of how life had abruptly juxtaposed his role; for it was this same apartment which had been purchased for Dex years ago—he had been young and very svelte indeed—by his benefactor, a charming man, a prominent banker, now deceased.

And so this afternoon could not have been more grizzly. Dex, pacing the parquet of the apartment's library, had fumed: he had not, if you please, reached that point when he had to make any such extravagant gestures for anyone's companionship!

David had pushed back his chair from the polished fruitwood desk, to answer him: "Since when am I supposed to be just anyone?"

No rational reply; Dex had been too bitter—not with David so much as with life, though it was David against whom he railed: that short memory of his, had he already forgotten what Dex had done for him? My God, it was just over five years ago when David had been nineteen, that Dex had found him. Doing what? Clerking in that musty Lexington Avenue bookshop, pandering to ladies who used the rental library and bought greeting cards with those coy sentiments dedicated to growing old or convalescing from some grizzly operation. But here was this absolutely charming but cadaverous young man, David Freule from the Middle West, impecunious and infatuated with New York. So that Dex had made all those trips back to the shop and had bought enough books to start a public library, and had finally convinced the boy to quit. He sent him to that first-rate secretarial school, and later took him abroad for a four-month tour. And never mind all the little baubles from Tiffany's and Valencort House, and the wardrobe and the rest, plus a chic roof over his head. David, it was true, turned out to be a supremely efficient secretary, and all personal considerations aside, Dex knew he could not easily function professionally without him. Yet none of this had mattered during that perfectly vile storm this afternoon; it had gone on until almost six o'clock. Over then. Or almost. Just silence between them.

"All right. Finish up your work," Dex had commanded then. "It's getting late."

"Oh, for Christ sakes, what do you think I've been doing!" David had thumped his hand down on the big typewriter.

"The Grovenours are due at seven," Dex had temporized. "And the cook—"

"All right, all right. I've only got a page or two left," David had said. "After all, it's not the Prince and Princess of Bourbon Balls coming—"

"Rosemary Grovenour happens to be—"

"Yes, I know."

"I think you need a drink," Dex said. Then: "I have every intention of helping her get under way here and—"

"Isn't she a little old to be making her debut?" said David.

"Let's not, hmm?" Dexter invoked the old soothing tone.

"My only point, Dex, is that I don't see the point in your going overboard for her just because you've got this fix on your dead mama!"

"Never mind that, David."

"Okay. Okay." David turned and presently there came the muted shudder of the electric typewriter.

Dexter moved back to the younger man. "Look, baby—"

"I said okay, Dex."

In the Chinese Chippendale wall mirror above the desk, Dex saw the reflection of his face, and he hastened away from it.

Fortunately, with the arrival of the Grovenours a little later, and with the drinks and the dinner, a truce grew rapidly enough, and Dex had even believed a new felicity existed between them.

Until now. Midway in the evening at The Discothèque. And again David's inquisitive glance had gone to that same table, that same person in the center of the room, and then this sudden, sullen departure for the john. It was simply too much to shrug off. Of course he needn't have subjected himself to this, he needn't have taken David along tonight. But he knew if he hadn't, David would probably have gone to that loathsome movie theatre patronized by all those loathsome Queens.

Or was he reading too much into all of it? For now, in almost no time at all, there was David, returning, out of the foyer, passing the bar. Returning.

Dex controlled the need to sigh. He lit a cigarette. And then he noticed with a rejoicing of the heart that that person at the other table was leaving with his friends. Ah, farewell. *Adieu. Arrivederci.* And now David was back, sitting down opposite him once more. And once more life was regaining something of its luster, however stained.

Grove noticed the change, the way Dexter Knight's eyes, murky, opaque, seemed to have altered, slowly to soften, and, after a while, to glisten. He was becoming more expansive, as he'd been during dinner. Dex said to him, "Aren't you two going to dance?"

Grove had no passionate urge to convulse himself to the cacophony of the discothèque, the big beat, the electric guitar, the jungle or mountain or backstreet cries. But he hesitated, looked over at Rosemary.

She said, obviously obliged to account for his lack of enthusiasm, "What Grove didn't tell you before was that he had a hard day."

"Not all that hard," said Grove. "Just two committee meetings and one short speech." It had, however, been the third time in a month that he'd left his duties at Edwards and Osgood to wade into those projects for which he'd volunteered or been recruited.

"No picketing, though." Rosemary recalled that Sunday of many weeks ago.

"No." He shook his head. "Such a goddam shame, seeing the wrecker's ball swing into action on Penn Station. I often wonder what would happen if the Italians had this mania for tearing down. Can't you just see the Colosseum making way for a Park-It-Yourself Garage? Or Hadrian's Villa flattened out for a Howard Johnson's?"

"O obscene thought," said Dex.

"The thing about my husband—all you have to tell him is that you've got some civic problem or project, and he's up, all claws bared—"

"For doomed causes," Grove said.

"What about the old Morley Mansion and that tavern on South Street? You got them spared, they're still on their historical little feet, aren't they?" said Dex.

"Well, yes. I do slip occasionally," said Grove.

"I think that's terrific!" This from David, in a rare burst of interest. "I adore those old places, but it would never occur to me to do anything about it."

"Don't talk too soon, David," said Rosemary. "You might find yourself working for him before the night's over."

Grove, looking at her, was still mildly astonished, impressed by her appearance, the remarkable transformation (for so many years she had been all shirttails, shorts, jeans, bedticking skirts, tweedy capes). But even this new façade of hers had been part of a special presentation.

Too special: when he'd come home to the apartment today, he had taken a hasty shower and when he'd gone into the bedroom, Rosemary in a half slip was sitting on the edge of her bed about to put on her stockings, and he had bent down and kissed her, and playfully tongued her breast, wanting then to make love to her.

But no. Too late. They had to be at Dexter Knight's shortly, and besides she had something to show him and it would take time. It was the new dress. And a new narcissism?

"Why don't you two dance?" Dex suggested again.

"Hell," said Grove, "I go way back to the Paleolithic days of the Twist and the Cha-cha, and all those other square-type shakeups."

"If that's all that's holding you back, why don't I see what we can do about it?" Dex was on his feet at once, moving with that suave springing style of his; he vanished behind the wall with its *trompe l'oeil* version of the Place Vendôme. And before very long he made his return from the *disquaire's* booth. "I tried to get Roy-boy to break all the rules, but nothing doing for the nonce. He did say, however," Dex added, "that he'd keep my request in mind."

In less than five minutes the roar of rock became subdued, though this reversion to the less fashionable music of a few years ago did not seem to discourage the crowd.

When he and Rosemary were dancing, she said, "You'll have to admit, this is kind of fun."

"Yes."

"Shall I get out my Nostalgia Pills?" she said.

"Better not." He pressed his hand hard against the small of her back.

After an interval she said, "Are you minding this? Truthfully now."

"Hell no. Why should I mind it?" Once or twice or thrice a year would suffice for him.

"Of course," Rosemary spoke lightly, "considering all the beauties in here, I suppose you can put up with it."

"Haven't noticed. I was sitting with my back to the floor." Grove glanced around.

A moving, swerving mural of women who, after how many hours under how many hair dryers or the hands of how many masseurs, how many ounces of ointments and dyes and scents, how many fittings before how many mirrors, had at last converged on this excessively small arena to present for the salivary delectation of the males, and for each other, the pretty faces and the hair sculptures and the cared-for bare shoulders and slim arms, the dresses cut to proclaim the swell of bosoms, the dazzle of jewels challenging the flesh—all remarkably or pathetically producing the illusion of youth. All these figures of all faiths with but one true religion, the worship of Youth (the battle against gravity). Age, like old buildings, could not be tolerated. Age, like even the most handsome and memorable architectural landmarks in New York, had to be disguised, effaced, demolished. "Yes," he said then, "I guess there are a few choice parcels here."

If he had denied it, she would have become agitated, even suspicious, despite the obvious fact that the preponderance of attractive women could only be ignored if you were blindfolded or blind drunk. He always had to keep his balance in these seemingly trivial skirmishes. He was more or less used to it now. It touched everything between them. His involvement last year with Corlis Wilbur, regardless of how it had happened, would never be out of Rosemary's consciousness: sometimes she would see in some totally innocent woman a threat that did not exist; it hadn't even existed with Corlis.

"I'm not sure," Rosemary was saying too jocularly, "if I shouldn't have kept us in Connecticut."

"Maybe you should have." Grove attempted to match her tone.

"There aren't quite so many goodies there," she said, but once more using this lighthearted manner to remind him of his defection.

"Come on, Rosie, we don't want to get hung on that," was all he said.

"Oh Grove . . ." And immediately close to him, "I'm sorry."

Sorry. That made it worse, since her remorse stemmed from something she herself had started.

"That was bitchy of me," she said then.

He didn't answer.

"I'm sorry, Grove," she said.

Something in her tone caused him to draw back, look at her, and he saw in her eyes what had not been at first noticeable in her voice.

He said, "Why don't we go home?"

"What?"

"We own that great 'gracious' bedroom and we haven't even initiated it yet," he said.

"We can't." She nodded toward Dexter Knight. "How can we?"

"Yes, I know." The logic was always on her side. Sometimes, like today when he'd come out of the shower, her logic was irrefutable, wasn't it? For a while, living at the hotel during the interim period when they were waiting to move into 1027, when she was occupied with decorating plans and the thousand details of altering or supplementing their furnishings, Rosemary had seemed very happy, ebullient. Yet the instant they'd gained possession of the apartment, she'd become suffused with self-doubts, waning confidence, uncertainties, suddenly not sure if the apartment really looked right, not sure if she'd done the right thing by declining Dexter Knight's subtle suggestion that a decorator friend of his might be a bit helpful, a gesture which she knew Grove would have opposed. She'd always had good taste, she'd done their Connecticut house with imagination and wit, no reliance on any of the S and S touches. But something had happened and something had corroded all her initial excitement; whereas Grove, who'd resisted buying the apartment, found himself immensely pleased to be there and particularly pleased with the prospect of his work on the terrace. So that on their first night of official residence, their feelings had seemed to have been reversed, and the experience had lost luster.

Tonight, however, her old spirit seemed to have taken hold again: the dinner in Dexter Knight's apartment this evening, the new clothes she wore, the easy elegance with which the evening had been introduced, the delight with which she'd greeted the diversion here at The Discothèque, her almost girlish pleasure when they'd begun to dance—all of this was certainly understandable, and he was glad for her. But then beneath it all was the familiar and dark presence of her anxieties, or one of them: for this exposure to such a clutch of narcissistic and glossy women in highest fashion and lowest décolletage, all this true or artfully contrived beauty and palpable sensuality, had finally undermined her gaiety, her confidence.

He could say he knew what made her like this, yet he was

tired of having to lean against the too-convenient post of her past, the bitter times or near traumas of childhood. (But whose childhood wasn't like that?) He'd been through so much of it, and another orgy of remembrances would not solve anything for her.

Or for him.

Not anymore.

"Grove . . ."

When he looked up, Rosemary shook her head and withdrew whatever it was she'd been about to say.

Instead, he heard the others now, the intellectual eddies of cross-talk—those utterances darting between partners or couples dancing around them in a cloying miasma of *Calèche, Miss Dior* or *Le Dix* provided a fragmentary counterpoint of the most profound nature:

"—Dee-Dee and G.G. will co-chair the committee—"

"—and if I never *see* the St. Regis roof again—"

"Bobbsie-Ann!"

"Ducky Lynne!"

"—just a teenyweeny sitdown dinner for forty—"

"Baby Jane—"

"—Fiona was there and Ira and Irene, all in Irene's pants."

"—and there was Robin among all those pushcarts—"

"See if Bill and Amanda can come—"

"—I said Billy Baldwin or Vincent, but why, Sister?"

"Isabel and Freddie simply took over."

"Lydia is putting Nonie up—"

"Tony Ammonds, you *are* a camp!"

"That boutique was discovered by Babe."

"Courrèges at her age?"

"They're talking to Dexter Knight—"

When he and Rosemary returned to the table, Grove felt unsettled, his spirit gritty, the evening's designed smoothness now pocked. He was almost thankful to find other people at the table talking to Dex. The Boggsens: Mr. Boggsen, a young man who seemed to be lost in the penumbra of his wife's vivid sun-spotted presence. As for Bobbsie-Ann Boggsen, Grove had no way of knowing she'd once been very plump, for now she was as fatless and linear as those plastic mannequins one sees in department store windows: she had wide gray hyperthyroid eyes, a cheekline photogenically concave, fine wrists, long talon-tipped fingers and a child's waistline. These features were rendered more fragile by the massive mane—the blond Niagara Falls, as Dex had called it earlier—which rose from her pale forehead in an imposing sweep and then plummeted heavily to her almost brittle shoulders. From a short distance she was not an unchoice parcel, Grove thought, though a basic vacuity in her face deprived her of any true beauty. She might have been aware of this, for when she spoke—and she was seldom tongue-tied—she set all her features into perfervid motion, the big vapid eyes taking on a certain frantic vitality, her undistinguished nose wrinkling, her mouth accenting her words with full pursings or taut twinkles; and then there was this habit or tic of cutely pitching the great blond mane to one side, letting it then fall back into place again.

It was easy enough, Grove supposed, to notice these flaws, though in honesty, or if he were in a better mood now, he might have admitted that in her way she was, or made herself, a not inconsiderable force of femininity.

Until she talked. Or rather, until she'd been talking for a stretch. Though there were hasty, breathy pauses when someone else might interpolate a monosyllable or two, Bobbsie-Ann Boggsen seemed capable of marathon soliloquies:

". . . what I said to Bill was . . ." an affectionate twitch toward her husband ". . . if Dexter Knight doesn't write something about my—I mean, the—Easter in Athens Ball for Cancer, I said I would end this long wild crush I'd always had on him." She looked at Dex and David, and dipped her polyethylene eyelashes demurely, though not without making it clear she was being humorous. "That's exactly what I said, and exactly what I meant. Because this benefit next Easter for the cancer crowd—I'm chairman of the Personalities Committee —is very close to my heart. You *will* do it, won't you, Mr. Knight? For me? For cancer?—Oh, listen to what Roy's got going now: the Rub. Almost no one can dance it yet. It's still too flash, people still insist on doing all those ancient wriggles like the Frug. Ugh. Not that I can do the Rub too well, I've only had one lesson from Roy." A toss of the blond mane, and then the big eyes dilating to radiate upon Grove.

"What about you, Mr. Grovenour? Would you help us out? I know you're an action lad, I've read about you and I know you can get some pretty fantastic things accomplished. I've got to make this Easter in Athens benefit the wildest cancer bash yet. Could I take the liberty of calling you?—Aw, is that fair?" A closer, moistly persuasive look at him, but then turning to Rosemary: "I can see I mustn't pressure your husband. I know how busy he is, but, fairly warned, I might press you into service, Mrs. Grovenour. I heard from—who was it now?—anyway I heard you are ensconced at 1027 Fifth. What luck. That view of the Dakota and all. I was telling Bill"—another gesture to acknowledge her silent, beaten mate—"that I think those nice old-fashioned buildings like 1027 are the ones that are going to be more flash in the end. Don't you think? Incidentally, Babe Burtley and Louise Javett have both promised to lend their presence to the Honor Table, come Easter. I can't let anyone escape. I suppose I'm going to dog people to death, but—well, said she modestly—I, we, raised ninety thousand dollars last year for the leukemia people, and I've promised myself that it's going to be a hundred thousand for the cancer crowd. If I need help you won't let me down, will you, Mrs. Grovenour? Oh, please don't feel pressed about it now. Mr. Knight was telling me you and your husband are in town to stay. I consider that a definite break for New York. Of course Connecticut's really become so Out, hasn't it? I mean, the really flash people are all *here*. I was telling Monica Loe—she's one of the new fashion editors on *Fig*—I was telling her last week between takes— I said, Monica, if it's the last thing I do, I'm going to do my share and more to make this cancer benefit the biggest ball game of all—!"

"Please excuse me, won't you?" Dexter Knight, whose composure was usually contained, looked unabashedly stern. He rose. "I've got to go over and kiss a very dear young creature."

"Isn't he really the ultimate in camp? There's only one like him." Bobbsie-Ann Boggsen's admiring gaze followed Knight as he moved to a nearby table to greet the friend who had just come in with three of her companions. "Oh, it's Sabina Clarke. Do you know her?" To Rosemary: "I believe—yes, her grandmother is Alfreda Peysen, she lives in your building, I believe—"

"Yes, she does," Rosemary said at once, with some authority; or had she spoken, Grove wondered, with the faintest trace of pride?

Bobbsie-Ann Boggsen, facing Grove again, leaned forward, and if there had been any kind of true beauty inside her bra it would have been in full fine view. "Mr. Grovenour, may I say something really wildly gauche? And promise you'll forgive me. Awful as it sounds, when you've got my sort of chairmanship, you've got to go all-out and enlist all the most well-known, I mean really distinguished names, people—you can. It pulls in public support. And I can't tell you how much it would mean to us if we had a Grovenour on our letterhead—I know you must hear this all the time, and I do apologize, but . . ."

"Mrs. Boggsen," Grove began, and despite the warning

Pan Am Building bleakly blocked off the south vista of Park Avenue like a giant tombstone) .

How to kill a city: get your free lessons here.

And so, turning his back on this sector of Park Avenue, this domain of the daily sidewalk jam and the coffee-break, this glut of glass testifying to the rapacious reach of realtors and builders, and the impotent thrust of city planners, Grove started his walk northward.

He moved in the fine November night, its clear rawness holding the foretaste of winter. Passing later Stanford White's beautiful Georgian façade, the old Calvert mansion, still intact, miraculously still intact and standing there now to confront him with its silent plea to be spared: he'd agreed, when approached by the Eastside Preservation Society, to try to raise the million and a quarter dollars necessary to tie up the property, to prevent it from falling beneath the wrecking ball of a builder who hoped to erect a thirty-one-story luxury cooperative on the renowned site. It was Grove's latest spare-time undertaking and he had had no luck at all yet, though he took hope from Peter Grimm's success in preserving the Pyne houses which, like the Calvert mansion, were among the few architectural beauties still gracing Park Avenue.

Onward now. Over to Fifth Avenue. Going along the Central Park side until he came opposite 1027, stopping then to peer upward, to see the parapet of the terrace on the fourteenth floor: a nimbus of light from inside; Rosemary would already have undressed.

Rosemary.

Soon now, he thought, as he crossed the street to the white and gold canopied entrance, he would be upstairs, taking off his black tie and the white pleated shirt, placing them not far from her new black pleated dress, these ceremonial vestments of their new life.

5. *647 Park Avenue*

The library of this cooperative apartment belonging to William and Bobbsie-Ann Boggsen is stridently contemporary: the art is today's pop; the furniture tomorrow's modern. Waiting for Mrs. Boggsen is a young woman, Joan Saunders (of Winn Associates, Public Relations).

As she waits, Joan consults the high mirror behind Bobbsie-Ann's desk to see if she looks properly Switched-On. No one is more aware than Joan of how temporal fashion cults can be, but she also knows that in her field she must invest in whatever the moment demands, and at the moment it's her above-the-knees, Little Girl sheath, the white Courrèges boots and, of course, the oversized white owl-like sunglasses worn not over the eyes but atop her black hair. Three years out of Mount Holyoke and looking the better for it, Joan is not pretty, her nose too sharp, the gray eyes too small; but she knows she gives the illusion of attractiveness, or at least the glossy personification of an Upper East Side wage slave.

Wages. She dips into her bag for cigarettes. Lights one. Glances out the window to the oyster sky of this midmorning in March. She consults her notebook:

Check Mrs. Boggsen. Committee replacement?
Grovenour?

Wages. Joan's income this past year has been double that of
her young husband, an avant-garde film maker. Her earnings
have leapfrogged her from the Village to uptown; her connec-
tions have led her to the lucky find of a high-ceilinged three-
room pad on East 68th Street, second floor rear of a once-grand
town house. She has already furnished the premises so ingen-
iously—a mélange of the conventional and the far-out—that
she's lured a magazine into doing a picture-story on it. Many of
the most expensive items in the apartment have been "gifts"
from undiscovered decorators who know that she can bring
them commissions from some of the clients she works with.

Joan's master plan is to sublet the place and find a larger one,
in a tonier building.

It is true that her work does keep her involved at the weirdest hours and cuts into the time she'd like to spend with her
husband. But it can't be helped. Either you swing or you don't.
He agrees. Joan and her husband are a Package Deal. Preg-
nancy would kill it. She vows not to let this happen. When,
now and then, she wavers, she only has to have lunch with one
of her old classmates: an hour with one of those decidedly hung-
up young wives from Wilton, Connecticut, and she comes away,
her convictions reinforced.

Perhaps that's another reason why she's running ahead in her
field. At any rate her recent assignment to look after Mrs. Boggsen's image is working out very well. She believes that success
comes with association. And she is very much associated with
Mrs. Boggsen.

"Sorry to be late, Joan. My flamenco lesson went overtime
this morning." Bobbsie-Ann Boggsen, with undaunted vivacity,

came into the library in slacks by Jax, shirt by Sert, her hair gold-grained long-swooped, this being her one brave rebel act in the face of the current (this month's) craze for Vidal Sassoon's scissory.

"Oh hi, Mrs. Boggsen." Joan Saunders rose and put out her cigarette.

"There's just no doubt about it, Joan," said Bobbsie-Ann as she reached her desk. "Flamenco gives me such a zoom, so marvelous for intestinal zip. If you keep at it your arms and underarms will never get that oogy droop. What time is your photographer due?"

"At eleven. About ten minutes, though this one has no sense of time," said Joan.

"Oh, before I forget—" Bobbsy-Ann reached into one of the side drawers of the desk. "I picked this up at the Parke-Bernet yesterday. I saw it and I thought of your new apartment right away." She handed the small terra-cotta sculpture to Joan. She watched her. She felt warmly disposed toward this P.R. girl; she was not only efficient but marvelously cozy.

"Why, Mrs. Boggsen—" Joan's smile was effusive, touching. "I'm *that* impressed. I—"

"It's just a little housewarming thing. It's supposed to be very much B.C."

Joan Saunders kept turning the Grecian figure in her hand. "I can't thank you enough. I adore it."

"Good." Bobbsie-Ann was pleased: if there was one thing she liked it was to give little Joys to people who didn't expect them. "Well, what's on the wild agenda for today?"

Joan Saunders put aside the gift and opened her notebook as Bobbsie-Ann, not unlike a business executive getting briskly to the work at hand, seated herself at the elegantly stark desk. A tilt of the head, and her hair, like a glittering hood, swung to one side.

"There are a couple of items, Mrs. Boggsen. I wanted to check with you about that replacement for your committee. We talked about your contacting Mrs. Grovenour."

"Yes."

"Also, since we have the cancer shots this morning anyway, I thought if it's all right with you, I'd like him to do the photographs for that Young Matrons of Manhattan feature. I know there's no rush, but I heard there's a chance of a strike at the photoengraving plant and I want to make sure we don't get caught."

"Yes. You're right. How clever of you. Marvelous idea, Joan."

"The clothes got here, didn't they?" Joan asked.

"They did," said Bobbsie-Ann. "And they're really terribly tish." The suit and evening gown were hanging in her closet; they had been donated for the Matrons feature by the new American designer, Lem Taite. Of course she could have worn clothes from her own wardrobe or purchased a few things, except that when you (or Winn Associates) made a tie-up with some Seventh Avenue couture house or designer you got the benefit of more press and magazine coverage. A snob like Dexter Knight might not write about it, but most everyone else would.

"I'd better try Mrs. Grovenour again." Bobbsie-Ann reached for the telephone whose *café au lait* tint matched that of the library walls. She pressed one of three buttons at the base of the instrument and then dialed the number.

Bobbsie-Ann Boggsen did not believe in the theory that you achieved more by doing less. Bobbsie-Ann did not believe in letting opportunity slip by untested. She knew that the kind of celebrity she now enjoyed had to be worked at. You had to coddle it, stroke it, study it, trick it, to fend off the enemy of her world: disinterest or boredom.

What she had, her special status in the New York scene, was something she would fight to hold, something that had not come to her easily: her two and a half teen-age years of oogy lumpy fatness in high school had given her an unforgettable taste of what it was like to be ungainly, to see people like her father, a vain and prosperous dentist, wince when he looked at her; to be unwanted, unpopular, uneverything.

Holding your place, she'd discovered, was more difficult than winning it. And to hold it she had to keep opening wider or newer doors for herself: she had to keep in mind that the end of her vogue could come with cruel suddenness. To prevent this she had to kind of infiltrate into territory that had not yet been possible for her; she had to begin reshaping her image.

How? By association. By osmosis. By always Being-With-It.

And why couldn't Rosemary Grovenour become her friend? Why not? Her instinct from the first time she'd met her last winter at Big D's told her that Mrs. Grovenour might not be as formidable as most women bearing a name of similar prominence. She'd only married into the name.

Only indeed.

But let's analyze what Rosemary Grovenour had going for her.

A pet of Dexter Knight, for one thing. Though that was just one of those lucky happenings of the past. Enviable maybe. And you had to remember, too, that Knight liked to have some pretty (but safe) woman to be seen with in public, and Rosemary was as safe as a sister. On the other hand, Dexter Knight could not necessarily be relied on until the end of time. He was known to turn on people, even on best friends. A person like Dexter Knight was emotionally erratic and extremely fickle.

Then there was Rosemary's husband. This was something else again. Bobbsie-Ann had already tried and failed to reach him the night at Big D's. Not by flirting, as such, but just by kind of projecting her natural female vitality. But Mr. Grovenour seemed unreachable. The marriage seemed tight, or at least as tight as most marriages. This then was a real asset for Rosemary. Yet wasn't there something, some hint or feeling of friction between them? Normally, Bobbsie-Ann might not have noticed it, but she was very much With-It that night and she did sense something. But what exactly? And why would it show? If Bobbsie-Ann were married to a man as tish as Grovenour, she would never permit *anything* to show.

But, if Rosemary could become her friend. Near impossible. There'd been nothing but setbacks. Mrs. Grovenour had turned her down flat last month when she'd invited her to lunch and the private showing afterward of the new film the cancer organization was about to release. Two weeks ago Bobbsie-Ann sent her a batch of literature, but this brought no response either.

Yesterday, however, something unexpectedly good had zapped right into her lap, that accident Minni Ogden Foote had had in Palm Beach. With Minni out, what better reason to call Rosemary Grovenour? Even though at breakfast early this morning Bobbsie-Ann's husband had urged her not to push it anymore. But she disagreed with him. She had long ago decided you could allow nothing to stop or discourage you; you had to ignore the advice of your elders, your loved ones, anyone in fact who thought negatively. (In her New Jersey high school annual, under PREDICTIONS OF THINGS TO COME, her schoolmates had written: "Barbara—Bobbsie-Ann—Storrs will be Mother of the Year with Four Children and a Kitchen known Far and Wide for its Homemade Bread and Pies.")

Well, as for that, her entire class had by now eaten their words instead of her baked goods. The square little bitches.

"Hello—" She gripped the telephone firmly. "Mrs. Grovenour? I tried to get you before, but you were busybusybusy! This is Bobbsie-Ann Boggsen—oh, how did you know? Aren't you marvelous. Don't think I've forgotten you've turned me down. I haven't. I'm coming right back again because—well, we're in a spot here, we've just lost one of our very best people. Tragic is the only word for it. But Minni Ogden Foote has had the most awful accident. Second-degree burns. Her husband called me late last night. They were in this restaurant near Palm Beach having crepes suzette, the waiter was clumsy or something and Minni's dress caught fire. Imagine. Now I'm minus my Minni, and she's been like a right arm to me, it's going to cave in my committee, the teamwork I mean. Anyway, could you by any chance have lunch with me tomorrow? I know it's last-minute, but this is one of those last-minute emergencies and I need help, I mean desperately, and I thought if you—You can? Oh, Rosemary—how very, very of you. Oh, please call me Bobbsie-Ann. What? Well, let's say one o'clock at the Trianon. Oh, wonderful, it'll be a fun ball game. I consider this a Red Letter day for cancer!"

Even after she'd hung up, Bobbsie-Ann felt that prolonged glow.

"Will you want a photographer there tomorrow, Mrs. Boggsen?" Joan Saunders' voice. "At Le Trianon?"

"Hmm?" Bobbsie-Ann kept staring down at the telephone. "She's such a charming gal. She can surprise you. Just charming." Then: "Funny how people can be sometimes. The last time I talked to her she—" But Bobbsie-Ann decided to let her feelings go unstated.

Joan Saunders said, "Will you want the photographer there tomorrow?"

"Oh—" A hasty, strategic decision: "No. I don't think so. It's too soon."

In an exceptional flurry of wifeliness, Bobbsie-Ann fixed her husband's Scotch highball that evening as soon as he came home from the day's labors at his downtown office. The maid hurried into the long living room and placed the Swedish silver dish of sunflower seeds (protein, energy) on the coffee table. And William Boggsen, his bland features brightening at all this solicitude, settled his sturdy frame on the sofa.

"Well . . ." he began after he'd savored the first taste of his drink and surveyed the room with an air of uneasy contentment. (The contemporary apartment had been furnished and decorated at a cost of $91,000—this did not include one still-unauthenticated masterpiece by a nineteenth-century English painter, and two absolutely genuine pop art pictures which Bobbsie-Ann had bought after being assured by an anonymous critic of the nation's guardian of culture, *Time* Magazine, that the artist was definitely "In." This expenditure for furnishings and décor came to more than the price of the apartment itself. This building, rising high above Park Avenue, had a façade of white glazed brick, automatic elevators, TV security system and interior walls not insulated enough to keep out the sudden cascade of bathroom sounds from the elegant duplex adjoining the Boggsens' on their left.) "Well, Bobbsie-Anne . . ." he said, "how was your day?"

"Just wait till you hear, Billy," she said: forgetting once again that she should have been the one to ask him how *his* day at the office had been. "Guess who I'm having lunch with tomorrow?"

"Give up," said her husband. "Unless it's Mrs. Grovenour."

"Darling, you just couldn't be more right!" Bobbsie-Ann was still standing in the center of the room—a habit she really had to break; she was wearing silver lamé hostess pants (size 8) and above her bare midriff a lamé bralike halter. "Tomorrow. We're going to the Trianon."

"How'd you do it?" Billy was agleam with her triumph: this was the nice thing about him, husbandwise, the way he was always so unselfish, proud of her accomplishments. Of course her doings did add some shine to his business life, did give him an aura of glamour among his associates.

She reported her telephone conversation of this morning. "It was the emergency with Minni Foote that helped, I suppose, but just between us, Minni is no great loss, I mean she let me use her name on our letterhead but she never showed up at committee meetings, never worked, never had time to have lunch with me—but anyway, Rosemary Grovenour couldn't have been nicer. Funny, isn't it? After the way she kept putting me off."

"Maybe her husband changed her mind."

"No. I doubt it. Grovenour really gave me a bad time. You remember that night at Big D's. He was unreachable," said Bobbsie-Ann.

"Yes. That's right. He's kind of an oddball."

"I suppose," she said, adding: "In his odd way, though, he's quite a wheel in this town. There was that thing in *The New York Times* the other day, six full columns, about what he's doing to save some landmark, I forget which—"

"Yes, you read it to me at breakfast."

"And yesterday I read he's raising hell about some plan to run an express passway right across somewhere. I don't know how he finds time for all this, do you?" said Bobbsie-Ann. "I'll never forget seeing him that afternoon near the Plaza and looking like—well, not a bum, but almost. He's one of those silver-spooners who go around hoping it doesn't show."

Billy nodded.

"Anyway, what I'm getting at is that if I get that name on my team, I don't have to tell you what that adds up to, do I?"

"No." He scooped up a palmful of sunflower seeds. "What's the menu for tonight?"

"Marga's fixing a marvelous little French dinner." This most recent cook-housekeeper was their third in less than a year.

"French? Why doesn't she do one of those Hungarian dishes she's good at?" he protested. "I'd just as soon go out and have a simple steak with Béarnaise sauce and a good baked potato."

"Darling, we're trying something more fun tonight. It's a recipe Dexter Knight wrote about last month. It sounds really tish. Billy, you've got to develop your palate, you can't go through life eating nothing but steak and baked potatoes."

"We've been married four years and you've never let a potato in the house yet," said William Boggsen.

"But isn't it really wild, the way it's working out?"

"Hmm? What is?"

"Tomorrow. The lunch," she said.

"Oh."

"Did you hear any weather report?"

"Cloudy. Cool. I think."

"I bought those two lovely suits and they've never been off the hangers," said Bobbsie-Ann, lips gravely pursed. "I wonder which one I should wear—my Norell or my Main—?"

But William Boggsen was suddenly distracted; he turned his head leftward toward the wall of the adjacent apartment: "There it goes again," he muttered. "Hear it every damn time."

6. *Le Trianon*

The fastidious, tyrannical restaurateur Claude Troube, of Le
Trianon on 64th Street between Park Avenue and Madison,
sees the two women, the *mesdames* Boggsen and Grovenour as
they pass from the foyer into his ivory-walled octagonal main
room which is ablaze with the glass fire of many crystal chandeliers. Twenty years ago he imported them from his native
France, a country he loyally loves but whose citizens, for the
most part, he loathes—though for that matter, doesn't he have
contempt for the majority of people who inhabit this earth?

As he goes to greet the ladies, his chill Normandy eyes are
quick to note if any waiter or busboy is guilty of even the smallest malpractice of Le Trianon's code. His attention is also sensitive to the welfare of the diners, particularly to those who are
new to his tables, those who might violate any of a number of
decrees: pipes and cigars are *interdit;* cigarettes are permitted
but not between courses. It is also to be understood that since
too many martinis before dining anesthetizes the senses, the
waiter will not serve more than one, possibly two, cocktails; but
not a *soupçon* more. As for the so-called health diets of some

Americans who fuss about the use of butter, cream or salt—such idiocies will not be tolerated here.

At Le Trianon one bends to his discipline, or one is apt to find the next time he telephones for a reservation that no tables are available.

"*Bonjour, mesdames.*" He favors Bobbsie-Ann Boggsen with his smile which is thin though lustrous, like his hair.

"*Bonjour, monsieur,*" Mrs. Boggsen answers. Then: "Are you going to let me practice my restaurant French this time?"

"No, madame. We will practice my restaurant English."

"This is Mrs. Grovenour—"

"Yes. I've met Mrs. Grovenour. With Mr. Knight," he informs Bobbsie-Ann Boggsen: for he would like to inform this *femme sauvage* that she is neither scoring a point nor being the first one to introduce this name to his establishment. On the other hand he is not unaware that someone like Mrs. Boggsen is necessary to the ambience of Le Trianon. Necessary, that is, for the present.

As for Mrs. Grovenour, though he is disposed toward her—she is *petite, assez belle, et s'habille à la mode française*—he must let it be known that she is still on trial despite the fact that Dexter Knight, whom he respects, brought her here to begin with. For it is one of the precepts of this autocratic warden of gastronomy that a restaurant's repute is sustained not only by the limited number of patrons who go there, but by the unlimited number who can't gain entry at all.

M. Troube is often called a snob. But this is too common a category for his loftily individualistic taste. He denies the accusation for the simple reason, he says, that *everyone* is a snob.

After the waiter had brought the watercress *potage*, Bobbsie-Ann Boggsen said to Rosemary, "I've been admiring that suit of yours."

"Thank you."

"It's terribly tish," said Bobbsie-Ann. "I've got to know where you got it."

"What?" But Rosemary was looking across the room: Corlis Wilbur with a man, a swift view before they were lost behind the decorative trellis. Corlis. What was she doing here? Whose husband was she with this time?

"—where you got it."

"Oh. Chez Martine," answered Rosemary. Just as well they were obscured by the trellis. Corlis. More than a year. She was more or less over it now, though even that merest sight of the Connecticut woman could start the agitation in her chest.

"French clothes are too subtle for me," Bobbsie-Ann was saying.

Rosemary tasted the watercress soup and said it was delicious. More than a year ago, a Good Friday, when she'd heard about it. Corlis Wilbur and Grove. A well-meaning friend had told her. Good Friday!

In disbelief and outrage she'd telephoned him at his office in New York: she had to see him. Now. Or as soon as he could get back. Her voice must have told him she knew. He came home on the early train, looking all crumpled, as if he'd been in the rain. Oh, it had been horrid, there in the living room of the eighteenth-century house, having it out, all that awful pacing to and fro across the wide uneven floorboards: Grove did not try to whitewash his action; nor did he try to imply that Corlis Wilbur had been the aggressor (which she had); nor did he accuse Rosemary of having failed him in any way (which she had); he only said that what had happened had been inexcusable and foolish and bastardly on his part, as well as unsatisfactory, harried, hurried, loveless.

Afterward there was that period when she couldn't speak to him and when he finally gave up trying to speak to her. They lived in this vacuum of unspoken recriminations until she broke it: in all her wifely outrage and righteousness she never thought she would be the one to compound the crisis, but that is exactly what happened. Early in June when Grove had had to go to Albany to attend a three-day meeting at the State House, she'd gone on Sunday afternoon to the Fairfield Flea Market and Antiques Fair. That's where she ran into Tom Birgen. Tom, who was circulation manager of a national magazine, always fussed over her whenever they met at local events or parties; he would always make mock sexual overtures to her, bizarre dialogue about the erotic dreams she inspired. When he found her alone that afternoon, he said in that somber-comic way of his, why didn't they get out of all this hot sun and have a cool drink somewhere? And suddenly Tom Birgen was the most charming and welcome human being she knew. She tried later to tell herself that revenge had nothing to do with that single weekend night, that she went into it out of an irresistible need to heal a battered ego, but certainly revenge was part of it.

And when she confronted Grove, she would tell him. They would be even.

But she never told him.

Instead she let him carry his own guilt, and he still carried it to this day.

Unfair, dishonest; all of that. Yet Rosemary feared telling him, a fundamental fear that some part of his male nature, though condoning his own adultery, however brief or meaningless, would never be able to accept it in her.

Not telling him did, of course, give her a kind of weapon, something to hold in reserve, a lingering satisfaction. But she also knew it left her too suspicious of him at times, and she knew that her self-confidence could be shaken by the merest feather of challenge.

Though she plunged frantically into more of her arts and crafts, more *papier-mâché* sculptures or collages or cocktail aprons, nothing turned out well. She and Grove slid into worse times; and her inability to have a child only made the climate in the Connecticut house more oppressive. While rumor and gossip in the community soon began to color even what artificial social life they had.

This is how it was until that last December when, before going to the annual eggnog party given by a neighboring psychiatrist and his wife, Grove without warning called upstairs: "Rosemary, can you come down?"

"I'm not made up yet," she'd said.

"Never mind." She heard him thumping up the stairs in impatient bounds. He was in the bedroom then. "Rosie, listen, I've decided I don't want to go to that silly goddam eggnog again."

"Hmm?"

"I said I don't want to go."

She turned from the mirror to look at him. He was in a dark suit; he'd pulled off his tie and his collar was open. "What's the matter?" she said.

"Nothing," he said, "that getting out of here won't help."

"What do you mean?"

"Out. From under."

How good it had sounded. But she said, "That would be crazy, Grove. Leaving here wouldn't change the—"

"You know what I want."

"I'm not sure I do."

"What I want is not to lose what we used to have, what we used to have is something I don't want to lose," he stated.

"If it was all that good," she said, "why did you—"

"For Christ sakes, you know better than that!"

A silence. Then: "Yes."

"Then goddammit, the first thing we've got to do is get out of this Connecticut sewer!"

"Where?" Rosemary said.

"Where? New York. Where I always said we should have been in the first place. I'll sell this place and buy us three thousand square feet of panacea in Manhattan."

For the first Christmas holiday in how many years they didn't go to the eggnog. For the first time in how many weeks they stayed together all night.

Grove had been right. Their mutual need to retrieve what they'd once had, to find something even better, did make the move to the city more exciting, more crucial. And the life there, as he'd predicted, did have stimulation and pace, and it did look as if they were on the way to something good.

Naturally there had to be flaws. And there were those droopy times when she felt weepy and inadequate. And suspicious.

And there were other problems: Grove had to be gone more often now: he'd become so enmeshed in his outside projects that his real estate activity at Edwards and Osgood was suffering, and he'd had to balance this by working at the company offices at night; this left her a little more free time than she wanted, though Dexter Knight took her to the ballet or to the theatre whenever he could.

Lately her chief uneasiness grew out of their social life. What there was of it. Grove's friends—a whole special little army of them—city planners, architects, Foundation people, were scattered all over the city, and she and Grove would play a kind of circuit ranging from the Village to Gracie Square, much wine drinking and much talk: rebuilding New York, creating urban renewal, developing Green Spaces, preserving landmarks, planting trees or just plain fighting City Hall. God knew it could make for some lively times. But the trouble with

these men was that they had wives, most of whom were so
bright or such outstanding careerists that Rosemary was getting
to feel woefully inferior, and out of this grew resentment, even
dread. Night before last when they were strolling back uptown
from Murray Hill—Grove was a chronic, compulsive walker—
she made the mistake of saying, "I think I'll skip that buffet dinner at the Orsons' next Wednesday."

"Why? We said we'd go," said Grove. "Don't you like the
Orsons?"

"Yes, I do."

"Or is it the others?" said Grove. "I thought you liked this
gang."

"I do. They're wonderful guys."

"Well?"

"I can't say as much for their wives. They're too opinionated
for me."

"You really think so? Well, maybe. Sometimes I suppose
they might be," he admitted.

"Sometimes, like most of the time."

"Aw, come off it, Rosie. What the hell do you care?"

"How can I help caring?" she said. "I mean, don't think
I'm going to take out my Self-Pity Pills, but they have a way
of making me feel utterly stupid sometimes. They make me
feel like a moron!"

"How can you say that?" he demanded.

"Just that. They're all so sure and successful or so super-
cultured I want to go crawl under the nearest Eames chair—
Why do they all have to have those Eames chairs?"

But her levity did not lighten the moment. And even as she
exposed her true feelings, she couldn't shake the way those
women often left her stranded with all her shortcomings and
failures. She'd begun so many careers in Connecticut and
they'd all petered out into dismal zero.

"Rosie, you've got to go easy or you're going to get yourself a whole fistful of hostilities."

He was right, of course. She let him talk her down and by the time they'd reached 1027, she'd changed her mind and said she'd go along with him next week.

But sleep was slow in coming to her that night. She knew the pattern of their life was a good one, even an enviable one. It was the only one, in fact. For she certainly no longer expected Grove to fraternize with any members of his family. As for those small dinner parties Dexter Knight kept saying he wanted to give for them (for her), Grove simply said NO.

Nonetheless, when she awoke yesterday morning she opened her eyes to a world that was negative, joyless, and she found herself already dreading next Wednesday's dinner at the Orsons'.

The tinsel of Bobbsie-Ann Boggsen's voice on the telephone yesterday morning had sounded much more welcome to Rosemary than she cared to admit. Just as accepting the invitaton to lunch at Le Trianon, with the implicit agreement to join the cancer program, gave her an undeniably pleasant sensation. She was ashamed of this. For she and Grove made no secret about what they thought of Mrs. Boggsen.

Yet there was in Bobbsie-Ann's voice a gaiety, a sprightly promise of the kind of New York Rosemary had, in all honesty, not tasted enough of.

The unexpected glimpse of Corlis Wilbur was a sudden blemish on the face of this new day. But even this, Rosemary told herself now, was made more bearable because she still had before her the "cozy" lunch with Mrs. Boggsen whose lively, freewheeling spirit gave Rosemary this involuntary pleasure.

"Are you all settled in at 1027 now?" Bobbsie-Ann wanted to know. "Was it a ball having it decorated?"

"I thought it would be," said Rosemary. "When I started doing it, I—"

"You did it yourself?" Bobbsie-Ann seemed surprised.

"Yes. But it's droopy, I'm far from satisfied."

"I know how you feel. It happened with me. I worked like a crazy thing doing everything wrong," Bobbsie-Ann offered with a show of sympathy. "It was a bomb. Then I got help."

"Oh?"

"Yes. I got Tony Ammonds. Or almost. He'd just come back from Palm Beach, just finished doing over the Vicomtesse Robiére from head to foot—her house I mean—and I said 'Tony, how would you like to work for a peasant like me? Just for the novelty of it?' He said he was booked. And also he refuses to do anything modern. Only French. He's gay as Charlie's hatband, of course. And he takes your eyeteeth. Anyway, he recommended one of his very tish friends, and I could get him for you—"

Rosemary said no, and thank you. "I think I'm going to have to work this out for myself. I always have before. I suppose I'm stuck with my own services."

"You know, Rosemary—can I tell you something? You've got flair. You're visual, aren't you? I knew the moment I met you, you had the touch—your hands show that. Your fingers are full of flair."

If Rosemary accepted the flattery without flinching, it was because she couldn't deny Bobbsie-Ann had spoken in such a warm, authoritative way. And it did give her a nudge, she did feel, at least momentarily, optimistic and determined.

"Tell me," Bobbsie-Ann began as soon as the soup plates had been removed, "do you go to any of the auctions at the Parke-Bernet or at the Madison Auction Gallery?"

"I haven't yet—"

"The reason I ask," said Bobbsie-Ann, "is I'm going next week. Wednesday. They're putting up a lot of Art Nouveau stuff which ought to be a camp. I love to go and see what I can pick up." A chuckle. "Once I picked up an English lord—no he was an earl—what happened was I outbid him, and later he came over and said could he take me to tea and he said I was his idea of what an American girl should be."

"Did you?"

"Go to tea? No," Bobbsie-Ann said. "But I invited him to our apartment. I said he'd like meeting my husband, who was my idea of what an American boy should be. He said delighted, but he never turned up. I think Billy doesn't believe me to this day."

In no time at all, thought Rosemary, this luncheon with Bobbsie-Ann Boggsen was somehow making her limp with ease and relaxation. She did not regret having come: this was turning out to be a bubbly day; as nice as those lunches she'd had with Dex Knight at Voisin or The Colony, even more enjoyable than the first time he'd taken her here to Le Trianon.

"Isn't this awful"—Bobbsie-Ann shook her head: her long blond hair stirred in dramatic undulation—"here I've been blasting away about everything under the sun except what's closest to my heart. And I don't have to tell you what that is, do I, Rosemary?"

7. *103 Beekman Place*

The arrival of Mr. Grovenour (carrying, for godsakes, what looks like a plant or shrub) at a party like this is rare, but the pianist playing at the far end of the long drawing room recognizes him from the past, though this is the first time he has seen Mrs. Grovenour.

The pianist, Chet Darnell, is curious to know why Grovenour has come here, since he is known to shun these *soirées*. Chet, however, is an inquisitive man; he is also somewhat bored. So that he welcomes a new face or two. Adds a fresh note to this kind of evening whose melodic line is usually bland and predictable.

It is a rather large party in the exceptionally large town house of Mrs. Helen Peysen Marmonier, who is a first cousin of Alfreda Peysen. Upstairs, after dinner, there will be dancing to one of Lester Lanin's smaller ensembles; and possibly later still, Roy Noonan might show up to lead the junior crowd in the Rub or the Skertch. But for now, before dinner, Chet, seated at the Steinway grand near the high French doors of the terrace with its spectacular East River view of the National Biscuit Company, plays his own brand of savage breast soothing: he ripples his fingers across the keys in a series of pre-World War II favorites, his middle-aged repertoire of early Cole Porter and Richard Rodgers to which hundreds of debutantes once tasted their first cocktail. Chet Darnell, as Dexter Knight has written, made the keyboard sounds for the *Jeunesse Dorée* of a whole era.

Chet, who was born in Plainford, Wisconsin, and who came to New York with his composer's portfolio, somehow got side-tracked playing *other* composers' music in the fashionable warrens of too many East Side bars. He is a juvenile of forty-six, a hearty figure whose complexion, nurtured on cigarette smoke and the total absence of sun or fresh air, is unblemished, firm and pink.

The services of Chet Darnell—a flat fee of one hundred dollars—are available to Helen Peysen Marmonier or any other persons of similar credentials. Perhaps this might limit his range of employment, but he cares little. The Upper Establishment, square or not, is where his particular gift is appreciated and paid for. He does not want to be a fad, he wants to be a tradition.

There are times, of course, when Chet kind of wishes he was part of the jazzier New York scene, parties where the East Village mixes it up with the Upper East Side: beards and ducktail, goggles and boots *vis-à-vis* Jerry's trims, diamonds and Sarmi—yes, but there is nevertheless something about a traditional evening like this, dominated by the remarkable Mrs. Marmonier, that comforts him, gives him a sense of continuity and the status of vintage necessary to his livelihood, the monies of which go toward the rent of his East 78th Street duplex, his collection of obelisks, his two pedigreed poodles, his two Siamese cats and his one adoring bedmate—a lank-haired, opal-eyed young woman whose father is a prominent minister of High Episcopal persuasion.

"Chet, baby—" A girl he scarcely knows leans over the keyboard; she is the daughter of one of the outstanding debutantes of the 1940 season. "My mother wants to know if you'd play—what's the name of it?—oh yes. 'You Do Something to Me.' Or something like that. Do you know it?"

"Yes—" A rueful smile for the girl. He lights a fresh cigarette. He notices the Grovenours crossing the drawing room. "Yes, baby, I know it."

Coming to this S and S party—Mrs. Marmonier was giving it for her recently married granddaughter and her husband—Grove was not without a grain of guilt, knowing he would probably not be here tonight if he hadn't needed Helen Marmonier's help. The last time he'd come to this Beekman Place house had been four years ago when he'd paid a call of sympathy after Mr. Marmonier's death, the old gentleman having been a friend of his grandfather's and father's. Since then he'd run into Helen on occasion, and he knew her granddaughter Deborah slightly; but these people for the most part were not in his orbit of interest, except, ironically and frequently, when he needed them, as he needed them tonight. He had telephoned Mrs. Marmonier today after the crisis on the Calvert mansion, but she'd been unable to see him then and had instead insisted he come to her party.

"Rosemary"—he'd had to call her in haste—"get yourself together. We're going to a wake. Black tie. Et cetera."

"When?"

"Tonight."

"Tonight?" Rosemary had said. "Whose party, Grove?"

He told her. "I'm sorry to expose you to this. But I have to try to charm the old lady out of a big wad of green." Then: "What's the matter?"

"Nothing," said Rosemary, "it's just that when you call like this and announce a party, it's so unlike you."

"No choice, Rosie. I'm already breaking out in a blue funk allergy, feel it in my navel and knuckles and my shanks."

"It can't be that bad, sweetie." And Rosemary added that luckily she'd gone to the coiffeur day before yesterday when she'd had lunch at Le Trianon with Bobbsie-Ann Boggsen.

"It can't be that bad, but it probably will," he'd said. "Though I have a crazy or misplaced kind of affection for Helen." On his way home he'd stopped at his nurseryman's and bought the fire thorn shrub.

And now, standing in the woman's drawing room, as soon as he introduced her to Rosemary he presented the green-leafed, orange-berried plant.

"Helen," he said to Mrs. Marmonier, "I remembered that garden of yours and by way of trying to bribe my way into your cautious heart, I want you to have this *Pyracantha coccineau*. It's all ready to plant. It can also be espaliered."

"Grove—I suppose you can really be very nice when you want to. It's beautiful. I love fire thorn and I haven't a single one." The elderly woman was dressed to the nines and wearing what for her was quite a show of heirloom jewels.

"We ought to stash it in something damp," said Grove.

"Yes." Mrs. Marmonier took the shrub to her cutting room next to the butler's pantry. The old girl was really quite an anachronism, Grove thought. (It was said of her that she still persisted in her habit of using the Social Register instead of the telephone directory when she wanted to look up someone's number or address.)

As he waited for her to return, Grove noticed the pianist across the room and said to Rosemary that Chet Darnell had changed comparatively little since those days in 1947 when Grove would motorcycle down from Cambridge and some-

times end up at the bar where Chet played; he could sign the
tab there, he said, and, as it sometimes happened, meet some
divorcée who could make a harassed or overworked junior forget Harvard. (As well as Radcliffe.)

"Now Grove—" Mrs. Marmonier was back; her eyes
sparkled with azure shrewdness. "Grove, I'm absolutely tickled
with that fire thorn. As nice a bribe as I've ever been given. And
I think it's only fair to tell you straight off that my dreadful
lawyer is just in the process of disposing of that dreadful department of internal revenue, and I'm scratching my name
from all charity lists."

"Helen"—he swung his arm roughly around her—"I weep
for you, but you've got to hear me out. I'm in a bad corner, can
we go somewhere quiet and neck for a while?"

Mrs. Marmonier said, "This is a party and you haven't met
anyone yet. I believe you know my granddaughter Deborah,
but there are any number of people you don't. Now you two
come along."

The introductions took more time than he cared to part
with. The indomitable Mrs. Marmonier, a social parliamentar-
ian of considerable force, steered them around the immense
drawing room which was walled in lime *moiré* and which ac-
commodated two marble fireplaces; she presented them to the
newly married couple and to most of the others, a mixed bag
of different generations. He knew a few of the guests, faces
to whom he'd been nodding for years. Alfreda Peysen was there
and so was Dexter Knight.

"Well, Rosemary—" Knight's stance, his always rather
baroque dinner clothes, his large carved ivory cigarette holder,
combined to divert the eye from his stoutness. "For someone
like your husband who keeps telling me he has no time for
those exquisite little dinners I want to give for you, for someone like Grove to beg off all the time, and then come running

the minute Helen Marmonier throws a few snacks on the Louis Seize table—all I can say is: *ce n'est pas gentile* on your part."

"Listen, Dexter," said Grove, "I'm here on business."

"You vulgar soul, I don't believe it."

"He really is," said Rosemary.

"See here"—Knight touched his silver-streaked hair—"I know you, Grove. You're a snob of the worst kind, the kind who's a traitor to his class." And going on then, as he often did, transposing the Knightian present into the Proustian past: "You effect all this preference for the Elstirs or the Bergottes, but the instant the Duchesse de Guermantes gives a gala, you come flying, don't you?"

Yes, Baron, Grove might have said, taking some license. Instead, he answered, "I'm strictly a last-minute guest, it's all strictly business."

"That's true, Dex," said Rosemary.

"Bless you, darling. You're a dutiful wife," Knight said. "And if I didn't love you I'd let it be known all over town that you had lunch with Bobbsie-Ann Boggsen at Le Trianon. For shame. Now I've nothing against her, as you know. That is, she's all right if one is impressed by temporary phenomenon. *Chacun à son goût.* But if one is concerned with permanence, well, that's different. People ask me why do I persist in measuring society with an obsolete yardstick? To this I reply, someone must maintain the basic currency. Now it is true that certain of these *jeunes femmes* like Bobbsie-Ann are only interested in wild antics and clothes or acting in little underground pop movies, or going in for anything they like to call 'camp'—an expression, by the way, despite its pretentious elevation in the *Partisan Review,* that every gay little chorus boy used to use as far back as 1925. All this is well and good, but your friend Bobbsie-Ann Boggsen does not deal in true, classic, official currency.

And that, *ma chérie,* is still preserved at the Fort Knoxes of the Helen Marmoniers and Alfreda Peysens. Now if we all flew off trying to be young and camp, buying every new wildness, every new style, every new chic, we would be socially bankrupt. Someone must maintain the currency. But people lose perspective, don't they? Even a bright little entertainer like that Chet Darnell over there, who should be brighter, said to me earlier, didn't I think this sort of thing—these people here tonight—didn't I think they were a slowly vanishing breed? 'My dear boy,' I said to him, 'the fact that Venice is slowly sinking into the sea doesn't diminish its beauty, does it? On the contrary it makes it all the more precious.'" He paused. "Oh, please do excuse me, I just remembered I promised to call David."

Rosemary, watching him leave, shook her head. "This keeps happening to him now, the way he suddenly takes off to make sure David isn't out somewhere on the loose."

"What happened to Helen?" Grove was preoccupied; he kept looking around the crowded room. "She's trying to stall me, you know that, don't you?"

"I suppose she is, but you shouldn't press her too hard, Grove."

"Rosie, if I don't get that wadful by Monday latest, that chimney of the Calvert house gets the wreckers' ball and—"

"Sweetie, don't work yourself up," Rosemary said.

Grove nodded. He beckoned over one of the white-coated waiters and ordered a bourbon on the rocks for Rosemary and a vodka martini "straight up" for himself.

"There's one thing about these wakes," Grove said after the man had brought their drinks, "at least the booze is first-rate."

Mrs. Marmonier's granddaughter, Deborah, in a one-shouldered dress stopped by and introduced them to the woman she was with, a Mrs. Stelward. Christine Stelward, who seemed to regard herself as quite a parcel. Which, he supposed, she was.

As the S and S small talk got under way, however, Grove kept his attention alert for sight of Mrs. Marmonier.

"—well actually," he heard Rosemary saying to the two women, "I'm afraid I've got myself pretty much involved with the Cancer Fund."

"Don't we all— in one fund or another?" replied Mrs. Marmonier's granddaughter. Her arms and the swath of bare shoulder were deeply bronzed.

Mrs. Stelward took out a cigarette and Grove lit it for her: unlike Deborah Marmonier, she was untanned, her skin being pale, probably delicate; her dark titian hair was long and thick and swept back into a Grecian chignon which was circled by a small band of pearls. She wore an emerald bracelet with matching earrings. (Weren't they wearing more of the real stuff now than when he was a kid? And he thought of that great choker of pearls his mother had come by via an inheritance from his father's first cousin, Anne Grovenour. The gift had come in a box lined in gray velvet and partitioned so that in one slot lay the genuine pearls, in the other the false set in perfect imitation. Grove's father, whose inherited income allowed him to be a law professor first at Columbia, later at Harvard, used to say he wished he could pay the real estate taxes on their old East 87th Street house, since sold, by giving the city "one pearl per annum.")

He was finishing the martini when he heard Rosemary saying, "Mrs. Stelward, I've been admiring those pearls, I mean the way you've done them in your hair. It's—it's really terribly tish."

Grove looked at her: he was sure he had not heard her correctly.

"Thank you," Mrs. Stelward said. (Miss Porter's, Welles-ley, was Grove's guess and he was seldom wrong.) "But they come loose and I lose them. This one is from Woolworth's."

"Our gang," Mrs. Marmonier's granddaughter (Foxcroft, Sweet Briar) resumed the conversation, "is going mad planning that theatre benefit for the Arthritis Association. Though I wasn't much help this year, and I feel awfully guilty about it. All the real work was done while Jim and I were at Montego Bay, and—"

Another young woman, in a strapless gown and accompanied by her husband, was beckoned into the group by Mrs. Marmonier's granddaughter.

"What was everyone talking about before George and I burst upon the scene?" said the strapless one (Ethel Walker, Vassar) .

"Mrs. Grovenour's cancer work and my finking out on our arthritis program," said Deborah.

"As a matter of fact," said the strapless one, whose fleshy young throat was adazzle with diamonds, "my darling husband here just got through telling me that if he put in the time and effort for his company that I do for cerebral palsy and arterio-sclerosis, he'd be a rich gent today."

Ah, Grove thought, the chic little white lies are popping to-night. Restively, he turned to the Woolworth pearls: "And what good charity do you toil for, Mrs. Stelward?"

"What?" She peered at him. "Oh—none at all."

"Really?" He found himself not undeservedly stranded with his pompous question.

"Mrs. Grovenour," the strapless one said, "who's doing the decoration for your Easter in Athens thing?"

"Mr."—Rosemary puckered her brow—"Tony Ammonds. I hear it's going to be wild. I haven't seen the sketches, but the other day I"—another hesitation—"but it's going to be not at all what people expect, I mean it's going to be real camp."

Grove regarded her anew, more sharply this time. He murmured something unintelligible and turned away to catch up
with another of the white-coated lackeys. Presently he was
downing his second vodka martini.

Just what, he asked himself in dismay as he moved off in
quest of his hostess, did Rosemary think she was trying to do?
Why the hell was she trying to sound like everyone but herself?

He found Mrs. Marmonier at the foot of the hall stairway, but
she was on her way to confer with the man from the catering
service and Grove did understand, didn't he?

At half-past nine dinner was announced. And so into the
dining room with its walls of resplendent chinoiserie. Here he
and Rosemary parted. There were four great round tables each
seating twelve, and a long table of fourteen; each serviced by
two waiters, each featuring a different kind of china (Grove's
was Lowestoft), silver and crystal. All tables held fresh-cut
flowers and were dominated by two gold candelabra.

Ah, he thought, the old girl had emptied the family closets
and coffers tonight. Strictly for the Undiluted. The Sure of the
Sure. Not one of those evenings when she spikes up the tepid
brew with a visiting symphony conductor, prominent politician
or celebrated playwright. No, this was Interbreeding Night.
And strange bedfellows would not be made or mated.

Grove found himself seated at a distance from Mrs. Marmonier. He was set squarely among some of the finest roses in
the S and S flower garden, including Mrs. Woolworth-pearls
Stelward, whose escort, he discovered, was a friend of his,
Henford (Hank) Hartley, a dilettante in the arts but lineage
unsullied. As for Mrs. Stelward, she did not say much to Grove,
either because he'd managed to insult her earlier or because
she had nothing profound to contribute except her quite choice
frontage. Or because it was not easy to get a conversation fired

up here against the table-babble which at this poignant moment, between the inevitable smoked salmon and the breast of
Cornish hen, was fraught with all the cosmic significance of a
travel poster:

". . . but in Positano you simply never get the sun in the
afternoon."
". . . the Greek Government dug out a new harbor there,
so we are able to sail right in."
". . . there's this darling little primitive island off Palm
Beach that Minni Ogden Foote told me about—"
". . . the thing about the Corviglia is after dinner you can
ski by torchlight—"
". . . I really responded to St. Anton."
". . . the Monte Carlo crowd at the Hôtel de Paris, I mean
for sheer hilarious vulgarity. . . ."
". . . but even in April, Rome is bursting with busloads
of Germans—"
". . . and there's this cunning boutique in St. Moritz that
sells those divine string bodices—like Sir Hillary's under-
vests, you know?"
". . . but even at Cap d'Antibes you can see the campers!"
". . . the thing about Yugoslavia, it's all very interesting,
but bleak, my dear, I mean for sheer bleakness—"

It wasn't until after eleven o'clock, when the Lester Lanin
ensemble was piping forth upstairs, that Grove was able to corner Helen Marmonier.

"Grove—" the elderly woman said as soon as they were
seated in the morning room at the rear of the second floor, a
small room with one small, perfect fireplace and paneled walls
tinted ivory—"Grove, now let's see how fast you can get on
with this. By the way, I think your wife is quite spiffy."

"Thank you, Helen," he said. "Okay. I'll plow right in."

But where to start, how to begin? He'd juggled a number of tactics, too many, so that he was not really certain which was most advantageous. She had already served warning to him about her taxes and no more charities for the present. This lively woman whose wealth (sugar and railroads) and whose late husband's fortune (shipping) was incalculable, and therefore all the harder for anyone to reach. He glanced up to the fireplace wall, to the portrait of the late Mr. Marmonier stiffly sitting beside a globe of the world.

"Let me say, Grove, if I may, that if you hadn't gone out of your way to alienate your family, they would probably have helped you now, far more than I ever could. It's been a perfectly dreadful year, you know. Not only taxes, but—"

She was into the second chorus of the perennial Blues-of-the-Rich.

"Helen," he said, "just let *me* say, if I may, that I had no choice. Those Grovenours who are still alive and dyspeptic today are not, as you know, on my side of the line, and they are so perniciously feisty as to embarrass me. They've embarrassed me ever since I was old enough to—"

"Now you are sounding just like your father," said Mrs. Marmonier.

"I am?" Grove knew that a few more words and he would succeed in getting her finely curved Roman nose out of joint. "Helen, you know I wouldn't be stupid or rude enough to foul up your party with this problem unless the situation was critical."

"Of course I know that," she said. "Forgive me."

Into this gracious leeway Grove plunged at once. These gracious moments of the Marmoniers of the world were charming and welcome, but he was all too aware that good manners or *politesse* was as natural to them as were their sudden jabs of impatience, cruelty, indifference or glacial coldness. "Helen" —he leaned forward in the black and gold Directoire chair; he'd decided on his course—"first off, I'm not trying to put the bite on you for a Giveaway program, nothing like that." He paused. "I'm not going to give you the old bacillus bullfosis." He paused again. "And this matter happens also to be something more than just a tax deduction, it's a hell of a lot more consequential than that. You know the Calvert mansion on Park?"

"Of course."

"Did you know it's going to be torn down beginning next Tuesday at exactly eight A.M.?"

"No, I didn't know that, Grove. What a pity. But heaven knows it's happening all the time," said Mrs. Marmonier.

Happening all the time. People thought that merely by saying it, they could shake off their responsibility.

"But to happen to a great Georgian house like this, Helen! This is one of those Stanford White babies that are practically extinct!" he declared.

"There's no point in raising your voice, Grove."

"Listen, Helen, Tuesday morning, unless I get action before that, the Mike Tavelli Wrecking Company sets up the scaffolding for the sidewalk shed and proceeds to slug down the chimneys and tear open the roof and let the weather in. Do you know why they do it that way and that quick? To ruin the place before any movement starts up to save it. I've been working on this for over three months, Helen, and today, this morning, before I called you, they dropped the knife on me. Can I tell you about it?"

He'd been in his office on the 38th floor of Edwards and Osgood on Madison Avenue less than an hour this morning when John Waine Edwards, the Chairman of the Board, asked to see him and gave him the sorry word: legal counsel for the

Calvert family had advised the realty firm that they could wait no longer for the property to be saved. "Now I know, Grove," Edwards had said, "that you've taken a personal responsibility about this. I know—and I readily go along with you—how you feel about getting that house into the proper hands and preserving it. But we still have our buyer. Ben Yurkas is, after all, in the business of building."

Yes, Grove said he knew all that; he'd been the one who'd brought Yurkas into the sale, but the man had bought the house with the promise to Grove that he would hold it for a minimum of four months before tearing it down; that if Grove could tie it up for preservation before that, he would release it.

"Well," Edwards said, "what's happened is simple. Yurkas has simply changed his mind. He doesn't want to wait anymore, and the Calvert family has given him the green light to go ahead and start his building. He's got Mike Tavelli squared off to begin demolition. I interceded for you, Grove. I've got the Calvert family to give us this weekend, plus next Monday, to find a buyer who's willing to take it over. Yurkas has promised he'll wait until then and if you can't bring in a bona fide offer from one of your leads, it's farewell to the Calvert place. I'm afraid, Grove, that's about it."

The day was frantic, one of the most frantic Grove had ever gone through, and during which he telephoned, taxied, walked, ran all over Manhattan backtracking to all the people whom he had approached earlier. He got nowhere. He turned then to the last source: the city. Downtown again, and desperate sessions with people from the Planning Commission and the Preservation Commission and the Commission for Foreign Service Development; it was out of the latter that he found his single lead, a foreign consulate who would need new headquarters: the Calvert property would be ideal.

"But of course, Helen," Grove reported now, "that consulate

has such a hell of a lot of red tape to cut through, it would take at least a month, minimum, to get a money signature from them. But I'll get it. However, what happens in the meanwhile? I've got to put a deal into Mr. Yurkas' fist by no later than Monday night, or it's no cigars."

"You haven't told me the price."

"A million, two four five." Grove lit a cigarette, going on immediately, carried forth by what he felt was the first breath of encouragement. "The thing is, Helen, if they tear down the Calvert mansion, that will kill the corner and then the two houses adjacent will go. That's the pattern. Historically, aesthetically, a famous, entire Park Avenue block front is destroyed, not a brick or a stone left and—"

"I see," said Mrs. Marmonier. "But you know, Grove, I've simply reached the point where I'll have no more part in these hopeless—and they *do* all seem hopeless—campaigns to save something or someone. New York has to learn to look after itself. It's a big girl now. It doesn't need a nanny rushing about every time it wets its panties or falls down."

"But this is not one of these long-range projects, this is temporary, Helen. A month or two. Your money can't possibly be tied up longer, unless you—"

"What I'm trying to say, Grove, is that it's really too discouraging, too tiresome, you've no idea how tired I am having to pull other people's chestnuts out of the fire. And aside from the loss of all that interest on—"

"All right." Grove abandoned his appeal to the lofty side of her character, and turned to something more pragmatic. "All right. Then I'd like to tell you one more reason, Helen, why you ought to put aside your objections, though I know in your case they're justified enough. But there's another aspect that cannot be ignored: every time one of those great last-standing landmarks gets cut down and a white brick junk heap gets put up, the houses and apartments of all your family begin to depreciate. This is something no one thinks about. It's invisible now, seemingly no connection, it's all so gradual. But in fifteen years from now, incredible as it may seem today, this section of New York can suddenly look like a high-rent slum, glutted with high-rise eyesores, a graveyard of speculators and shortsighted people who should have known better. Suddenly then, 740 Park or 940 Fifth or One Gracie Square—and, Helen, 103 Beekman Place, plus your son's new house on Sutton Place, plus your other son's duplex on 69th Street, just to mention a few we know—do you know what's going to happen to all these properties the minute people realize that the neighborhood they always thought was impeccable is falling apart? Do I have to tell you what could happen? In other words, Helen, the money I need now is for more than just a noble act of goodwill, a hell of a lot more, isn't it?"

He waited. Helen Peysen Marmonier's face was grave.

"I understand," she said then. "Why didn't you tell me all this to begin with? At least there's some constructive point to the whole thing. Too bad though, such a poor time for me, I just wouldn't dare call my lawyer or the bank, they're cross enough with me as it is." Presently an afterthought: "Have you talked to Alfreda about this?"

He said he did not know Alfreda Peysen well enough.

"If you'd like I'll talk to her," offered Mrs. Marmonier.

"Would you?" But then he said: "I'll get her here. Don't move, Helen."

He went upstairs. At the opposite end of the long room where the orchestra played, there were half a dozen gilt-painted café tables. But Alfreda Peysen was not among the people there. He did happen to see Rosemary, however. She was dancing the Twertch or the Swilch with the husband of the strapless one. She looked gay enough, if not almost beatific.

Grove hurried down to the drawing room then. He found
Alfreda Peysen sitting near one of the fireplaces, flanked by her
granddaughter Sabina Peysen Clarke, a young man and Dexter
Knight. The old lady was immersed in conversation and he
could see he couldn't break it up, at least not then. He returned
to the morning room.

By the evening's end the best he could walk away with
was Mrs. Marmonier's promise to talk to Alfreda Peysen tomorrow. "A whole goddam night of double-barreled effort
and all I've got to show for it is a pale, polite promise," he stated
as soon as he and Rosemary were in the taxi, homeward bound.
He did not feel like walking.

"Oh, I wouldn't be all that sure," said Rosemary.

"I am though."

"Don't be so pessimistic."

"The energy, the manpower I wasted!" Grove slumped
lower into the seat, and there was silence. Then out of his
rampant discouragement and irritability he said, "By the way,
what were you supposed to be constructing tonight?"

"What do you mean?"

"I mean those sounds I heard you uttering, like something
out of a cartoon. I couldn't believe it was coming from you,
the way you were talking to that gang of S and S charity sisters."

"Well—what did you expect? I was self-conscious enough
as it was," Rosemary protested.

"But why?"

"Why? Because I knew how you felt about most of those people and you were watching me, looking over my shoulder. I became so inhibited, I didn't know what I was saying—except that
whatever I would have said would have been wrong as far as
you're concerned!"

"Aw, come on, Rosie, you can't seriously—"

"I happen to be very serious."

"But why the hell would you worry about that crew, much less about me?"

"Well, I do worry. I mean I don't like to look like an utter ninny," she declared vehemently. "And that's what I felt like, the way you kept watching, and I knew what you were thinking—"

"I wasn't watching you," said Grove. "I was just kind of paralyzed when I heard Bobbsie-Ann Boggsen and it turned out to be you."

"Oh, shut up."

"All I'm trying—"

"Please shut up!" A defiant movement, the small figure hunched up against the side of the seat.

Grove touched her arm. "Look, Rosie, what I'm trying to say is—"

"Do we have to go into it again? I had a rotten time tonight, if you must know, and thanks to you." Her eyes straight ahead, shoulders rigid.

"You didn't seem to be having too rotten a time when I saw you dancing with that pink-faced dumbdumb of a fop who—" began Grove.

"He's not a fop at all. Anything but," said Rosemary. "And while I think of it, I suppose you're going to say you didn't fall all over the place when Mrs. Stelward—"

"Who?"

"Mrs. Stelward. And don't—"

"Oh." He'd totally forgotten. "You mean the Woolworth pearls?" He paused and he did not restrain his sigh of resignation. "Yes, I guess you're right, I fell all over the place."

"It was obvious so don't try to sound like a martyr, it's not at all funny, it's about as funny as everything else that happened tonight. Instead of having a little enjoyment, all I had was—"

In exasperation, he said, "Enjoyed it? Will you please tell me what possible enjoyment you could get out of that predictable marionette show? Since when are you—"

"It happens to be interesting to me. Now and then. If you must know"—her tone was more than defensive—"it's fun for a change, it's amusing. You keep forgetting it can get pretty dull for me sitting around on those Eames chairs and everyone talking half the night, those Olsons and the others who—"

She had reached for that again, he thought. "Now listen, Rosie, if you don't like the Olsons, that's one thing, but let's not compare them to this mob tonight." Then: "All right, let's forget it. All I object to, Rosie, is you sounding like everybody but yourself. Why the hell should you let them give you a bad time?"

But the Rosemary on whom he was centering his puzzlement and dismay was obviously a Rosemary who no longer seemed to quite fit into the frame in which he'd held her image all this time. Though this was not the first occasion when he'd had to admit to himself that there were aspects of her nature which he hadn't known existed. And to all the neurotic itches that had developed in Connecticut there were now added others. What disturbed him most was the disparity between the Rosemary he thought he'd married and the Rosemary of recent weeks, of tonight.

When or how had this change begun?

What had happened between tonight and that day when he'd first met her? A summer weekend when he'd come to Connecticut to participate in a New England seminar on Regional Planning. He'd stayed at the house of one of his associates and on his last day, a Sunday, his host had given that slate wiper of a cocktail party to clean up social obligations in the neighborhood —eight years ago and Grove could still see that dreary group, composed of local garden club stalwarts, as well as knobby-kneed City Chaps in madras and their wives in toreador pants plus white cardigans caped over the shoulders.

But there in the midst of this rural nest of S and S'ers, was this attractive, small-boned, dark-haired girl.

Smoking a cigar.

Creating a hell of a rumple among the Bulb-and-Seed Set.

Including himself.

To her, he made a fast path. Who was she? What was she doing here?

She was Rosemary Stubbins. (Out of Pennsylvania.)

And that stogey in her little fist—to Grove it was like a small scepter regally showing her indifference to the public or private opinion around her.

What was she doing there? Well, long story. She worked in New York, studied nights at the Art Students League, and recently through another student she'd been given free use of a converted barn and she came here every weekend to paint. She was enthralled with the beauty of the Connecticut countryside. She was trying to get a job out here. She wanted to leave the city for good.

Grove was enthralled with the beauty of her frontage and intrigued by her character.

Grove was a Planner. He replanned her life.

Once, a few weeks after they'd met, it occurred to him to ask her if she'd given up smoking cigars.

Oh, actually she didn't much like them.

She didn't?

No.

But that first time he'd met her—

Well, she supposed she just smoked for the hell of it.

It took him a long time to decide that smoking the cigar, like other impulses she'd acted on later, was her way of bolstering

her unsureness, her fear of being overlooked, her need to make
an impact. He loved her, he was moved, touched.

Then he discovered there were other impulses: her tendency
to flirt or to make outrageously shocking remarks. This usually
happened when they happened to be within a safe or conventional circle of people, but never among those whose sophistica-
tion might seriously challenge her.

Putting this together now in the taxi, Grove could see certain parallels between her actions tonight at Mrs. Marmonier's
party and those other times of the past: grimly, and with that
edge of disenchantment that often scores such questions, he
asked himself how much the Rosemary beside him differed
from the Rosemary of the early days, from that initial image?

If she'd succeeded in creating an image, he himself had probably helped to enhance or perpetuate it. He'd seen her not only
as she'd hoped to be seen but as he'd chosen to see her. So that,
dismayed as he might be now, he could not even have the comfort of knowing she'd changed without his collaboration.

At least the skirmish, the post-party battle between them
in the taxi now, put them on a new level of awareness of what
might be happening to them, to her.

"Well, they did give me a bad time," Rosemary was saying,
"and it did bother me. I wouldn't have cared maybe, if you
hadn't made me so damn self-conscious."

"I'm sorry to hear that, Rosie." He put his arm around her.

She wrenched herself free. "Well, it's over and I'm glad of
it. My whole evening was ruined and I'm not going to go
through anything like that again!"

"Now you're making something altogether too—"

"Too what?" She turned to him.

"Nothing. Never mind. This is god-awful, Rosie—" He lit a
cigarette and it tasted bitter in the bitter silence between them.

Presently, as the taxi slowed, approaching 1027 Fifth Avenue,

Rosemary in a quietly controlled way said, "Incidentally, I forgot to tell you, while I was having lunch with Mrs. Boggsen the other day, I saw a friend of yours."

"Who?"

"Corlis Wilbur."

"Oh," he said.

"Yes," she said.

And the last round, he saw, had been won by Rosemary.

Wordless. They went to their apartment on the 14th floor. In the living room, out of habit, he crossed to the telephone and dialed the Answering Service: *Call Mrs. Marmonier.*

Normally this might have augured well, this immediate response. But in his present state he could only anticipate frustration or defeat.

Defeat it was: Helen Peysen Marmonier had talked with Alfreda Peysen right after Grove had left the party. She was very gracious, kind, sympathetic.

But no prize in the S and S crackerjack.

He hung up. He heard Rosemary moving in the bedroom. He turned and made his way to the terrace. He pulled loose his black tie. Leaning against the stone parapet he stared out to the opaque March sky, to the city's towers—opaque shafts randomly shot with squares of light. The view tonight yielded him little. He stirred then; dispiritedly he walked around the terrace; absently he touched an evergreen tip of his Japanese black pine, and then he found himself looking around among this abundance of flowers, shrubs and trees he'd planted, and thinking: no disappointments here; here, unlike his marriage, all came up love; here, unlike his work to spare the death of the Calvert house, all came up life.

8. Mr. Lorio's

Within the Roman ambience of his hairdressing salon on East 65th Street, a scissor's reach from Park Avenue, Lorio darts into his office. Despite the morning's hurryhurry he must have his momentary solitude, his espresso, his daily newspapers. Let everyone wait. This is his ritual. Lorio is emperor to his harassed employees. More importantly he is emperor to the band of fashionable women who pay his outrageous fees and who depend on his art (as well as his advice on makeup, clothes and even, frequently, their most intimate problems) to help shape their social destinies.

Lorio, a satyrlike man of forty, is beak-nosed and deceptively warm-eyed. His hipless frame is snugly, somberly clad in black cuffless trousers and a white shirt whose austere elegance is relieved by a burnt orange tie of op art design. He fled Naples at an early age, but he has mastered and nurtured a Roman accent—he jets annually to the Holy City—and it remains profitably with him. Why not, he muses, if so many of these silly bitches are charmed by it?

Okay? That is how it is. His salon is *molto* snob.

And let some people keep talking about "certain men" who

are trying to make freaks of women. Such talk. For doesn't everyone know that without the Lorios these women would be lost? The Lorios of *haute coiffure* and *haute couture* are the ones who are turning the American woman from a flat-heeled, over-scrubbed, dull-suited, tight-curled nonentity into a chicly shod, clad and coiffed creature of infinite allurement—well, maybe that is going too far. But the Lorios are the ones who are making the miracles.

So let the people talk. Lorio keeps going to the bank.

Now, as he sits at his desk in splendid isolation in his small rococo office, he sips his freshly made espresso and resumes the reading of the papers which he has begun at breakfast. He likes to bring himself up-to-date on world affairs—that is, the affairs of *his* world. The newsmakers are often his clients or their husbands. Every day there is something. Though today there is nothing so far. No. But here, yes. His eye spies it out, this name. Grovenour. At the bottom of a boxed column.

B. B. Grovenour.

Whose wife is due here today, isn't she?

He scans the feature piece:

> Is New York becoming a city without a past? How many more historic landmarks will have to be destroyed by the wreckers' ball before New Yorkers awake to the continuing annihilation of their city's past?
>
> Latest of the structures which have fallen victim to the speculator's demolition squad is the renowned Calvert mansion on Park Avenue, about which Ada Louise Huxtable has said—

Lorio scans downward to the final paragraphs:

> —Mr. B. B. Grovenour, who is known to have given his services to preserve this singular residence by Stanford White, could not be reached for comment. Once more the citizens of

New York have shown their apathy, and once more these same citizens are crying: Why doesn't somebody do something about this?

Why, indeed?

Ah, these Americans, Lorio reflects. When will they face the truth? That America has one philosophy: change. Change itself is the very way of life. This Grovenour, he is trying to fight change, or at least arrest it. *Molto bene.* He wants to keep something of the old. It is a losing battle though. Only change, newness, novelty, is what talks to the people here. Still, they want the old too, they want the tradition too, they want even some kind of aristocracy too. They want want want. But what they buy is change. Just as Lorio himself offers them change, newness, novelty.

He finishes off his espresso as his assistant, Mr. Charles, steps in to report: Mrs. Guest will be ready for combing in five minutes; Mrs. Boggsen ready for tinting in ten minutes; Mrs. Renssaeler waiting for consultation. And Mrs. Grovenour's appointment time is past due.

Che peccato, murmurs Lorio.

Rosemary could claim little contentment on this June morning; she'd come here nettled by doubts and grievances. Yet there were times like this when for some reason being at Mr. Lorio's gave her a mild or soothing sort of pleasure. Part of it, she supposed, was simply the environment itself, the handsomeness of this reception room with its black and white wallpapered mural of ancient Italian *piazzas* and *palazzos,* this room with its splashing Roman fountain in the center and the flattering gauzelike lighting and the subtle pink fabric of the sofas and the tables of pink-veined marble. And too, there was the mild distraction of glancing through all the foreign fashion and art magazines, as well as *Fig*. She leaned back and leafed through the latest issue of *Fig* with its focus on a fantasy world—the elegant photographs of incomparably beautiful models or young matrons in incomparably beautiful French clothes, the pretty portraits or vignettes of pretty people in their prettily decorated habitats. Of course she'd been a subscriber of the magazine for years, and she'd always been amused by its glossy style. Lately though, she was beginning to feel a little more at home with its pages, less remote. Not that she was one of the *Fig* people—far from it—but she supposed her attitude toward the magazine was somewhat less critical now that she was a little closer to its milieu.

In spite of Grove.

For almost every move she made these days seemed to antagonize him. Even so innocent a step as joining the Clinton Club. Though Grove could not really accuse her of instigating the move, for that had come from Mrs. Osgood, wife of the senior partner of Edwards and Osgood. She had sponsored her, and Rosemary had appeared before the Board of Governors last month, gone through the entire process, doing it well, and coming out of it unexpectedly conscious of a sense of pride. The Clinton was still one of the best of the old-line women's clubs, and though it was stuffy, it was no longer as rigid as The Colony. What Grove had objected to was the thousand-dollar membership fee and the annual dues of six hundred. But even Grove, who was known to break quite a few rules at Edwards and Osgood, had to adhere to protocol in this case: the elder Mrs. Osgood, he said, was one of the evils that came built into the job.

Actually Rosemary found the club to offer more than the usual advantages: among other things she'd found to her astonishment that Bobbsie-Ann Boggsen had been quick to snatch up the invitation to go there for lunch last week. The Clinton was surely the last place in the world you would have thought Bobbsie-Ann would want to go, but that was the thing about Bobbsie-Ann, you never could be quite sure what to expect from her.

However, there was no doubt about what she could expect from Grove: he'd been perfectly horrid when that first picture appeared in the papers, the photograph of her and Bobbsie-Ann lunching at Le Trianon, discussing the cancer benefit of the Easter in Athens Ball. Since then there'd been the other pictures in the press, the fashion show for the benefit of the Liver and Kidney people, and again recently when as co-chairman with Bobbsie-Ann of one of the committees of the Rheumatic Fever Foundation, she was photographed having lunch at Le Pavillon by no one less than Peter (Sonny) Sahn of *Fig* Magazine; and she had even appeared with Bobbsie-Ann on a closed circuit television program on behalf of the Rheumatic crowd.

She did not like to admit, any more than did he, that the move to New York, while solving some problems, seemed to have created others. What he wanted their life to be was turning out to be not at all what she was beginning to want for herself. And whatever she wanted, Grove seemed opposed to and detested.

She realized of course that much of the unpleasantness lately had stemmed from Grove's disposition: you could trace it back almost two months, to his failure to save the Calvert house; and now there were the new difficulties he'd run into with that protest movement in Staten Island.

It was the Staten Island trouble that had led to the arguments yesterday. He'd telephoned her yesterday afternoon and asked her to give up the benefit auction at the Parke-Bernet they were going to attend last night. He had to be up very early in the morning, he had to be at Staten Island to lead the sit-down protest, he'd said, and he didn't want to get caught up in the late hour of the auction.

She'd been desolated: the affair at the Parke-Bernet was being sponsored by the Rheumatic Fever people, and wasn't it perfectly natural, being involved in the program along with Bobbsie-Ann Boggsen and the others, that she should feel a proprietary interest in the occasion? She wanted to participate, show her face, be in the forefront of those present. (And it wasn't merely because she would be among those photographed.)

But now for Grove's sake, she'd agreed to cancel out the evening.

When Grove got home from the office last night and they were having their drinks in the living room before dinner, he'd said, "Look, Rosie, I'd appreciate it if you could go out to Staten Island with me in the morning—"

"Tomorrow?"

"Yes. I can't stay out there all day and you could help me—if you'd be there, there's a job that—" Grove had gone on to tell her in detail, his voice taking on that familiar urgency, of the scheme for the next day's operation: as one of the leaders of the protest movement which hundreds of Staten Islanders were going to launch, he needed all the help he could get to coordinate the action; there was to be a massive sit-down directly in the path of the bulldozers; evidently whole clusters of old trees were going to be uprooted on a sixty-five-acre site which was owned by the borough, and which had been designated as a future park or green area, but which instead had been acquired by doubtful means by a realty syndicate for the purpose of starting a large, non-site-planned development of cheap, non-architect-designed houses. The blight to the island (already suffering from unsightly architectural fungi) and to the adjacent residential neighborhood would be beyond redemption.

Yes. She understood all of it.

And she felt about it the way Grove did.

But she couldn't, she just couldn't bring herself to cancel out her entire day; she'd already canceled the affair at the Parke-Bernet. But the next day was one she couldn't give up. "I—I don't see how I can, sweetie," she'd said. "If I'd known about this earlier—but I have these appointments for—"

"For what?" Grove demanded; he stood in front of the sliding glass doors of the terrace, the vodka martini in his hand still untasted. "For what?"

"For . . ." She had to pause: she couldn't say for having her hair restyled at Mr. Lorio's; she knew she couldn't say it was for her lunch and her afternoon with Bobbsie-Ann Boggsen. "Well, I have an appointment for a fitting at Martine's, if I expect to have that dress in time for the Olsons' dinner party. And"—she had to improvise or reshape the truth again—"and I definitely have to be at Waldo Stryker's studio downtown to check with him on that charity lecture series for the Phlebitis League; he's going to try to get Andy Warhol for us." It would have been anathema to Grove if she'd admitted she was going with Bobbsie-Ann, who was to take part in the latest underground film which the pop painter was shooting.

"The only thing is, Rosie, strange as it may seem to you, there are a few things which might just be a little more crucial than—"

"Oh, do you have to be so damn patronizing!"

But he'd turned, put down his drink and telephoned his secretary at her home: he told the girl to rearrange his business appointments and to put off the major one until late afternoon so that he'd be free to spend more time on Staten Island. When he hung up he retrieved his glass and downed the drink a bit too fiercely.

Rosemary said, "If you called her just to make me feel more muddy, you succeeded! But—"

"I did it because it seemed the simplest thing to do." His voice in that tight deep pitch which belied the reasonableness of his words.

Rosemary didn't want to let that pass, but she decided she'd better. Without saying anything else she went into the kitchen to check on the dinner: the maid stood smoking a cigarette and looking out the window to the rear façades of the Park Avenue apartments to the east where other uniformed maids could be seen in other kitchen windows.

At half-past seven Rosemary lit the candles on the dining room table and they sat down to eat, but it did not go very well and there were too many spaces of silence between them. From the Fifth Avenue windows the cinderous dusk had given way to night, and the checkerboards of light grew sharper in the apartments on Central Park West.

After dinner Grove had more telephone calls to make in preparation for the Staten Island action; and she seated herself on the floor, on the pale gold linen-fibered rug, at the foot of the sofa. She glanced through the evening papers. But she could not concentrate: she felt restive, suspended; she kept picturing the event at the Parke-Bernet which would be getting under way about now. The more she thought about it the more sullen and disconsolate she became. She looked over at Grove at the desk. It was going to be another of those awful nights.

Another stalemate.

"What's the matter?" Grove said when he came over and sat down at the end of the sofa. "You look like you've got the blues popping right out of your eyeballs. You know I didn't deliberately go out of my way to foul up tonight for you—"

"I feel awful." She did not look up at him. "If I'd known about tomorrow sooner, if you would just have told—"

"It couldn't be helped."

"Yes."

He lit a cigarette. After a while he said, "Tell me something."

"What?"

"Aren't you getting a little fed with that whole mob?" said Grove. "I should think, Rosie, by now you'd—"

"I haven't been doing all that much," she reproached him.

"Seems to me you've been in there swinging with the best and the worst of them."

Oh God, how unfair could he be? "Why shouldn't I?"

"No reason," said Grove, "except that most of those dames you see are the—"

"Is that supposed to refer to Bobbsie-Ann Boggsen?" She leaped too hastily to the defense.

"Not necessarily," said Grove.

"In other words, yes." She rose and went to the Saarinen chair, as if she needed its enclosing protection. "At least Bobbsie-Ann is lively, she at least tries to be original—" What Rosemary was trying to say, without saying it, was that of all the people she'd met in the city, Bobbsie-Ann Boggsen had proved to be the kindest, most generous, gayest, most enterprising; every time she was with her, another door to another experience was opened—though sometimes, if Rosemary wanted to admit it, when that door opened she found herself wedged behind it, her personality dimmed, shadowed, undeservedly obscured by her more spectacular friend. "Do we have to start in on Bobbsie-Ann again?"

"No. I'm sorry, Rosie."

"I mean really, Grove. I can't seem to do anything or see anyone that pleases you. You won't have any part of what you call her mob or any part of the S and S mob. It's only *your* mob, isn't it?"

"I've never said that."

"That's how it comes out though." Listlessly Rosemary rubbed her brow. "I don't know what's wrong with us, Grove." She peered at him. "It would be awful if we'd reached the age when we're so damned inflexible we won't give in to each other."

"Is that what you think?"

"I don't know."

"Because that's a pretty grim prospect," said Grove.

"Yes."

"I don't know if it's that or if it's something beyond that." He was watching her more intently. Then: "I don't know what the hell you want to get out of all this, Rosie, I really don't."

"What do you mean?"

He hesitated. "Look—I have to get to sleep early. Let's forget it." But then he said, "No, what I mean is I don't quite dig what it is you're after. What all this tearing around town is supposed to represent."

"Would you prefer to have me sit around making us needlepoint cushions with my gold needle?"

"You know better than that, Rosie."

"Why do *you* tear all around town?" she countered. "You're pressed for time in your own business, but that doesn't stop you from taking on all these other projects. I grant you it may be more purposeful, but that doesn't give you any right to throw this at me this way—"

"Certainly it doesn't," said Grove. "All I asked you was what it is you're after. What it represents. If it's a question of asserting yourself or getting your face in the papers or staying young forever—"

"Grove—"

"Or do you think you're being especially hip buying all that bacillus bullfosis people like the Boggsens or the—" He stopped. "Let's admit you were vegetating in the country too much of the time, but at least when you did occupy yourself with something it was kind of creative or thoughtful—"

"Oh Grove, for God sakes, can't you understand, all I want— I mean, it's just that I'm enjoying I don't know what you'd call it—it's a feeling of participation—" She shook her head; frustrated, she got up from the chair.

"Participation in what?" said Grove.

"What?" But she was too agitated or impotent to express it precisely.

Except that she knew that somehow she was beginning to feel for the first time a rebirth of self-confidence, even identity.

In all those seven years in the country, all her dabs and daubs at painting, writing, ceramics, decoration, all those artsy-craftsy efforts of hers, had added up to a muddy nothing; *she* had added up to nothing.

She'd never been a personality. A force. When she walked into a room nothing ever changed. But now she was becoming aware that she was capable of creating change; at least she was participating in the life around her and even being regarded, occasionally, with interest or esteem. People were beginning to recognize her, newspaper and magazine people, photographers were commencing to give her that look of attention she'd never known before.

No matter how "creative" her activities in the country might have been, they'd been failures and they had never altered the world's view of her, a housewife, a creature who happened to be Mrs. B. B. Grovenour.

That was beginning to change now, wasn't it? You couldn't classify her quite so readily now, could you?

Why?

Something Dexter Knight had talked about: there was a whole new breed of women who, though being essentially housewives, were achieving a special kind of celebrity, something, he said, which could not have happened years ago. In the past you were either an established "society woman" or an established woman in a special field.

Today in New York, women were breaking the old pattern: their very way of life was becoming celebrated. If Bobbsie-Ann Boggsen was an extreme example, there were countless others who in less bizarre ways were also becoming stars in the New York heaven, others like herself. Soon—how soon she didn't know—but possibly soon, Rosemary Grovenour might conceivably represent something, might set a style, a trend, create a change, a new action.

How? She didn't know. But wasn't it exhilarating just to contemplate?

"I don't know what I want," she'd finally said, unable or unwilling to articulate what she'd been trying to form in her mind. "Except that I want the chance to find out for myself."

"In other words, without any suggestions or interference from your husband. Is that it?"

"Oh Grove, that's not it at all!"

"All right." Shortly afterward he'd left to take his shower and go to bed.

For a while she remained in the big living room, going out then to the terrace. But the night air was gritty and she stepped back inside. She could not rid herself of the presence of guilt which had come upon her after Grove had gone into the bedroom. Belatedly, but no less genuinely, she felt she had let him down. Which was bad enough in itself, but she'd let him down, lying to him, stating reasons which she knew sounded trivial, superficial, absurd.

It wasn't as though he asked her help all the time. He'd never asked her before. And it only meant the loss of that one day; she could lose her appointment with the inspired if arrogant and temperamental hairdresser, and the world wouldn't come to an end if she failed to go downtown with Bobbsie-Ann for the afternoon, for that underground movie.

She switched off the living room lights. When she reached the bedroom, Grove's lamp was out, though she knew he wasn't asleep. "Grove—"

He stirred. "Hmm?"

Rosemary sat down on the bed. "Grove, I don't know what got into me, I mean, those appointments aren't all that important—"

"Doesn't matter—"

"Yes, it does. There's no reason on earth why I can't go out there with you in the morning. Do you know, I've never even *seen* Staten Island?"

"Oh, forget it, Rosie." He sat upright. He was naked. He never wore pajamas, not even in midwinter, just as he refused to put on a heavy coat or a hat in the bitterest February weather. ("Grovenour blood," he liked to say, "may be diluted by arrogance and smugness and cold with greed, but for sheer heat it's like active lava.")

"No, I'm serious," said Rosemary. "I insist I go."

"Forget it. I don't know why I made so much noise about it."

She touched his shoulder. "But Grove, it's absolutely ridiculous my thinking I couldn't go out there. I want to be with you."

He swung around to face her. "It doesn't matter. Anyway, Rosie, it's nice of you to change your mind. But it'll probably be a rough day there and why in hell should I drag you into it?"

"I insist, Grove."

"Look, Rosie"—he turned on to his side—"about what we were talking about before. About what's happening to us."

"Oh, I—"

"I've been thinking about what you said."

"Grove, all I meant was—"

"And while I was thinking about it," said Grove, "it occurred to me that I keep forgetting that one of the main reasons I wanted us to move to town was so that you could get a whole new deal." He reached over and turned on his lamp. "And I suppose my idea of a new deal and yours maybe aren't the same always. Which is all right, too. I don't say I necessarily go along with what you want to do, but I sure as hell shouldn't stop you from trying it."

This admission coming from him, after all these months of protest, left her disarmed. She said, "Grove—you talk as if it were all your—"

"Oh, I know you've had your innings too, Rosie."

"Yes." She felt impelled to say more, to clean up all the scraps and pieces of black and white lies, black and white resentments, but somehow she couldn't.

"The trouble is we let these things hang on, instead of—"

"Oh sweetie." She leaned down and kissed him on the corner of his mouth.

"What?"

But she couldn't summon the sort of statement she knew he was hoping to hear.

She kissed him again.

Seeking what? Substituting that for what?

Rosemary was conscious of what was slipping from her and what she might have gained: she was losing the chance to clear and clean the air, the chance to state her truest feelings; out of this she might have won Grove's total understanding or sympathy.

No.

It was something else.

It was the unevenness of the score that scratched at her. Uneven, all the odds were on Grove's side: Grove was the one whose activities she could not truly find fault with. What could you say? That the only love he held, outside of loving her, was this passion of his for a city that was indifferent to it?

What else, what deeper than that?

Yes, that was the worst part. She couldn't even charge him with his one infidelity, for she'd lost that right by her own act of unfaithfulness; though he didn't know about it, that didn't change matters.

If there was something, one specific thing about Grove she resented, it was that his character seemed to be made of better stuff than hers. Not that he was too good, but that she was not good enough.

At heart, this was what she deplored in him, and in herself.

She might have been able to tell him everything that was on her mind, she might have been able to unburden herself of all the small lies and deceits if only Grove were less decent, if only Grove showed the greater weakness, if only Grove were more ignoble.

Yes.

Then she might have told him everything, even told him how she truly felt about her life here and what she wanted out of it now.

Instead, tonight he had been willing to admit his errors, he'd at least attempted to show understanding and sympathy. So that now, of course, she was too ashamed or embarrassed to match even his preliminary candor.

Kissing him now. Again. Wanting somehow to isolate the moment as it was. Leave it there. And making him believe, mistakenly, that sex itself was all that was needed to seal the beginning of better times between them.

So that Grove, as if he too wanted to herald the moment,

pulled her down to him, and then his hands were under her dress in that playful and exaggeratedly wicked way, and then she got up and took off her clothes.

"Mrs. Grovenour?" The girl in the pink tunic beckoned to her, holding open the black lacquered door which gave into the labyrinth of Mr. Lorio's salon.

She took off her sheath in the private dressing room and the maid hung it up, and then Rosemary went into the booth. As soon as one of the girls had settled her in the chair and protectively swathed her in the monogrammed smock and cape, Mr. Lorio appeared.

"*Buon giorno,* Mrs. Grovenour," he greeted her.

"*Buon giorno,* Lorio."

He carefully put on his large black-rimmed glasses. "I must tell you, it is always such a pleasure to have you here. Why? Because you have a freshness, an outlook that is refreshing. I think many women must envy it."

"Lorio, you're certainly in a high mood today."

"Don't worry. It never lasts."

But Rosemary proffered her warmest smile: she was becoming so fond of the master hairdresser; he was a kind of counselor; he was like a wise older sister or a sophisticated aunt. Though he could be as cruel as he was kind. She supposed she shouldn't have spoiled him with that gift last month, but Bobbsie-Ann assured her that the favored few never hesitated to lavish lovely little presents or "campy little nothings" on him.

No sooner had Lorio turned back the French cuffs of his shirt than Bobbsie-Ann Boggsen, her blond hair still in rollers, looked in. "Excuse me, maestro," she said, "but I have to have a word with my friend here." To Rosemary: "There's been a switch, we're not going downtown. They're going to shoot the picture at Hank Hartley's place. Would you mind if we gave up the Trianon and ate here instead?"

"How can I say no in front of Lorio?" said Rosemary. Mr. Lorio had an arrangement whereby food was sent in from a nearby restaurant, the Nature Table, in which he owned a half interest and which served, at indecent prices, organically grown vegetable dishes he claimed were notable for their low-calorie rating and high-health and beauty index. (The agonizing thing was that Lorio himself, thin as a thistle, often lunched on mounds of spaghetti or rigatoni which he moistened on their way with half a bottle of choice wine.)

"Good," said Bobbsie-Ann. "Hank Hartley's man is coming by for us here. Probably in the Edsel." She laughed. "I mean, he's got that marvelous Bentley and a Jag, but he still insists on using the Edsel. He's one of those people who just refuse to admit they ever made a mistake. But you'll like him, I promise. He's really terribly gussey. Incidentally, he knows your husband, and when I told him you'd taken me to the Clinton Club for lunch he said it didn't sound like any wife of Grovenour's—"

Rosemary had been perplexed once again, though pleased, by the way luncheon had turned out, not only because Bobbsie-Ann had been eager to go to the Clinton with her, but that she had regarded it with such unabashed delight. "You know something, Rosemary," she'd said, "I love this place, I mean it's so creepy, so Peck-and-Pecky, it's almost a camp. Sort of like going back to the womb, so womby, and for two cents I'd love to apply for membership, but of course somebody might be prejudiced, I mean they might think I'm too much of a nut to ever make it."

Surely, Rosemary had thought, she was being facetious. Obviously. But she discovered later that this was not quite the case. "Not at all, Bobbsie-Ann. Why wouldn't you make it?"

Rosemary had stated in a spirit of sincere conviction, indifferent at the moment to the ring of attention the women around them had been giving Bobbsie-Ann, whose great blond lion's head and blue-eye makeup and high lizard boots sent a shiver of excitement among the ladies that day.

"Sorry to hold you up, maestro," Bobbsie-Ann Boggsen apologized now. And before turning to leave she wiggled her fingers and gave him the parting Italian shot: *"Ciao."*

"Now then." Mr. Lorio had grown impatient. "What is on Mrs. Grovenour's mind today?"

"What's on my mind? A coiffure I'm getting bored with, Lorio," she stated. But less resolutely then: "Or do you think we ought to stay with this?"

"You want my honest opinion?"

"Yes."

"My honest opinion, Mrs. Grovenour, is you're right," he said. "Women forget that Lorio can get just as bored with their coiffures as they do." He kept studying her image in the mirror.

She waited.

"All right," he said then. "I know what we'll try. You'll trust me?"

"Oh, certainly." But she was a bit disappointed, for she'd hoped to discuss it with him. Though she did not in any way want to imitate Bobbsie-Ann's coiffure, she did harbor hope that she might in some way suggest something that might give a similar effect.

"For one thing"—Lorio addressed the mirror—"this Mt. Vesuvius must go! Too much for a person your size. I wanted to give you extra height, but now that I know you better I think you are not the type for that. And also the bouffant, it must go too. I'm going to simplify. I'm thinking of something old, like Garbo used to wear it, but with Lorio's flair. Bangs sweeping to the eyebrows in a curve, everything else straight, not too long, but straight. We'll have to get rid of the zigglies. I'll iron them out, and then just swerve up the ends in a half flip. You understand? *Simplissima, bellisima.*"

"Well . . . yes. Yes. All right. We might try it."

"It ought to be lightened a tone, just a tone," he went on. "And while I think of it, Lorio was worried about something the other day, Mrs. Grovenour. Your picture in the paper with Mrs. Boggsen."

"Oh?"

"Your lipstick. It's too pale. That's for the kids. For you, with that fine face, it's not good." He paused. "For Mrs. Boggsen, the no-lip lipstick is maybe amusing." Another pause. "But before you leave today we'll try something Lorio has just imported, a new color."

"Good. Let's gamble." But Rosemary knew that what she'd been hearing was Lorio's way of reminding her that she was no longer all that young, that in fact she was several years older than Bobbsie-Ann Boggsen. God, he could be nasty when he chose to. He meant well, she supposed, and he certainly knew his business, but there were those mean little slashes now and then. . . .

It seemed to her that being made to look attractive was no longer enough in New York. There seemed to be a kind of desperate race. You could notice it on the streets, the way even the commonest secretary got herself up these days. Everything seemed geared for a big beauty race and unless you ran fast you would lag behind. More and more women were pressing, straining to win that race: the hair, the eyes, the lips, the skin, the race for the youngest skin, the slimmest bodies, the firmest bosoms, the tints and shades, even the dimensions of the heels you wore. ("There is nothing more pathetic," Lorio had said a few weeks ago, "than seeing ridiculous high heels on women of the menopause brigade, they look so sad clicking and tottering their way down the street.")

It just seemed sometimes that no matter how much you tried, there were always so many girls and women who suddenly could make you look droopy, dowdy and a hundred years old. My God, she was scarcely thirty-two, but . . .

Rosemary said, "Lorio, sometimes you just love to be brutal, don't you?"

"Brutal? Lorio brutal?" he protested. "Such talk, Mrs. Grovenour! Now then. When we're through today, your hair will be *bellisima.*"

"Marvelous, Rosemary! That Lorio is pure genius, isn't he?" said Bobbsie-Ann when they met later in the reception room of the salon. She peered at her hair with approval. "I mean, it's really terribly gussey."

Rosemary, whose spirits seemed immeasurably improved since that morning, said, "Would you mind if I changed my mind about going to that thing with you? I think I'd like to go." At lunch over the trays sent in by the Nature Table, she'd feared she might be too much of an outsider, not knowing any of the people who were going to make this film at Hartley's apartment. Now, however, she felt more adventuresome.

"Oh good. It ought to be a ball and a half! They're strictly underground, you know. Terribly *avant* and wiggy, but definitely a real film art form."

"I have to call Gristede's and order something for dinner. I'll have to get home by six latest. That's the worst time for a cab—" Rosemary immediately regretted her prosaic concerns. Bobbsie-Ann Boggsen never seemed to be hampered by these domestic considerations. Once Bobbsie-Ann had said, "Oh, it doesn't matter if I'm late. My jewel of a slavey takes care of everything. And my husband, well, I've trained him to relax and wait until I'm back. He used to be a clock watcher, but I got him over that."

All of which would not do for Grove. Rosemary's day might be one thing, but after six in the evening she wanted to be right on hand and have everything functioning perfectly: the succession of maids she hired through the housekeeper at 1027 left much to be desired.

"We'll make it in time. Fear not," Bobbsie-Ann said. "Maybe we'd better wait outside. Woody might not be able to park when he gets here." Bobbsie-Ann started to the door, looking, Rosemary thought, not without a sting of envy, unlike anyone else. She was clad in vinyl: over her white vinyl sheath she wore the leopard-spotted vinyl coat and the leopard-spotted vinyl boots. This ensemble, with her long bright hair, did not make her an inconspicuous sight out on the sidewalk in front of Mr. Lorio's.

Who was Woody? Rosemary wanted to know.

Woody was Woodward, Hank Hartley's chauffeur and general factotum.

"Any minute now—and I'm sure it'll be in the Edsel—he ought to be bombing along," said the indefatigable Bobbsie-Ann Boggsen.

Rosemary peered up the street toward Park Avenue: sheer exhilaration already shaped her anticipation of the afternoon.

She glanced at her reflection in the glass of the adjacent shop-window: the sassy flare of the gray Nina Ricci spring coat and the silhouette of her new coiffure did make her appearance decidedly—well—decidedly gussey.

All part of a new life, a new way.

All shining.

Except that now as she stood there beside her white vinyl-veneered friend, she grew more aware that the emanation she was sure she radiated for all the world didn't seem to exist; for the people passing by ignored her as if she were as prosaic or lowly as that nearby fire hydrant. Everyone's attention seemed to be fixed on Bobbsie-Ann.

But surely Rosemary should have been accustomed to that by this time. And as Bobbsie-Ann's most frequent companion, shouldn't she have continued to feel pleasure merely to move in the dazzling aura of her friend?

Yes. But then why was it that she felt something else?

A feeling she couldn't quite define. It couldn't have been resentment, nothing that strong. It seemed the merest sensation, but like a taut thread it cut finely.

9. *958 Fifth Avenue*

In the Chauffeurs' Waiting Room, a subterranean chamber in the garage of this cooperative apartment building, all the men now waiting are full-time, bonded, insured, uniformed chauffeurs. All except Woodward.

Woody, a dour and dumpy man of fifty-two, used to drive for Mr. Hartley's parents, and after they died, he continued working for their son, Henford (Hank) Hartley. But he doesn't drive very often nowadays; only when young Hartley is too busy with other matters, or if he is ill or if he has injured himself skiing. So that Woodward has become a kind of butler-house-man-cook who, with the part-time maid and the charwoman, looks after Hartley's domain, the duplex on the nineteenth floor.

But he's pleased today. Today he'll be driving again, even if it is the Edsel instead of the others. Since he's early, he stops off at the Chauffeurs' Waiting Room. He'll see who's there. Sometimes, like today, he gets lonely for other times.

Several men are seated on the two long leather-padded benches, and he knows most of them, though he only addresses the two at this end.

He greets Malone, who has driven Alfreda Peysen here from

1027 Fifth Avenue, and who is waiting for her to finish her visit upstairs.

He greets Parker, whose employer is a high official with the United Nations, and who lives here.

These three men—Woodward, Malone, Parker—are tacitly recognized members of the chauffeuring elite. They have rank and interests in common: their employers are prominent citizens; they own Rolls-Royces or Bentleys.

These three do not converse too freely with the other five chauffeurs sitting on the bench across the room, for the employers of the five are less distinguished and the cars they own are only Cadillacs or Lincoln Continentals.

Seated alone, at a remove from the others, is Johnston, to whom the rest speak only occasionally: he is young and he is a Negro, and the car he drives is a Chrysler Imperial. Johnston is preoccupied now: he is finishing the daily crossword puzzle of *The New York Times.*

"Not the Edsel again?" inquires Malone, his tone intimately ironical, since he is privy to the fact that the Hartley stable also includes the Bentley and the Jaguar.

"Yes," says Woodward. "Mr. Hartley wants me to pick up some friends."

"The fair sex, hmm?" observes Malone.

Parker, the third of the trio, says with ponderous weight, "These young fellas, what else have they got on their minds today except having a good time?"

Malone nods. "When Mrs. Peysen's husband was alive he worked from morning till night, around the clock. I used to drive him down to The Street every morning at seven-fifteen."

A grave silence as the men look through the glass partition to see driving down the ramp a woman at the wheel of a black Mustang convertible. Woodward recognizes her. Mrs. Christine Stelward. She lives here.

"My boss's son has a Mustang, the fastback," ventures one of the Cadillac chauffeurs. "He used to have a beautiful G.T. Sting Ray, but he smashed it up in Central Park, so the old man's punished him: the kid has to drive a Mustang now."

"Tough titty," mutters someone.

Mrs. Peysen's chauffeur, Malone, bites off the tip of a fresh cigar, and one of the Lincoln Continental men helpfully offers him a light, and the room's not too fragrant dampness becomes enriched with the aroma of the premier-leafed cigar.

Parker is saying, "That was the first time we were ever at the Union Club when there wasn't even double parking."

Uninvited, one of the Lincoln drivers insinuates himself into the conversation: "Union? I don't know about that. But that hotel—the Park-Regent—try to wait by that place!"

"We always take care of the door at the Park-Regent," Woody remarks. "Parking is no problem."

An attentive silence now as a Rolls Royce Phantom II town car, with liveried chauffeur at the helm, rolls down the ramp.

"Rental," Parker observes loftily. "Who do they think they're fooling? With that number on the plates, gives 'em away every time."

Mrs. Peysen's chauffeur asks Woodward, "Young Hartley still got that art gallery of his?"

"No, he had to give it up," says Woody, adding, "But we'll write it off, taxwise."

Malone nods. "That magazine, the literary one, he's still running that, isn't he? Or financing it?"

"Yes. But that's not in the black either." Woody frowns. "Mostly what he's doing, like today, he's making, or helping them make, movies. Special ones. They're only shown in private." A rising note of optimism asserts itself as if he hopes that this time his employer's venture will yield some kind of financial profit instead of merely the same old failures which give him nothing but tax deductions and a lot of handclapping from weirdies and rich people who you'd think would know better.

"These movies"—Malone arches his brows—"nothing for my lady's eyes, hmm?"

"No." Woody knows it is time to leave. He carefully tightens the knot of his black tie and tugs down his black cap. "Well, better get that piece of iron on the road."

He leaves the waiting room and goes into the garage. He drives the old Edsel downtown to pick up Mr. Waldo Stryker at his studio, a loft far over on East 9th Street. Stryker, a bearded young man, is, according to the newspapers, a pop artist. One of his latest paintings, "The Toilet," was purchased by Mr. Hartley. And Woodward, even though he is used to it now, still grins with embarrassment when he passes it, and the charwoman always works with her back to it. However, Mr. Hartley calls it fresh, and fine. (And it will probably end up at the Parke-Bernet or Madison Auction Gallery, auctioned off like many of Mr. Hartley's other acquisitions from time to time.)

Waldo Stryker sits in front with him, and then they move uptown to East 65th Street and draw up before the white and black façade of Mr. Lorio's. Woody steps out and tips his visored cap and opens the rear door to admit Bobbsie-Ann Boggsen and the young woman with her whom he has never seen before.

He will drive them back to 958 Fifth Avenue and then collect some of the other people.

Though none of them knew it, this "underground" film they were making in Hank Hartley's duplex apartment (and with H. H.'s funds) was to be the apogee of the pop period, a phase which was to perish soon to make way for something else, something newer, a change—always that change which seemed so necessary for survival in any endeavor of American life. In the view of the vanguard, Hank Hartley had learned that the instant an American painter or writer attains his artistic zenith, he becomes old hat; and the credo of scientists, he decided, could also apply to art: *If it works, it's obsolete.*

So that Hank himself would always be the first to jettison today's painter or writer or personality for tomorrow's, he would always look for a *new* new young artist or a *new* new young group; he too made what Harold Rosenberg called a "fetish of birth dates and watched the clock to count the hours of decline" of the latest darling of the arts or, for that matter, anyone else who occupied the fragile throne of chic.

To Hartley's credit, however, it could be said that though he had absolutely no creative talent, he had taste, judgment and sometimes, quite fortuitously, daring. He had a nose for the nuances in cultural trends just as his father had had a nose for the nuances in the stock market.

Hank Hartley might have been just another lackluster rich boy, another stenciled product lost in the striped mosaic of the Ivy League except that he chose as far back as his undergraduate days at Harvard—he was a class behind Grove—to follow, study and then play the culture circuit. This took money and enthusiasm. And though he could be very generous with his funds, he could also be inexplicably penurious and niggardly. And if he had boundless enthusiasms he also had maddening fits of inertia. He chased after people with the same determination that he later hid from them.

At the age of thirty-five and after two disastrous marriages he was still regarded as one of New York's most eminent bachelors, and if he had developed a paranoic attitude toward candidates for the conjugal bed, it could be understandable since his previous marital errors had cost him well over a million dollars. His current or newest interest in women was directed at Christine Stelward: with her of course there was no financial opportunism to fear, but she presented other aspects which were even more formidable. Christine Stelward lived three floors below him, and though, unlike some of his other friends, she had not participated in Waldo Stryker's pop film today, she was coming later this evening for the private showing of Waldo's previous movie.

"Hank—hey, Hankypooh!" Waldo Stryker was calling out from the balcony which overlooked the vast living room—"I'm still going here."

"Still going?" Hank turned from Rosemary Grovenour with whom he'd finally found time to talk. He surveyed the debris of his apartment in the aftermath of the pop film Waldo Stryker had finished shooting a few minutes ago. "I thought it was over, Waldo."

"Nothing is ever over, matter is infinite," pontificated Stryker from his balcony Parnassus. "And I wouldn't want to miss what's going on now." Then he bellowed: "Light up a Kent, you've got a good thing going!"

"We have a budget going here, too," Hank reminded him.

"Yeah, but with all the equipment still here, I don't want to miss this," declared the bearded painter.

"This" was the cocktail party now in full heat, the inevitable transition from one function to another, except that now more people had dropped in and Woody was having to dispense more drinks. And everyone was talking about Stryker's film "Mouths" which had taken only two hours to shoot today. Many of Hank's friends had formed the cast; they were shot in a variety of actions: brushing teeth, kissing, yawning, laughing, nibbling corn off the cob.

But the most outstanding scene had been Bobbsie-Ann Boggsen who, instead of doing what she'd been told, namely sitting down and putting on her lipstick, had removed her leopard-spotted vinyl dress, revealing to everyone's joy, leopard-spotted bra and panties; then, standing before Hank's three-paneled dressing room mirror, made up her lips, shifting her stance and her flamboyant hood of hair while Stryker, his camera aimed at her backside, recorded the long sinuous process.

Now as the Dave Clark Five gave way to The Stones, as the stereo exploded in the high room, Bobbsie-Ann Boggsen, still in her bra and panties, was again becoming the focus of the occasion, this time dancing the Rub and the Twitch with the novelist, Giles Folor.

"Here, let me get you another, Rosemary." Hank Hartley guided her over to the bar, a seventeenth-century, carved Gothic pulpit from a French church which his decorator Tony Ammonds had installed for him. As Hank replenished Rosemary's bourbon glass he said, "You might still find yourself in a Stryker epic if this keeps up."

"*You've* been avoiding it so far," said Rosemary Grovenour.

"I'm not as photogenic as you," said Hank.

"I think that's more Mr. Lorio than me," said Rosemary, but despite the modest reply, he noticed her smile had acquired more radiance; she regarded him more attentively too. That was the agreeable part of talking with her; unlike so many other women he talked with you didn't have the suspicion when she looked at you attentively that what she was really looking at was the Chase Manhattan Bank, chief repository of the Hartley trust.

"I've decided," said Rosemary, "that Bobbsie-Ann is right about you."

"Oh?" He noticed her glancing at his grubby denim work shirt. Though most of his suits were tailored by Weatherill's, for today's event and others like it he purchased his clothes at the nearest Army and Navy Surplus Store.

"You're a Social Register Dropout," said Rosemary. "Like my husband."

He laughed. "How is Grove these days? The last time I saw him was at the club and he talked me into going to Penn Station and picketing. What's he up to now?" Then: "Staten Island, isn't it? I read something about it yesterday."

"Yes." She told him about the sit-down protest. "I called him at the office a little while ago but his secretary said he still hadn't come back. I left your number. I never know with Grove, he makes it home for dinner sometimes, and sometimes he doesn't."

"Call him again, why don't you?" Hank said. He invited the Grovenours for the buffet later and the showing of Stryker's previous pop movie. "No one has seen it yet. I'm running it here because the police raided the last showing at Waldo's loft. I've invited a few more people in but for obvious reasons I didn't tell them about the film."

"Hey—" Waldo Stryker had come downstairs and approached them: he was stripped to the waist now, barefooted, and wearing around his neck a thin chain from which there dangled, like a St. Christopher's medal, a BMT subway token. "Hey, Rosiepooh," the pop painter cried, "you're not going to be an off-frame character this time, this time I'm going to get you!" But his perfervid gaze had returned to Bobbsie-Ann Boggsen who was still dancing in her leopard-spotted undergarments, still in wild contortions with Giles Folor who, not to be outdone, had removed his ankle-high country shoes, his coat and shirt, revealing the premature paunch of his whale-hued belly. "Oh, Bobbsiepooh," Waldo cried, "this is visual ambrosia, baby you are the cube root!— Hey, don't stop, keep going—!" He glanced around looking for one of his assistants; instead he saw the big gnarled face of his producer, a young man named Michael O'Leary. "Hey, Mike, put on my new record, I've got a massive idea, put in on, willya, Mike?" To Hartley: "Hank, wait till you hear this record. My first. They're going to put out a hundred thousand."

"What is it?" asked Hank. It was not always easy to keep up with the myriad projects in which Stryker was involved and from which he was deriving an income said to be sizable enough to cause other artists to disparage him as a hoax and hack.

"All I did was tape a whole slew of radio and TV commercials, put it all together. It's called 'The Sounds of America's Soul.'" Stryker's calculated gaze took in the figures of the cocktail party: the dancers, the game-players, the covert lovers, the earnest little culture clusters. "What I'm going to try now is shoot the party as it goes and grows, shoot it like a silent, but letting the commercials blast over all the shots willy-nilly—"

"Use the commercials for the sound track, is that what you mean?" Hank said.

"You're With It, Hankypooh." And Waldo Stryker was gone, his slender arms flailing, his faun's face flushed as he shouted instructions, as he set up the tripod near the room's now-frenetic center.

—MISTER CLEAN!
—PARTICULAR PEOPLE LIKE PARTICULAR FLAVOR
   IN THE GOOD TASTE OF PALL MALL.
—NEW DASH CLEANS YOUR LAUNDRY LIKE
   IT'S TEN FEET TALL—PFSSHH!

Voices singly and in choral groups, cries, shouts, pleas, coos and other sounds of orgiastic ecstasy came in counterpoint to the Rock 'n' Roll and the bursts of conversation.

"My nearest neighbors"—Hank said to Rosemary Grovenour and jabbed his thumb toward the floor—"fortunately they're still in Europe."

LIGHT UP A KENT. YOU'VE GOT A GOOD THING GOING.

Woody returned to the pulpit-bar to assemble more drinks. "Easy, Woody," said Hank, giving the man the familiar warning: he needn't dip into any more of the premiere brand Scotch, it was time to pour the bargain brand. Woody nodded, confirming the message.

As now Waldo Stryker moved his camera in for a closer shot to cover the pelvic arabesques of Bobbsie-Ann Boggsen.

NEW AJAX LAUNDRY DETERGENT IS STRONGER THAN DIRT—PSSHHH!

"Hank, darlingest. KissKiss!" A young woman, Daphne Bernlinsk, lively and intense, with the dark eloquent eyes and the curly dark hair of a French poodle, arrived, leaned forward and touched his cheek, while, her lips pursed, she kissed the air. Then she threw her white motorcycle helmet onto a chair: "I know I'm late, but my Honda broke down right in front of Parc Cinq and that doorman damn near had a coronary." Daphne was already looking at Rosemary Grovenour with the shrewd query bright in her poodle eyes. Hank introduced her, and then Rosemary excused herself: she wanted to call Grove's office again.

Daphne watched her for a moment, then turned back to Hank. "You'll have to fill me in." She drew from her handbag a notebook and a slim gold pencil. "I'm going to block out my piece before tomorrow. We lock up Friday." Daphne Bernlinsk was a passionate culture queen. And an associate editor of *Hipman,* a magazine dedicated to the cult of IN. She was determinedly on her way to becoming in cultural circles what Dexter Knight was or had been in the upper realm of society, without, however, the latter's historical sense or his grace. Her father, a missiles parts manufacturer and a prominent art collector, had purchased and given her a twelve-room cooperative apartment on Park Avenue which Daphne promptly sold and, with that contrived nonconformity common to people who use snobbism inversely to gain recognition from those who are born snobs, she bought an apartment on Central Park West. Later, however, she became even more daring and sold the West Side apartment to return to one on the East Side, where her salon flourished.

Hank Hartley felt about her somewhat the way he felt about the English: he admired her without necessarily liking her. But even Hank accepted her form of subtle blackmail, going to her salon occasionally, for she saw to it that laudatory or informative articles as well as reliable news items about him appeared from time to time in *Time, Hipman, Fig, Vogue, Commentary, Esquire, Playboy, Partisan Review, Harper's, The Paris Review* and *Women's Wear Daily.*

Now as Rosemary Grovenour came back downstairs, Daphne said, "I'd like to talk to Mrs. Grovenour later. I've been hearing about her. I wouldn't be at all surprised if she isn't very much my cuppa." Daphne kept watching her. "I wonder why?"

"I don't know exactly," said Hank.

"Well, that's just it, Hank," said Daphne Bernlinsk not without a flash of arrogance in those bonbon eyes, "when you know *too* exactly, there's seldom much interest, is there?"

—HOW CAN JUST ONE CALORIE TASTE SO GOOD? BECAUSE THE COCA-COLA COMPANY KEPT THE FLAVOR IN TAB!

Daphne waited until Waldo Stryker had finished shooting Bobbsie-Ann Boggsen and Giles Folor, then she pounced upon them, for after all it had been at least a week since she'd seen them last, and there was much KissKiss in the smoke-swirled air. How Daphne adored these moments, these vignettes in these environments: oh how delicious to function in this high duplex room with its bold new paintings by all the bold new painters; how she envied Hank Hartley's brand of snobbism which allowed his living room to display only that art which was currently, fashionably IN, while in his splendid bedroom suite upstairs, for the delectation of his closest friends, he showed the paintings of those artists whose works already hung in the Modern Museum, the Whitney or the Guggenheim: Dove, Tobey, Davis, Pollack, DeKooning, Kline, Ernst, Rinehart, Ajay and some of the others, and the priceless Calder which floated in impudent beauty from the ceiling.

"Giles! KissKiss!" She greeted the Boston-born, red-haired novelist who, breathless now and spent, leaned against a Jensen cabinet. She had already composed a nice paragraph about him for her piece; he was among the IN people listed in *Hipman* for the months of April and May. As for June and July— that was anyone's guess. (Daphne had to single out Giles Folor because, after all, hadn't he and his charming mistress Irene had her out to Long Island for that winter weekend, put her up at that elegant inn, cocktailed and little-sausaged her, wined and roast-beefed her, had that colossal party of roaring and besoused literary lions, and hadn't Giles read aloud a chapter from his nearly finished novel which, by a happy chance, seemed ideal to abstract for a future issue of *Hipman?* And hadn't Giles in the spirit of good horseplay kissed and fingered her wetly in the kitchen while his girl was answering a long-distance call from an old Dartmouth buddy of Giles' whose career had bombed out dismally, so that Irene naturally had to get him off poor Giles' back?)

"Daphne," said Giles Folor in his stentorian voice, "how is

the black lady of the social sonnets? Could I get you a *soupçon* of booze?"

"Not now, but thanks, Giles." Turning then to Bobbsie-Ann Boggsen, who like Folor was, thank God, still on the current list of IN people, "Bobbsie-Ann! Umm. KissKiss! I'm consumed with envy. Where'd you get that bra and panties?"

"I didn't get them from Peck and Peck," said Bobbsie-Ann, and then as Rosemary Grovenour joined them she said, "Oh, have you met Mrs. Grovenour?"

"I have indeed," said Daphne. "And am I ever consumed with curiosity and envy. Where'd you get that dress, Rosemary?"

"Martine's."

"Umm. I should have known. But that's just too chic for poor me." Daphne giggled enough to reassure her audience that they need waste no pity on her, and making a mental note to give more attention to Martine's in the near future, for it seemed to have developed into a definitely IN boutique: Daphne had underrated it because neither Amanda Burden, D. D. Ryan, Catherine Milinaire, nor even Jane Holzer bought their clothes there.

"Rosemary," Bobbsie-Ann was saying, "you're not thinking of leaving are you?"

"No, not yet," said Rosemary Grovenour. "I tried Grove's office again, but he's still not there. I left word for him to call me here. But I ordered a few little Gristedelies in case we have to picnic at the old homestead."

Daphne laughed: her omnivorous chocolate eyes on Rosemary, studying her, examining her equipment, needing to decide swiftly if she should be thoroughly cultivated and brought into the Daphne Bernlinsk consortium of culture: the name for one thing would add a distinctive fillip to her salon; the rather special cachet of her husband's figure in the New York civic landscape would also provide a certain relief from the internecine gang of literateurs; and too, Rosemary made for the kind of chic Daphne had become hungrier for: that dress of Rosemary's was a little Parisian cameo, the hair was inescapably Mr. Lorio, and that long chartreuse-stoned necklace she'd made herself *was* a change from all the Jean Schlumberger glitter around these days.

What else?

She was obviously the closest buddy of Bobbsie-Ann Boggsen, and beyond that Daphne sensed intuitively that she must possess, in one form or another, a certain artistic flair: this blending of gifts was definitely what her salon might well use.

Yes, putting it all together, what she'd heard about her, what she'd read, what she'd seen today, Daphne decided Rosemary Grovenour was definitely slated for IN.

And yes, that was Sonny Sahn, the INmost photographer of *Fig* Magazine, taking Rosemary's picture.

Yet—and Daphne was caught in a helpless agony of indecision—she was reluctant to go all out and make the commitment. She still had to be wary, her position was still not all that secure: one false move and immediately people might begin saying Daphne Bernlinsk is slipping, sliding into Dullsberg, Gaucheville, Old Hattown or Straight City.

—DON'T WAIT TO BE TOLD
YOU NEED PALMOLIVE GOLD!

Daphne therefore decided to hold herself in check, cool it, keep her attention on what was going on around her, to the way Waldo Stryker, who loved her, and his assistants, who loved her, kept changing the camera setups, recording the variegated antics of the cocktail party—yes, they all loved her: she was a bachelor girl and already twenty-eight years old—they all loved her and not a real male in the lot, except for Stryker's producer, Michael O'Leary, beside her now, huge and astute, and saying in a half whisper, "Daphne, you can believe me, this thing to-day that Waldo's doing is going to end up a cinematic saga." He paused to follow the direction of her gaze. "What do you think of her? Her name is Grovenour."

"Yes, I know," said Daphne. "I'd say she's pretty much my cuppa."

"Very much mine, too." A concupiscent grin was bold on O'Leary's coarse-grained face.

"Hey—!" Waldo Stryker's voice boomed out in warning.

It was precisely at this moment that Rosemary Grovenour while moving across the room accidently struck her foot against the camera's tripod, knocking it over, the camera falling to its side on the carpeting, the rods of the tripod askew like the stiffened legs of a dead animal.

"Oh, I'm sorry!" said Rosemary Grovenour. "Is it—"

"Yeah, it's still running." Waldo Stryker reached down to pick up the camera.

"Look—why don't you—I mean, what would happen if you just left it there, running like that?" Rosemary Grovenour said out of what must have been either embarrassment or a des-perate attempt to turn the mishap into an asset.

"Hey—why not?" Waldo Stryker stepped away. "Rosiepooh, that's exactly what we have to do." He fumbled with the BMT token at his frail chest. "Hey—look what we've got going for us here!"

The overturned camera, Daphne saw then, was focused up-ward to the window seat where Nina ver den Kahr and her fiancé Jake Harowitz, the painter, were playing dominoes. "No—don't move, keep playing, Ninapooh," urged Stryker. (Nina ver den Kahr was a post-debutante who was going to marry Harowitz because, as she told everyone quite freely, "I'm sick and tired of people saying I'm anti-Semitic.") It was clear now what Stryker wanted to get: Nina ver den Kahr was sitting cross-legged, her Little-Girl sheath crumpled well up above her knees, the flesh of her thighs forming a columnar milkiness fading into pubic darkness.

"Oh, this is visual ambrosia!" cried Stryker. "Don't stop, keep pushing those dominoes, baby. This is the cube root."

—BORN A BLONDE? NO—BORN BLOND!

"Hey—" Stryker exclaimed to Harowitz, "hey, Jakeypooh, she's going to look greater than La Jaconde!"

"Screw you, Waldo," growled the other painter, "everyone knows what you're trying to do to the American woman."

Hank Hartley came over to Daphne and the others: he was taking orders for a pickup dinner—peanuts, popcorn, maybe some caviar. Was Bobbsie-Ann staying or was her husband Bill home waiting for dinner?

"He'll wait," said Bobbsie-Ann. "He's on a TV kick now, nothing but Westerns. I stopped looking at Westerns when I was sixteen. All the camp was still in them then."

"You're staying, aren't you, Daphne?" Hank said.

She nodded. "Is Christine Stelward coming?"

"Her name's not on the list," replied Hank irritably.

She leaned closer to him: "What about Jackie? I heard, I don't know where, that Jackie might be coming later. True or false?"

"True and false," said Hank with that maddening vagueness he often invoked just to keep people palpitating with curiosity about his public projects or private parties.

"Oh," Daphne Bernlinsk reproached him, "how you cherish your cool."

—WHO'S DRINKIN' ALL THAT DIET-
RITE COLA? EVERYBODY!
—MISTER CLEAN!

"You see, Rosemary, what we're after here is not just movies, not what the term means in Hollywood or Europe, but what Waldo is trying to—" Michael O'Leary, the producer, kept his arm above the back of the sofa, letting it graze Rosemary's shoulder from time to time or letting his hand fall casually, intimately against her arm—"what Waldo is after is the spiral essence of the cube root, so to speak."

"Spiral essence? What is that?" asked Rosemary.

"The core of the essence, the groiny grain extracted from the cube root of total spontaneity," said O'Leary.

He must have thought she was an idiot, Rosemary reflected. She turned to see him staring down her bosom like a man in a trance.

She shifted her position and looked at her watch.

"Of course"—O'Leary resumed his observation of the filming of the party—"of course it isn't every day you get a natural personality like Bobbsie-Ann Boggsen. I mean, look at that, look at her!"

But for some reason she could not fathom, Rosemary did not want to look at Bobbsie-Ann, who had commenced a new dance, leading it this time with Jake Harowitz and with three other couples circling her like disciples in a primitive rite. But Rosemary decided she was tired of watching Bobbsie-Ann. Was there nothing else or no one else to watch? She addressed O'Leary: "What is your connection with this movie, Mr. O'Leary?"

The wail of The Stones had been replaced by The Hermits who were now replaced by the latest rock group, The Creeps.

"My connection?" Michael O'Leary let his fingers play

lightly, absently against her arm. "I'm Waldo's producer, though our films are never produced as such, if you know what I mean?"

"Yes," said Rosemary, her attention adrift.

Incredible: Bobbsie-Ann Boggsen was dominating the entire party. How? She'd already been in the film they'd shot earlier; anyone else would have let it go at that. Not Bobbsie-Ann. That energy, that ego, that drive was without end. Nothing counted. No one else mattered. Incredible. And now here she was once again pacing the proceedings.

Rosemary looked at her watch for the second time: she really had to get herself out of here; obviously Grove wasn't going to call. She had to get herself back to 1027, be there, be on hand when Grove arrived: the very least she could do, particularly after that uneasy night she'd had with him, particularly after the decent way he'd been, making every attempt to be fair about her, taking on more than a fair share of the blame himself. She had to leave.

Then why did she keep sitting here? What detained her? Was it merely because of the attentiveness shown her by so many people? Surely not just that.

"Where do you live, Rosemary?" the importunate O'Leary was saying now.

"What?"

"Where do you live?"

"Oh—" She borrowed from Grove. "Near the Metropolitan Museum."

"That's not too far from my establishment. Ugly word. I'm on East 86th," said O'Leary.

"I have to leave now, as a matter of fact." Rosemary did not move: a faintly disagreeable sensation seemed to have insinuated itself upon her.

"Let me ask you this, Rosemary. How come you've kept yourself off-frame all this time? People get the idea just because the police have raided Waldo's showings, that all we want are kicks, all this jazz about our being pornographic—oh sure we've had some nudity and a little sexual byplay, but it is always natural, spontaneous, pure even, that's what Waldo is after, the cube root, don't you see?"

Rosemary picked up her bourbon, but suddenly the smell of it sickened her. She wished the lights weren't so damn bright, and all that noise.

"Oh great—great, look at her now!" O'Leary's cloying interest in Rosemary was diverted as he turned to stare, like the others, at Bobbsie-Ann Boggsen.

—GO GO GO WITH THE STRENGTH OF
CHEERIOS—BANG!

An explosion of laughter erupted into the high apartment as Bobbsie-Ann left Harowitz and, going to the end of the noble Fifth Avenue windows, took hold of one of the draperies, pulled it to her and began imitating in that marvelously uninhibited way, a burlesque stripper caressing between her thighs the proscenium curtain.

Laughter ricocheting around the room.

And Rosemary suddenly standing up.

"Anything the matter?" Michael O'Leary was beside her.

"No, it's just that—" she couldn't say she felt this nausea—"I think I'll see if I can get myself some tea. I have to leave, but if I could get some tea—" She started for the kitchen.

"Here, allow me, madame." O'Leary accompanied her through the long pantry and into the stainless-steel expanse of the kitchen. "I know this place almost as well as my own." His statement was more braggadocio than reassurance. He put on some water to boil, then moving back to her, took hold of her hands. "Are you sure you're all right, Rosemary?" His big unwelcome arm around her in bracing but extremely personal solicitude.

"Actually"—Rosemary stepped back and swallowed—"actually I feel all right. It must just have been—"

"Here, sit down." The gallant O'Leary brought over one of the black iron Italian chairs which circled the white table by the windows.

"Oh—no. Thank you. Actually I'm fine now, I don't know what it was." She even smiled at him. She knew it couldn't have been the bourbon, nor was it anything she'd eaten, and after all hadn't she really been having a glorious time here today?

Or had she?

Surely—surely it couldn't have been that spasm of resentment over Bobbsie-Ann Boggsen's exhibitionism a few minutes ago.

It couldn't possibly be that.

And immediately Rosemary was conscious of that same sensation, though worse: hot and debilitating.

No. Absurd. It couldn't be jealousy. Absurd. Why would she ever be jealous of Bobbsie-Ann whom she loved, who had been so wonderful to her, who—

But why wouldn't the sensation leave? It seemed to burn in her bones and—

Michael O'Leary said the water was about ready. He was fussing at one of the long counters, and she looked up to see him opening all the cabinet doors and she saw shelf upon shelf of canned goods, jars, boxes, bottles, a miniature supermarket.

"A miniature supermarket," she heard herself say.

"Hmm?"

"Nothing."

He brought over the cup of tea, but she didn't taste it. She kept staring at the rows of packed shelves and at the debris on

the counters, the empty or half-empty boxes and cans and cigarette packs and bottles.

And she could almost feel tone and color coming back into
her cheeks: "Look—"

"What?"

"I was just thinking"—Rosemary could no longer resist the
impulse—"all that stuff, I was just wondering if I couldn't just
fool with it—"

"What stuff?"

"All this—" She moved to the counter, absolutely ex-
hilarated by the way this impulse kept working in her.

Why not? A costume, a kind of pop dress. For the pop party.

And from out of those dismal suburban years, all those abortive creations, being the belle of amateur arts and crafts, out
of all that unrewarding experience, she found herself happily,
agilely putting together now what was becoming a costume
that would match the very sounds that assailed her from the
next room.

Yes, if she could make it work, and yes, it had to work: those
two cardboard boxes, one had held cocktail crackers, the other
a soap powder; she could cut them into the shape of shoes and
—where were there any scissors around?

O'Leary pulled open drawers. He found a pair.

She pulled off her Paris dress.

He was watching her then. "Hey, how about that!"

She said, "Could you dig up some wire and string?" Fortunately Woody, only mildly startled, came into the kitchen then
and she put him to work at once, and soon with the gift of her
facile fingers, her natural dilettante's flair for the cottage arts,
she was right back in full form: improvising pendant earrings
out of Schweppes bottle caps, a tin brassiere out of two empty
cans of Martinsons coffee, a necklace from which she hung a
book of S & H green stamps (Hank Hartley, she learned, saved

them assiduously). For a skirt she used sections of that morning's *Herald Tribune* and *Times,* cutting, patching, pasting fragments so that the skirt, six or eight inches above the knees, formed a collage of Sulzberger and Lippmann and Prescott and Jimmy Breslin and Ada Louise Huxtable and Maurice Dolbier and Eugenia Sheppard and James Reston and Art Buchwald. She made a hem fringe of clothespins and with five empty cans of Campbell's tomato soup she fashioned a towering red and white chapeau.

Woody had been indispensable, while O'Leary, pork-fingered and clumsy, his hulking presence hovering around her, kept muttering, "Oh great, the cube, baby, the cube!"

She completed the change in the pantry, and then moved gingerly as far as the threshold of the living room; she floundered there, her feet unfirm, spongy, her heart in a frenzy of throbbing: all the inspiration and zeal of her kitchen episode now congealed into a gelatinous dollop of fear and self-consciousness.

O'Leary, however, in that basic way of his, pushed her forward and out into the cavernous white-walled room, and there she stood unseen, unnoticed, obscured, feeling just as she'd felt at other times when she entered a room in the company of Bobbsie-Ann Boggsen, except more foolish.

Where *was* Bobbsie-Ann now?

Wasn't anyone noticing Rosemary?

Yes—people were aware of her, but in a peculiar or hesitant sort of way; there seemed to be some sort of indecision.

Yes, that was Bobbsie-Ann darting into the powder room.

But the others—yes now, and oh God she wished she'd stop this trembling.

There—yes, Nina ver den Kahr seemed to be watching for Giles Folor's reaction, but Giles was studying Daphne Bernlinsk's face, and Daphne was surreptitiously watching Hank

Hartley, while Hank Hartley was furtively eyeing Waldo Stryker.

Where was Bobbsie-Ann?

"Hey—!" It was Waldo Stryker who courageously leaped forward. "Hey, lookit, lookit!" the pop painter cried out. "Rosiepooh, it's lovely, I can't bear it—such ambrosia for the retina! The cube root, the penultimate, baby. Baby, don't move until I get you!" He went for the shoulder harness to which he now attached his camera.

"Rosemary Grovenour!" Now Daphne Bernlinsk ran to her, a brave heroic figure, brimming with love and courage. "Darling, how inspired!" She closed in on her and tilted her poodle head against Rosemary's cheek. "Umm. KissKiss! Darling, is this ever my cuppa!"

Where was Bobbsie-Ann?

Nina ver den Kahr and Harowitz clapped vociferously, generating wild applause all around.

—NEW WISK—PUTS THE STRENGTH WHERE THE DIRT IS!

And slowly, deliciously now, Rosemary's fright, her unsureness began to dissolve, though Waldo Stryker's whirring camera around her was unnerving: he was shooting from below and now from the rear and now from up on a chair and—

"Did I miss something here?" It was Bobbsie-Ann Boggsen; she was fully clad again. "Rosemary! I mean, when did all this *happen?* Oh, what a—I mean this is really something—" She kept fussing around Rosemary, at a loss for the first time, the spectrum of her vocabulary momentarily constricted. But then her hyperthyroid eyes became aflash with solicitude and she was *With It* once more. "Oh, wild! But here—let me fix this, it's coming apart—" And placing herself directly in the path of Stryker's view, so that her mighty mane of hair was like a brilliant gold shield between Rosemary and the camera, she bent to the task of tightening or readjusting the thin wires which held the coffee-can brassiere in place.

"Oh, that's the cube, baby!" shouted Waldo Stryker.

"The cube!" echoed Mike O'Leary and several assistants.

"This ain't high, it's *orbit* camp!" declaimed Waldo Stryker.

"*Orbit* camp!" cried two socialite sub-junior cosmetic editors of *Fig,* who'd arrived a few minutes before.

"*Orbit* camp!" cried the latest arrivals, Mr. and Mrs. Leikis, a young pair whose hundred-thousand-dollar Park Avenue apartment, which might have been just another conventionally fashionable one, had been given national magazine and newspaper coverage because they had chosen, being obviously very *Switched On,* to hang the dining room, the foyer, the living room, the bedrooms and the bathrooms with paintings of monumental cheeseburgers, colossal Coke bottles, cans of baked beans, soaring syringes, F.B.I. posters, ceiling-high photos of Clara Bow's face and Elizabeth Taylor's mouth, and many other fine artworks of this genre.

"Rosemary—" The red-haired novelist Giles Folor pushed his way through, cigar majestically in hand—"Rosemary, I'm going to lure you out to my plantation on Long Island this summer! We'll have a wee cotillion in your honor." He turned, and assigning his next silver-chased words for Daphne Bernlinsk's ears, so that her piece in *Hipman* would more accurately record his presence at H.H.'s party, said, "Rosemary, as far as I'm concerned you are the queen of the 1964 tournament of terror! Let me christen thee." He bent forward and with mock rituality, kissed each of her coffee-can breasts.

The cocktail party had come to a halt: the camera had ceased; gone was the cacophony of Rock and conversation and the TV commercials; gone, at least for the instant, was the gravitational force known as Bobbsie-Ann Boggsen.

For when Rosemary looked around, Bobbsie-Ann had moved off: and Rosemary felt almost ashamed for the triumph which pulsed and tickled inside her like a suddenly healing wound.

"Hey—Rosiepooh, it's for you," called Waldo Stryker.

"What?" she said.

"The telephone," Stryker said.

Hank Hartley said, "Take it upstairs, Rosemary."

That would be Grove now: she felt a twinge of regret, even hostility, that he was drawing her away from this rich, sensual niche of admiration in which she found herself.

Carefully she climbed up the spiral staircase, wanting to keep her costume intact. What, she wondered now, would Grove have said if he could have seen her?

Upstairs in Hartley's master bedroom with the master bed and the master works of art, she picked up the telephone. It was not Grove.

"Mrs. Grovenour," said the voice of woman, a young woman obviously.

"Yes?"

The caller identified herself as Edna Mitchell, one of the sit-down demonstrators in Staten Island.

Grove was in jail. That was why the woman was calling. Many of the demonstrators had been taken to jail, though they'd all been released now. Except Grove.

"Why? What did he do, what happened?" Dismally remorse seized her; dismally she looked down at her costume.

"I believe there are several charges—resisting arrest, assault and battery—" The woman reported that in the course of the scuffle as police tried to break up the demonstration this afternoon, one of the patrolmen had been unnecessarily rough with

Mrs. Mitchell—she was four months pregnant—and when they got to the precinct station, Grove voiced his objections again and got into a violent dispute with the man and had slugged him right in front of the desk sergeant.

No, Grove was not hurt. Only the policeman.

Five hundred dollars bail. Checks were not acceptable, said Mrs. Mitchell, and Grove did not wish to use a bondsman. His attorney was out of town, and he did not wish to involve Edwards and Osgood. He wanted to keep this as quiet as possible, though the press was already on to the story. Would Rosemary get the cash from the wall safe in the apartment and taxi down and bail him out at once?

"Yes—yes, I'll get right down there, tell him I'll be down as soon as I can."

Apologetically the woman said she was sorry, and that Mr. Grovenour was a "perfect doll" and if there was only something she could do—

As Rosemary started downstairs, the sounds of the cocktail party had resumed, risen, the voices and the dance music and again Stryker's strident TV tape, merging with a decibel force that was almost shattering.

—YOUR SEWER SERVICE—AND AWAY GO TROUBLES DOWN THE DRAIN—ROTO-ROOTER, ROTO-ROOTER!

"Rockefeller's ordered a meeting on it for a day after tomorrow," Grove was telling her. "Which I hope will get some action out of those miserable bastards."

"Isn't that getting action awfully fast?" asked Rosemary. He noticed, on this taxi ride from Staten Island to Manhattan, the sharper edge of her concern and interest; she looked livelier, in fact, toned up, a flush of life in her face which was unmistakable and which he felt, not without a degree of pleasure, might have been generated by his involvement in the day's events or drama. And it seemed to him too that their talk last night in bed had helped to clear the troubled air between them. "How were you able to do it?" said Rosemary.

"Because I sat on that telephone until I got on to the Lieutenant Governor, and then I got through to Rocky with whom I've never had the greatest relationship in the past—but today he came through, very cooperative. Do you still want to go to Hartley's?"

"I think it's just what we ought to do. It'll force you to relax. Otherwise, Grove, you'll never unbend. I promised Hank I'd bring you back alive."

"Well, let's see how it goes." When the cab made the swing around the Pan Am Building—Park Avenue's high-rise obituary —Grove gave the driver the address of Edwards and Osgood. "I have to stop at the office, I won't be long, Rosie."

Clouds, delicate and the hue of the pink peonies on his terrace, looked incongrous, innocent in the New York sky, and the June sun, though dying, still flung back the clouds' color, washing with this pearly tint the western flanks of the midtown façades.

It was shortly after seven when she and Grove entered the office building on Madison Avenue. She accompanied him to the 38th floor (Edwards and Osgood also occupied the two floors below) and she waited while he went through the memorandums on his desk. He signed a number of papers and he had to telephone his secretary and one of the other officers of the realty firm before he was ready to leave.

"Look, Rosie—I don't think I can face anyone yet. I need at least one, possibly two drinks, before I do anything."

"Of course. And you must be starved." Rosemary's way of reminding him of the dinner at Hartley's.

"Only for a drink, and maybe some sexual advances of a low-down order," he said. "Let's go in here and discuss the situation." He led her into the nearest bar, the Pewter Mug, which was put together by a Madison Avenue decorator to look like a venerable English pub: the mirrors and the bulbous crystal lights, the red plush and the oaken beams (made of plastic). The soft banquettes, however, were designed less for the hardy ascetic Britisher than for the American's more pampered and flaccid backside.

As soon as he inhaled that first vapor of his lemon-scented vodka martini, and as soon as it had cooled his tongue and his spirits, he was able to discuss the day more fully and answer more of Rosemary's questions.

"Of course," said Rosemary later, as they started on their second round, "when that woman—Mrs. Mitchell?—called me, I got the scare of my life. I thought oh God now what's happened to Grove?"

"That's what I like to hear, Rosie, a wife in a high state of feminine fear for her messed-up mate." He glanced at her. "Incidentally you look pretty jazzed up, I mean you look different than when I left this morning. I meant to tell you before."

"Mr. Lorio's fine Italian hand," said Rosemary.

"Oh, I didn't know you were going there—" An indefinable disquietude touched him.

"I didn't either—" She reached for her glass. "I mean, it was just one of those freak things. I was with Bobbsie-Ann and she had an appointment and he took me on too—last minute." Then hastily in a rush of solicitude: "Grove, what I wanted to know, I mean did you really have to hit him?"

"What?" He looked at her; he decided his apprehensions might have been unwarranted.

"The policeman," she said.

"Listen, Rosie—after all, it was just a scuffle, a lot of noise. It wasn't Selma, Alabama, you know."

"It was awfully crucial to you last night," Rosemary re-minded him not without some justification.

"Yes. But that was only in our own backyard."

"Anyway—you still haven't told me how it happened, I mean exactly."

He lit another cigarette. He exhaled a long cone of smoke. He peered ruefully at the knuckles of his right hand. "Exactly, I'm not sure myself." It was soon after eight o'clock that morning, he recounted for her, that the group, about ninety people, started the sit-down, forming themselves into a human barri-cade in front of the heavy machinery which was being used to drain the large, tree-studded building site: there followed the quiet, futile discussions with the workmen, and then the less quiet argument with the foreman, and later the highly volatile threats of the president of the contracting corporation who noti-fied the police. Within ten minutes the "bluecoats," led by the chief of the parkway patrol division, arrived and ordered every-one to leave.

"No one budged," said Grove. "Then some of the bulldozers started revving up. We all just sat there. We linked arms."

"With Mrs. Mitchell?"

"She just happened to be next to me. There was a rabbi on my other side, so you see we were properly chaperoned." Grove paused. "The chief ordered us to leave a few more times and when we kept refusing—I told him there wasn't a prayer of our leaving, everyone was too goddam mad about this entire un-wanted project. After that, there was a long hiatus and I took off for the nearest telephone and called Albany. That was my first call, and I got nowhere. When I came back I saw that more flics were on hand, and then they started pulling the lines apart. You never saw such a twisting mass of arms and legs, guys were falling right and left, handbags flew open, eyeglasses got crushed—my friend the rabbi was in there swinging and lost his toupee—it was the goddamdest rumble you ever saw, and then more cops got there and not a single United States marine to save us. They started to carry everyone bodily to the paddy wagon, and that's when it got roughest, that's when this hot-head cop gave Mrs. Mitchell all the trouble. When I tried to break it up, two of New York's finest took care of me. It wasn't until we got to the station that I saw what kind of shape Mrs. Mitchell was in, I got a good look at her wrists—they looked like red rope, her forehead was bruised and—well, let's just say I lost my good manners and I got hold of that son of a bitch and—you know the rest. The precinct boys didn't take me too seriously when I asked permission to call Albany. At any rate Rockefeller has set up the meeting so that both sides will have a chance to present their case, and believe me there's enough rotten apples in this legal basket to keep the District Attorney's staff picking away for months. Meanwhile the Lieutenant Governor has ordered all work on the project temporarily suspended." Not until now, having summed it up, did Grove feel that rewarding sense of gratification. "I think I'd like another vodka martini."

"Grove—" She finished making up her face and handed him the silver compact which was a bit too large for the small beaded evening bag she had brought along from their apartment. Absently he dropped the compact into his side pocket. "Grove, why don't you hold off? Maybe we ought to go home. After all this, it would be stupid of me to insist we go to Hartley's now."

"Hell no," he asserted. For her sake. Reciprocity. The new deal. She had, after all, given up the affair at the Parke-Bernet for him last night. "I promised you we'd go to Hartley's, and we're going." He summoned the waiter of the Pewter Mug who was costumed in a way that made Grove wish that instead of seventy-five cents, he could have tipped him five shillings.

Like 1027, this neo-Renaissance marble and limestone co-operative at 958 Fifth Avenue, where Hartley lived, was another of those S and S palaces typical of the period just preceding World War I. Yet it did sustain a certain aura of the city's past, and Grove thought again of how few of these buildings were left, and of the handful of older, finer town houses of the nineteenth century still standing in this sector. But in the last six months alone three of the most perfect of these houses on Fifth Avenue had been demolished and new high-rise apartments, high in price, low in architectural distinction, were already on their way. (Not very far beyond, northward, in Harlem, this speed of demolishing the old and erecting the new seemed not to exist; northward in Harlem there was paralysis where action was desperately needed, while down here around Fifth, there was the swiftest action where preservation was preferable.)

He and Rosemary started up in the recently installed elevator, its interior appointments so contemporary, its attendant so ancient, though moving gingerly enough in his slate-toned uniform and the white pique stock stiff beneath the wattlelike flesh sagging from his jaw. The car stopped at the 11th floor, and a woman stepped in.

"Oh—hello," she said.

He couldn't recall her name.

"How are you?" said Rosemary at once. "You remember Mrs. Stelward, don't you, Grove?"

"Yes."

"Helen Marmonier's party," said the woman whose perfume, though surely as unique or expensive as Rosemary's, dominated the car. It seemed to happen like this very often, this unawareness of Rosemary's scent, whereas the fragrance of another's perfume was something he was immediately conscious of. "Are we all going to Hank Hartley's?" said Mrs. Stelward.

He nodded. The elevator door slid open and he followed the two women into Hartley's foyer, a commodious room of white marble flooring and white walls, darkly accented by the only American heirloom pieces in the apartment, the two high-backed Chippendale chairs by Chapin; on the half-round wall table reposed a sensually sinuous sculpture by Arp.

"You saved me again, Rosie," said Grove as Mrs. Stelward advanced into the living room. "How'd you remember her name?"

"Oh, come on, Grove, why do you insist on saying you never remember her? That figure and that hair, and the rest of it—"

"I recall it now all right, but I didn't when she suddenly popped into the elevator like that." But he saw that Rosemary still regarded his protestation dubiously: she liked to get her teeth into a nugget like this. She seemed to have forgotten that the night of Helen Marmonier's dinner party, he'd had nothing in his head except the Calvert mansion, and he could have come face to face with Sophia Loren, Jeanne Moreau or Julie Christie without the impression being necessarily imprinted on his then-distracted mind.

"Grove!" Hank Hartley, in one of those workman's garbs he liked to effect, greeted him. "I'm delighted you could come or that Rosemary could drag you up. I understand there's five hundred bucks on your criminal head—"

"Oh?" Grove frowned.

"It was on the seven-o'clock news, also," said Hank. "Let me get you a drink, we haven't had a notorious character in this place since . . ."

Grove asked to use the phone and went upstairs to call the elder Osgood who, more than anyone else in the realty firm, always gave him the most difficult time about his outside activities. When he returned from this disagreeable duty he passed

Rosemary, who was standing near the foot of the spiral staircase: she seemed to be virtually suffocated by what looked like
a band of admirers. He was hesitating on the edge of the palpitating group when Rosemary saw him, and when she came over
he told her about the call to Osgood.

"Hey—Rosiepooh—" a voice intruded—"let us not flake
out!"

"I'll tell you more about it later," said Grove.

"Grove"—she turned to the others—"I'd like you to meet
Waldo Stryker. And this is Daphne Bernlinsk—" She also introduced him to a further assortment: Giles Folor, Nina ver
den Kahr, Mr. and Mrs. Leikis, a chap from Lincoln Center
Film Foundation, a P.R. girl named Joan Saunders and her
husband; a raven-haired woman who was a genuine American
Indian in a genuine Yves St. Laurent dress.

It didn't occur to him until a few minutes later that Bobbsie-
Ann Boggsen was not present: but who was he to be ungrateful
for big blessings?

He was just retreating from this tight little circle when Hank
Hartley, who was standing nearby with Christine Stelward,
beckoned to him. "What do you think of the way your wife
walked off with our little cinematic gasser today?"

"I—that is, Rosemary hasn't had much of a chance to tell me
about it yet." He was a fraction put off, but in his attempt to
ignore it, he said cheerfully, "The husband, as you know, Hank,
is always the last one to hear."

"Well, she created quite a stunt, I'd say. I was just telling
Christine about it." The way Hartley looked at Mrs. Stelward
suggested his interest in her went beyond that of being a good
host or neighbor. "You've met, haven't you?"

Grove nodded.

"I believe this is the third time," declared Mrs. Stelward,
"though I'm distressed to say the first time Mr. Grovenour tried

to put me in my place or what he thought my place was. Isn't that quite true?" But her smile was absolutely even, the clear green eyes without malice.

"I'm afraid I was a little shook up that evening," said Grove. "As a matter of fact"—he could not resist grinning—"I'm not exactly in top form tonight, either."

"From what I've heard, I don't wonder," said Mrs. Stelward. The dark russet hair was not masterfully piled up on this occasion, no chignon, no Woolworth pearls, and no emeralds. Tonight her hair hung to her shoulders, straight and just as casual or outdoorish as the last time it had been stylized and elegant: he was mildly astonished to realize how much he had retained about her, but that, he supposed, was probably because Rosemary had so often and so pointedly dwelled on her features.

Hartley's houseman, Woody, came by and Grove asked for a vodka on the rocks, and then he said, "Hank, you'll have to give me the report on Rosemary."

"Well," said Hartley, "while you were beating up that gendarme today, Rosemary gave the pop art movement something of a beating—either that, or she gave it another dimension."

As he listened to this account of her exploits, Grove was surprised, and yet not surprised; he was pleased, and yet not at all pleased. On the one hand it was fine that she could have created and carried through an idea and that she had stirred this mob into admiration; on the other hand, it was also pretty goddammed silly. Of course it was consistent with these exercises in dilettantism that Hank Hartley always found irresistible.

Grove kept watching the group around Rosemary, and he wondered how she could take them all this seriously, this mob which was trying so hard to stay Switched On despite the feeble current they had to work with.

When Hank finished describing her antics and the subsequent applause and endorsement by the clan, Grove belatedly recognized why she had seemed so keyed up, accelerated, on the drive back from Staten Island; what he thought had been her revitalized interest in him had, of course, been born of something altogether different.

But Rosemary, he conceded, couldn't be blamed if she took her triumph in such an outsized way: she'd had meager pickings much too long. What he regretted, though, what discouraged him, was the extent to which he and she differed as to what was consequential and what was not.

"Hank," he said, "I think I'll get myself a little more of this inferior vodka of yours." He left him and Christine Stelward, and moved off to the seventeenth-century Gothic pulpit and poured himself a robust double.

"Hey—" he heard Waldo Stryker say in joyful imitation of Rosemary, and with that happy inflection of discovery: "I think I'd better stop taking those 'Ego Pills.' "

Laughter: the clan had evidently found yet another gambit of Rosemary's to titillate them.

As now Daphne Bernlinsk was lighting Rosemary's—no, it wasn't a cigarette; it was a cigar which Rosie had playfully taken from the novelist Giles Folor.

In wonderment, Grove watched her: not merely because he hadn't seen her smoke a cigar since those Connecticut weekends eight years ago before they were married, when she'd done it before an audience who might be easily impressed or shocked, whereas tonight among a different set of people her gesture represented the very opposite, reflecting a new sureness, control, and her pleasure at being on top of a situation.

He turned away: he cautioned himself to take this vodka with only moderate haste, though it was not long before he was telling Woody to fix him another double. But then trying to reason that if Rosemary was emerging with a new or different personality, it might be to the good, it might be an answer; perhaps if her hunger for what she desired was sufficiently appeased or glutted, she might end up wanting no more of it.

Let us hope.

By the time Woody with the help of two virginal and uniformed Irish girls—they must have been shanghaied from Schrafft's—had the buffet dinner under way, Grove was feeling primed enough to wear his best social face. A dozen more people had arrived and the evening was beginning to take on a different shape. Whereas earlier there had been a certain homogeneity to the party—that is, Hartley had achieved what he always strove for, that felicitous admixture of S and S'ers with so-called creative or bohemian people—now, however, when the dinner had been finished and he and the others were having espresso, Grove noticed what at similar parties in the past sometimes occurred: the interlocking and interloving crowd had somehow become untangled, had somehow parted, each group ending up in its own corner. It had not happened in any arbitrary way but rather like an inevitable act of nature, like pebbles and stones being dispersed by the tides.

He was standing somewhere on the periphery of S and S land, talking with a Briarcliff girl who was serving her first strenuous year with *Vogue*, and who was wearing bell-bottomed party pants, when Hank Hartley called for quiet.

"We're going to show Waldo Stryker's latest film now," Hank announced, his hands thrust boyishly into the pockets of his rough Army and Navy Surplus Bargain denim work jacket, "and for those who don't know about it, I'd like to say that though I haven't seen the finished cut, I did see some of it being made at Waldo's place, and I think it represents a bold push forward in the art of movie making. Waldo's films, in addition to being a permanent part of the Cinema Society's library, are becoming increasingly popular with intellectual groups on many university campuses. But rather than discourage the police, this seems to have sharpened their suspicions and they seem more determined than ever to prevent these showings. Anyway, I assume we'll be spared any trouble tonight. Okay, Waldo? I think we can start——"

"Okay, Hankeypooh." Assistants had set up the screen against the fireplace wall, and Stryker now took his place at the rear of the room by the projector.

The scattered islands of guests began to drift together again. Chairs and sofas were being occupied. Grove saw Rosemary and some of her friends and admirers settling themselves on the floor. He waved to her. She waved to him. He might have joined her but he had had his share of squatting uncomfortably on the embattled ground of Staten Island. He glanced around. When he saw Christine Stelward sitting on one of the two long sofas, he decided to deposit himself beside her.

"I thought," he felt obliged to say, his words vodka-honed, "if you didn't mind, I'd favor you with my ungracious presence once again."

She smiled, saying nothing. He drained his espresso cup and placed it down on the floor. After a moment he said, "My wife turns out to be a great fan of yours, Mrs. Stelward."

"That's very nice to hear."

"I'm merely trying to show you that I'm capable once in a while of saying something inoffensive, even flattering." He tried to remember, but couldn't, what he'd heard about her at Helen Marmonier's party. She was married—the ring was there—but she obviously was not making it her life's work anymore. Nor was she, he judged, despite her disarming way of smiling and the fact that she went around without her husband, one of those ladies who play the Upper East Side Boudoir Circuit: his attention moved to her legs, and immediately he was aware of a fugitive flurry of uneasiness—for even as he looked up again, he could see the back of Rosemary's shining new coiffure a few rows ahead of him.

He lit a cigarette.

"Hold it a moment, Waldo—" Hank Hartley, who had come around and was about to sit down on the other side of Mrs. Stelward, turned and crossed behind the sofa and moved to the foyer door.

"My dear Hank—" It was Dexter Knight, gray hat in hand, his pigeon-gray suit double-breasted and double-vented, a dark and perfect red carnation in his lapel. He stood shaking hands with Hartley. "Hank, what are you all dressed down for? A meeting at the Teamster's Union?" He paused. "You know David, don't you?" He nodded toward his youthful secretary, though already Knight's seal-black eyes were peering with practiced ease and avidity around the large duplex apartment making that inventory of faces familiar and unknown. "I hope I'm not too late. You know, Hank, I'm very tolerant of you and your cultural shenanigans and *tout ça*, but if Rosemary Grovenour hadn't called and passed on your good invitation, I—oh, hello, Rosemary—" he called out, "no, don't get up to greet me, it's a sign not of your energetic youth but of my advancing age." As he edged forward: "I understand via two travelers who were passing through Ankara, Turkey, that you've done the most delicious things in this pop thing—well, do them if you *must*. And bless you, darling." He greeted Nina ver den Kahr and a few others. Then: "Oh, hello, Stryker, how are you?" But a faint frostiness invaded his voice as he addressed the painter, that chill that often marks the recognition in public of one homosexual of another.

"What can I get you to drink, Dex?" asked Hartley.

"A brandy, thank you," said Dexter Knight. "I hope from

now on you will stop telling people I'm reactionary about going to parties like this. You see, I can be quite flexible if I choose. Grove—my God, you. What's happening? I thought they'd be tucking you into some varmint-filled little police cell in darkest Staten Island. David—?" He glanced around until his gaze rested on his slender and golden-thatched companion who had joined Rosemary's group on the floor. Knight then moved blithely to the chair alongside the couch where Grove and Mrs. Stelward were sitting. "Ah, Christine—" He extended his hand to her. "Darling, seeing you is an utter tonic. I adore your hair that way. Long and loose. It's too natural to be natural. Who did it? Mr. Lorio?"

"Mrs. Stelward," said Mrs. Stelward.

"You know, Christine, you're one of the few women I know —and I've known you since you first set your little debutante's foot on terra Plaza—but you're one of the few women who can *do* your own hair and *talk* about it without making me cringe."

She laughed. "I only do it myself when I remember that going to the hairdresser's takes four hours out of a day, which is a stupid waste, isn't it?"

"Darling," Dexter Knight sat down and crossed his legs, or rather wrapped one leg around the other in that rubbery, cozy way common to men of his kind, "darling, there's more Puritan in you than I realized, though thank God it doesn't show."

Hank Hartley brought him the brandy, and then seated himself on the other side of Christine Stelward. The lights were turned off and presently the sixteen-millimeter film began. In the flickering darkness Mrs. Stelward took out a cigarette, and Hartley, a nonsmoker who always kept a packet of matches in his pocket, lit it for her.

The title of the picture, *Communion # 3*, and the credits were shown in the almost illegible longhand script of Waldo Stryker:

not written by Waldo Stryker
not produced by Michael O'Leary
not directed by Waldo Stryker

There followed a shadowy view of an amorphous room which contained a bed on which lay a long-haired, pock-faced girl in white leotards; she was reading a book and she would wriggle around sporadically, and then putting the book aside would stare languidly to her left. The camera would hold on her for what seemed an interminable time as she stretched her body and began undulating in a clumsy and prolonged exhibition of sexual frustration or, if you chose, desperate longing for human recognition and affection. Alternating with these views, the camera would swing leftward to show nearby a brutish young man of outsized shoulders and biceps, attired in the glossy black deep-sea-diving gear of a frogman, as he kept checking his twin-tubed oxygen tanks and his elongated spear gun, working away with total masculine preoccupation.

In silence the film's monochromatic images continued their alternating rhythms with absolutely no variety and with no regard for time until the final shot, which was sustained for nine minutes as the camera held on the girl's blemished face, the only relief coming when a fly, which touched down on her cheek, caused her to twitch the insect away.

A storm of superlatives shattered the quiet now as the lights were turned on and everyone, or almost everyone, cried out their praise to Waldo Stryker and his crew, as well as to Hank Hartley.

And Rosemary gave Stryker the accolade of several sisterly kisses which seemed to delight him. Two photographers—one in a jump suit and Beatle mop—whom Grove had not seen earlier, appeared and kept flashing away at the barechested, barefooted Stryker as he talked with Rosemary and some of the others.

The spectacle, like that of her smoking the cigar, continued to spark his curiosity, his wonderment and, though he tried to resist it, his dismay.

"What did you think of it, Mr. Grovenour?" he heard Mrs. Stelward asking.

He turned.

"The film," she said.

"Well"—he was thankful now for the diversion—"for a while there it had a kind of nice ugly sexy ambience, but then something happened, it fell apart. Maybe it's just overexposure—"

"Yes, very likely. But that poor girl." Mrs. Stelward shook her head. "One thing can be said anyway. It's doubtful if this picture will advance the case of the American female."

"Or the male, for that matter," said Grove.

She turned to Knight: "What did you think of it, Dex?"

"Hmm?" Knight was peering across the thronged apartment to where David was talking with one of Stryker's young assistants. Then: "Oh, the picture?" With disciplined control he smiled and said, "Well, let's just say I liked it better than *The Greatest Story Ever Told.*" He chatted on and then excused himself, rose and, after an elaborately innocent detour of the party, paused as he came upon his secretary and the other young man.

"What can I get you to drink, Mrs. Stelward?" asked Grove.

She would be grateful, she said, for a little Scotch and much ice.

While Grove stood waiting by the pulpit-bar for Woody to prepare the drinks, Dexter Knight sauntered over. "I'll say good night to you, Grove. I'm afraid I've had enough of Hartley's mélange. I'm just waiting for my sometimes talkative secretary to talk himself out."

Grove said, "I didn't know you knew Mrs. Stelward."

"*Mon cher,* why not?"

"I was going to ask you a question—"

"I never say anything indiscreet. What is it?"

Regret and embarrassment seized Grove. Yet he heard himself say, "I was just wondering about her, that is, I've seen her around but—"

"*Sans* husband?" said Dexter Knight. "I told you, Grove, I never speak out of turn, but since I happen to trust you and being inordinately fond of you and your popular wife, the situation with Christine is—" As he lowered his voice his dark eyes took on for the moment that glinting zest people often reserve for announcing some fragment of bad news about a friend. "It's one of those unfortunate Catholic involvements. Her husband —Howard Stelward—is simply holding on to her. He's always been an indifferent Catholic. Until Christine wanted to divorce him. Then he became holier than His Royal Roman Holiness. But as I understand it, it's Christine's father, who's very much an R.C., who—"

The recital was broken off, for it was then that he saw David following the other young man up the spiral staircase. And, like that night at The Discothèque last winter, Dexter Knight's face underwent a helpless transformation: age and sorrow, which discipline had temporarily shielded, now appeared to weigh down his flesh and extinguish the vivacity in his eyes. Nevertheless, when he gained control again, he hastened away, managing to walk with his customary *élan*. And Grove saw him ascend the spiral staircase, but when he came down he was alone, and alone he departed.

Grove brought the Scotch to Mrs. Stelward. She was standing

alongside the sofa, smoking a cigarette. He supposed he was looking at her differently, that is, seeing not only what was obvious—the green eyes, titian hair, the curve of her calves —but what he hadn't observed earlier. So that now through the lens of knowledge or partial knowledge he'd just acquired, he could see in the tone of her face a patina of something else; sensing, in the fair tissue of her skin, a darker texture of melancholy.

"Thank you." She took the drink. Then she said: "I've been admiring you, I mean I was thinking how after the kind of day you must have had, you can still find the energy to come here and be—"

"Ah"—a sudden mischievous grin—"that's because when I go to parties like this, I'm inspired, and energy pops out of my fibula, my left ventricle and from every follicle of hair in my head—"

"Grove—oh, excuse me—" Rosemary had joined them. "I just remembered you still have my compact."

"So I have." He brought out the square silver compact from his side pocket. "Whenever I carry this I sort of list to starboard. It's like ballast. I suppose that's no way to talk about a birthday present—"

"Anniversary present," Rosemary corrected him.

"Yes, I meant—" But the unfortunate words had escaped him.

"Next time," said Rosemary, "I'll bring our Memory Pills." Then: "I'd better get back to the—I didn't mean to interrupt—"

"You didn't at all," said Mrs. Stelward.

"Rosie, do you want a drink?" he said: aware, as Mrs. Stelward must surely have been, that the question of Rosemary's immediate need of the compact was highly debatable.

Yet this was one occasion when her possessiveness startled him, for she had certainly not gone out of her way to be with him during the party and she had certainly preferred instead to remain happily enclosed by the parentheses of her most recent friends.

Or was he being unjustly critical of her because he had resented her intrusion and her betrayal of jealousy in front of a virtual stranger?

(But since Christine Stelward was in fact a stranger, why in hell did it matter one way or the other?)

"Yes, I'd love some bourbon, Grove. If you wouldn't mind," Rosemary was saying.

He was turning to leave as a young woman, Joan Saunders, in white Courrèges boots, white skirt and enormous owl-like dark glasses, stopped by on her way out. "Then I'll check with you tomorrow, Mrs. Grovenour?"

"Oh—yes. Yes," Rosemary said in haste.

Joan Saunders, he recalled now, as he made his way through the clusters of Instant Celebrities and INsters, to the pulpit-bar, was the P.R. girl he'd met earlier, the one who worked for Winn Associates. And what in the name of Jesus would she be checking? What now on Rosie's agenda?

At the bar he looked back and saw Rosemary speaking animatedly (overanimatedly), to Mrs. Stelward. He knew what that meant.

He sighed: there would now be another of those noisy polemics with Rosemary on the way home tonight; it was only a short walk from here to 1027 but it would be like ten miles, and even as he contemplated the prospect, the muscles of his jaw grew taut, and the weariness he'd managed not to yield to overtook him.

His spirit, moreover, was not elevated by the debate now in

full heat directly behind him. It had all begun in such a civilized way, Daphne Bernlinsk and the others absolutely agreeing that this obsession with who was IN or who was OUT was merely an idiotic manifestation of America's immaturity—yet within no time at all, the partisans were at it hot and heavy, comparing their sacred lists, giving to this esoteric concern all the fervor of their Promethean intellects:

"D.D. is In—"

"V.V. is Out—"

"C.Z. is In—"

"According to *Harper's Bazaar*, Plimpton is—"

"The *Times* says Bellow is—"

"According to Eugenia Sheppard—"

"E.E. is Out—"

"He was In until *Time* put him on the cover—"

"No, *Vogue* says she's back In—"

"Susan Stein as of now—"

"De Gaulle's definitely In—"

"Nixon was *always* Out—"

"Mimi is In—"

"According to Diana Vreeland—"

"But according to Gloria Guinness—"

"In, but not Chic or With-It—"

"With-It and Chic but not In—"

"Baby Jane—"

"Rauschenberg's In—"

"Minni is Out—"

"Isabel Eberstadt is In, *toujour*—"

"Little T is—"

"Warhol is, at least through July—"

"According to *Esquire*—"

"Sybil still is—"

"According to *Hipman*—"
"Bobbsie-Ann—"
"B.B. is Out—"
"In—"
"Out—"

10. La Boutique Martine

Situated on East 62nd Street, irresistibly near either The Colony or Le Trianon restaurant, this fashion enterprise of Martine Volier's is regarded as a shrine of chic by those women (mostly under forty) who buy their Paris-imported, custom-adapted clothes there.

If the prices are brazen, one doesn't mind; for what one pays for is Martine's singular flair, the way she takes a French suit or dress and adapts it brilliantly to the body and personality of the individual buyer, and then proceeds through the exacting craftsmanship in her workrooms to produce the final garment flawlessly to one's taste. So that her clientele, despite her prices and her sometimes outrageous tongue, is devotedly loyal.

And profitable. Though her business expenses are formidable, and involve discreet distribution of folding money among a line of dedicated civil servants from various departments of the city's government, including the police, Martine lives quite simply. She is thirty-seven and her needs are basic: good food, fine wine and, rarely, a gift for some young man who proves himself to be masterful, undemanding and unsentimental in her bed.

In every sense this Paris-born and indomitable woman knows what she's after and what she's not after: she does not, for example, try to win over those ladies who would perish if they didn't purchase their wardrobes at the collections in the French capital (and who, in addition to needing to be among the first women of the world to acquire the newest models of the *haute couture*, also find it comforting, if not downright delicious, to be perched on a tufted little chair amidst Gloria Guinness, the Baronne Alain de Rothschild and Eugenia Sheppard).

Nor does Martine go sleepless fretting about those patriotic ladies who pride themselves on "Buying American," and who—Martine often mimics them—are heard saying: "Why go to France or Italy when I've got Norell right here?" or "Bill Blass is my boy!" or "I just couldn't live without my Lilly!" or "I'd die without John Moore."

Now and then, however, one of the "Buy American" enthusiasts will defect and escape bravely across the fashion frontier to seek asylum at Martine's.

Like this young woman, Mrs. Boggsen, who has just entered.

But she will have to wait. Everyone is busy, and Martine herself is talking with one of her *femmes fidèles,* a client of many years standing.

Martine is an independent-minded woman whose harsh early life is seen in her lively but unsoft brown eyes. She often confounds new customers by the way she dresses, preferring the skirt and sweater favored by the ordinary *vendeuse* at Dior's and other Parisian houses. Just as the walls of an art gallery are unobtrusively gray or white to feature the paintings, so it is that Martine dresses simply to center interest on the clothes she sells.

And this September is turning out to be an exceptional selling month, bringing as it has a number of new people, among whom there was that bright, overtalkative girl, Daphne Bernlinsk, whose money must be as abundant as her taste isn't, but who came here because she admired the chic of Rosemary Grovenour.

Bon.

Now here is this creature with the blondest and the longest hair, another of those persons whose antics in New York, whether one wanted to notice them or not, have become familiar to Martine.

"Yes?" Martine at last advances into the front salon to greet Bobbsie-Ann Boggsen. "Can I help you, madame?"

Help?

If there was one thing she wouldn't turn her back on, thought Bobbsie-Ann Boggsen in a spasm of humility, help was it. At least from the outside in, she'd decided she needed some assistance. Which meant clothes. She'd always carried the banner for the Seventh Avenue boys, but now the French *haute couture* had taken on for her an almost mystical need. And even though Rosemary did shop here, why should that stop Bobbsie-Ann? After all Rosemary was just one of countless others who patronized Martine. Of course, coming here wouldn't be the same as having Seventh Avenue come to you—her closets were packed with models she'd helped publicize for American designers— there would be no free Tricks and Treats in this low-key, high-priced establishment.

But it was fall. And every fall she was consumed with the spirit of fashion, the lure and love of it. But plus: she needed a change of pace this time, a change of style; she needed *something* to ward off this prickle of fear that her life was being subtly, slowly undermined, a suspicion that her place in her world had somehow altered, just the smallest bit. Not even noticeable to anyone else.

Maybe she was being supersensitive. Maybe she was being superresentful of that special festival of films at the Museum of

Modern Art this summer. Waldo Stryker's picture of Hartley's party (titled *Popumentary*) in which much of the action around her had been cut out, and more footage given to Rosemary Grovenour. And after that, of course, there was that sickening rash of pictures and stories in the New York press depicting Rosemary at functions not only in East Hampton and Southampton but, weirdest of all, attending ceremonies at the opening of a new City Rehabilitation Center, and at the Housing Bill rally in front of City Hall, and a dinner party at Gracie Mansion.

Not that Bobbsie-Ann had been out of the ball game, very far from it, baby. For example, hadn't there been that wildest and campiest of parties on Sybil's Floating Discothèque on Long Island Sound? And at another party, hadn't that publisher talked to her about doing a book on what he called "your life in the Popsie Generation"? Yes. Even though he hadn't followed through, never called her since then. And she'd be dead before she called him!

"How do you do? I'm Mrs. Boggsen," said Bobbsie-Ann to the Frenchwoman. "I've decided that it's time for me to start thinking about Paris clothes."

"But we have no other kind," came the cool put-down from Martine, and for two cents Bobbsie-Ann would have walked out right then and there and gone to Bergdorf's or Chez Ninon.

"What I mean," she said, "is I'm interested in a complete wardrobe for the whole season, or at least to start the season—"

"I see." As they talked, the woman kept coolly studying her, and wasn't there something unnecessarily unkind about the way she was appraising her hair? "I understand. Yes." Almost human now. "Why don't we have a little coffee. We can discuss the problems in my office."

Spoken like a psychiatrist. Down on the couch: last night I dreamed I was in my Paris-made bra.

But Bobbsie-Ann almost docilely followed the slim, dark-haired Frenchwoman through the next salon.

Oh, wasn't that D.D. and Isabel and Jean over there? Yes. She waved to them. New home week.

And now into the long wide hallway which like the salons was scented with St. Laurent's *Y;* delirious! She had to get some while she was here.

As they were about to turn into the office, a woman from the fitting room nearby called out, "Oh, Martine, could you look at this now, please? I'm in an absolute twitch of indecision!" It was Rosemary's voice.

Twitch of indecision.

Martine opened the office door for her and said she would be back in "just a *petite seconde.*"

Bobbsie-Ann hesitated: should she peek in and say hello to Rosemary or not? Not. She could hear them talking, and then she heard Rosemary say, "You're not at all yourself today, Martine. Is anything the matter?"

"It is nothing," said the woman in her lyrical Parisian accent, "I am only a little sad. This nice boy stayed with me last night. But it's no good."

"Oh, I'm sorry—" said Rosemary.

"All I wanted, you see, is a little fauck, but he insists on a serious relationship."

"Martine"—this time the voice was Daphne Bernlinsk's—"Martine darling, you're wonderful, you're definitely my cuppa!"

Bobbsie-Ann stepped into the office and shut the door. Martine soon appeared followed by a black-smocked girl with the coffee. Martine sat erectly on the chair by the gilt-encrusted Louis XVI desk. She sipped the coffee and said, "I thought if we talk first, Mrs. Boggsen. After all this is not a question of a few cruise clothes, is it? You are speaking about a serious wardrobe."

"What it is with me . . ." But Bobbsie-Ann floundered.

Martine proffered an almost tender smile.

"I mean, what I want, what it amounts to is a whole new feeling," Bobbsie-Ann declared.

The woman nodded. "Good. When you do business here, the talk is always between us. Privately. Women like that. Just as they like to make changes, they like—as you say, a whole new feeling sometimes. There can be so many reasons, a personal situation, the marriage or a love affair—"

"It's nothing like that," Bobbsie-Ann interceded at once, even though the interview now amused, even comforted her. "Nothing like that at all, Mrs.—"

"Please call me Martine, Mrs. Boggsen."

"Please call me—Ann." Bobbsie-Ann heard herself saying it for the first time, an experiment.

"Ann?" The woman seemed puzzled.

"Yes. Ann," stated Bobbsie-Ann.

"Very well. Now first, Mrs. Boggsen, I want to know some things, and I would like to get your precise measurements—"

When Bobbsie-Ann was settled in an alcove off one of the salons, she began her program by looking at some Chanel suits. Martine stood beside her while one of the saleswomen began to bring out the models for inspection. She selected a white one, braided with navy and sparked with gold buttons and chains. She regarded herself in the mirror and she was overwhelmingly pleased. The saleswoman, at Martine's order, brought in a pair of Chanel shoes for her to try on. The ensemble was complete: she virtually looked like a new personality. She had a new skin. Seven hundred dollars.

Yes. Martine agreed. It was right for her. "Except for one little thing, your hair, Mrs. Boggsen. I admire it—it is different, it is sexy, *n'est-ce pas?* And there is nothing wrong about that. People make the mistake of sometimes thinking wrong about sex, don't they? People are so quick to call one a whore. I have a friend like that, and I always tell her: 'I may be bed-minded, but darling, I am not a whore.' " Martine paused. "Yes, I admire your hair, but for these clothes, for the Chanel silhouette for example, it is not right. May I?" She moved behind her and lifting the thick long golden tresses, worked them with a hairdresser's dexterity into a different form, closer to the head and shorter. "Like this, perhaps, if you see how I am thinking—"

The entire ritual became ever more fascinating to Bobbsie-Ann. And long before it was over—she'd ordered the white Chanel and a suit by Yves St. Laurent, three Givenchy dinner dresses and one town coat, two Balenciaga ball gowns and a white plume-ruffed evening coat, two pairs of Chanel shoes, three pairs by Roger Vivier, and three handbags—she felt euphoric. A super euphoria suffused her newly born being.

She tried to hurry Martine about the alterations and fittings, but the woman refused to be pressed: two more fittings would be necessary and the times specified.

"Martine"—Bobbsie-Ann could not resist rhapsodizing—"as far as I'm concerned this is one of *the* days of my life, I mean the way you dig fashion is a revelation."

When the woman left her, Bobbsie-Ann decided to move to the rear room again and have another look at a Cardin dress she'd seen before. After the saleswoman had brought it for her she held it against her and consulted the mirror. Well, maybe not. Not for her. But her hair. That had to go. Martine just couldn't have been more right: that mass of brassy fur had to go. Exit.

Along with half her name.

Oh what a day. Historic!

In the mirror then, she saw that Rosemary Grovenour had

come into the rear salon. Bobbsie-Ann turned, smiled, crinkled her nose in smiling greeting: "Rosemary—hi—"

"Oh—hi—" said Rosemary not without some surprise. "I didn't see you—" Her hair was lighter in tone, more chestnuty now, and she was wearing a cinnamon Dior suit.

"I've been here half the day," said Bobbsie-Ann, but her words sounded superfluous somehow.

"I was here earlier," said Rosemary. "I just came back to pick up a package." This too seemed sash-weighted with effort.

"I love that suit, Rosemary. It's terribly swig."

"Thanks, darling."

"Well—" Bobbsie-Ann was determined not to notice the slight drop in the room's temperature—"marvelous running into you—"

"Yes. Is this your first time here?"

Bobbsie-Ann nodded. "That Martine, what a touch she has. Don't you adore her? Wild."

But another silence which neither of them seemed to know how to break. However, when a girl brought Rosemary her package, a gray and white box tied with gold cord, the stiffness of the interval eased.

"Oh, by the way—I was going to call you, Bobbsie-Ann. I hope you're not busy the 19th—that's two weeks from Saturday night. I'm having a little dinner."

"The 19th?" Bobbsie-Ann said as if she hadn't known about the party. "Oh, what a shame, we're penciled in for that night." She'd decided days ago that she had no alternative except to be inaccessible.

"Really? Oh that *is* a shame," said Rosemary. Then the crumbs of consolation: "Well, maybe it's just as well, you could be bored, sometimes that civic mob can be Dullsville Incarnate."

But if that were the case, why had Rosemary already invited Dexter Knight, Hank Hartley, Waldo Stryker and Daphne Bernlinsk? And God knew how many others. The fact was that Bobbsie-Ann had called Hartley last week to ask him to her theatre benefit party for the 19th, and he'd been unable to come. Now she knew why.

"Wouldn't you just know it?" said Bobbsie-Ann. "That's the one night we're going to the theatre. And Arthur afterward. We bought a slew of tickets—it's for the Cerebral Palsy crowd —and we invited a slew of people." Bobbsie-Ann's guest list, however, had not been put together until she'd heard about the Grovenours' party, from which, obviously, she and Bill were to have been excluded. "Well, anyway—let's be in touch. *Ciao.*" But then her gaze arched beyond Rosemary's shoulder: "Minni!" she cried to Minni Ogden Foote, her briefly one-time cancer committee colleague, a blond young woman in a pale gray Paris suit, black alligator bag and black alligator boots.

"Hi, Bobbsie-Ann." Then in a burst: "Oh, Rosemary! How are you?" Minni came over.

"Oh—do you know Rosie?" said Bobbsie-Ann, and unflinch-ingly put her arm around Rosemary's shoulder in a gesture of intimate, almost possessive affection: but oh how incredible that she should find herself having to cozy up to Rosemary in order to woo a creep like Minni Foote. "I didn't know you two knew each other."

"We met this summer," said Rosemary.

"Met? I should call it more an explosion," declared the fair and athletic Minni, who could be as authoritatively horsy and tweedy in the country as she was authoritatively elegant in town. Wasn't it the Minni Footes who in the end seemed to survive every kind of social climate? Bobbsie-Ann mused wist-fully. "Why," Minni was saying, "I daresay half of East Hampton is still talking about it." Minni expounded, "Rosie arrived in this absolutely spectacular white dress with black lace pantaloons, along with Waldo Stryker and a blind guitarist, as well as Grove and two members of the City Zoning Commission, and my, how that evening changed, didn't it, Rosie?"

"I guess we did get up some voltage," came Rosemary's airily casual reply.

Then Bobbsie-Ann said, "Minni—remember when you had that accident with the crepes suzette in Palm Beach last year? Well, Rosemary here is the one who took your place on my cancer committee. I must say it was really a fun ball game, wasn't it, Rosie?"

"Umm," said Rosemary. Low voltage. Glancing at her watch. "I'm meeting Grove here." And after a moment in which she took on the breath of the old cordiality, she said she did have to run. And there was that hasty cheek-pecking.

Minni Ogden Foote, who had started into the nearby alcove, looked back and called to Rosemary, "Bye darling, see you the 19th. We're in an absolute twitch of anticipation."

Bobbsie-Ann turned to confront her image in the mirror: "Oh," she murmured to herself, savoring Martine's accent: "Fauck zem all!"

Within Grove's sight was the windowless gray façade and white door of the French boutique: he could see it through the glass wall of the art gallery near Park Avenue where he was now with Christine Stelward. It was close to the boutique, though not too close, and it gave him more time to be with her, since he had to pick up Rosemary at five o'clock. The sheer necessity of making such an arbitrary, callous arrangement did not, of course, in any way soothe the sting of his guilt: for that ailment no scientific cure or balm seemed to be available.

It was almost five, he was saying.

Christine nodded: her eyes grave green ovals of contradiction above the gaiety of her smile.

They were still standing before one of the op paintings near the front, but not really examining it since their interest was elsewhere, this being a crucial day for them. Until very recently none of their encounters had been prearranged, at least not by her.

How comforting euphemisms must be: "God." "Fate." "Life."

It had been Grove who'd commenced it when he'd seen her in Central Park that Saturday afternoon a week after Hank Hartley's party last June. Bicycling. Exercise. He'd been the one who'd stopped her as she was pedaling past the lake; he'd been the one, who, on the following Saturday, rented a bicycle so that he could see her again. The third weekend she did not appear. It was obvious why.

But he ran into her twice after that, once at 66th Street and Lexington Avenue as she was coming out of St. Vincent Ferrer; though she was a renegade Catholic, her father was devout, and she accompanied him dutifully to church whenever he felt well enough to go. (The following Sunday he found himself, with a helpless, juvenile idiocy, walking, skulking near the church in the foolish hope of seeing her again.)

Not until that Long Island party at Minni Ogden Foote's, whose husband had been a fellow member of the Hasty Pudding, did Grove get to see Christine for any length of time. At that party Rosemary and her inseparable Waldo Stryker were creating so much frenzied action around the pool, diverting, among others, the two gents from the Zoning Commission, that Grove was able to corner Christine, be with her, talk to her for that isolated and heady hour. Not enough time for him, yet long enough to grasp unmistakably that the unruly emotion going on inside him was, despite her disciplined poise and manners, also alive within her.

Nothing, neither his conscience, nor his guilt, nor her resistance, could deter him from telephoning her the next day: could he see her? Anywhere, any time?

No, Christine had said. Surely under the circumstances he must know how impossible that would be.

Yes. He knew it. Of course he knew it.

In that case, she said, she was distressed to have to hang up.

After that, without protest and to Rosemary's astonishment, he willingly participated in or at least attended most of the social events on her calendar, becoming, he supposed, something just short of a Fop, a Swinger—all in the wild hope of running into Christine again.

When he did encounter her, however, it was without contrivance or design: this was in August when he'd just left behind him a meeting with the trustees of the Guggenheim Museum— he'd been there as a realty consultant—when he almost collided with her on the main floor of the ramp-walled rotunda. She could not object if he joined her, could she? Starting at the top and winding downward along the *via* Frank Lloyd Wright, they moved from picture to picture, not seeing them, not speaking, until without warning she paused and looked at him and said wasn't this being decidedly foolish? And he'd said yes, decidedly, but didn't she know how he felt? Couldn't she see?

She knew. Yes. And she could see: her hand touched the side of her auburn hair, and he noticed a movement, like a tremor, in her throat as she turned away from him. She moved down the ramp and out of the museum.

Settled. Over. Demolished with one stroke. The swing of the wrecker's ball. Finished as sure as Penn Station or the Calvert mansion.

All the proper moral action was on her side.

Well, he could be decent, too, couldn't he? He could be an

admirable chap, show that he too had that good old American moral fiber.

He therefore never telephoned her again.

Not until the middle of September, when the disease collapsed the last strand of American fiber.

He was braced, prepared for the next strike of the demolition hammer, but when he heard her voice it was unfamiliar, uneven, and she said in a breathy rush of resignation or relief, yes, she'd meet him. Where?

They met twice briefly. Each time in a public place.

And today in this gallery.

As now he said: "I think I'm getting more deceitful and clandestinish every day."

Her smile was unsuccessful.

"It's true," he said.

"I'm distressed to say, Grove, as much as I don't want to, that I just don't know what to do about it anymore."

"My whole goddam metabolism is kicking up," he stated.

"Yes," said Christine.

He stepped closer to her: but their closeness became so unsettling they finally had to move on to the next painting to try to find some distraction.

"I suppose," said Grove, "the sooner one recognizes himself as an ordinary swine, the better."

Christine stared at the painting. "Oh, I should never have let myself—" She stopped.

Into the wasteland of silence he said, "Where can we go? When?"

"I don't know," she said.

"Somewhere. Out of town. Any place." His voice, with its foolish, harsh, classic call of craving, was scarcely recognizable.

Movement again. The next picture, whose brilliantly calculated optical configuration must have seemed clean and clear compared to the chaos that swirled in him and in Christine.

"—all those people," she was saying then, "all those people one always hears about or knows—all those furtive couples who have to hide out. I just can't think that we're like they are. Or are we?"

"Yes, I suppose we are," said Grove. "That doesn't change anything though, does it?"

Christine looked at him: that hopeless, helpless, devastating green gaze, except that now into the always pellucid eyes an opalescent mist was gathering. "I think," she said, "you're probably late, Grove."

"Yes."

He crossed Park Avenue and continued the short distance up 62nd Street toward the boutique.

Not slinking, except in his mind.

No, he found he was walking briskly, an innocent and purposeful figure: but how facile he was becoming at deception, how easily you can acquire the gift. His brief fall from grace with Corlis Wilbur in Connecticut, though it could not be condoned and though it had been a hasty and loveless lapse, had never demanded this sort of serious subterfuge.

Was it an immemorial instinct?

Was it a gland in the body put there, secreted there, lying quiescent until the time it was called upon to function?

Function it did: he was discovering that he could be as shoddy and ignoble as the next man, couldn't he? A vice-president of Edwards and Osgood, a figure of civic responsibility, he could now add to these distinctions that of being just another ordinary adulterer—even though adultery as such had not yet occurred.

But if its fulfillment was imminent and your need or desire was too powerful for you to stop it, the act of infidelity was already yours. Bravo!

He opened the white door and entered the boutique. He saw Rosemary among the several women there; she was holding a package. He was struck anew by the metamorphosis which was taking place in her: a year ago she might not have been noticed among this cluster of fashion-dedicated women; today she was outstanding. It was more than her exterior—her hair was much lighter and higher, the bangs more dramatic, the skirt of her suit was well above the knees—for now even her stance was commanding, and the gaminesque glint that had marked her eyes had given way to a certain acuity, though it was more pleasurable than cunning.

How objective he could be now. Alas.

Ah, Rosemary.

She stepped down the three stairs into the front salon. "I was just going outside to look for you, Grove."

"Am I late?" he asked: the stalwart, considerate, hero-husband.

"Not for you," she said.

"I hope you spent a wadful here," said Grove: nothing like guilt to turn a man into the most prodigal of spenders.

"I'll bet you do." She smiled.

It was true that with the spiraling success of her life, the costs of her wardrobe and other expenses and indulgences had recently almost doubled: but of course mum's the word for the errant husband.

As now Madame Volier paused on her way through the room to greet him, and he said (ah, wasn't he the sensory kid today), "Martine, what smells so delicious in here?"

It was the St. Laurent perfume. "*Y.*"

"You mean why, like in a question?" Grove went on with the smallest of talk, finding that he still needed that extra measure of time to make the transition from palpitating culprit to calm and hearty mate.

"No. The letter Y. For Yves," she explained. Then: "Would you like to see your wife's new dinner dress?"

"I'll wait to see it on her." The gallant spouse.

"It's the Courrèges I told you about, Grove," said Rosemary.

"Oh—?" Looking vague: the very spitting image of the bumbling American male.

How many other roles could he play to dramatize for Rosemary, and the world, their felicitous marriage?

The irony of all of it, the unbearable irony, was that lately their marriage could be said to be better than it had been in many years.

Further irony: after his despairing of Rosie's lack of enthusiasm for his interests, her reluctant but dutiful participation in his life, she seemed now to be becoming the epicenter of it.

More than that: she was helping him in a way he would never have expected. Undoubtedly her motives might be questioned, but he couldn't deny that she was creating all kinds of benefits for him.

She had, in a word, driven in; a new force, a virtually new Rosemary. And if her dinners and other activities were extravagant, they seemed to be thawing out or warming up quite a few of his friends and other wheels within civic circles who normally put up stiff resistance to some of his plans, projects, fund campaigns and myriad long-shot dreams.

But if Rosemary's antics and her recent popularity had drawn the interest of a whole fashionable gang of New York hedonists, it had also attracted the very people he would have sworn would be indifferent or impervious to it. Whatever this proved about human nature was not very complimentary. (Though the same could be said, these furtive days, about his own nature, couldn't it?)

As they stepped out into October's late afternoon, Rosemary

said, "Are we walking there?" Then: "I should know better than to ask that."

"Unless you'd rather not?" said Grove—a most considerate man, and becoming more so every hour.

"What time is this reception?"

"The drinking part starts any minute now." He took her arm as they moved eastward toward Park Avenue.

(The gallery had already closed.)

Though he frequently talked about the state of the streets, he threw himself into this favorite topic with even greater zest now so that he might generate a sense of normalcy: these olive-toned sycamore trees were among the city's best, weren't they? And why didn't more residents emulate 62nd Street's fine show of windows and balconies laced green with ivy and spattered scarlet with geraniums?

A sight for Mary Lasker.

How was he sounding? Rosemary did not seem to detect in his excessive effusions a single counterfeit breath.

"How long do you suppose it'll last?" asked Rosemary.

"Until the booze gives out."

"I don't know why you look so glumsy," she was saying as they reached Park Avenue. "After all you went through last June, it's nice to see you get the sweet end of the stick for a change. I should think you'd want to take out your Red-Letter Day Pills."

Christine. Back at 958 Fifth Avenue. Alone.

He nodded. In a few minutes they'd be at the Waldorf and that reception would be under way for the recently formed Inter-Borough Planning Association of New York, at which he, among a few others, was to be honored for his "leadership and accomplishments" in the Staten Island crisis.

"My trouble," said Grove, "is I'm too unaccustomed to suc-

cess to take it gracefully." Just at that instant as he looked southward the length of Park Avenue, through the gray veil of dusk,
the long broad thoroughfare was startlingly stippled with red:
all the traffic lights at all the corners flashed red, and crimson
glowed from the rear lights of a thousand halted cars, while
atop the Pan Am Building a helicopter hovered, quivered, its
red lights blinking, so that the aircraft looked like some me-
chanical and monstrous night insect.

11.   The Park=Regent Hotel

Hard by the geographic center of the Upper East Side's social preserve, on Park Avenue at 70th Street, stands this anonymous mass of limestone from which at the sidewalk level the flat, mulberry-colored canopy juts forth like a haughty and impertinent tongue.

This hotel is a stronghold, a meeting-place, eating-place, drinking-place, coming-out place and living-in place (daily rate for a double-room: $40 to $55, though half the units are suites ranging from three to nine rooms). It is a bastion in which political destinies have been shaped, high business negotiated; where debutantes have been presented and deflowered, and where their mothers and fathers before them have known the inevitable progressions from courting to divorcing or simply from flirting to fornicating.

Mr. Alfred Shurle, the hotel's bland, Swiss-born Assistant Director (the Director is in Bermuda convalescing from a nervous breakdown) in his sober vest and short coat, his striped trousers, his deceptively mild blue eyes behind the anonymous glasses, moves on cushioned feet across the starkly understated lobby and up the six steps into the main barroom. It is a tepidly beige chamber, without daring décor, without an exotic name, being known only as the Park-Regent bar—in the manner, if not quite the spirit, of the Ritz of olden times.

It is half-past five on this misty November afternoon and the barroom is handsomely peopled and gratifyingly busy. Mr. Shurle is anxious to greet Dexter Knight, whom he has seen entering a few minutes earlier. Though Mr. Knight needs the Park-Regent, it would be more accurate to say the Park-Regent needs Mr. Knight. (The public relations staff on the mezzanine floor, though chiefly occupied with news releases and photos of dinner dances, committee meetings and charity balls, has already been notified that Knight is on the premises. He is among the chosen few to whom the management each Christmas sends a Tiffany-purchased gift.)

Personally speaking, Mr. Shurle does not much care for Knight. Personally, he has never liked that kind, though in recent years they seem to have proliferated fantastically, and he has become accustomed to them. However, Mr. Shurle has always known that a hotel careerist, like the perfect Call Girl, never permits his private taste to govern his business life: he has acquired the charming, enigmatic smile, the casual solicitude, the subtle arrow of admiration for his clientele that seldom betrays his true feelings: even his wife, during the most intimate moments in their boudoir, sometimes wonders if he really desires her or if he is merely serving with a smile.

"Mr. Knight, how does it go today?" he inquires as he reaches the table.

"How does *what* go today?" Dexter Knight retorts: he is obviously in one of those sullen moods of his; he keeps glancing impatiently across the crowded room to the entryway.

Mr. Shurle, who knows enough not to let himself be impaled on the spike of Knight's sometimes cruel wit or disposition, blandly changes the subject. "I understand we'll be having the pleasure of seeing you again for the December 16th evening." He is referring to the International Hunt and Race Society's annual ball—for the benefit of World Cardiac Research Foundation.

"Yes," says Dexter Knight, "but I hope we see a few less German faces this year."

"The Princess Firna Birenzia is already in from Rome and the Comtesse Jacqueline de Rocheferron arrived yesterday from Paris." Shurle thus evades any answer that might get back or offend the German aristocracy who will be residing at this hotel; at the same time he is giving Knight a piece of information.

"Oh really?" The first stroke of pleasure is seen brushing Knight's roseate cheeks. "I adore them both. They are both narcissistic, of course. I do prefer Rocheferron, though. She is a coldblooded and ruthlessly beautiful female, not only an excellent horsewoman but a dedicated clotheshorse."

"Have you ordered your drink yet?" asks Alfred Shurle.

"I have," said Knight, "but I suspect the waiter must have gone over to the Delmonico to get it."

Shurle heels around at once. The captain is not to be seen. But luckily the source of the lamentable service is now on his way and Shurle gives this waiter, a new one, the silent, stern reproach that tells him this gentleman is to be given serious and flawless attention.

"Good God, Alfred—" Dexter Knight nods toward a table near the piano where two women are seated, obviously awaiting their husbands. "You're letting just about everyone in here these days, aren't you?"

"I beg your pardon?"

"Those two—" Dexter Knight squints in disapproval. "They

must have just disembarked from Lake Forest, Illinois. Page-boy bobs, Davidow suits and the circle pins. I daresay they're probably wearing invisible hairnets."

Shurle's smile suggests agreement even though he knows that the Park-Regent, like the Plaza or the Regency or the St. Regis or the Delmonico, needs these outsiders, members of the pushing and irrepressible army of affluents from all over the U.S.A.

He turns to see if Knight is satisfied with his Scotch and soda. He signals silently to the captain to dim the central chandelier. The pianist has seated himself. "We've persuaded Chet Darnell to play here during cocktails. Started yesterday."

"Yes, I know." But Knight is once more glancing with impatience toward the entrance of the bar.

After murmuring a final pleasantry, Alfred Shurle, his bony shoulders erect, his features bland and precise as a watch face from his native land, takes his leave.

Dexter Knight had almost finished his drink by the time he saw his tardy secretary make his appearance in the room: at least forty minutes late. Why? Where? With whom?

How charming he looked, too charming really, in that newest English suit, slightly pinched in at the waist, and those high vents giving his tall figure such verve, such chic. God, he shouldn't let him run loose like this. Wicked.

But at least he was here now. How nicely he moved across the room, blue eyes earnest, and the finely curved mouth; and now there was breaking that faintly taunting smile as he neared the table. Meaning what? His thick hair, as he passed beneath the discreet sparkle of the crystal chandeliers, became a dappling of gold.

What a different boy from that cadaverous book clerk he'd discovered how many autumns ago?

"I thought you'd be coming directly from the apartment, David," he greeted him.

"Could I at least have a drink for God sakes," David settled himself and studied his virile fingers, the chunky gold ring Dex had recently picked up for him at Van Cleef and Arpels. And what about the gold cuff links purchased at Valencort House?

After the waiter had departed with the order, Dex, unwilling to forsake his suspicions or fears, said, "If you weren't planning to stay in, you might have told me."

"I had a few personal errands. Would you like to have it play by play. For God sakes, Dex, is this your idea of a—"

"I merely missed you a bit, David. If that's a crime, I apologize." Still, Dex had to know. Time unaccounted for. He'd telephoned the apartment two hours ago in the midst of that charity fashion show at the Carlyle and the maid had said David had left. Where? What errands? With whom?

He ordered another Scotch when the waiter brought David's vodka.

"Anything special come in?" Dex asked, business briskness dominant in his tone now. It might ease the moment or disarm David, and then he'd loop around to the subject a bit later.

"The usual." David brought from his inside breast pocket the sheet of monogrammed memorandum paper.

Dex put on his black-rimmed reading glasses and studied the notes—telephone messages from friends or public relations people and social secretaries and others:

Mimi Strong called re: release for Dec. issue.
Le Trianon. Tomorrow lunch. Rosemary G.
Alfreda Peysen. Still ill. Delaying return from Middleburg, Va.
The Colony. Gene will make it later.
Daphne Bernlinsk. Wouldn't say what or why.
La Caravelle. OK. Thursday dinner.

Joe Tankoos. Re: Wine Cellar bash for Princess d'A.
Diana V. returned your call.
April in Paris Ball people. (Again!)
Send congrats. Eugenia Sheppard.
Lucile Sloane. Handling Boggsen acct. Omit "Bobbsie." (!?!)
Helen Marmonier's secretary. Dinner 25 Nov. Black t.
Chu-chu Tew. Wants private word. Tomorrow A.M.
Call C.C. at N.Y. Times.
Sent extra photos Cee-Zee Guest.
Jerry Zerbe. Call. Photos.
Minni Ogden Foote. Dinner Nov. 29.

He removed his glasses and handed the paper back to David: surely enough time had passed to soothe the way to truce. But as he looked at him he noticed that the interval of silence had only seemed to aggravate his secretary: there was that familiar brow-knitted signal of dissatisfaction, the mouth drawn into a fine line of anarchy and that trick of his, twirling and twirling his glass, grooving circular patterns into the beige table cover.

"May I ask," he said, "what's got you in such a thing now?"

"Hmm? Oh—what difference does it make? Can't we enjoy a drink without all this royal inquisition for God sakes?"

"I happen to care about how you feel, David. In case you didn't know."

David shut his eyes and passed a fatigued palm across his forehead.

"Are you tired?"

"No."

"If you think you've been working too hard—" Dex began anew.

"Did I say anything about that?"

"Not directly. But what is it?"

"Nothing."

Therefore Dex had to revive the ancient theme: "I mean if

you think you've got such a dreadful lot, it's only fair to remind you that most people have it infinitely worse. Odd as that may seem to you." But he could not dam back the bitterness: at first when David had come to work for him, live with him at 1027, the boy had joyfully cried out his gratitude from morning to night. Of course since then he'd grown soft, spoiled. Dex had really spoiled him wickedly. Yet, why not? Though one did want some reward, some indication that David, despite any minor grievances, appreciated the level of life to which Dex had elevated him.

"Let's not get carried away, Dex. For God sakes stop making like the Royal Master and the Orphan Footman."

"I wouldn't exactly call that being quite fair. Personal matters aside, David, you work for me, yes. But I am simply your employer. You even possess a Social Security card."

"I have the card but not the security," came David's immediate rejoinder.

"Meaning?" Though Dex knew too well.

1027. The apartment. Again. Back to that.

This was the third time in a year David had the brutality to hint at it, and Dex was left so incensed now that he said, "There are all kinds of easy jobs around, pensions and benefits, all the security the welfare state can bestow. Why don't you go out and see for yourself what the world has to offer?"

"I happen to know what I can get. If I want to."

"Oh?" It had never come to this.

"If you don't believe me, I can give you a sampling."

"Why not?" said Dex imperiously, coughing to conceal the tightness in his throat.

"Well for one thing," said David, "I've been given a marvelous chance with Tony Ammonds' firm."

"Tony Ammonds?" Dex should not have been shocked: he should have known that Tony Ammonds, whose interior decorating Dex himself had made so popular and fashionable with so many of his friends and in the many magazine pieces he wrote —he should have known that in the last analysis, Tony was just another immoral, promiscuous, opportunistic, untrustworthy, insatiable crotch-crazy queen!

"Yes. Tony is very anxious to have me join him," said David. "As a matter of fact he even has a place I can live. A place of my own. It's a little apartment practically on the East River, across from the Brearley School, and a perfect dream of a—"

"Well, by all means," said Dex, "I think you ought to snatch it, a flat of your own. What more can you want? And on a clear day you can look out and see all those dear little trolls dashing out of Brearley—"

"Okay, Dex. I was only telling you. You asked me and I told you."

"My, my." Dex swallowed. If it was the last thing on earth he would never under any circumstances deed over the apartment at 1027 to David or anyone else. Not as long as he was alive: once the apartment were in David's name and ownership, Dex knew his hold on the secretary would lose its traction. Even if David's now brutal pressure represented the kind of act Dex himself had once committed years ago, even if Dex had cruelly forced his one-time elderly benefactor to will him the apartment, he refused to let himself become the victim of the very same demand.

"It so happens I turned Tony down," said David then.

Relieved beyond measure, Dex's sarcasm returned: "That must have taken high courage."

"Not too," said David. "I had a much more interesting offer elsewhere."

"Oh?" Then: "Why, I had no idea, David, I was harboring such a rare prize, keeping him caged up so pitifully—" And lapsing into another of his Proustian parallels: "Don't tell me that all this time our Albertine has been straining at the bonds of captivity, and sneaking out to make all manner of obscene and wicked rendezvous?"

"Drop it, why don't you!"

"What better offer now?" Dex insisted.

"Mrs. Jason Calisster."

"You mean Marion Calisster?"

David nodded.

"And what did she offer you, dear? You needn't look at me like that. I'd really like to know what that vulgar soul suggested."

David said, "She needs a personal secretary. Mainly."

"I see. And you'd like me to give you a reference?"

"She's chartering a yacht," David resumed, a gauzy softness filtering his voice. "She's chartering it for next May and cruising the Greek islands—the Aegean ones mostly—and she needs someone to handle all her work and, well, be a kind of companion, man of all seasons, that sort of thing."

"How can you resist it, David?"

"It's a flat ten thousand for the trip."

"I see. That *is* putting it on the line, isn't it?"

"I admire her honesty," said David.

Into the dismal pause came the sounds of Chet Darnell who was tapping out his nostalgic evocation of Cole Porter's "Just One of Those Things."

"And tell me, David"—Dex selected a cigarette from his case —"what happens on that yacht when you aren't island hopping? In other words, who hops Mrs. Calisster? Of course I know she had her face lifted in Zurich a few years ago, but I can't help wondering about the rest of her alluring anatomy, knowing as I do that even that little man in Zurich can't perform any further miracles of levitation. As for that little moustache of hers, even though it keeps growing back, one doesn't always notice it for all those diamonds she keeps slung around that unfortunate corrugation of withered skin she calls her neck."

David said, "You always resort to bitchiness when all else fails."

"All right, David. I'll try to be realistic then. But let me say, as someone who knows something about horse flesh, that ten thousand dollars is an awfully cheap price to pay for a first-rate blue ribbon stud."

But David had by now fortified himself against the onslaught. With a maddening calm, he turned and offered Dex a light from the 18-karat-gold Dunhill lighter Dex had presented to him three years ago (and which Dex had received as a gift from Mr. Lorio a year before that; while the hairdresser undoubtedly had been given the lighter by one of his innumerable and ardent lady clients).

Dex beckoned the waiter: another vodka, another Scotch and soda. He fitted the lighted cigarette into his ivory holder.

"I'm sorry, baby," he murmured. Greece. He'd had the identical plan himself. Less than a week ago. The fancy had taken hold then, but he had decided not to discuss it until he was certain he wanted to carry it out.

"To tell you the truth," David said very calmly, "I've been itching to see the Greek islands, there's a shop in Mykonos run by a young guy named Niki who—"

"I got the impression," Dex broke in, "that what you were itching to see was a deed of ownership to the apartment." Spoken at last.

"For God sakes, do you have to put it that way?"

"You're the one who's put it that way. . . ." Dex paused; he sensed, sniffed victory: time for a turnabout. "Let me say, David, that my worldly possessions are not many, but the apartment at 1027 is more than just a possession to me. It is my only dependable love—outside of you perhaps. It's all I truly possess. It's the one thing I can always turn to, come back to, when the world bores me or when on those very rare occasions I let myself admit that nothing but misery and tragedy awaits the best of us—" He had not intended to go that far. "Of course, I'm overdramatizing, aren't I? But you understand, David, that aside from this, there is nothing of mine you can't have any time you want it." And even before he could check it, he gave way to the thrust of his impulse: "The funny part—it always happens like that—but the funny part, David, is that one of the things I wanted to talk about today, why I thought we could have a festive little drink here, was that I stopped in at Ports of Call last week and I talked with Stein and entourage, specifically about doing the whole Greek circuit, including Istanbul—and then you let fall those wicked little offers, or should I say propositions? from dear Tony Ammonds and dear Marion Calisster, and I thought I'd be damned if I'd ever mention Greece again." He waited, peering at his cigarette holder. "But then, why not? Why shouldn't I? If it's a competitive world, why shouldn't I put my bid up over theirs?"

No response.

"How would you feel about that, David?"

He waited, but from a nearby table there intruded the conversation of two men who, in their passionate concern for the particular British cars they owned, had let their voices rise to an indiscreet and un-Rolls-Roycean loudness: "No, no, I tell you, Jim, the *only* way to run the air-conditioning pipe through that Rolls is to have the ashtray section removed!"

"David?"

"What do you want me to say?" David's tone was disturbingly glacial. "Would I like to go to Greece? Obviously. But that's not the whole point. My situation isn't at all what it should be.

Everyone I know around my age is already established, on the way up. Secure and—"

Exasperated, Dex said, "Oh, come now. One minute you talk about dropping anchor with Marion Calisster, and the next you're talking about being established, on your way up. As for all this vaunted security—" But even now, at this painful juncture, the sight—spectacle—before him was such that he had to break off. Was it that no crisis, however personal, would ever transcend his obsession with the vagaries of the social scene? "Are you seeing what I see?"

Dexter Knight was still watching with total absorption the incredible tableau forming at the banquette less than a dozen tables away from him.

"Yes." Even David was drawn away from his truculent rebellion. "I see it. But what is *she* doing with *her?*"

For there was Bobbsie-Ann Boggsen, more elegant than splashy, and sitting down beside her now was her companion, Princess Firna Birenzia, the young Roman beauty about whom he'd been talking with Alfred Shurle not more than an hour ago.

"I don't know," Dexter Knight murmured. "Is it Bobbsie-Ann who's with her or is she with Bobbsie-Ann? There *is* a distinction. But in either case, I must say it's a stopper, isn't it?"

"Yes."

Within these few seconds Dexter Knight had taken on an unexpectedly fresh interest in Bobbsie-Ann Boggsen. As he observed the women, Firna Birenzia's mischievous eyes found his and immediately she waved, and Dexter, who had never dreamed he would be publicly seen going to Bobbsie-Ann's table, rose to do just that.

"It's Ann—not Bobbsie," David whispered the reminder.

And Dexter left, feeling even more charitable toward Mrs. Boggsen—Ann—because it was her startling arrival with the

Italian noblewoman that had quite naturally, if temporarily, restored the comradeship between him and David.

"Ah, Firna—" He leaned down to kiss her. "*Amore mio, tesoro mio!* It couldn't be a whole year, another year, and you look even younger, if that's possible."

"Please sit down with us, Dexter," said the young princess.

"Ann—" He used the recently truncated name with an ease that suggested he'd never addressed her in any other way. "How are you, darling?" He settled himself on the chair across from them, his back to the room, a position he disliked and to which he was quite unaccustomed. "I didn't know you knew Firna, who's always been one of my secret vices."

"Oh, we are friends," said Firna, who in Dexter's opinion was notable for the young decadence of her face and the faintly cynical slant of her eyes which imparted a sultry interest in what is euphemistically known as the more worldly pleasures. Her dark hair, parted on the side, was lustrous and long and fell provocatively to curtain half of her left cheek. "You know what has happened, Dexter? I was on the *Michaelangelo*, the second day out of Genoa, when I received from my charming friend here a cable to invite me to stay with her. I have known —Ann, I have known Ann for several years, many times I have met her in New York. I am an admirer of hers, she is the most American girl I have known."

Dexter turned to the "most American," whose once dazzlingly blond hair had taken on a conservatively tawny tone. "Ann," he said, "I adore that Chanel on you."

"It is so chic for her. I always regret I am not the Chanel type." The Princess Birenzia's French and Italian wardrobe was almost as extensive as the Duchess of Windsor's, though more flamboyant; she was given to going to parties in those swirling, voluminous pajamas designed by her friend Princess Irene Galitzine.

Firna's titled husband resided in Rome and it was said that they saw each other mainly on the two or three chief religious holidays of the year.

The more Dexter Knight thought about it, the more he realized that this unlikely confrontation between the two women was not as unlikely as it appeared: for like many of the European nobility, the youthful princess was predisposed to having part of her way paid for her by American friends; she would give a thousand-dollar check for a little dinner dress but she would be agreeably pleased to save the fifteen hundred dollars her stay at the Park-Regent would have cost her.

Her position, in other words, was so impregnable that regardless of where she lived or with whom, people accepted it; in fact, they found innumerable reasons for admiring or envying whatever she did.

"Dex," Ann Boggsen was saying—"and by the way don't worry about dropping the Bobbsie. It can't be done overnight. I dropped it because I've suddenly had it up to here!"

"But I find it charming," said Firna. "Names should be like wigs, we should be able to put them on, take them off. It is the nice thing about America that one can do it."

"Well," said Ann Boggsen, "I didn't want Dex to think I'm completely ticky." More intently then: "What I started out to say was I'm going to give a little dinner for Firna a week from tonight. Could I count on setting a place for you?"

"I can't think of anything more delightful." Dexter's smile was candidly ironic.

"You see"—Ann Boggsen turned to the Italian—"he would never have come to dinner before. But now with you here, Firna—"

"Darling," he said, "you mustn't get paranoiac about it. I've been a snob all my life and with people in higher places than you. As for those functions of yours, they've been much too wild for me to cope with. Or approve of. But now, with our mutual friend here, you are finally reaching me. And bless you for it, darling."

"Bless *you,* darling," said (Bobbsie) Ann Boggsen.

On a subsequent day that week in the Park-Regent bar, Rosemary Grovenour, wearing owl decals on her fingernails, her hair longer and subtly streaked a smoky blond, was finishing her second bourbon: she was being interviewed by this young—mygod, she couldn't have been more than twenty-four—newspaperwoman.

In the true American anti-snob tradition, the two were already on a first-name basis: Rosemary, because she was snobbish enough to feel she must be charmingly informal; the young woman, because she was snobbish enough to feel she mustn't show any special deference toward her subject.

Continuing now was the ping-pong of questions and answers:

Q: "—in other words, Rosemary, the whole idea of manufacturing the dress came as a complete surprise to you?"

A: "Yes, it was a complete bolt, Betty. When the company asked me for permission to use it, I didn't think they were serious. Left me in an absolute twitch."

Q: "One thing. Do you know how it was done, the whole process from the start?"

A: "Mainly what happened was that this friend of the manufacturer happened to see me in Waldo Stryker's little pop film. He got the idea from that, and then he got hold of the film and worked from there. They had to make a silk screen print and then they were ready to print it on different fabrics."

Q: "And the design of the dress is exactly like the one

you made at Mr. Hartley's party—the coffee cans, the strips of the *Times* and the *Tribune*, the S & H green stamps, the clothespins—the whole thing?"

A: "More or less. Actually though, I didn't think, with all the pop and op designs around, that this one would mean much. But I seem to be wrong."

Q: "Which is a nice way to be wrong. Do you think the success of it is partly due to all the stories we've heard during the summer—the way the whole party got put on film and all the rumors about certain of the shots having to be cut out?"

A: "Oh, I'm sure that's probably part of it, Betty."

Q: "And your modeling it yourself at that fashion show last Friday must have helped, too. A very personal question. You don't have to answer it, of course. I understand the manufacturer is paying you a royalty. I assume that's true."

A: "Yes, it is. But I'm turning over half of whatever I get to a little charity of mine."

Q: "I see. How does Mr. Grovenour feel about all that's happening?"

A: "Oh, he's been terribly larky about the whole thing."

Q: "Do you think you might do anything else along this line?"

A: "Not as far as I know. But I never know from day to day."

Q: "You were saying earlier, Rosemary, you've had some art training?"

A: "I used to paint. I studied at the Art Students League. And in Connecticut I used to dilettante around with all kinds of projects and mediums. Ceramics, plastics—nothing much ever came of it."

Q: "I don't think you can quite say that anymore. One thing. People have been talking a lot about your dinner parties. Do you have any special formula?"

A: "No. I stopped using my Formula Pills. I think it's more kicky to play as you go, I mean building each party around a different idea, depending on who's coming or what the occasion is. Like the little party we're having tomorrow night. Actually it's just a little dinner for a friend of my husband's—Eliot Noyler. He's left Harvard's department of architecture and planning to take a new post with the Planning Association of New York. What I started to say, Betty, was that Mr. Noyler is a billiard buff, and so I've taken over Gus O'Hanlin's pool parlor on Second Avenue for the evening."

Q: "Gus O'Hanlin's parlor. Second Avenue?"

A: "Yes. That way there'll be enough tables for everyone. Gus and his son will be around to give lessons, also. And I'm having lots of pretzels, chewing gum, beer, candy bars, oh, all kinds of tackytackies. Plus champagne."

Q: "Do you know what you'll be wearing?"

A: "Actually, it's a shift. I designed it myself. Green baize with big polka dots like pool balls."

Q: "Sounds like quite an evening. Could you tell me who some of the other guests will be?"

A: "Well, let's see. Hank Hartley is coming. And Christine Stelward. Daphne Bernlinsk. Waldo Stryker. Minni Ogden and Ralph Foote. Nina ver den Kahr and her husband Jake Harowitz. Mr. and Mrs. James Orson. Giles Folor. And there's a little pair of Rock singers, The Spooks, I found them hiding their talent under a Yorkville bushel basket—oh yes, and Caesar Mattos.

I don't think anyone knows about him yet. He's an
artist but it's hard to describe what his work is like—"

Q: "Oh?"

A: "Actually I met him this summer in the offices of the
dress manufacturer on Seventh Avenue. He works there
as a slavey in design. But his work is really terribly
tony. It's totally fashion-oriented. I call it Fop Art. He
uses very elegant materials instead of everyday little
ordinaries. He puts together wonderfully weird feminine figures with scraps of mink, chinchilla, sable, cloth
of gold, beads. Or male figures with weskits of ermine
tails and thick hair mops of hound's tooth check, Harris
tweed, brocades—but I'd rather you didn't mention any
of this, I mean I did promise the *Fig* people I'd give
them a first on it—"

After she had gone, Rosemary noticed on the banquette the
copy of the newspaper Betty had brought with her when she'd
arrived: it lay folded open at the page of "Metropolitan Social
Events." And there, smiling up at her now, in an understated
Givenchy cocktail dress, her hair without dazzle, was Bobbsie-
Ann Boggsen with "her house guest, the Princess Firna Birenzia
of Rome," shown at the Park-Regent Hotel last night where
there had been a reception for some of the foreign visitors here
for the International Hunt and Race Society's Ball.

Since this was the second time she'd read it, and since she'd
already heard about it at least six times in the course of the day,
Rosemary beckoned the waiter and asked for another bourbon:
"Just on the rocks this time, please."

Christine Stelward, at the end of that same afternoon, met
Hank Hartley for a drink at the Park-Regent bar, and as soon as

they were settled, and before other matters could be discussed, she said, "Hank, that dinner at the Grovenours' tomorrow night —I'm afraid you'll have to get someone else. I won't be able to make it."

"You won't?"

"I can't." The lie, not a very big one, came readily enough: her father, she said, was going to the hospital tomorrow evening in preparation for a new series of tests the next day, and she had to be with him. She did not say the move to the hospital was to be in the forenoon.

What else could she have done?

How simple to have simply said she could not comfortably be a guest of Rosemary's and Grove's; she could not sit at the same table or in the same room with them.

Not anymore.

As for Hank, he would have no difficulty in getting another partner: it was the particularly attractive thing about their purely social and undemanding friendship, this freedom they enjoyed, though he hadn't ever been completely reconciled to it.

He consulted his watch: he'd have to call someone shortly, get another date, and he'd have to check with Rosemary; this sounded like it would be one of those evenings of hers he wouldn't want to miss.

"I'm sorry about it," said Christine.

Hank understood. If his brother George, a United Nations official, was still out of town, he'd ask his wife to go with him to the Grovenours'.

"I must say," Christine began after she tasted her Scotch, "I can use this. It's been one of those days that are never long enough to get everything done." She reached down to the banquette for the manila envelope of manuscripts, which she handed to him. "I brought these back, you lucky man."

"Oh, thanks. I don't know why you're suddenly trying to do so many things at the same time."

"I guess," said Christine all too truthfully, "with me for some reason or other, it's always been a feast or a famine."

He glanced at the thick envelope. "I feel as if I'm exploiting you."

"That's good. That'll give me someone to blame." This fall she set a program for herself that was undoubtedly crowding her. Which is what she really wanted. She began her days in Morningside Heights at Columbia where she'd commenced, rather belatedly, the studies for her M.A. Plus working three afternoons a week (without salary) for Hank Hartley's *Poetry Review*. Though this little magazine which he financed continuously lost money, it was becoming a showcase for new poets here and abroad. (It was also a tax-deductible way for him to make his periodic safaris to London, Paris and Rome.) Christine ran the office, which was wedged into an air-conditioned *cul-de-sac* on the 57th floor of the Wall Street brokerage house of Hartley, Plimson and Rhodes, the firm in which Hank's father and brother were active.

For a while now, as she and Hank had their drinks, as Chet Darnell rippled forth his familiar versions of Richard Rodgers' show music, they discussed current problems of the magazine; and when they'd finished he excused himself to make his telephone calls; he walked across the pastel-walled barroom, and his gait, his tall muscular figure, seemed somehow too athletic for the hothouse ambience of the Park-Regent.

"Luck?" she asked when he returned: academic question, yet she knew that despite the many girls who would be only too available to him, he'd become fussy and cautious; his private life seemed as conservative as his public participation in the arts was progressive.

"Well, fortunately," said Hank, "Sabina Clarke was free. She's on the young side, but last minute, you know." As for his sister-in-law: "She's booked. Going to 1040, another Kennedy dinner of the groupy-group."

Christine decided to order another drink. When the waiter had departed, Hank Hartley said, "Chris, something I've been wanting to ask you which is none of my business."

She recognized the unbantering tone, but she said, "Oh, go ahead, you know me well enough to ask embarrassing questions."

"Don't throw me."

"I tried, at least," said Christine.

"What I mean"—Hank hesitated—"is . . . well you haven't seemed to be the Stelward of yore."

She opened her cigarette case. "Maybe that's good."

"I'm serious, Chris."

"Well, all right." She invoked her sprightliest smile. Or made the attempt. "In what way am I not of yore?"

"It's nothing I can rattle off, just a feeling is all." Hank lit her cigarette.

"Masculine intuition. That's what you've got," she countered. But when she saw he wouldn't be put off, she said, "I think it's nothing more than you're unaccustomed to seeing me in such a rush of work, or what passes for work. You have to remember, Hank, I haven't gone to school for a long time. I'm rusty." She'd been graduated from Wellesley in 1955.

"Could be," said Hank. "Or maybe I'm just reading something that isn't there. Maybe all it is, is that I resent the idea of your moving out on us at 958."

"I haven't moved out as yet. But thank you anyway, Hank." However, she had notified Edwards and Osgood, who handled the management of the cooperative, and she had also informed the building's Board of Directors that she wished to put up her apartment for sale. She'd been looking for another location, one less conspicuous. For reasons self-evident and imperative. She was on the track now of something that met her needs: the purchase of a small brick town house on 83rd Street between East End Avenue and the East River, in the rear shadow of Gracie Square. The ground floor was a shop occupied by a dealer of antiques whose sign on the door *To The Trade Only* eliminated retail traffic. The three floors above were structurally sound, though there was replastering and painting and decoration to be done. There was a roof terrace and a small private garden area at the back. The price, $195,000, would not be much more than what she would receive for her present apartment at 958 Fifth Avenue. But what she would be buying, among other necessary and desirable qualities, was privacy.

"I wish you no luck," said Hank. After they'd begun another set of drinks, he came around to yet another matter of concern: Howard Stelward. "I take it that no news from your husband is still bad news."

"Oh, very much so." If she sounded almost cheerful, it was because she was that relieved to find that Hank Hartley did not know what she feared he might have known or suspected.

"I keep wondering how long you can go on like this, Chris."

"What can I do? Send my petitioners to Vatican City with a wadful"—she hadn't meant to use Grove's phrase—"and say how's about an annulment?"

He nodded. Then: "I don't know why I keep thinking there'll be a break in this."

Not while her father was alive.

"Will you please tell me," said Hank, whose two previous divorces had been obtained by the simple, if agonizing, process of separating himself from an abundance of money, "will you please tell me what Howard is holding out for?"

"What the hell does he want, what's he think he's holding out for?" Grove had asked the same question less than a week ago when, against all resolve, he'd come to 958 where he might too easily have run into any number of friends, but heedlessly, without discretion, knowing only it was her maid's day off, he'd risked it. And she had not stopped him. "Will you tell me, Christine? Why doesn't he give up, what would he have to lose?"

"Possibly his job, for one thing. After all, Howard is still running the foundation, and he does enjoy his seventy or eighty thousand a year." The Wyman Foundation was a Catholic-directed philanthropic organization endowed by Christine's father, Francis Spence Wyman, and her mother, the late Mary Van Raevler Wyman.

"But who cares?" Grove protested; he pushed the bedsheet back. "Let him have the job, give it to him for life."

"You don't know my father. He doesn't work that way," Christine said. "That's why Howard still passes himself off in front of him, and half the world, as the most devout gent in town. Marriage is a holy sacrament, and even our separation, almost two years now, even that doesn't exist without permission from the Church."

Though Grove was well aware of the basic dilemma, they had deliberately eluded talk of it until that afternoon last week; until then neither of them had had the will to discuss it in any of its disagreeable ramifications.

Until that afternoon last week:

He'd come up, after telephoning her. He'd stepped into the foyer. They had stood there locked together breathless, in the tremor of that first-time touching.

They'd gone half blindly through the apartment to her commodious and overimmaculate bedroom with its four-postered, canopied, neatly feminine bedstead. Neither of them thought to dim the daylight, to lower the blinds or draw the curtains or drapes. And afterward, the prim expanse of her room was happily unrecognizable: the debris of their clothes lumped in wild chaos on the white carpeting.

"It's so goddam immoral, what he's trying to do to you!" In Grove's indignation he was quite oblivious to his own irony. He lit a cigarette and placed the ashtray on the disordered sheet between them. "Just as immoral as what I'm doing to Rosemary —except with me, or you, it hasn't been calculated or malicious."

"To us, yes that's true, Grove. But to anyone else—"

"One thing is beginning to get me down," Grove said. "I mean I don't really have a serious claim against Rosie. She may be doing a lot I happen not to like, but she's not in the same league with Howard Stelward."

"No one is," she said.

"What about him, incidentally? Do you mean to tell me he's been living like a good celibate monk all this time?"

"Until recently I was never interested enough to find out," said Christine. "But the last time I went to his place—I had to go there on some business—I did get a glimpse of the new housekeeper he's installed."

"I see." Grove looked at her. "And he knows you won't or can't do anything about it. That's what's so goddam—" He stopped. "What would happen if you told your father, I mean if you put it in such a way that he—"

"Grove, how can I?" Christine said. "How could anyone?" She stubbed out her cigarette in the ashtray. She sat upright then. "Our only trouble, Grove, is we're just about one decade too old."

He turned to her. "Only one?"

"Maybe less," she amended. But how much easier it would be, she mused aloud, if they could be the same people ten years from now: the Church or its hierarchy would conceivably have come to honest terms with modern realities, the Pill would be long-perfected, social patterns would have altered, and religious dicta would be far less constricting. Abruptly she looked up. "What was that?" She kept listening. "Did you hear anything, Grove?"

"What?"

"You didn't hear anything?" she asked again.

"No."

"I thought I heard a door—but it couldn't have been." She listened again. Silence. Into which, more clearly, returned the snort of traffic far below on Fifth Avenue. She sighed. "Gave me a scare. I was sure it was something."

"It better not be," Grove said. He extinguished his cigarette and replaced the ashtray on the bedtable.

She said, "I keep thinking of what we talked about that day in the gallery—worrying if we were going to end up like all those other furtive couples I've always been so uncharitable about—"

Grove said, "When I was on my way up here in the elevator I felt as sneaky and shoddy as God knows how many other guys in the same bind; but there I was chatting amiably with the elevator attendant and handing out the bacillus bullfosis with the best of them." He glanced at his watch. He had an office meeting at half-past three.

Christine said, "I'm distressed to say my performance was just as admirable. An old friend of mine called and said she'd just come by two tickets for the ballet for this afternoon, and could I join her? She knows how I love ballet. But surprise. I said no I was really all jammed up today with rewriting my lecture notes. I sounded so absolutely scholarly and conscientious that she apologized for disturbing me."

"Well, we're learning, aren't we?"

"We seem to be." Christine noticed then that his rather rueful smile was becoming something else: his hand was warmly on her thigh and again the play of his fingertips stroked love (and her long abstinence) into almost immediate, helpless desire for him. She slid down to meet his mouth, and to feel then, in a swoon, her breast touched by his breath.

The sun had lowered: through the bank of western windows it rudely spattered, aroused them with its hard, clean, winter-bright intrusion.

Grove was the first to stir. "How'd it get to be after three?"

"Oh," she heard herself protest like how many of the others she deplored, and who, like her, also had to hide from time. "Does it have to be that late!"

"This table," said Bobbsie-Ann Boggsen to her husband, in the columned ballroom of the Park-Regent Hotel, "is *molto bene,* isn't it?"

"It ought to be," said William Boggsen quite cheerfully. For this December night's event, the International Hunt and Race Society's gala, he had paid five hundred dollars for the table for ten. It was an admirable and tax-deductible gesture, though the evening's noble purpose of charity might have seemed secondary to the loftier business of social intercourse and the competitive display of female figures, fashions and jewels, the coiffures, bare backs and the fleshy flash of bountiful bosoms.

The decoration, by Tony Ammonds, was in the *fin de siècle* spirit of Deauville (Ascot, Longchamps and Saratoga having been the unsurprising motifs of the previous years).

Despite the environment of horse flesh Bobbsie-Ann, like many of the other people here, was unacquainted with the equestrian art; though recently she'd begun riding lessons with a teacher no less accomplished than her Roman house guest, Princess Firna Birenzia. And now, as she viewed the long white ballroom crowding and coloring with couples, she saw that Firna, who with her escort Tony Ammonds had stopped to talk with Dexter Knight, was making her way to the table.

And as the Princess and Ammonds neared the Boggsens, a photographer stepped in to immortalize the moment: Bobbsie-Ann's ball gown by Givenchy, a blazing white faille, whose simplicity gave way at the hemline to a flamed circle of scarlet ostrich feathers; but even this must have seemed dim compared to the triumph dazzling in her wide eyes.

"There's just one person I miss here tonight," she murmured to her husband, "and I'll bet you'll never guess who that is."

"Never, honey." William Boggsen smiled.

Oh, if only Rosemary Grovenour were here now!

What a touch—or, as she might have said no more than seven months ago—what a fun ball game tonight would be!

What she wouldn't give to dig Mrs. Grovenour's puss tomorrow when she picked up the newspapers and saw the Boggsens with their distinguished Roman friend and Tony Ammonds and the three other couples who were their table guests.

Wow! Pow! Bobbsie-Ann couldn't help invoke the lusty, outmoded cries that had marked her vocabulary two years ago.

And tell me, Mrs. Grovenour, why is it you're looking on the greenish side? Sick? Nausea?

But why, Rosiepooh?

Just because, after all I did for you, after all I did to snatch you from your mousy, funky funksome world, you showed your gratitude by aping and eclipsing me?

Not with all your little Gristedelies!

But wait.

For you don't know—not yet—how it feels to be the number

one pumpkin, the pet of the town, The Pet, and then wake up one morning to find you're no longer tall, but as low as the pooch who pees on your doorman's shoes!

Yes, and suddenly the faces of all your chums get that yellow murk in their eyes when they try to look at you, and suddenly your old Royal Station table at Le Trianon is occupied by someone else, like for example, some Bitchypooh like Rosemary Grovenour.

Well, *mia amore,* as we say in Italy, before you take your boots off you are going to witness your former friend Mrs. William Boggsen moving up once again.

Yes, and all this time you'll be jazzing around being the New Pet, the pumpkin of the month, until one funky day you'll blink to find you too have been eclipsed, and suddenly what are you?

You are no longer Daphne Bernlinsk's cuppa.

And no longer Waldo Stryker's pooh.

And that face on the cover of *Hipman* or *Fig* is someone else's.

And all those dress designers and decorators and hairdressers who were licking the decals off your fingernails, those dear boys will suddenly droop with indifference when you've been stripped of your IN and are standing naked in your OUT!

Yes, that's the way it happens. It almost happened to me. Almost.

Yes.

But behold me, baby. Mrs. William Boggsen, a *molto* chic signora indeed, is making the kind of scene that matters. Here is where they deal in basic currency, as Dexter Knight is always saying. Like, for example, my Roman friend, and like, in case you're thinking she's only at my place for the free ride, you hear she's invited me to be *her* guest in Palm Beach next month.

(She hasn't yet, not officially. But she'd better!)

"Bobbsie-Ann," Firna was saying now as she sat down at the large circular table, "Dexter Knight told me to tell you how much he admires your dress."

"Oh—thank you," said Bobbsie-Ann. "I must admit it really is quite a nifty little *numero*." As she looked over and waved to Dexter Knight she saw that her other table guests were arriving. In a month or so they too would be ensconced in the Florida winter resort.

"That talk of Firna's, inviting you down—" Bobbsie-Ann's husband had said earlier. "Sometimes I've wondered if she's sort of holding that over your head. She isn't, is she?"

"Oh no," said Bobbsie-Ann, though after what had happened late this afternoon she couldn't really be positive.

It didn't matter anyway. When the countdown was over, all that mattered was blasting off for the South, the invitation confirmed: after all, it was the Princess' idea to begin with, wasn't it? Just a week ago she'd said in that charming, offhand way, "Bobbsie-Ann, you must come down, be my guest."

The vision immediately took fulll fat form on the wide screen of Bobbsie-Ann's Technicolor mind: to be down there for several weeks in January or February, that was nothing. But to be there as Firna's guest! In that nifty Palladian house loaned to her by old friends (who had places in New York, Paris, St. Moritz, and Acapulco, and who would be away all winter overseeing the construction of another house near Montego Bay).

Yes, but Firna had never mentioned the visit again. And there was this odd, this oddish thing this afternoon at the apartment when she and Firna were preparing to dress for the evening: Firna had sauntered into her bedroom wearing, as was her wont, merely a bra and those lace, bikini-cut panties. She was out of face cream and could she borrow some? Of course. They talked idly for a while and when the subject of clothes came up, as it did so often, Bobbsie-Ann saw a natural opportunity to remind her house guest of what, in all her frivolity, she might have forgotten; yet Bobbsie-Ann hesitated, fearful that it might be the wrong move. In the end she decided she had to snare the chance. "By the way, Firna, I was just thinking, there's no point in your taking your entire wardrobe south. You can leave the rest of your clothes here."

"Oh," the Princess had said, "I don't know. But that is so generous of you, Bobbsie-Ann." She started to leave and then turned back; and then in this playful way, she reached out and so lightly touched her fingertips to Bobbsie-Ann's lips.

After Firna left, Bobbsie-Ann decided that it wasn't really all that odd. When you thought of how she did all kinds of things which seemed curious at times: but wasn't that one of the reasons why having her here was so kicky, such a kicksome experience? Her whole approach to life was different from Bobbsie-Ann's, and in fact her views on morals generally were —well, not weird, but typically Firna. Like when she joked about Americans and the sex revolution, she liked to quote the Frenchwoman who, when asked a too personal question about love, answered: "I make it often, but talk about it never."

(For that matter, Bobbsie-Ann mused bitterly, Firna talks about Palm Beach never.)

Which was just too dragsome for Bobbsie-Ann's dynamic nature. She had to be *numero uno* in a situation.

Well, she would be. Soon. She had to be.

Now, as her other guests appeared at the table, she noticed that even her normally passive husband, even Bill, showed a flush of gratification, or pride, as he stood up to welcome the others, all of whom were friends of Firna's whom she saw from time to time in Europe or Palm Beach or New York.

They were now also Bobbsie-Ann's friends.

Oh, and by the way, Rosiepooh, have a look at this tableful. Rearrange the meeting, put the couples together, and you'll see, reading from left to right: Mr. Tony Ammonds and Princess Firna Birenzia. Also, there is Mr. Joseph Jannus, the New York industrialist and his wife, the former Italian contessa, Benedetta (B-B) Frouchini; they live on Sutton Place. (This is the second marriage for both.) And Mr. and Mrs. Marshall Jones III, stables in Long Island and Middleburg, Virginia; his wife, Diane, a New York girl, modeled for Chanel in Paris; they live on Fifth Avenue. (This is the second marriage for both.) And Mr. and Mrs. Gillon Findley; he was with the U.S. Embassy in Rome and is now a foreign film importer and distributor; his wife, Joan, though no blue-ribbon beauty, has been one of the real Go-Pots with the Junior League of New York; they live on Park Avenue. (This is the third marriage for both.)

Yes.

Quite a tableful, wouldn't you say, Rosiepooh?

And look who is politely, mildly waving from that table over there—couldn't be Minni Ogden Foote. But it is: nodding discreetly in her diamonds and in that unhorsy St. Laurent.

Bene.

For more than an hour the dinner conversation, like the wines that accompanied it, sustained its body and bouquet. And Bobbsie-Ann decided that so far as the Princess was concerned, she would play it on the cool side of the centerpiece. Anyway, Firna was still zestfully exchanging gossip with the other women. Bobbsie-Ann used the interval to get on to other business.

She turned to her right to resume her talk with Tony Ammonds. There was still much to talk about before dancing broke up the evening. "Tony—"

But the eminent decorator's eyes were slitted in critical appraisal of the ballroom in which his firm had installed two hundred pounds of foliage and several miles of yellow and green bunting (the Society's colors), as well as all the materials necessary to re-create the thatched-roof Norman houses and stables, the *auberges,* the casino, the track and paddocks, Les Toques—the whole range of landmarks familiar to the Normandy resort. On either side of the bandstand, where the traditional Meyer Davis group would be playing shortly, were replicas of the gambling rooms where croupiers would be stationed later to raise further monies via chemin-de-fer, roulette and baccarat.

"Umm?" Tony Ammonds was still appraising his handiwork. "What is it, dear?"

"That apartment I started telling you about before—"

"Oh, yes," said Ammonds, murmuring to himself, "I think this will be my last charity ball, projects like this are only for madmen." Then: "That apartment, what about it, Bobbsie-Ann?"

"Well, I didn't think I'd be able to get it at first," she reported. "I mean, after I heard about it and called Edwards and Osgood last week, the man I talked to was such an utter poop, all that evasive dialogue—I mean dullalogue—about he wasn't sure if it would be available. But then this morning someone else from Edwards and Osgood called—a perfectly divine specimen—who said he would arrange for me to get a look at it day after tomorrow." To Bobbsie-Ann's ear, this sounded right, very right. Yes. As Dexter Knight was always writing, it was the basic currency that mattered, and she was definitely in love with basic currency, even though she wasn't really too sure what it meant.

"Where is it, Bobbsie-Ann?" asked the interior decorator.

"958 Fifth Avenue," said Bobbsie-Ann, who'd decided there was nothing you could do about losing the "Bobbsie" among people you'd known over a prolonged period; as for outsiders, strangers and the press in general, it was now definitely just plain, four-square, true-blue Ann Boggsen or Mrs. William Boggsen.

"Lovely old building," Tony Ammonds said. "Whose apartment is it?"

"Christine Stelward's," she answered.

"Oh, Christine's?" His fox-brown eyebrows arched in a first thrust of interest. How *could* he be such a snob? You would have thought in his position, he'd be beyond that. "Yes," he was saying, "I know it quite well, though I didn't do it. Is it large enough for you and Bill?"

"Ten rooms, I believe. And there are three bedrooms, three baths, and a powder room. And this man from Edwards and Osgood said the drawing room is definitely of party proportions."

"Yes, it is," said Ammonds. "And it *is* a drawing room, not a living room, I can assure you, dear."

"What I was wondering, Tony, knowing what an elusive specimen you are, what I was wondering was would you go there with me to look it over day after tomorrow?" She laughed. "This is a proposition, Tony."

"Why don't we check my calendar in the morning," he said, "and if there's time I'll nip over and we'll have a peep at the premises." He would nip over, she knew from her experience with him during the Athens ball, in his silver-gray Rolls-Royce. (He always had it waiting and when he took on a job, he would be chauffeured on his way, followed by one or two station wagons with the younger men who, under his direction, did everything from taking measurements and photographs right through to scale drawings and watercolor renderings with swatches of fabric and papers stapled on to suggest alternate color schemes.)

"That would be *molto bene,*" said Bobbsie-Ann in a surprisingly creditable Roman accent. She glanced across the table to her husband, who was speaking with Joseph Jannus. "I haven't told Bill much of this yet. It's too soon. I'd rather wait until you give me all your ideas. And the estimate."

"Which is apt to be considerable, dear." His way of reminding her, if she needed to be reminded, that if he took on the project he would charge the Boggsens his customary steep percentage of the entire cost of the job; plus astronomical mark-ups on all the small *objets d'art* which he would seek out for her (and which came from his own warehouse).

"What would you think, Tony, in going really far-out and doing the whole thing in French period?"

Ammonds smiled enough to show he got the joke: for he did all apartments in seventeenth- or eighteenth-century French furniture and furnishings: you had no choice. He did nothing else because his clientele, for the most part the Undisputed Social Elite, would *have* nothing else.

"Baby," said the decorator, "even if I were doing over Firna's *palazzo* in the heart of Rome, everything from the *boiserie* to the *bidet* would come from France."

"What? Who is saying that? You, Tony?" The Princess turned and blew him a kiss, her eyes lowered in that sultry, mischievous way. "What did I hear you say?" She leaned forward, exposing what little had been left unseen by the décolletage of her ball gown, a Balenciaga of lilac *gonflé* satin and white mink. "Was it treason, Tony?"

"Yes." The concept that interior decorators must look willowy or fragile was false if you took Tony Ammonds for your model. For he was a vigorous and virile figure. Elegant, of course, but none of that flamboyance in clothes or gesture that people often associated with those who worked in this *métier*. Tony Ammonds was, in fact, married. And you'd often hear him speak with touching affection of his wife, though she could no longer hear his loving sentiments because she was undergoing an extensive cure in a West Coast sanatorium. Her nervous breakdown is said to have occurred shortly after her marriage to the decorator. But whatever the reasons for the psychic damage, she had been thoughtful enough to provide for him before the nuptial night, so that Tony had had the necessary capital to set himself up in a splendid complex of studios, workrooms and offices on East 66th Street, where his weekly payroll was formidable and where for many years he had been flourishing with phenomenal success, taking his place along with Billy Baldwin, Vincent Fourcade, Stephane Boudin and others, as one of the master interior designers to the *haut monde* of the city.

"Firna—" said Bobbsie-Ann. "I want you to come with me to see something day after tomorrow, something special. A place—"

"Oh, I am not sure," said the Princess. "There is suddenly so much to do before I must be in Palm Beach."

"Oh?" But Bobbsie-Ann heard no more. Not another word. And now, too soon, the music had commenced.

Marshall Jones III said to his wife, "Diane, the first dance is mine. Every deb has the first one with her poor old father, you know."

Diane Jones rose. "Funny."

"Bobbsie-Ann?" The sturdy William Boggsen moved around to her chair: how relaxed and beatific he looked: how she counted on Bill, loved him for his always imperturbable and comforting presence.

Tony Ammonds escorted the Princess to the floor, followed by the Joseph Jannuses and the Gillon Findleys.

And now the thatched-roofed and worm-timbered world of old Normandy was caught in the sudden storm: the lightning flashes of emeralds and sapphires and diamonds, and the swirling winds of satin, brocade, lace, lamé and cut-velvet ball gowns.

Bobbsie-Ann, dancing with her husband, said, "Bill, you hear anything more on your end of the table from Firna or the others?"

"No, nothing special," William Boggsen said. "Maybe she just assumes you're coming down."

"Well," said Bobbsie-Ann, "in the meantime I'm not setting in a line of sunglasses and beach sandals."

"At least she can't say we haven't done more than our share," William Boggsen said. "Money's been flowing like Chianti, but what the hell, I'd say it's been quite an eye-opener and a good time all around. And some of those Italian dishes she cooked, never put anything in my mouth I liked more. And the way she does it, in the kitchen in those dressy gold pajama-dresses. Beautiful. Can't understand how her husband lets her out of that *palazzo*." His broad palm pressed the small of her back and he tilted his head to look with purest admiration at her white Givenchy ball gown. "I think she's really crazy about you, Bobbsie-Ann. But then who isn't?"

"What?"

They were now dancing far from the bandstand and she heard herself saying to him, wasn't this the straightest experience, dancing like this, but a novel, funsome thing, no shaking, no jerking, no rubbing, no twitching?

While dancing around them, all these couples, a whole crowd of inter-Continental friends, whipped talk to and fro, and it had a golden and irresistible ring to Bobbsie-Ann's avid ear, even though at times it seemed too esoteric:

"—only Senior's stable could draw a tag like that."
"—a spotter hoisted the price."
"—the Phipps and the Englehards and—"
"—and the Alfred Gwynnes—"

"—all the Raymonds and all the Winstons—"

"—highest for a bay filly—"

"—chip off the old Bostwick."

"—Ira, Jacqueline and Peggy—"

"—you have to bring your own mount."

"—Peggy, Jacqueline and Ira."

"—was the second Rothschild winner."

"—I mean it's not like it used to be, I mean just *anyone* and *everyone* is getting horse-minded!"

"—C-Z—"

"—B-B—"

"—Prince Charles swears by it."

"—Can't sell a yearling without the Whitneys."

"—sired a line like that."

"—I must say, Louis XVI costumes for a lousy partridge shoot is a bit much!"

Oh, it was a glorious, a really kicksome evening. And after they left the Park-Regent, they all went to The Discothèque (it was uncrowded, impossible to believe that Big D's, the sacred shrine, was already losing its IN). They only stayed ten minutes and went to Cheetah, and then to El Morocco where Marshall Jones III and Diane played hosts, abetted by the best champagne and brandy in Elmo's cellar.

It was past 3 A.M. by the time the Boggsens got back to 647 Park Avenue. Bobbsie-Ann shuddered at the white-glazed brick apartment building with its tissue-thin walls and the second-rate modern décor. *Uggh!* Oh, it was utterly *ugghsome!*

If they could buy that Fifth Avenue apartment of Christine Stelward's—

As for Firna, she couldn't have been more vivacious. She was really indefatigable. And when Bobbsie-Ann and Bill were in their bedroom undressing, she knocked on their door and said would they like a very small something to eat? She was in the mood.

Of course, said Bobbsie-Ann.

Though William Boggsen, regarding his recently expanded girth in the mirror, was forced to decline this time. "But Firna," he called out, "I expect a raincheck."

"What is that, a raincheck?" asked the Princess when Bobbsie-Ann, in a dressing gown of palest organza, came into the kitchen.

Bobbsie-Ann told her. "What are you going to make?" she asked then.

"Oh," said Firna, with the pleasure of all cooks who never have to cook except now and then in the spirit of caprice. "Oh, something for the tired eyes. In Italian cuisine, it's true what people say, it's for the eyes, the colors simple—risotto is yellow, bright green lettuce and red for tomatoes—like a child's painting."

In the livid brilliance of the fluorescent kitchen, Firna stirred up a whirl of savory smells as she put together a small skilletful of rice, cheese and peppers, a fine little salad and of course the filtered black coffee. Coffee never kept her awake, nor did rice or pastas add an ounce to her slender body. However, it was also true that riding or swimming and massage was an invariable part of her regimen.

The Princess moved about the kitchen in the gayest, blithest way, relieving the occasion of its normally mundane aspect: for this cooking stint tonight she merely wore minute flesh-colored panties, a green silk pajama top partially buttoned, and a pair of gold Fiorentina shoes. "*Alora,*" she said when she'd finished her work and had washed her hands. "I won't have fun like this in Palm Beach because the chef is Parisian and he's king of the house. No one's allowed in the kitchen."

(Oh, if Rosiepooh could dial in on this scene!)

Carefully now, Bobbsie-Ann said, "I wish you weren't rushing off. We're going to miss you here, Firna."

Waiting then: could she have made it any plainer?

"Oh, everything you say and do, Bobbsie-Ann, is always so generous." Without warning then, the Princess leaned forward and there was that sudden dart of warmth, Firna's swift, casual, playful touch of a kiss just beneath Bobbsie-Ann's ear.

So casual, swift, indifferent almost, that Bobbsie-Ann was embarrassed for feeling peculiar, for even *thinking* there was anything dikey about it when all it probably was, was another of Firna's impulses of affection.

"What is it, what's the matter?" The Princess was peering at her.

"Why, nothing, Firna—" Bobbsie-Ann must have been frowning or her voice must have unwittingly conveyed reproach, for her house guest moved away from her rather abruptly.

Glancing around, the Princess said, "Where did I put my cigarettes?" But the voice held impatience or boredom.

12. The Museum of New York History

The photographer Peter Sahn, who is known as Sonny in the hothouse realm of *Fig* where he flourishes, asks Mr. and Mrs. Grovenour if they would now move to the central doors of the auditorium, away from the throng in evening clothes who, long-stemmed champagne glasses in hand, are clotting the marble lobby of this museum on upper Fifth Avenue. The fête now in progress is to celebrate the first anniversary of the Inter-Borough Planning Association of New York of which Bayard Burton Grovenour has recently been made president.

It is a Tuesday night in February. Tuesday is the day the museum is closed to the public, though now and then it is opened for certain private social or civic functions.

Fig will feature this evening's event, which is why Sonny has been given the assignment: there are other photographers as gifted as he, but none more sought-after, more in demand, more highly paid and more talked about. Some people say it is because his handsome books of color photography (subjects as diverse as ballet, pre-Columbian sculpture, American pop art) are part of the coffee-table surfaces in most recognizedly chic drawing rooms; others say it is because of his notoriety, his repute for bedmanship, for despite his frail frame he is known to keep two or three women a week in an ecstatic flurry of anticipation or blissful languor. Others, yet, say it is because of his manner of dressing: he is a fashion faddist who (circa 1965-'66) favors the dandyistic suits of the Faubourg St. Honoré, Paris; as well as the wildest whims of Carnaby Street, London; 4th Street or Madison Avenue, New York. Tonight he might be considered conspicuous in this crush, for he is wearing a black and white zigzag-striped shirt, a black fur tie, black double-breasted blazer with eight Coldstream Guard buttons, claret-red corduroy pants and black patent leather cowboy boots.

"Rosemary," he says, "if you and Mr. Grovenour could just move back, by the doors there, yes. Just a bit forward, Rosemary. I know you didn't wear that dress to hide it." It is black, sleeveless, cut low, short, simple and utterly unadorned except for—you have to look twice because at first you might not believe it—the thin chain from which is hanging what from a distance seems a dark, abstract-shaped amethyst, but which on close inspection turns out to be a purple plastic miniature sports car. Even Sonny has been charmed: "Where'd you get it?" he has asked.

"Oh, it's just one of those dinkytinkies I found in a Cracker Jack box," Rosemary answered.

But the effect is surprisingly decorative and a far shine from the diamonds, emeralds or sapphires confronting you from every woman's earlobes, throat or décolletage.

Sonny, the fact is, enjoys a real empathy with Rosemary, though unlike his relationship with some other women, this is all he enjoys: it is fairly obvious that the Grovenours have one of those good marriages in which love hasn't been splintered by the divergent activities of the partners. Sonny ought to know. He moves around. He knows where a number of skeletons in a number of closets are. Including his own.

Rosemary Grovenour, he feels, has to be admired. In a sense she's been a Cinderella, creeping out of the Connecticut woods with nothing but her name going for her and becoming a kind of anti-belle of the ball. From a follower she has become one who is followed. Her entourage, many of whom are here to-night, are devoted to her: Daphne Bernlinsk, Waldo Stryker, Giles Folor, Nina ver den Kahr, the just-divorced Minni Ogden Foote and her husband-to-be Mitchell Valencort, Hank Hartley and probably Hartley's friend Christine Stelward. (He must get to Christine in a hurry; she's talking with Dex Knight now, looking so casual, so un-got up, almost indifferent, yet near-dazzling in that green dress and the auburn hair loosely piled up, playfully touched by the circle of pearls. He must get over to Christine.) And there is Judge Zachary Cunningham, the main dragon of tonight's event.

Everyone, as they say, is here tonight. Except for Bobbsie-Ann Boggsen. (Though Dexter Knight recently granted her celebrity by mentioning her flatteringly for the first time, he could not, however, resist identifying her as "Mrs. William Boggsen, the former Bobbsie-Ann Boggsen.") She is now defi-nitely forsaking (or has been forsaken by) all her old friends in preference for what some headline writers still call the In-ternational or Jet Set. It is no high-echelon secret that she and Rosemary Grovenour are no longer great comrades. Yet Sonny is fond of both of them: his appreciation of pretty or provocative females is more steadfast than his belief in their permanence in the shaky pantheon of New York's popular elite, and he hopes he will be around long after the city's current crop of darlings has turned to fat or been exiled to Outsville.

Banishment to Outsville can befall even the mightiest. Who knows this better than Sonny? Just as he knows some people here tonight might be offended by his clothes, but it is better to offend than to be ignored.

"Mr. Grovenour," he says now, "that smoke from your cigarette is going to give us more cloud than face."

"I don't mind. Unless it bothers you," replies Grovenour who, Sonny thinks, is being much more agreeable or relaxed now than he'd been the last time he'd seen him: it was at 958 Fifth Avenue, one afternoon a few weeks ago. Sonny had been up to Hank Hartley's to shoot Waldo Stryker and some of his paintings, and afterward when he and Waldo were on their way down, the elevator had stopped and Grovenour had stepped in. He'd seemed irritated at seeing them though that was probably because, as he'd said, he'd been in the building on some harassing business for Edwards and Osgood who managed the cooperative. Couldn't have been one of Grovenour's good days. But tonight he seems more amiable. Or perhaps his features appear less perturbed now because, after all, he's wearing his honors tonight. This event is important to him. It is the new organization's first official effort to stimulate public interest in its cause. After the crowd has been properly juiced up with champagne, Grovenour is to make the chief address in the auditorium. And there is to be a fashion show or pageant depicting styles from Manhattan's early years to the present day. Rosemary Grovenour is responsible for this, and she will even participate at the end, wearing several of the clothes with which her name is becoming associated: the poptail dress, the poolroom shift and the fop-art pants.

Sonny stirs: to his practiced but still zealous eye he raises the camera.

Not long after the photographer had left them, Grove and Rosemary moved into the auditorium, walking along the left-wall aisle on their way backstage. Without warning, she said, "Do you think anything's wrong—about Christine, I mean?"

"Christine?" In less than ten minutes he had his speech to

give; but of course Rosemary's question, innocuous as it might be, rocked him. "What makes you think something's wrong?"

"She seems to be going out of her way to avoid us. Tonight was the second or third time she couldn't come for dinner."

"She's here now, though."

"You know what I mean."

"No, I don't. Do we have to discuss it now?" It was time to show the gruff impatience of any culpable husband.

"Well"—Rosemary touched the plastic sports car dangling above the declivity of her bosom—"it struck me again tonight. I've been asking myself some questions."

"And answering them I trust—Rosemary, this is no time for fun and games."

"I mean, could it have been anything I've done? Or we've done? When you think how different she used to be when she first came to the apartment with Hank—all chumsy and chirpsy."

"I don't find her all that different," Grove said. An implausible answer was better than none.

"Maybe you don't see it," she said. "After all, Christine is a fan of yours."

"I didn't think you'd even had time to notice, Rosie." He was certainly getting more agile at varying his responses. "You're the one in the family who has all the fans."

"If I am," she replied, "it hasn't hurt you any, has it?"

"I didn't say that." He held open the metal fire door that led to the backstage area. "Of course it hasn't hurt me. On the contrary." This had to be admitted: no one had worked harder than Rosemary in the preparations for tonight's event, as well as for many other occasions when she'd created a new climate in which his outside interests might best be served. (And certainly no one worked harder than Rosemary to create a new climate for Rosemary.)

Times were often, however, when Grove wished he had more to rebel against: nor could he complain of her excesses, or her ego, swelling now like a gland. He knew she was still compensating for her past failures.

So that when he was with Christine, he didn't even have the legitimate or traditional grievances against his wife that can help make adultery more palatable to the atavistically puritan American male.

"Rosiepooh!" cried the bearded Waldo Stryker: he had designed the background panels for the fashion pageant.

(There now hung in the Grovenours' apartment at 1027 Fifth Avenue a painting by Stryker, one of his more notable pop works whose design included a loaf of Bond bread, a jar of peanut butter on a cabinet shelf illuminated by a fluorescent light tube which could be turned on or off. Rosemary had bought it partly with the monies she'd made from fashion royalties. The cost was $2000.)

"Oh, darling! Umm. KissKiss!" Daphne Bernlinsk ran up, her poodle-eyes agleam, her head bobbing forward, lips pursed, peckpecking the air: it was as if she hadn't seen Rosemary for a week instead of half an hour ago in the auditorium lobby. "Waldo was just showing me what you two have been up to back here. Couldn't have been more surprised. Came just like a bolta."

"Hi, Grove," Waldo Stryker said.

Grove greeted the pop painter, absolutely convinced Stryker would mention having run into him at 958. Stryker and Sonny in that elevator with him: who could ask for anything less!

And almost immediately, as if the painter had been taping his apprehensions, Stryker said, "Before when I saw Sonnypooh, we were saying—"

"Waldo, do you happen to have a cigarette?" Grove interrupted him gingerly. Stryker and Sonny were probably two of the most active gossip pigeons in the entire Upper East Side.

"Anyway, we were saying, and this is the true cube root, baby—" The artist held his lighter for Grove.

"Thanks, Waldo." He glanced out to the stage and then in a flurry of haste, stamped out his cigarette: he saw that some of the other officers of the association were seating themselves on the platform. "Looks like my time has come," he said and, though it was still too soon, escaped onto the stage.

He waited, sitting there until Judge Zachary Cunningham, the chairman of the evening's program, introduced him. Grove rose and stepped to the podium.

". . . and what we're here for," he addressed the audience wryly, "is to celebrate, among other things, the insane buildup of traffic in the streets and the maniacal tearing down of New York's landmarks. Not that anyone cares. That's the nice thing about living here, we don't have to care. Let somebody else worry about what's happening. After all, it's a big city; one of those clowns down at City Hall will manage things somehow. In the meantime let's ignore it. One look at our waterfront, and what do we think? We think how soon can we get a plane for Venice? New York has three hundred and fifty years of history, but for a historical tour, where do we go? Paris or London. The sights are all there. Of course we New Yorkers could boast in our own way if we wanted to: don't we have one seventeenth-century house in Brooklyn still standing? And suppose it *is* choked off by weeds and overgrowth? It's there, isn't it? But don't lose heart. We still have a few remnants of the eighteenth century. It might take some doing to find them, but they're there *somewhere*. And if they're being torn down, you might still see the fragments in some New Jersey swamp or a dumping grounds in one of the Rockaways." He paused to consult his notes. "We've tried to keep it a secret, but New York was the first capital of the United States. The Congress sat here, George Washington was inaugurated here. Where? Well, that's part of the secret. You see, we got rid of the local White House. Martha Washington also had some real estate in town, a mansion on Broadway between Morris Street and Exchange Alley. But as we all know, the value of Manhattan property became so high that they did the only sensible thing, they tore the house down. In Paris, for example, they aren't that shrewd or progressive. Don't have our Know-How. Real estate is allowed to lie fallow; in fact the Government won't even permit historical landmarks to be touched, thus preventing a lot of enterprising speculators from making a decent living. So that today almost anywhere you go in Paris, you can still see the places where kings, queens or cardinals once lived, or the houses where Voltaire, Balzac, Flaubert, Hugo, Baudelaire, Stendhal and Proust did their work. But Europeans seem to be getting tired of all that. Forget it, Charles, the French are saying. And they're now coming over *here* as tourists. This reversal of tradition is creating great economic benefits for cities like New York: a tourist comes here once but he has to come back the next year because while he was gone, countless buildings were demolished and new ones erected in their place—

"What has all this got to do with city planning? For one thing, as Ada Louise Huxtable has pointed out, 'until city planners have a combination of historical knowledge and aesthetic sensitivity to equal their good intentions, planning is a lost cause in this city'—"

As he spoke, as the speech drew more response, as he rode more easily with it, he found his view of the audience losing its massed or anonymous blur; he was becoming more conscious of certain faces, certain people. He also found himself trying to avert a leftward glance to where she sat:

Second row. Left. Watching him. Prominent. Among the more than two hundred people. The auburn hair and the pale green dress. Too vivid between the black of Hank Hartley's tuxedo on one side of her, and the tuxedo of another man on her other side.

Yes: he could speak, and think while, contrapuntally, another part of him could communicate with her. If he allowed it.

While Rosemary, also prominent, her coiffure now the color of champagne, sat in the center of the first row.

". . . but there are all kinds of aspects which those of us who are mad enough to be concerned with city planning should become more aware of. I am thinking, for example, of what Charles Abrams has said. Mr. Abrams of Columbia University, who is head of the city planning department of the School of Architecture, has noted with a humanitarian and humorous eye that many young women are, surprisingly enough, no longer being attracted to New York. Women fresh out of college or small towns are shunning the city partly because we are destroying places where they could meet young men and be courted. Parks are dangerous and to be avoided, and buildings are not designed to allow young people to sit and talk. The city, he maintains, should be a 'trystorium'—"

There'd been two trysts at Christine's since she'd taken possession of her still uncompleted house on East 83rd Street. She'd moved in sooner than planned, a considerate gesture to accommodate William and Ann Boggsen, the purchasers of her

Fifth Avenue apartment, who needed to get their complicated alterations and decoration under way.

It had been just the other day, late afternoon, when he'd gone to see her again, arriving almost on the heels of the departing maid, the carpenters and the painters. She was standing outside the living room door on the second-floor landing, and as he bounded up with rather overyouthful haste, he was unaware of the stairway's freshly sandpapered handrail, unaware of the acrid smell of fresh paint drifting down from the third floor, anticipating with wildest impatience the touch, feel, scent of her closeness: they stood together, their mouths in fierce communion for a long time.

When she took his coat and hung it in the hall closet, she said: "You know, I just got back myself less than ten minutes ago. I'm not going to drive anymore. The streets were simply paralyzed with traffic." There was still that pressing schedule, going for postgraduate work at Morningside Heights, as well as downtown to the office of Hartley's poetry quarterly. "I'm still in my work clothes," she was saying as they went into the high-ceilinged, nineteenth-century living room. Dustcloths covered the furniture preparatory to the replastering and painting. But all Grove noticed at first was that there was a blaze of cheer in the fireplace: Christine's quick simple way of bringing charm to disorder.

As soon as she closed the door, he was holding her again, unbuttoning the jacket of her suit, and through the silk shirtwaist, savoring the thrust of her breasts against him; and again kissing her, drawing back then, looking at her, the dark coppery hair hanging loosely to her shoulders, the eyes misty green, agitated.

Presently she said, "I'll get you a drink."

"I don't think I need one yet," replied Grove, adding, "A real boulevardier would have said he didn't need one because he got intoxicated on you." He sat down on the long muslin-sheeted sofa. He looked around. "It's going to be a hell of a handsome room one day. In spite of all the S and S equipment."

Christine nodded, crossed her legs. Then she said, "You know something perfectly horrible just occurred to me—"

"What?" He leaned over and kissed her and decided to re-acquaint his hand with the delicious feel of her thigh (almost but not quite shutting out the ubiquitous vision of Rosemary).

"You're always harping on anything or anyone too S and S. What about me?" She paused, watching him. "No, seriously. There's probably no one you know who's more S and S than I—"

"You?" He laughed. "Of course you're not. Not at all."

"But I am. Think about it," she said. "And if you'll remove your nice warm concupiscent hand from my person, you'll see how S and S I really am." She proceeded to remind him of some of the labels that marked her life: from Miss Porter's School to her debut at the Plaza to Wellesley, to the marriage with Howard Stelward at the Church of St. Vincent Ferrer. "Et cetera, et cetera."

"Oh, sure. Superficially that's true," asserted Grove. "But you're not that way at all. I mean, good Christ, you're not an S and S'er at all. You're using your mind for something more than figuring out what to wear and where to be at the right time and the right place. You get around a lot and you always look outstanding, but with you that's not an end in itself."

"If you're trying to set me up for the next few days, you're succeeding." Christine smiled. Then she said, "Anyway, I've got incontestable proof that I *am* one of the unmentionables."

"How?"

"Simply that here I am entertaining a man in the official and accepted clandestine manner, exactly like all other countless S and S'ers."

He lit a cigarette. "It's not the same. Look at the narrow ground you have to stand on. Your father on one side, Howard Stelward on the other."

"At least I do have you in between, don't I?"

"Properly speaking you don't even have that."

"Properly speaking," Christine said, "I've always done everything properly all my life. I deserve a break." She took his cigarette, drew in deeply. "Everything with me has always been so perfectly proper. But"—a grim smile—"I'm completely churched-out, golfed-out, Junior Leagued-out, charityed-out, bridged-out, sailed-out, skied-out. I'm everything except Groved-out." She handed the cigarette back to him, going on then to tell him about last night's hospital visit to her father, and how the ailing man had again pressed for a reconciliation with Howard. "Reconciliation? My God, Grove, imagine trying to answer him at this point!"

"Is he talking more about it now?"

"It depends," she said, "but Howard had been by the day before and whenever Howard sees him, once or twice a week, he always wears his best Catholic face and goes through the whole business, ticking off his rosary of complaints and how can he get our marriage restored. Sometimes, I'm distressed to say, I'm almost driven to telling my father the truth. But of course Howard knows I can't or won't ever do anything like that."

Grove rose and moved to the high windows which overlooked the rear garden below, now bleak and bleached by winter, the single sycamore leafless, skeletal. "At least, Christine, you're caught up in a situation you can't change." He turned back to her. "Which is not the case with me."

"But what's the point of changing it, Grove? There's no point telling Rosemary. At least not now. If I can't get free, what's the point of it?"

"Even if your hands are tied," Grove asserted, "mine

aren't. If I were free it would certainly be fairer to Rosemary. And also, you and I would have to carry only half what we do now. But goddammit, how in hell am I going to tell her?" He moved absently around the room. "Assuming I have the guts. And assuming I ever get three minutes privately with her. She's putting in a twenty-five-hour day. She's just at the peak of her power after too long a time on the outside."

"Then do you think it would be better to tell her now? Now that she's apparently found herself? I'm not suggesting it, Grove, I'm only asking, wondering. I loathe all the deception, I can scarcely face Rosemary anymore—"

"I don't know," he said. "I could tell her. Sometimes I think she's tough enough to take it. But other times . . . I just don't know."

"Yes."

Abruptly Grove said, "When I think how far off I went—"
"From where?"

"I mean, when I think, Christine, how Rosemary and I wrote our own lease for a whole new life here in town and how jazzed up I got believing it."

"Rosemary still believes it, doesn't she?"

Even more, he thought, than he would have liked to say— and he could not bring himself to tell Christine. For Rosemary, ever since last week when Judge Cunningham had hinted something to her about getting Grove to turn and face the Mecca of City Hall, ever since that first overture from the judge, Rosemary was running a new temperature.

The possibility—and that is all it was—of Grove one day becoming a candidate for Mayor of New York had set a fire under Rosemary.

Of course.

But this was something Grove had no taste to discuss with Christine. Not now. He knew her well enough to know or fear what she might do. He knew she would attempt to clear out, leave, vanish, exit.

Grove said, "I think I'll have a drink after all."

"So shall I."

He was back at the windows. "If I lived here, you wouldn't have that wilderness of a garden down there. I could make that patch of neglected real estate into a paradise in winter."

"Could you?" She brought him his drink. The flat gray light of February touched her: except for her lips she wore almost no makeup, yet her complexion, the pink of *Malus floribundi* held a subtle out-of-doors sheen.

"This spring," he went on more extravagantly, "I might do some work down there for you. Put in moonflower or tobacco plant, which has a great night odor, and get a nice daytime fragrance of dianthus and some thyme between the flagstones—"

"I can't possibly wait," Christine said.

"Why in hell did I leave Connecticut?" he declared, adding fiercely and facetiously, "If I lived out there now I could make the classic telephone call and announce an urgent meeting in town." He looked at her. "This way I don't even have the classic *modus suburbia* to go by. Just guilt. Bursting out in every direction, out of my pancreas, my kneecap, my eyeballs. Or if I could just feel guilty for not feeling guilty. But no. I just feel plain guilt period." More of his martini. "Incidentally, since I'm suffering, when is the upstairs going to be finished?"

"If you are trying delicately to refer to the master bedroom, they won't be through until tomorrow," said Christine. "The smell of paint is still all over the place. Next they'll be coming down here to paint and we'll be forced to go upstairs. To answer your question."

"I see." Rather wistfully he glanced to the hall door. He looked at his watch then, deploring the way time has, being laggard and oppressive for the wretched, while for the joyful or the wicked it is all too elusive and swift.

". . . as for the new building code," he was telling his audience, "whatever happened to those bonuses the city was going to give out to encourage builders to surround structures with open spaces or plazas? When a serious architectural and planning contribution like the Seagram tower comes along, what happens? The city fathers showed their appreciation by assessing the building with an even higher rate. But I suppose I mustn't cavil. I ought to be more constructive. I ought to remind us that we are said to have all the outstanding technical and artistic geniuses right here in our own city. Which makes for a provocative mystery: for if they're all here why do we have to go to Boston, Chicago or Philadelphia to see what's bold or inspired in architectural planning and urban renewal?"

"You're right," he declared abruptly. "Totally right."

"About what, Grove?"

"If I'm going to tell her, this is the time." He finished his drink. "It has to be. It can't wait."

That had been three days ago. And still it had to wait.

13. 863 Park Avenue

Her backside does not require massaging, the masseuse admits, not at the age of this young woman. It is firmly curved, shapely, though unlike the rest of the sun-bronzed body, it bears the skimpy band of white skin branded by the bikini she has worn all during March on the honeymoon in Acapulco. The masseuse keeps working, kneading the young flesh of Minni Ogden Valencort who, until her recent divorce, has been Minni Ogden Foote.

But the masseuse is accustomed to this, working on the same body while the name keeps changing.

The new Mrs. Valencort is naked, flat on her flat stomach on the high portable massage table which is set up three mornings a week in the mirror-doored, mirror-walled, gold-ceilinged dressing room of her apartment, formerly the quarters of her new husband's previous marriage.

Like most people, the masseuse, Dolores, had no idea that the former Minni Ogden Foote was unhappily married. She suspected it now and then when she would come in the morning to work on her, and would overhear harsh words. But Dolores has been in this business too long not to know that silence and complete discretion is what endears one to the clientele. If she wanted to talk, ah, there would be enough to fill many books, wouldn't there? However, Dolores has strived hard most of her life to reach her present status, and she is not going to jeopardize it by trading in gossip. The contrast between her life and that of most of the women she serves couldn't be sharper, but if she has learned anything at all, it is that she doesn't necessarily envy these women who are envied by most everyone else.

When Dolores, a sturdy, vigorous widow of dyed blond hair and a natural, if bleak, sense of morality, left her native town, a suburb north of Madrid, she went to Paris. She was seventeen. She got employment with an American family while learning much of her craft at the Université de Beauté, École des Soins Esthétiques. After coming to the United States she spent several years with Elizabeth Arden and Helena Rubenstein. For the past six years she has been in what she likes to call "private practice." Even though she might have an open schedule now and then, she will not take on any new clients. Not unless they are people whose rank she respects. Some of her colleagues regard her as a snob, and one woman whose demand for services she spurned called her a snob's snob. But Dolores doesn't know about all this foolishness; all she knows is that someday her hands will not longer have the necessary strength and then she will retire and transfer her savings account to a bank in Arizona.

She has looked after Minni Ogden Valencort for almost three years, though people who didn't know Mrs. Valencort's problem would wonder why she would ever need this kind of therapy. But one has to remember that her mother is one of most beautiful women in New York. One is always seeing her picture in the newspapers and reading about her. This has not been easy for the daughter, who goes out of her way to keep physically fit and trim: she'll have no flabbiness or sag when she becomes middle-aged. It is a war for her, this living up to her mother's reputation, competing with it.

Now, Dolores deftly dips her fingertip into a jar of the special Arden cream and then works it into Mrs. Valencort's upper thigh. Of course, she reflects, the best thing that has happened to this young woman is her new marriage. He is very nice, Mitchell Valencort (it is his family who has always owned Valencort House, the jewelry firm whose fine old stone-fronted store on Fifth Avenue has been a New York landmark since early in the nineteenth century). Young Mr. Valencort must be a good lover. One can usually tell by the wife's disposition, health, glow of skin, how good a lover her husband is. And he is different from many of the husbands in this class. He is a sportsman, yes, and he is an enthusiastic pilot—he has his own helicopter so that they can go to parties in the country. But he dresses differently than most of the other men, or at least he does now, since his marriage to Madame. And now his hair is very long, and he only wears American clothes daytimes when he goes to his office at Valencort House.

Cute.

That's what the young Valencorts are. The two together are cute. The former Minni Ogden Foote has had her long blond hair sheared off and wears it very, very short like a little boy. And she wears pants now. Almost all the time. Last week when Dolores happened to see the couple on the street, from half a block away, it was not easy to tell who was Mr. Valencort and who was Mrs. Valencourt.

"Oh, Dolores—that feels lovely. Right there. It must be that I need it," Minni Ogden Valencort says. "That food in the Greek place last night. Even those belly dancers can't stay thin. I think I'll need a pedicure today."

"Yes, madame."

"My mother, you know, wears a size eight, and she doesn't even *bother* with massage. Tell me the truth, Dolores, do you really like my no-hairdo hairdo?"

"I'm sure I will," answers Dolores. "I'm not used to it yet."

"No one is. Except Rosemary Grovenour. They all think it's too masculine."

"Madame could never look masculine," replies Dolores honestly. But she knows this is the first serious attempt to show in public the break with the mother.

"Hey—sweet potato—" comes the voice of Mitchell Valencort from the adjacent bedroom. "Are you finished in there?"

"Almost. You can come in. Can't he, Dolores?"

"Yes." Dolores replaces the white sheet across Mrs. Valencort's backside.

Mitchell Valencort appears. He is not tall but he has powerful shoulders, narrow hips and fine hands. His black hair is straight and thick, ledged across the forehead, richly fringed at the back of his neck. "I'll trade jobs with you, Dolores. Okay?"

Dolores smiles politely, but bends more steadily to her task.

"Darling," Mrs. Valencort raises her smoothly blond boyish head and squints up at him, "you look like a kind of chic Beatle." He is wearing a tweed Norfolk jacket, matching tweed cuffless trousers and a brocade vest spanned by a thick gold watch chain which once belonged to his great-grandfather.

"Funny, at the office they don't have that attitude." He turns to peer wryly at himself in one of the mirror-paneled closet doors. (The twenty-foot-long closet contains Minni Ogden Valencort's spring wardrobe, 38 pairs of shoes, 20 pairs of boots, sweaters, shirts, pea jackets, half a dozen new beaded evening gowns, and mostly the full complement of pants: sport slacks, daytime slacks and the countless pants for evening wear— ruffled, feathered, laced, beaded, jeweled.) Mr. Valencort studies his top-heavy, mop-heavy face. "My barber's going to miss me, but think of the money I'll save."

Dolores finds him much more simpatico than Ralph Foote.

He lights his great curved calabash pipe. It juts from his mouth like a miniature saxophone. He sits down on the white-fur-upholstered dressing room stool. The maid, Jenny, comes in presently with his coffee. The extension telephone rings and the girl goes to answer it on the other side of the room. The center section is given to a recessed, gold-fixtured makeup alcove flanked on either side by the long counters of Carrara marble beneath which are the tiers of drawers for undergarments and a concealed jewel safe.

"Mrs. Valencort, it is for you," says the girl. "Mrs. Grovenour calling."

Minni Ogden Foote Valencort, a touch of Foxcroft, a dash of Junior Assembly, a bit of Briarcliff and more than a rash of rich Ralph Foote (once when she commented on the price of dinner at Lutèce, Dexter Knight chided her, saying, "I know how it is, dear, you're just living from hand to Foote"), stretched out her slender arm and took the telephone from the girl and placed it on the massage table.

"Rosemary, darling! I called you twice yesterday, you rat! Oh, all right. No, it's not too early. Dolores is here doing me. And my super-duper darling husband is all dressed, if you must know." Mitchell Valencort belonged, sartorially speaking, to the same club as Sonny Sahn, Frederick Eberstadt and others. She saw that Mitch, his legs crossed, was still wearing the slippers she'd given him, the lovely black velvet ones with his initials embroidered in metallic gold thread. "What?"

"I called," said Rosemary Grovenour, "because I've just invited Mitch's father to lunch. And he's breaking an appointment to make it. But there's much news since yesterday. Much! Anyway, Mr. Valencort is meeting me at Le Trianon, it's a larky day for me, and I'm celebrating. I wanted you and Mitch there too. Big secret. It's going to be rompy, I promise."

"Oh, damn, I hate to poop out on you, darling, but this just couldn't be a worse time for us. Otherwise I'd love to. What's up? Can't you tell me?" But Minni was almost certain she knew: it would surely be about the absolutely wild and wonderful new kind of costume jewelry Rosemary had recently been making, experimenting with. Mitch had told his father about it just before they'd left for their wedding trip. "Rosemary, really darling, aren't you even going to give me a hint?"

"It's too good to waste on the phone, Minni."

"I just can't manage it," said Minni. "What about Grove?"

"Grove is all jammed up today. He's involved in one of those long hasslegassles with Hoving and Huntington Hartford."

"Of all the days!" Minni would have changed her plans in an instant, but she knew Mitch would never put up with it; he'd taken the day off and he had it fully planned. "I just couldn't, darling. My darling husband gave himself a holiday. He's in an absolute twitch. We're going shopping for a new car. We have an appointment at Inskip at noon, and then we're taking off in the old copter for the Island. But look—" Minni tried to keep muted an excessive show of eagerness— "I trust we're still having dinner with you tomorrow night, aren't we?"

"Of course, Minni."

How she looked forward to it! Even though Mitch sometimes accused her of trailing after Rosemary like a disciple, being with her was always a peak experience for Minni: it was all part of the new life since she'd married Mitch. She and Mitch had a place in Rosemary's circle, but it wasn't just an ordinary place, rather special really, since Minni, unlike most of the other women, was almost always with her husband. Some people, she suspected, might joke about her and Mitch being such a constant twosome, but that was just too damn bad. It was a new way for Minni. She'd been alone, always on her own, while she'd been married to Ralph Foote; she'd always been just another of those New York women who go everywhere and do everything without any visible means of a husbandly presence.

"Come on. Please. Tell all," Minni persisted. But when Rosemary continued to refuse, she decided not to push it. "By the way," she said then, "I suppose you saw the papers today—"

"I only had time for a quicksy look," said Rosemary.

"I meant that thing about Bobbsie-Ann Boggsen."

"Oh."

"Are you going to her little housewarming dinner-dance, or needn't I have asked?" said Minni. Ever since she and Mitch had become a devoted part of the Rosemary Grovenour cult, Bobbsie-Ann had gone out of her way to demonstrate her disapproval. "We weren't invited either, and I'm desolated. Hawhaw!"

"I suppose," said Rosemary, "one won't be able to get in without a passport."

Minni's laughter was vociferous in tribute to the cutting precision of Rosemary's remark.

"Well, we wouldn't have been able to go in any case," resumed Minni. "Mitch and I are having our own little blast that night. We decided in bed this morning. Yes, the twenty-ninth of May. Unless that's bad for you. Oh good. What? Well, we're going to put all the furniture and paintings in storage for three days if you can imagine anything sillier. We'll just hole up in the Princeton Club for a couple of nights while we get the apartment ready and all that. We're going to turn the whole place into a— Well, I'll tell you about it tomorrow night. Anyway Mitch and I decided not to use a decorator, we're doing the entire party all ourselves. Did I tell you Mitch and I are almost finished with that needlepoint bedroom rug we started in Acapulco? And—" Through the partially open bedroom door, Anthony, their giant English sheepdog, thumped in. "Oh, Anthony my big baby just came in. He must have heard us talking about our party. Anthony"—she reached out to fondle his woolly head—"my sweet super-duper dollop of dog, you! Oh, speaking of Acapulco, the night before we left there, who do you think flew in from Palm Beach? None other than Firna Birenzia. True. I swear. On a stack. Firna simply walked out of that big barn of a villa in Palm Beach, said it was too boring and the temperature had dropped to 57! So she accepted an invitation from the Longman Scotts. They sent their plane for her, and she showed up just in time for the last round of Coco Locos and then dinner at Armando's, and afterward she made it to Gloria Guinness' party. Incidentally, I heard yesterday that the Boggsens are having an agent scouting a villa for them down there for next winter."

After the briefest hesitation, Rosemary said, "That'll be the end of Acapulco."

"Oh, don't say it," Minni protested.

"Maybe it won't happen," Rosemary said, "maybe they won't find a place."

"I'm afraid they will. I was at my cooking class at Michael Field's, and Sabina Clarke told me there's no doubt of it. The last stick of French furniture has just about been put into the new apartment and here she's already got Bill all exercised about snapping up the first super-duper joint that comes on the market down there. If that fails, they're going to build."

"Well, I wish her the besta." Then: "Oh, excuse me, Minni, my other line is buzzing."

"I'll hold on."

Mitchell Valencort was on his feet now. "If you two have finished, Minni, I want to talk to her. I have to hear the news."

"Sorry," Rosemary said when she returned to the phone. "I made the mistake of promising these people I'd go to the opening of their new boutique, and they've been such nestypesties ever since. I think I'm going to have to get a new unlisted number."

"Yes," Minni said. "My darling husband is trying to snatch the phone from me. He wants to talk to you. He wants to hear your news."

"Nothing doing."

Mitch lifted the telephone from Minni's grasp. "Rosemary, we can't wait until tomorrow night. Can't you open up now? You know one of the reasons I married my darling wife was because she is your friend. How's that for starting off the day with the right way to cultivate the people worth cultivating?"

"Really, Mitch, it's much too good to waste on the telephone. And if you were at your office now instead of playing hookey, your father would have told you all about it."

"Not necessarily. We're not always on the best of terms," Mitch said. "Anyway, I hope it is what I think it is." He saw Minni, the square of sheet wrapped around her middle, get off the massage table and seat herself on the gilded Steinbergian wicker chair; she set a foot into the white oval porcelain bowl on the floor, as Dolores prepared the pedicure. "Come on, Rosemary, after all, didn't I introduce you to my father? He was a fan of yours, I know, but I did lead him by the nose and—"

"Are you trying to shame me into it, Mitch?"

"Yes."

Minni leaned forward, watching her husband.

"Oh, really?" Mitch was saying. "Well, I suppose he can be nice if he chooses." He kept nodding as he listened. Then: "Why, Rosemary, that's phenomenal. That, as they say, is the way to sell the product. And all I did was predict it would happen."

"Did it?" Minni demanded.

"Yes. The Old Man is terrifically impressed. He's going to help her get it off the ground."

"Whoops!" cried Minni Ogden Foote Valencourt.

"My darling bride just said whoops in case you didn't hear," reported Mitch. "And so do I. I don't have to tell you how long he's resisted costume jewelry."

"Oh, he still resists it," said Rosemary. "I mean, he wouldn't touch it for your company. But he did say he'll try to see that it gets to the proper people."

Minni, her feet dripping, hastened over and captured the telephone again. "Rosemary, darling, I'm enthralled. I think the news is absolutely—I think this jewelry kick of yours is going to make you gruesomely rich and we can all say we knew you back in the days when you were merely famous!"

"Listen—" Mitch regained the phone. "I don't want to downgrade my Old Man, but I want you to remember, Rosemary, no matter how kind or helpful he may seem, if anything comes of this he'll see to it that more than a few pennies end up on our side of the IBM ledger."

Shortly before noon that April morning, Minni Ogden Foote Valencort, in gray pants and white car coat, her husband in his tweed Norfolk-jacketed suit, each of them hatless and making a vivid study in tonsorial contrasts, were waiting for a taxi beneath the white canvas canopy of 863 Park Avenue. As they waited they watched their maid Jenny as she took, or rather accompanied, Anthony the English sheepdog on his unwanted, citified constitutional.

Near the canopy a chauffeur was feather-dusting the hood of a black Bentley limousine. And at the corner, two of those dilapidated, wheeled delivery contraptions favored by the better groceries and markets of the East Side almost collided.

While the doorman, stepping off the curb, blew his nickel-plated whistle in the hope of luring a cab; he kept chirping away, joining the pipings of the other doorman on both sides of the block who were on the same mission. And there arose in the violet swirl of smoky spring air that familiarly shrill musical composition heard three times a day along the upper reaches of Park and Fifth avenues: the Concerto for Whistle and Taxi.

It was not quite tragic, yet, as it sometimes happened, there were three major parties on the same night. Thus, on the evening of May 28th, when the Valencorts gave their party, Bobbsie-Ann Boggsen had hers; and downtown in his loft apartment, Waldo Stryker was holding a summit conclave of the pop clan. Each party was heralded as the Ultimate.

When the blue chips were down, however, the Valencort party, though outstanding and lavishly celebrated in the press, reflected a kind of final code of the young of their class: the party was chic, jazzy and inventive, yet never so far out that it could be called shockingly bizarre.

Though Minni Ogden Valencort felt euphorically emancipated from the conservatism of her marriage to Ralph Foote, and though her new conjugal partnership with Mitchell Valencort inspired her to undertake a more enterprising social life, she was, like her husband, always rooted to her past: no matter how high or freely the Valencorts might fly their kite it would always remain attached to earth by the umbilical string of their heritage.

Yet, as Dexter Knight would soon say, and Daphne Bernlinsk soon perceive, it was just this dichotomy that attracted so much attention to the event and its striking young hosts. In other words, the occasion offered that irresistible combination of social indifference along with sheer social cachet. There was another aspect which made the evening unique: it was not confined merely to the young generation, but was a neutral ground where the young and the not-so-young, as well as the decidedly old, seemed to fraternize with comparative ease.

True to their word, the Valencorts had had most of their furniture and rugs removed to storage, and while the large apartment was being decorated for this party, they camped out at the frigidly façaded Princeton Club. Though they had in all sincerity planned to design the party and do all the work themselves, it had been necessary in the end to call for help: Tony Ammonds (who decorated the duplex apartment of Mitch's father, Pierre Valencourt, as well as the premises of the Fifth Avenue store) consented to send over three of his young assistants to give the couple a hand. After all, Minni and Mitch did move in the major league of party-givers, and they knew that Rosemary Grovenour, among others, gave parties not simple to eclipse. However, the Valencorts were blessed with the kind of security that could compete with utter casualness: they kept their party budget to just under seven thousand dollars. Even their invitations held a casual tone (though the paper and engraving were from Valencort House) saying merely: *We're having a Café-Dance. Wear what you will; anything welcomed. Except Black Tie.*

The only person who defied this injunction was Dexter Knight. He arrived a fraction later than most of the others, wearing his dinner clothes; he had a carnation in his lapel and a black tie was vivid at the collar of his discreetly ruffled white shirt.

"Oh, Dex—" Minni Ogden Valencort greeted him in the immense entrance foyer which was to be part of the dancing area. Her short blond hair was combed forward into long slanting bangs; her earrings, designed by Rosemary Grovenour, were

elongated, asymmetric triangles glinting with bits of tinted mirror; her pants ensemble, a Paris adaptation by Martine, was
aglitter with white and silver paillettes. "Dex, really, what a
super-duper reactionary you are!"

"Darling—" Dexter Knight resolutely surfaced his desolation
with an extravagant smile—"darling, you surely ought to know
by this time that I'm the last of the great conformists."

Even now, during this hideous hiatus since David's departure,
despite the despair shattering him, he could still command a
vestige of his style, a facile manner.

"I'm not sure if we should let him in, Mitch," Minni said.

"We can always take it to the Admissions Committee," said
Mitchell Valencort. He wore, Dexter noted, one of his less work-
aday costumes: tight faded levis and a high-buttoned black velvet Edwardian jacket on which he sported a large metallic daisy;
his dark hair seemed longer, thicker, more wildly fringed.

"Tell me, Mitch," said Dexter to this sprightly heir of one of
New York's most venerable families, "are you by any chance supposed to be Richard the Lion Hearted or Prince Valiant?"

The Valencorts laughed. Minni said: "We were disappointed
about David, hated to have him poop out on us, Dex."

"Yes, I'm afraid he did, as you so exquisitely put it, poop
out." Dexter was thankful for the gambit. "But as I told you, I
have been overworking him this year and I had to ship him off
to sea—" the merest hesitation— "or rather to Marion Cal-
lisster's ship."

"I'm so sorry, Dex, I mean I'm glad for David of course, but
I know how you depend on him." Minni Ogden Valencort was
being tactful. Too tactful. He wondered if Rosemary had said
anything to her: it was a mistake sometimes to confide in Rosemary; these days she could be quite unreliable.

"I hope," he was regathering his poise, "I'll see a few unfamiliar faces tonight, Minni." He peered beyond his hosts. "I see your father is here, Mitchell. He was just dashing across the room or whatever that is in there. A café, I take it?"

A butler, dressed like the rest of the hired help, in the coarse apron, black pants and white shirt of a European waiter, took his coat and hat.

"We'll take you on the tour, Dex," said Minni. "If you'd like."

"If ultimately it leads to a Scotch and soda." He followed them. She and Mitch were sparkling with eagerness to show the final fruits of three days' labor. Those past three days in which he had not seen a soul except the delivery boy from the liquor shop. Two weeks since David had flown. Gone.

What now? He followed the Valencorts. What manner of invention, effort, money, had these two poor dear things put into an evening's divertisement? But bless them for it. What would he have done tonight without fantasies such as this party?

The parquet floor of the great drawing room was left clear along the center section for dancing. But the rest of the room was now a New York summertime café, more beautiful than realistic, more beflowered and flower-scented and prettily devoid of soot; low green hedges separated the dancing area from the rows of tiny tables.

"What exactly is that, my dears?" Dexter paused to look at one wall: it was given to posters and old advertisements, but mostly it was zigzagged in childlike markings—the chalk and crayon graffiti often seen on fences and walls in city neighborhoods. Scribbled or printed were the names of many of the sixty guests in a variety of facetious connotations. Some of the inscriptions read:

PIERRE VALENCORT IS A GIRL'S BEST FRIEND

Christine Stewward is teacher's pet

DAPHNE BERNLINSK NIGHT OR DAY – CALL → 789-9668 ←

DEBORAH MARMONIER RAND LOVES JOHN LINDSAY

Dexter Knight Voted by Village Voice as hippie of the year

4 SALE! 1955 EDSEL. SEE H. HARTLEY

Sabina Clarke is hung up on you know who

Minni Loves Mitch

JUDGE CUNNINGHAM CAN FIX IT!

THE GILLON FINDLEYS SHOW DIRTY MOVIES

GILES FOLOR FLUNKED ENGLISH!

BUY YOUR SNAPSHOTS OFF SONNY SAHN

Rosemary H Loves H Grove

NINA VER DEN KAHR HAROWITZ IS A RAT FINK HA! HA!

"Charming," said Dexter, adding unkindly, "It's all so simple and spontaneous."

"Isn't it," replied Mitchell Valencort blithely enough.

"Come see where the eats will be," said Minni, indulging in that common pastime of the private school elite who enjoy spouting the patois of the streets.

The dining room, he saw now, had been converted into the sculpture garden of the Museum of Modern Art—or a terraced segment of it, prepared for alfresco dining. A long buffet table with fountains of fresh flowers and jets of white tapered candles would be laden later with the food being sent in from Le Trianon. Though this was taking a bit of license with the museum, the sculpture in the room provided a more authentic aspect: pieces by Zorach, King, Nevelson, Giacometti and Henry Moore —gifts, Dexter knew, from both the Ogden and Valencort clans. "I see," he said, "that you two are using the old family hand-me-downs."

"Oh, we have a few of our own too—" Minni pointed to a Segal and a Marisol.

David—the thought pierced him—would probably be on the isle of Mykonos this evening, seated at a café table on the waterfront sipping ouzo with his menopausal patroness.

The Valencorts continued the tour, showing him the library now become the café of the St. Moritz Hotel; going on then to show him one of the guest suites which had been transformed into a replica of the Bitter End coffeehouse; and a second guest suite which, Minni and Mitch assured him enthusiastically, was the latest of the East Village bars: the New Order Bagel. In here some musicians were playing New Order Rock. The sounds drove him out. He was then taken to the rear, to the master bedroom, now metamorphosed into the Parisian sidewalk café of the Hotel Stanhope on Fifth Avenue. There were even copies of

Le Figaro on some of the tables. "I think I'll settle here," said Dexter. "It's convenient to the Metropolitan—"

"Dexter—" Rosemary beckoned from one of the tables. "Come, join us."

He hesitated: a drink alone would be preferable. He had played out his charm for the moment. However, when he saw that Rosemary was with Mitch's father, Pierre Valencort, he decided to move. The whole purpose of tonight was not to be alone, to come to this party and perhaps later look in on Bobbsie-Ann Boggsen's little sideshow. He would see the Comtesse Jacqueline de Rocheferron there. That would make for diversion. He rose and went to the other table. "Why, Mr. V.," he said to the prominent jewel merchant, "if I'd known you'd be here I would have worn my splendid Valencort studs." He kissed Rosemary. "Darling."

"You needn't apologize, Dexter," said the elder Valencort, whose agile but portly frame was draped in a fawn-gray suit, double-breasted vest and foulard tie. He wore no jewelry whatever. "After all, look what our friend here is wearing."

"Umm." But Dexter could not resist frowning. "I see we're back in that scruffy poolroom again, aren't we?" For Rosemary had on an updated version of her baize shift.

"No, I was referring to that—" Valencort indicated another of the pieces of costume jewelry she'd designed: a multi-hued necklace of miniature pool balls, each with a number on it.

"Just one of those dinkytinkies made by loving hands at home," said Rosemary with a modesty perhaps more cultivated than genuine. Her blond hair was now cut shorter, rather briskly shaped like a young lady executive's.

"I believe we'll be seeing those 'dinkytinkies' in at least a dozen department stores before Christmas," said the elder Valencort.

"Dex, you haven't seen this yet—" Rosemary moved back, tilting her leg upward and revealing—yes, her feet were bare, but figured in a tracery of fake amethysts, opals and sapphires.

"And what," asked Dexter, "is it?"

"I call them Lotus Footsies," said Rosemary. "They're the only ones I've made so far."

"Darling," said Dexter, "now that you're going into vulgar commerce, I'm not sure I approve. My God, those dresses of yours are getting so common—I daresay I see hundreds of them every time the Seagram Building disgorges all those little secretaries. And now we seem to have all manner of"—he winced—"'dinkytinkies.' You know, one day we're going to wake up and find the New York woman who is the most chic is the one who does absolutely nothing."

He saw, gratefully, Minni Ogden Valencort directing the waiter with the Scotch to his table.

Rosemary said, "Have you heard much from David?"

"Just a cable. The poor lad is really there to get away from the typewriter, you know," he answered with calculated lightness, though his eyes, fixed on Rosemary, held less warmth: he particularly resented her question; she knew perfectly well he hadn't heard from David and she'd deliberately, cruelly imposed the subject because she couldn't bear his indifference to her popularity or her swift rise as a careeerist: amid so much adulation she couldn't bear his disapproval. Dexter had from the beginning tried his best to set a direction, a tone, for her, but she had only gone so far, and then she'd skittered off on her own without his advice, without his benediction!

Or was Rosemary's poisonous jab meant as a reminder that she was not the only one who failed to remain cowering in his commanding shadow, that David too could free himself?

Not that it mattered. Nothing mattered. He was positive he would never recover. He raised his whiskey glass, and favoring

Rosemary with one of his most satanic smiles, said, "Bless you, darling."

But the whiskey seemed raw, stinging, carrying with it no balm.

For forty-eight hours after David had left him, Dexter had remained locked in his bedroom at 1027 Fifth Avenue with only brandy as his chief nourishment. He'd never punished himself or his intestines with such a stupid excess.

Catharsis, he'd thought. Just as he meant to purge the lingering spirit of David's presence by going to his clothes closet and taking the rest of David's wardrobe and stuffing it down the incinerator: only to discover that the closet had already been emptied. David had evidently removed his entire wardrobe and all the costly accessories, taken them elsewhere before leaving for Greece and the sagging bitch who awaited him aboard her ship in Piraeus Harbor.

Well, bless her. And bless David. He wished them nothing but luck: may that boat crack apart in a violent Aegean tempest!

The only tempest, however, was in his heart.

And the whiskey did help, didn't it? But only a respite.

If he was left with anything it was his pride in knowing the apartment had not changed hands. It was still his. Inviolate. Forever. He had not succumbed to the younger man's black-mailing demands; he could at least tell himself he had not been bilked. Unlike his own one-time benefactor, he retained his identity, his pride, his integrity.

Was it worth it?

No.

He'd erred. David gone. Dexter knew it was a hideous vain-glorious blunder. He would never recover.

In the New Order Bagel, listening to the New Order Rock as if there simply was no other kind of music fit for IN-Ears,

Daphne Bernlinsk, the city's busiest and buzzingest culture bee, wearing a scarlet sari by Count Ferdinand Sarmi, sat at one of the small tables, nodding her poodle head, rolling her chocolate eyes and tapping time with her feet. Her escort, a glandular-eyed young man with literary pretensions, was in the adjacent room, the Bitter End, lapping coffee to sober himself up from all the martinis he'd had at Daphne's West Side apartment this afternoon. He drank, she realized, because he couldn't quite accommodate her in bed; what was worse was that he was sobering up now because he wanted to be clear-eyed enough to enjoy the spectacle of all the attractive young women present. As far as Daphne was concerned, this was indeed the bitter end. Of him.

Yet she found herself not unhappy: this party—she hadn't expected it to be on such a fresh level; in fact she might not even have gone if she hadn't known Rosemary Grovenour would be here. But the party had a quality, and there were not a few INteresting people. It was, after all, a bonus. She would possibly come away with an attractive name or two to add to her list, to give to her salon both chic and artistic respiration.

She waved now to Christine Stelward and Hank Hartley when they came into the murkily lit room with the young Valencorts, and presently the New Order Bagel began to explode with new spirit, for Minni and Mitch started dancing the Bird, which was still recent enough to be considered acceptable.

But how adorable they were.

How they really magnetized the others in the room. How they drew them to the floor. The young Valencorts—their movements were supple, subtle, yet emanating an aura of sexuality, the two of them touched each other in that provocative way, and look at them, their hairdos, that amusing masquerade in reverse, male and female, charming.

Soon the New Order Bagel café was thick with figures in a kind of spastic harlequinade. The clothes women wore had such variety that the effect was that of a costume party: short skirts, ball gowns, pants, pajamas, nightshirts, pea jackets, cutouts and see-throughs, striped skivvy shirts and nude dresses with patches of glitter for sweet modesty.

And the young Valencorts led the pack: this same girl who a year ago was still Minni Ogden Foote whose parties in Long Island, until the advent of Rosemary Grovenour, were strictly Old Westburyhampton Old-Line. The Old Oaken Bucket in the Old Social Well.

Yet when Minni and Mitch combined, a new chemistry happened.

Sparking the party with SUCCESS.

Yet not doing anything except being themselves, absorbed in themselves.

"I can't understand those two," Hank Hartley said at the adjacent table. "You'd think they were the ones who *discovered* marriage."

"Maybe they are," said Daphne.

Christine Stelward in a short Nile-green dress, her auburn hair hanging straight to her shoulders, kept watching the couple. She smiled with that unabashed candor of hers. Or was it wistfulness? "I think," said Christine, "there's enough love there to go around for everybody."

"Yes," said Daphne. "It's the one thing they're really fulla." And she wished a little might come her way.

But look at them. With a painful blend of envy and admiration she watched Minni Ogden Valencort and her husband perform, the slim, shimmering, sleek-headed Minni and the Beatle-mopped, elegant INdividualist Mitch, together made such a— what?

A touch. News. For Daphne.

Maybe, possibly, a piece for *Hipman?*

Daphne could be, again, the first with the word.

Possibly.

How?

What was there to hold on to? Not Togetherness, surely not *that* for God Sakes!

But of course. Just that. It was so old, so gauche, it veered on Camp!

Togetherness raised to a new and sophisticated level: SEX-UAL TOGETHERNESS. LOVE IN ACTION. WEALTH and WITH-ITness. BLUE-BLOODED HIPSTERISM.

Daphne was becoming so captivated she almost wet her panties.

Yet—she had to restrain herself. Not get carried away. Was she in any condition for shrewd judgment? Not after this afternoon.

Yet—

Wait. Check. Cross-check. Feel.

Yet already even a tough baby like Hank Hartley was getting part of the message. And a bright female like Christine Stelward was certainly reading it.

It had to add up to hallmark material. Look who was here tonight— Yet none of them would be able to articulate what was happening. Daphne could do that. She could be the first with the word.

And first to build an evening at her salon around them?

Wait.

Yet: wasn't Dexter Knight more than civilized to them? Wasn't Rosemary Grovenour virtually tonight's guest of honor?

Wasn't that Hallmarktown? Yes.

And wasn't Pierre Valencort present?

And Grove?

And look at Joan and Gillon Findley. And Giles Folor and several other writers and artists. And *Fig*'s Seeing Eye: Peter Sonny Sahn.

John Lindsay was supposed to come if he got back from Albany in time.

And Jackie would surely look in. (Ohhhhh!)

And Bobby. Or Sargent. There was talk of others popping in later: Amanda the B or George the P or Robin the B or Truman the C or Eugenia the S or Gloria the G or Norman the M or Susan the S or Lydia the M.

(Earlier when Daphne asked Dexter Knight if he'd heard that Stanley Kauffmann, the drama critic of the *Times*, was coming, Dexter had replied: "No, he covered it last night.")

Of course not all of them would make it.

And something else: who was at Bobbsie-Ann Boggsen's party tonight?

Also there had to be more than a quorum of Hot Ones down at Waldo Stryker's now.

Daphne turned to Hank Hartley: "Hank, you're going down to Waldo's later, aren't you?"

"Waldo's?" For some reason Hartley seemed perplexed. "I'm not sure. Why, Daphne?"

"I'm supposed to go," she said cautiously, "and I thought I could hitch a ride."

"I'm not sure. I'll let you know," said Hartley in that maddeningly vague or enigmatic way of his, and turned to watch the writhing mass of chic humanity clotting the floor of the New Order Bagel.

"Dance?" It was the voice of Mitchell Valencort; he had stopped dancing with his wife long enough to do his hostly duty.

"What?" Daphne looked up: though she preferred to be regarded as the mistress of her salon of culture rather than merely a social or frivolous creature, she found herself uncommonly pleased to be singled out by Mitchell Valencort.

But as she was about to rise, she saw that it was Christine Stelward whom he was addressing.

Daphne went back to her drink. How crazy this was, wasn't it? She of all people. She, Daphne Bernlinsk, the Honda-hopping Avant-Gardist, the Recorder, the Cultural Matchmaker—had she forgotten the role in life she had so assiduously created for herself?

She had almost lost her Cool, hadn't she?

She brought her attention, her chocolate bonbon eyes, to Mitch dancing with Christine, and her admiration for him, which might have declined like her pride, mysteriously rose. And when the dance was over, she saw him collect Minni and begin yet another round of the Bird, and there was much mouth-to-mouth pecking whenever they came within touching distance of each other.

Incredible, those two. The golden storm they were whirling up in their own party.

INcredible! Daphne murmured it to herself or to her world at large.

"Are you sure you don't want to go, Grove?" Rosemary asked. "I told Waldo we'd be there—"

"I'd prefer not to, Rosie," Grove said. They were standing beneath the great arch between the living room and the dining room. "On the other hand, I don't particularly think you ought to go down there alone this late."

Rosemary stared up at him. "Why, Grove, what is this?"

"What is what?"

"Your being suddenly all protective and papa-like," she said.

"Oh? Was that what I was being?" He'd floundered again, again stubbed his toe on the stone of his guilt.

"Yes. But it doesn't matter. Daphne is coming along," said Rosemary.

"Oh." Grove swallowed. It was shortly after the late supper. The salmon mousse and the curry of duck, among other plain fare, plus the two wines, were already making a searing assault on his insides. It wasn't the supper as such. It was the rush of affection Rosemary had seemed to show for Christine, the way she'd insisted she sit at the same table. This did not make for digestive calm. "You take the car. I'll walk home."

He noticed that Christine was talking to someone in the dining room—or sculpture garden of the Museum of Modern Art. He looked rightward then to the flowered café of the immense living room. Behind the low fence of green hedge, a Rock quartet (Old Order) was stationed, playing for the dancing now under way there and in the foyer. Three electric guitars and drums kept their decibel madness down to a din.

"Would you like to dance?" Grove asked: as considerate and gracious as any husband on the premises.

"I really have to get downtown."

"You've got enough time," Grove said.

She did not answer. Nor did she leave.

"The Valencorts"—he was made uneasy by Rosemary's prolonged silence—"they're certainly a juiced-up pair, aren't they?"

"Everyone here seems to be," Rosemary said, adding then: "Or almost everyone."

"Yes" was his inadequate reply to her thrust, if that is what it was? And immediately he found it absolutely necessary to give the party his most intensive survey: Minni and Mitch Valencort were undoubtedly the centrifugal force of the evening, their exuberant choreography inspiring the horde. There was Giles Folor, the russet-matted Boston novelist, visibly perspiring as he Birded away with his newest mistress, a former slavey with the *New York Review of Books*, whose reedy figure and delicate features were dramatized by a Sassoon haircut and tight tangerine pants around which was slung a cowboy belt and twin holsters jutting with menacing rhinestone revolvers. He saw Hank Hartley in his Army and Navy Surplus Store denims and work shirt, doing an antediluvian twist with Sabina Clarke, who looked like his young sister or niece just down from Farmington. Dexter Knight, who rarely danced, was performing a stylish foxtrot with old Helen Marmonier (ah, how she'd failed Grove the night of another party, how long ago? when he'd gone to her Beekman Place residence to lure from her the wad to save the Calvert mansion now long gone and replaced by that thirty-story pile of white subway toilet brick) ; Mrs. Marmonier, who had dropped by tonight after the opera to have a visit with Minni's mother, Mrs. Ogden, both ladies being fellows in perpetuity of the Metropolitan Museum of Art. He saw Helen Marmonier's granddaughter Deborah and one of the elegant New Order Rock musicians bobbing their brains out doing the Jerk. A tall sinuous *Fig* model with a curvaceous rump, being careful not to disturb her coiffure as she danced in unfashionable closeness with Sonny Sahn. Gillon Findley, ex-attaché to the U.S. Embassy in Rome, and currently importer of foreign films, was dancing with his wife in perfect and modish Birdesque. Pierre Valencort, short, stout and stately, held an old party of nineteen whose vinyl skirt was mid-thigh and who wore silver-foil flowers in her hair. There were at least a dozen young couples he did not know. He saw signaling to him now Judge Zachary Cunningham, former jurist and currently one of the mayor's advisers, dancing with enthusiastic indifference to the Rock beat with his wife, a gay woman much of whose wealth and time was given to the Whitney Museum and the Bursitis and Arthritis Foundation.

"Have you talked to him yet, Grove?" Rosemary said.

"Judge?"

"Yes."

"No. I've eluded him so far."

"You mustn't."

"I've had City Hall until it popped from my pores and my navel."

"He's serious, Grove. He told me he's going to work on you. I don't see why you're so anti."

"The Judge wouldn't be hounding me if you hadn't encouraged him," Grove said.

"Why not? I really think, in spite of anything you might say, you'd make a marvelous politico. And you—"

"Listen, Rosie—"

"Grove, what's happened to you?"

"What?"

"I mean the way you're trying to turn your back on all you said. I'd like to remind you," Rosemary spoke more rapidly, "of what we talked about, what you talked about, when you wanted to make the move to New York, all you said you could do here, all the potential you were going to take advantage of—why, you definitely told me you would even make up and hold hands with City Hall, and all during this past year, everything I've done has been to help you. I just can't understand how you stand here and reverse everything you—"

"I'm not trying to reverse anything, it's just a question of—"

"It's a question of wanting to ignore me, for one thing, isn't it?" Rosemary said.

"What?" Hurriedly he turned to wave to someone in the dancing crowd who had not waved to him: unfortunately his eye happened to single out amidst the chalked graffiti on the wall Rosemary loves Grove.

At once he glanced away, back to the Museum of Modern Art sculpture garden: unfortunately he saw Christine leaving the room, moving in the direction of the archway.

Abruptly he turned to Rosemary. "Sure you wouldn't like to dance?"

"No. I'm just waiting to say good night to Minni and Mitch."

He was immoderately relieved to see that Christine had paused to speak with another woman. But the curry of duck had lurched again.

"Grove," said Rosemary, "you won't forget to talk to Judge—"

"Look, Rosie"—he drew in a deep breath of fine smoky air—"the talking I have to do is with you. Why don't you give up the Waldo Stryker party and we'll—"

"Are you mad? How could I?"

"Every time I suggest we have a talk you're in such a hell of a sudden hurry to get some place," Grove declared.

"I am? I think you must be imagining that, Grove." Rosemary's small-boned features seemed constrained, rendered, he felt, more noticeable by the sharp or alien blondness of her hair. "After all," she was saying, "we talk every night at dinner and every morning at breakfast—"

"If you can call that talking," said Grove. "You're on the telephone during breakfast, and you're on the telephone half the time during dinner or you're gone, giving an interview at some store or having to show up for the opening of another new boutique or just tucked away in that back room of yours with your pliers and plastics and—"

"Why is it you've never mentioned any of this before?" she asked, not unreasonably.

Because, he could have said, he obviously would rather collect grievances than have to confront her with the truth. "I never mentioned it," he temporized, "because in the face of Madame's frantic schedule how could I?"

"Oh, how you exaggerate. Why do you exaggerate like that, Grove?"

Why? Because, how else could he justify his endless and unjustifiable procrastinations?

"I mean," she went on, "unless it's something you've got on your mind that has you all buggsied up—"

"What do you mean?" In lighting his cigarette now, Grove almost singed his index finger.

"For one thing," said Rosemary, "you keep making it sound like I'm some kind of wicked witch who's trying to avoid you—but maybe it's— Are you trying to avoid *me?*"

"You make it easy sometimes," Grove answered. Then: "Look, Rosie, this is not the place for—tomorrow's Sunday—and tomorrow we're going to talk—"

"Tomorrow?" Rosemary's brow puckered. "Oh, I forgot to tell you I'm lunching at Mr. Valencort's house. It's the only free time he'll have all week. And afterward—there's that cocktail reception—"

"What reception?" he asked: her schedule at times tended to give him vertigo.

"At the League of American Crafts."

"Well," said Grove, "why don't we just try to pencil me into your agenda for sometime next year."

"Grove." She reproached him. She fingered the chromatic miniature pool balls of her necklace. "Oh, Christine!" she called.

He looked up. Passing beneath the archway between the two rooms, Christine paused: even under disagreeable conditions the sight of her stirred up his entire arterial system. (She did not look thinner, though she claimed she'd lost four pounds during the past eight months shuttling between Hank Hartley's magazine office on Wall Street and her graduate studies at Morningside Heights. To his eyes it did not show.)

"Darling—" Rosemary was beckoning to her.

But now Grove could feel a kind of glacial lurching within his stomach: the salmon mousse had congealed.

"Christine," Rosemary was saying, rippling now in brightest cadence, "would you mind taking out your Good Deed Pills and dancing with my husband? I have to go downtown to Waldo's party, and I can't leave Grove like this— He's in one of those grumpley moods of his—"

As soon as he and Christine began to dance, he said, "I'm not making sense tonight. I can't make out Rosemary at all." He guided Christine to a less peopled corner of the foyer. He found himself holding her much less decorously than he should have. "Christ. You feel so good and you smell so delicious. I'm ready to commit mayhem."

"Grove, we—"

"Can you tell me why she's doing this?" Grove said. "Going out of her way to be all that cozy with you."

Christine shook her head.

"Isn't that something new?"

"And it's awful," Christine declared. "At dinner, we—"

"She's been throwing me one curve after another. And then her asking you to look after me," said Grove. "I wish you would, by the way."

"I don't understand it." Christine glanced away. "It was absolutely unnerving at times."

Dismally, he said, "It's as if she suspected or knew, and is trying to test us."

"If it was that—" Christine's hand tightened on his. Her father's image, he knew, was already summoned.

"I don't know, I can't tell," said Grove. "You'd think I'd know what she's like. But how in hell can I? She's like someone else now. Yet—how could she actually know? Unless—" Once again there insinuated itself that haunting sight of Sonny Sahn and Waldo Stryker, that dismal encounter with them in the elevator at 958 Fifth Avenue. "Unless Sonny or Stryker let it drop—"

"They had no way of knowing you'd been at my apartment," said Christine. "No, if anything's been said, it conceivably could come from another place."

"What? What place?"

"It didn't occur to me until yesterday, but"—Christine's clear emerald gaze took on a mist of apprehension—"but that European antiques dealer on my ground floor. I've discovered he does quite a bit of business with Tony Ammonds. French furniture. And some of those boys talk a lot. If he's seen you—and I suppose he's bound to have—oh, it's too awful to even contemplate."

"Do you think it could be anything like that?"

"It could be."

He looked at her: in addition to his niggling anxieties, it was painful to see Christine, who had her own dismal and hopeless situation to contend with, now having to bend beneath yet another burden. He said, "I didn't want to load you down with this. Half of it, anyway, could be in my head."

"Or mine," said Christine.

"Yes."

From the other room the Rock blasted and twanged the festive air.

"Unless," Christine said now, "it's something she feels instinctively and—"

"She's much too busy to feel anything instinctively." But Grove reconsidered: Rosemary could indeed have sensed what was happening. If, in fact, he reviewed the past, wasn't it curious that right from the beginning more than two years ago, the night of that big S and S *soirée* at Helen Marmonier's, the night he'd first met Christine, Rosemary had fixed on her, selected her as someone who had, even unbeknownst to him, invaded his consciousness? Grove stirred. "I'm going to get this over with." Then: "How many months since I said that?"

"It doesn't matter," she said.

"Let's get a drink."

"Please don't keep worrying about that part of it, Grove. It'll probably happen one day without your even planning it."

"Sooner or later it has to," he said. "And when it does I'll undoubtedly go gutless and chicken right out." He had in truth tried or planned to confront Rosemary several times, but, as he told her tonight, there was always some new plateau she was about to reach, some new rush of activity, some new personality to be won, some new and breathless wonderment which he never had the heart to kill.

Or rather, that he didn't have the will to speak up.

"How does it feel," he said, "to be in love with a truly heroic figure like myself? Tell me?"

"I dread having to tell you I *married* a hero." Her smile was grave. "And I couldn't possibly bear having two."

"Ah, you're so goddammed delicious I'm going to clear out of here and go to your place and let you tell me more. Why don't we do that?" he declared in an anguish of love and lust and guilt.

"Not after the way Rosemary acted tonight. It's an insane risk, even though, Grove, how lovely it would be."

"Christ." Heedlessly he pressed her to him. "It's an orange pekoe world!"

"What does that mean?"

"I don't know. Except it is. The way I feel. Like a goddam

oversqueezed soggy bag of orange pekoe tea! Let's get a drink."
But then he said, "Christine."

"What?"

"I've been thinking. Which is bad," he said. They stopped
dancing. "The trouble is it's too easy to kid myself. That's been
the trouble. Rosie is busy, yes, and she's pushing herself hard,
yes. But what I suppose I don't like to admit is that she wouldn't
be doing it if she didn't assume that basically I'm with her, that
she had *me*. Before she got into any of this, she was totally shaky,
and jealous to a frenzy. Now she's making it in a way she's
dreamed all her life. And she's secure. At least she's secure
enough not to let you or anyone else threaten her."

Christine said, "You really think that, Grove?"

"How else can you account for the way she's been, the way
she was tonight?" He paused to live with this melancholy prospect. "I'm afraid that's what's been underneath everything all
along, and I suppose that's why I haven't been able to bring myself to speak up. Let's get those drinks."

They made their serpentine way past the dancers in the floral-
bright café of the living room. Past that wall with all the graffiti
chalked up.

Rosemary loves Grove.

They waved to Hank Hartley who was still dancing with Sabina Clarke. They continued through some of the other café
rooms which were too clotted with guests. At the far rear of the
apartment the sidewalk café of the Hotel Stanhope (the master
bedroom) was virtually deserted. While Christine went into
the powder room he settled himself at one of the tables beneath
the too-immaculate awning, and gave the waiter the order.
He had scarcely lit his cigarette when he saw the rangy figure of
Judge Zachary Cunningham moving into the room. Grove contrived a hasty reach for the newspaper *Le Figaro*, but the former
judge was arrowing in on him.

"Alone, Grove?"

He said he'd just ordered a drink for Mrs. Stelward, who would be returning shortly.

"Good. I only want a minute or so. For now. I was talking with Rosemary before—" Judge Cunningham, who was legal counsel for the Inter-Borough Planning Association of New York, seated himself: he was a notably straight-backed man; his long grooved face was crowned with flat, center-parted silver hair.

The trouble with Cunningham was that he was a decent individual, and Grove could not put him off. "Yes, Rosie told me. She's on your side."

"She's on your side, too," said the Judge, not endearing himself to Grove or to his cause.

"As for me, Judge—" Grove began.

"I know what you're going to say," the man interposed. "You had six years with City Hall and you were not happy. I know. But you were too young then. And since that time—a lot of people, including the Mayor and Rockefeller—they've told me they think it's criminal for you to stay uncommitted to public life."

"You mean political life, don't you, Judge?"

"I'm serious."

"Is this your idea?"

"It started in the Mayor's council. They brought your name up."

"For what?" Grove regarded the elder man with a cynicism that had been born long ago.

"At the moment—for a new post we're talking about," said Cunningham. "Deputy Commissioner of Planning, Parks and Preservations. One of those all-inclusive jobs—"

"All-inclusive headaches."

Cunningham ignored this. "Naturally, Grove, so far as money is concerned, we can't compete."

"Maybe it's just as well, Judge."

"Don't glib me off, Grove. Your credits are too good. Your professional training, your real estate experience, your civic activities, and lately that help you've been giving Hoving, assembling parcels for his vest-pocket parks program. With credits like that, Grove—"

"Anyway," Grove said, "you know I like to work on the side. No fireworks. None of that. The kind of man you need is someone the public knows something about and who—"

"That might be true." Cunningham's gray eyes brightened rather slyly. "Except that ever since that Staten Island affair when you slugged one of New York's finest to protect Young American Motherhood, you are no longer unknown."

"She was only four months pregnant," said Grove.

"Don't quibble with me, Grove. I wouldn't be hounding you here, of all places, if I didn't have a lot of people counting on me to bring you in."

"I'm flattered," said Grove. "Deputy Commissioner of— What the hell is that again, Judge? Sounded a bit like the old official bacillus bullfosis."

"My dear friend," said the Judge, "you didn't for a moment think I'd waste your time, or my own, with this kind of job, did you? That is merely a necessary warm-up for something else. What we're getting at—those of us who are expert with the crystal ball—is the future."

"Future?"

"The Mayoralty." The Judge leaned back, folded his arms across his narrow chest.

"I see." Even Grove found himself silenced for an interval. "Yes."

"I see," Grove said again. The waiter appeared and placed the drinks on the table.

"I promised I'd lay this out for you," said Cunningham. "So that you'd know what some of us are up to. We'll talk about it later in the week." The Judge prepared to leave.

Grove detained him. He had lived with the tribute for a few moments, savored it. But then he said, "Judge, do you think anyone in his right mind would really want that job?"

"I know of one or two superior citizens who wanted it. And got it," said Judge Cunningham.

"Yes, I suppose."

"I told you, Grove, we're not asking you to make a commitment this soon. You have time on your side." Cunningham bent forward: a more solemn tone touched his voice. "Don't hand down a decision now. But promise me you'll think about it carefully. Will you promise me that?"

Grove heard himself say, "Yes. But—"

"I only want you to sleep on it for a few weeks," resumed the implacable Cunningham. "And there's something else you have to remember."

"What's that?" He was dismayed to find his ego beginning to prickle with response.

"You can't turn this down as easily as you might think. Because, Grove, you've got too much working for you: your public life—frankly—has been impressive, provocative and scrupulously honest," the Judge stated. "And of course your private life, thank God, is impeccable."

Grove saw Christine nearing the table. His movement, as he rose to hold her chair, might have shown a certain absence of grace.

14.   958 Fifth Avenue

The dinner party being given tonight by Mr. and Mrs. William Boggsen marks half a year of service for Lucile Sloane, who is Bobbsie-Ann's social secretary. Three days a week.

Duties? Oh, terrifically complex—handling the correspondence and writing the invitations and the bread and butters and what about the French lessons and hints on flower-arranging and which catering service or private chef and where to hire the right kind of bonded help and not just any florist but the proper one, or, if necessary, a flower consultant and where to rent the extra tables and chairs, the crystal or flatware and which markets for meat or fowl or fish and don't forget firmness, politeness or rudeness in putting down all those seekers for favors, money, testimonials and oh yes the hotel people and the new restaurant people and the new department store people and the new fur people and who to tip here in the apartment building and leave enough time to send out social intelligence to the press and reserve that table at Le Trianon or that time at Mr. Lorio's.

For these profound chores, Lucile Sloane is exceptionally equipped: she is thirty-two, attractive but not obtrusively so (complement but never compete with the woman of the house) ; she is rather bony but since she is also chic, her figure can be called svelte. Her clothes are not many but first-rate; fashionable but not faddish; she favors Bonwit Teller or Bergdorf Goodman. She has clear skin, short dark hair and her horn-rimmed glasses or circle sunglasses rest on the bridge of a refined nose that has the correct angle of Episcopal tilt.

Born in Mamaroneck, New York, resided in Europe and Manhattan, Lucile has been brought up in the genteel life. Until the death of her father. His demise, fortunately, did not come until she finished at Masters School, Dobbs Ferry, and at Briarcliff. He left a shocking pile of debts paid since by Lucile and her resourceful mother.

She has toiled for two prominent social-secretarial firms, quitting finally because she choked with boredom maneuvering and updating the endless lists of debutantes and extra men; she has also served a sentence with Winn Associates, Public Relations. But for the past two years she has chosen to farm out her talents to individuals. At present she has two other assignments besides the Boggsens.

As for the Boggsens: a nifty job. Yes. Or maybe not.

Might have been. But Lucile fears she has been having second thoughts lately.

She sniffs something malodorous in the near future.

Pity.

That's how it is sometimes.

Yet people envy her, don't they? This association with the rich or celebrated. Her path must be gilded. But Lucile knows better. Give your time and energy to making other people's social lives successful and what's left for yourself? Not even marriage. (She does have a friend, an escort, her lover, but she doesn't have enough time for him, and since he is a rather brilliant if rough-looking Jewish intellectual, he is naturally in terrific demand these days at all smart parties, so that her chances of keeping him faithful, or even in tow, are thin. Alas.)

Maybe she is cynical or unkind occasionally, but why not? It's little enough pleasure to indulge in when your personal existence is rather barren or your professional life somewhat disenchanting.

"Lucile—" It is Bobbsie-Ann Boggsen. Brought To You In Living Color. She has just come into the drawing room. "I hope you're not *trop fatiguée* to make the rounds." Mrs. Boggsen consults her diamond Valencort watch.

"No, not at all." Lucile smiles. Though it is already close to eight o'clock, she knows that Mrs. Boggsen is posing, waiting to hear her opinion of this newest adornment of her wardrobe. "It's perfectly beautiful," says Lucile. "And so perfect for the season."

Which it is: an understated Balenciaga gown with delicate tendrils of flowers espaliered on a sheath of palest lemon organdy. Her hair is darkly chestnut, burnished; swooping over one side is a braided torsade. By Mr. Lorio.

My, but this elegant dark sweep of conservative coiffure is an epoch away from the Bobbsie-Ann Boggsen who flaunted the great blond corona that catapulted her into the Farthest-Out Go Go Girl of the Wild and Woolly East. That amazing amalgam of Faith, Pop and Charity.

The metamorphosis has been remarkable. For part of which, credit Lucile Sloane who has properly guided her and properly saturated the hemisphere with the news that Mrs. Boggsen is now known to her intimates only as Bobbsie-Ann; to acquaintances as Ann, and to all communications media as Mrs. William Boggsen.

"Well," says Mrs. Boggsen, "let's go inspect the troops."

Code for hired help.

Oh well, it's touches like this that make the job bearable. The job, after all, has been a challenge of a kind for Lucile.

Unique. Different enough from the other assignments. Despite the drawbacks.

For Mrs. Boggsen, unlike some women who come to New York from the lube pits of Michigan or the oil holes of Texas, and who often require a mammoth task force as well as a bow from Dexter Knight to nudge them into "society"—Bobbsie-Ann Boggsen does not need this sort of campaign, for she is already well known. Her problem, technically, is not to enter, but to reenter; that is, to reestablish her celebrity in a new realm. One loosely defined as International. (Tonight's party is unquestionably being spearheaded by Comtesse Jacqueline de Rocheferron of Paris.)

Yet, for all this, something malodorous persists, some flaw mars this tableau. Lucile detects it. Lucile fears she will soon be taking her leave of 958 Fifth Avenue.

Even though, unquestionably, Mrs. Boggsen began her latest phase with notable success, beginning as she did by having Princess Firna Birenzia as her house guest last winter, having her as her guest of honor at that horse ball at the Park-Regent Hotel.

But something seems to have gone wrong since then.

That same high level has not been sustained. Not quite. Is Mrs. Boggsen aware of this? Does it reach her yet amidst her new life in this former apartment of Christine Stelward, this ménage properly French, properly Tony Ammondized?

Has Mrs. Boggsen had pause or perspective to suspect a fly in this Louis XV ointment?

Possibly not: look at her now. Bobbsie-Ann very bright and churning with chic and confidence as she glances around the drawing room, appraising professionally this area which is to be the setting for the after-dinner coffee and liqueurs.

"You know something, Lucile?" she is saying. "I feel like a five-star general about to go into battle."

Lucile must maintain or match Mrs. Boggsen's thyroid gaiety. Not always easy.

Face this: the job is simply not shaping up for Lucile; not forming, firming-up, into a top credit for her. Lucile must always be associated with people who show benefits, who plus-up from her assistance and Know-How. Lucile must witness sure success of her clients or employers. Remember, one failure, or even one semi-dud, and immediately your name becomes linked with it. And this, Lucile Sloane will not risk.

"*Nous allons!*" commands young Mrs. Boggsen as they start for the dining room, the first battle station. "Oh, I know, I know *absolument*, that it's going to be the greatest party, really kicksome!"

But Bobbsie-Ann wished her social secretary would get that funky face of hers brightened up. How dragsome it looked. Lucile could be like that at times. Her private life was probably out of joint.

Well, *tant pis!* How she loved to say it, a fling of the hair, an arrogant arch of the brow: tant peee! Too bad!

And on now to the final prepping, as Lucile called it. Bobbsie-Ann drew gaiety from the mere anticipation of this, her most stellar and staggering dinner-dance to date. Deliberately contrary to custom, she had not had the apartment especially decorated or festooned for the party, preferring instead to show off Tony Ammond's original design, the furniture and paintings. Many of tonight's guests had never been here before.

Now she and Lucile moved through the entrance foyer with its walls of toile, its marble-topped and carved console and the gold clock and the two paintings by Pissarro.

Into the long dining room: walls brocaded in ginger-colored silk, many small French Impressionist paintings and that one huge Monet—it was not one of his choice lily ponds, but the name *was* Monet, wasn't it? (A better investment than stocks, Tony Ammonds had insisted.) And wasn't it a little more art-some than, say, owning all those toilets and catsup bottles by Waldo Stryker? She and Billy got rid of them a year ago.

And look at the tables—round, five of them, each set for eight, with coral flowers and white tapers and organdy cloths of faintest pink. No primary colors except for the place cards which were in the form of flags of France, Italy, Luxembourg, Yugoslavia, Austria, Chile. And oh yes, America.

Bobbsie-Ann paused: it was a palpitating moment as she waited now, watching Mr. Lenoir, the chef and *maître de maison* (Lucile had engaged him three months in advance) as he gave the temporary staff of fourteen their final instructions, checking off his list in that brisk, haughty way of his. And then she and Lucile had their last-minute word with him whose fee was so formidable that even Billy Boggsen had balked and protested. Bobbsie-Ann adored this ritual of the pre-battle conference with Mr. Lenoir; he was such a haughty, moody man, a joy. He hadn't decided until three days ago exactly what the all-French menu would be; and then Lucile had had to rush in the orders to Wynne and Treanor's for the fish—*le turbotin à la régence avec sa garniture classique;* and to call to Shaffer's market for the pheasants—*les suprèmes de faison Rossini au foie gras de Strasbourg,* and there would be the truffles and the celery *braisés à la Chateaubriand.*

"Have we time for a small drink, Bobbsie-Ann?" William Boggsen had come into the dining room. He was ruddy-cheeked, and resplendent in his dinner clothes.

"Very small." She consulted her watch again.

"Lucile, join us?" Boggsen asked.

"I don't think so. But thank you," said Lucile. "I've got some paper work—" Party bills and the envelopes of cash for tips.

"And I want to get it out of the way now." She left to go to the rear of the apartment.

Bobbsie-Ann made her final survey of dining room, savoring again the conservative pink and white motifs of the five large round tables framed by the muted champagne tone of the walls which were so dramatically accented by the paintings, and gold candelabra.

Battle plan would soon be action: guests invited for 8 P.M; cocktails and hors d'oeuvres in the paneled library. At 9 P.M. dinner would be announced. (Mr. Lenoir would not permit more than an hour for the cocktail period.) Then coffee and liqueurs. A Lester Lanin group—Lucile had had to book them months ago—would arrive at 10:30 P.M. Dancing would commence.

"Well," said William Boggsen, "I take it we're about squared away?"

"Billy," said Bobbsie-Ann, "you couldn't be more right."

(And Rosiepooh, my *chère,* aren't you at the wrong party tonight?)

"I suppose," said William Boggsen after they'd had their hasty nips of Scotch in the library, "that Jacqueline will be late."

"She could be." But as they returned to the drawing room, Bobbsie-Ann, thinking about the Comtesse de Rocheferron, was possessed by a suddenly grim prospect: "You know what just occurred to me, Billy?"

"What?"

"I mean—what if Jacqueline happens not to like pheasant?" said Bobbsie-Ann. After all, she did not really know the Comtesse all that well. She'd met her last winter the night of the Race and Hunt Ball. She was a friend, or a friendly rival, of Princess Firna Birenzia's. (Ugh! How ughsome!) But she'd only seen Jacqueline twice since then, and when she'd invited her for tonight's dinner party last January, Jacqueline had been delighted to accept.

Delighted, the Comtesse had effused. *Ideal*, she'd said, since she would be leaving Acapulco late in March, returning to Paris and then coming back to New York this week, dinner at Bobbsie-Ann's, and the weekend at Newport, and then jetting back to Paris in time to take her two adopted children, by a former marriage, to Switzerland for the summer, so that she'd be free to join her husband in Venice, after which it would be Monte Carlo for Princess Grace's Red Cross gala and then to the family château near Blois.

"Don't worry about it," said William Boggsen, "I imagine all the French like pheasant." He lit his cigarette. "Though as far as I'm concerned, give me a simple thick cut of prime beef or—"

"You know, Billy, I do think you ought to make more of an effort with your French tonight," said Bobbsie-Ann, taking refuge from her anxiety in the view, the spectacle of her drawing room, nothing less than quietly, discreetly fabulous—the Aubusson rug and the *boiserie* of the walls tinted that subtle shade of linden green; and the four sofas, oval shaped with incurved arms, gilded wood: rare, flawless, mint-condition Louis XV, as were the many carved and curved chairs, and that divine *commode en tombeaux* decorated in marquetry. Veiling the high bank of Fifth Avenue windows were the lemon silk curtains. Almost the same tone as her gown.

"Why worry about my French, Bobbsie-Ann?" her husband was saying. "Everyone coming tonight speaks excellent English. Even the Americans."

"Well, Jacqueline, I know, prefers French," she reminded him.

"All the French prefer French," said William Boggsen.

"But I mean really, Billy, a few words, a phrase or two, just enough to show you aren't a total linguistic loss."

"What about my Spanish?" he said. "I thought we were going to get comfortable in Spanish. We're getting a line on that house in Acapulco now, but I don't want to go down there like just another joker arriving for a quick tan—"

"You're right," she said, "but tonight isn't next winter."

He said, "I think my trouble is that I hated that French professor I had in college, and now whenever I try to listen to those records Lucile got us, all I can hear is the voice of that arrogant son of a bitch—"

"The elevator," Bobbsie-Ann murmured, and after a swift, loving gaze at herself in the carved and gilded wall mirror, she advanced, a slim general sheathed in Balenciaga uniform, to the entrance foyer.

Without quite knowing how at first, Bobbsie-Ann's natural ebullience soon became undermined; it wasn't until more than half the guests had arrived, that she realized why some of the joy had slipped from her.

She recognized the reason then: she was greeting, observing each of her guests, not through her own vision, but through that of Jacqueline de Rocheferron's.

Yes: somehow imagined through the Comtesse's always cool, topaz eyes, Bobbsie-Ann saw her guests looming less and less desirable, less top-drawer or more second-rate.

Not all of them, of course.

There was the lively young Contessa Maria Brantogli in the Galitzine evening pajamas of orange and yellow silk; and there was that darkly virile young Chilean bachelor with his more elderly companion, Lady Sibyl Sykes; and there was that Austrian couple from the U.N. or the embassy—but he was a minor official.

In fact, now that she thought about it, there seemed to be quite a few other minor officials from foreign embassies or consulates: they always seemed to be available for any kind of dinner or reception. Lucile Sloane had pointed this out, but Bobbsie-Ann argued that they did contribute a funsome influence of the Continent.

Looking at them now, however, she couldn't help thinking of them as extras, spear carriers with foreign accents, colorful in a mob scene but strictly dragsome for the main drama.

Bobbsie-Ann did not delude herself: she knew that one name was the magnet; that the name of Jacqueline de Rocheferron had lured most of the others.

For example, she knew that Mrs. Joseph Jannus, the former Contessa (B-B) Fourchini, a really casual snob, would never have come tonight if there hadn't been the prospect of Jacqueline's presence.

As for her other buddies of this past winter—the Gillon Findleys were at Minni Ogden Valencort's party tonight. (As was Rosiepooh.) And the Marshall Joneses III had flown their plane from Virginia to New York to be house guests of the Jock Leggerts in East Hampton, who were having the Prince and Princess Boimand of Belgium for the weekend.

And to think Billy had paid fifty dollars a plate for the Findleys and the Joneses last December for that horsy charity ball, having them at the table along with Princess Firna Birenzia (ughh!).

But that's the kind of game it was, and it was worth it.

Or was it?

"Ann, darling—" The muted, warm voice of Dina Tyson Tetterley, age twenty-five. "How terribly cute of you to have us. You know us, we're such stick-at-homes that unless someone puts the invitation right under our nose, we'd never go anywhere except to St. Matthew's parish house and back, would we, Jimmy?"

" 'Fraid not," said James Allison Tetterley, age twenty-seven. They lived just down the street at 886 Fifth Avenue.

"Oh, of course," said Bobbsie-Ann to this most conservative addition to her newly conservative life—a desperate addition, since the Tetterleys could be very squaresome with their Episcopal Church gambit and all the charitable good works. But they did have one indisputable asset: their names. Dina was a Tyson, and like her husband's family, the Tetterleys, helped to write more than two centuries of American history and bank more than one century's wealth.

It had been Lucile who'd suggested Bobbsie-Ann invite them, feeling they might make for discreet balance on the social seesaw which would be overloaded with European gentry.

Bobbsie-Ann had resisted the idea and had only yielded when it looked as if her guest list might be shy the desired number.

The Tetterleys were only a year or two older than the Boggsens. Dina was very chatty, but she did *know* everyone. Her clothes were always flawless, perhaps too traditional, but Bobbsie-Ann was developing a quiet, new conviction about cardigans and pearls.

Too bad, the Tetterleys' being so dragsome when they got onto the Church. Yet, as Dexter Knight had pointed out once: "If it weren't for the younger members like the Tetterleys the Episcopal diocese of New York would lose not only its cachet but much of its cash."

Even Jacqueline de Rocheferron would not fail to respect them. Or their names. Even granting that Jacqueline was as snobsome as they came, she would surely sparkle when she met the Tetterleys. At least for five minutes.

The thing was to keep them off the Church. Bobbsie-Ann in

self-defense had already warned the Tetterleys that she hadn't been to church since she'd been knee-high to a pew. They took this gracefully; they did try to be funsome. But in Bobbsie-Ann's book, Dina Tetterley was filed under E for Emergency Use Only.

"Dina, everyone's in the library," said Bobbsie-Ann.

"Oh, *goody-goody*," said Dina, and looking around the drawing room, added, "Love this room, Ann. Love it. It's so right. Louis XV can swing if you do it right. When we were here last time there were too many people and I couldn't really appreciate it." She turned to her husband. "Makes our place look a bit shoddy, doesn't it, Jimmy?"

" 'Fraid so," said James Allison Tetterley, joining in his wife's little charade of modesty: the Tetterley duplex had been featured in the last issue of *Fig*.

"Mrs. Boggsen—" It was Lucile Sloane. "Telephone for you."

"Who is it?" Bobbsie-Ann asked as soon as the Tetterleys had sauntered off to the library.

"Jacqueline de Rocheferron."

"Oh?" Bobbsie-Ann quelled the thrust of her immediate fear. "I wonder if she's held up somewhere—"

"She didn't say," reported Lucile Sloane in that nasal, chic, funky tone which at times, like now, irritated Bobbsie-Ann.

Moving now to the east wing of the apartment to take the call, Bobbsie-Ann's breath came shallowly: the generalissimo's verve seemed to be waning.

When Lucile Sloane stepped out of the elevator and into the street lobby of the apartment building—it was shortly after eleven o'clock—she nearly collided with Dexter Knight, who was just arriving.

"Darling," said Knight, who shocked Lucile by his appearance: his always fleshy face seemed drawn, wasted, the vivid black eyes colorless as dust. "I've defected from the Valencorts' party to see what's being offered Chez Boggsen. How are you, Lucile?"

"Ready to drop," said Lucile.

"I must say the same. I've lost my dearest possession, as you know."

"Yes." She knew Knight trusted her; he often confided in her because she was known never to betray a confidence: discretion, in her kind of work, was the hallmark.

"Thank God for all the parties tonight," said Dexter Knight and removed his hat and his black dress coat.

"I was very sorry to hear David left," said Lucile.

"My dear"— Knight guided her away from the elevator attendant, and over to the Queen Anne settee which stood flanked by monumental plants against the smoke-mirrored wall—"what does one do when a thing like that happens? I'm lost. I was so dependent on him."

Lucile nodded. She accepted one of his cigarettes. She could see in the wall glass across the lobby the image of Knight and herself: like two forlorn passengers in a very elegant railroad station.

"I shall never recover from it," said Dexter Knight.

"Oh—"

"Never. Lucile, you must believe me, I've never lived through such a shattering time." Knight turned from her.

"I wish there was something I could do. But I know when something like this happens, no one is—"

"Darling—" he turned back to her. "Please forgive me. There's nothing more hideous than having to hear a— But at least I do feel you're more understanding than most souls." A restrained sigh. "The hideous part is I have to engage someone else now, anyone who is capable and loyal, but today where does one find that? I must get help soon though. Everything's piling up on me. If I could find someone loyal and capable and not merely out for the vulgar dollar and those obscene social security benefits—I must call an agency. But they produce such dreary uninspired numbers, don't they?" Then: "You don't by any chance happen to know anyone who might be suitable? I mean outside of yourself. I could never afford you, Lucile."

"I can't think of anyone offhand," she said. "But if I do, I'll call you. Oh yes, there is—there might be one possibility—"

"Oh?"

"There's this boy—not a boy, he must be twenty-four or so. I met him a few weeks ago at a party I was helping with." She paused. "Yes, he might be a definite possibility." She told Knight about the young man who had had some experience with a publishing firm and who was now secretary to an art dealer. "He might shape up into something. I think he must be capable, otherwise he wouldn't last with that gallery."

"Ah, yes. What's he like?" asked Dexter Knight.

"As I said," answered Lucile, "I imagine he must be quite capable. He's bound to have typing experience and he seemed intelligent—"

"Umm. Do you happen to remember, Lucile, anything else about him?"

"Oh." Lucile recognized the nature of the query.

"I mean what's he like?" Knight resumed. Then: "Is he, for example, fat, thin, light, dark—?"

"Lightish, I believe." But this of course had remote connection with the man's capabilities.

"Lightish? How light? Would you say mouse light? Or chestnut or corn-silk or on the sheer golden side?"

"I'm really not sure," Lucile said unkindly, for she recalled the young man accurately.

Knight pursed his lips. "Would you say he's average height or puny or one of those giant-sized numbers?"

"I'd say on the giant size, or near it." She noticed now that Dexter Knight was sitting more erectly in the settee. She could not resist adding, "But I'm not sure exactly if he's had short-hand experience or—"

"You say tall—lightish?"

"Yes."

"Would you characterize him," Knight persisted, "as exterior or interior decoration? By that, my dear, I mean would you say he's inclined to flabbiness or muscle?"

"Does it really matter, Dexter?"

"Oh, not really, but you understand, I am sensitive. I'm a terribly visual person, as you must know," he said, "and I function better, professionally speaking, if my eye is at least mildly, aesthetically stimulated."

"I see. In other words, Dexter"—Lucile's sympathy was running thin—"you don't want to look at his record, you just want to look."

"How incisive you can be, Lucile," said Knight. "But tell me, darling, where does one get a glimpse of this paragon?"

"He's with the Lievey Gallery on the second floor, Madison Avenue near 76th Street," said Lucile.

In a flick of a flash this man, who a few minutes before was stooped by sorrow and rendered bleak-eyed by a loss from which he would never recover, whipped out his gold pencil and gold-edged black leather notebook, and hastily, if not feverishly, was writing down the information. "His name—you didn't give me his name—"

"I only remember his first name," she said. "It's Derek."

"Derek." Knight printed it in his small, slanting style. Then he looked up at her: his saturnine face, the lackluster skin, seemed to have become luminescent as if some trapped inner light had been sprung and freed, its glow released. "Curious, isn't it? Starts with D."

"Yes."

"Sometimes I can be absurdly superstitious, but D—think of it. D. Derek." Knight abruptly stood up. "Lucile, I can't tell you how thankful I am for this suggestion. We must have a drink soon. Of course, I'll check into this. Who knows, perhaps this little meeting of ours might be—" He broke off, and suddenly as if he recognized the extent or potential of his quicksilver, feckless nature, he retrieved the visage of his inconsolable grief. "Lucile, my dear—regardless of what happens, I know you know how vulnerable all of us poor souls are, and that no matter what we might say or do, our most precious losses keep living inside us."

"Yes."

Presently Dexter Knight, as if with effort needing to drape himself with the cape of life's more prosaic concerns, said, "Well now. Tell me, how's Mrs. Boggsen's little gala upstairs? Have I missed much? How does Jacqueline de Rocheferron look, that divine porcelain-shelled Parisian clotheshorse. How I adore her. Narcissism incarnate, isn't she?"

"She isn't there. She isn't coming," Lucile said.

"Not there? But I thought she—"

"I don't know exactly what happened, Dexter. Except that she telephoned earlier. And Mrs. Boggsen simply told me she wouldn't be coming."

"Oh dear," Knight said. "I wonder what it could have been? I came expressly to give my poor famished eyes the banquet of merely contemplating the Comtesse. Now, I'm not even sure if I want to go up. Oh nonsense. Of course I will. I did promise Bobbsie-Ann, poor soul. Was she too miserable?"

"I really don't know, Dexter." Tactfully Lucile did not report that Bobbsie-Ann, after the telephone conversation with Jacqueline de Rocheferron, had vanished into her bathroom and had not emerged for half an hour, during which time William Boggsen, a resilient host, danced enthusiastically with the more pulchritudinous of the young European women.

Nor did Lucile mention what she'd heard B-B Jannus (the former Contessa Fourchini) saying to a compatriot: "You know, between us, I am agreeing with Firna—and yesterday when I saw Jacqueline she told me much the same thing—Bobbsie-Ann is charming, yes, but something has gone from her, she is not that same wonderful crazy American girl we all were amused and fascinated by. Now, I'm afraid, she's becoming just like too many other people we know. Such a pity—"

"Ah, well." Dexter Knight glanced toward the elevators. "Tell me, who else is there?"

"Oh—the usual."

"I see."

"And the Tetterleys," Lucile said. "But that was my doing, I'm afraid. I thought they'd help plus-up the local contingent."

"They will. They will. You mustn't downgrade them, Lucile," said Dexter Knight. "I adore Dina Tetterley and Jimmy. Why? Whenever I see them, it is like seeing the *ancien régime,* like being with old Helen Marmonier or Alfreda Peysen, but the Tetterleys are young, they are the continuum of youth, and it reassures me, reminds me that despite the mad, silly tempests and zephyrs of New York life—you know, all life in America has become a popularity contest—it's the young Tetterleys, among others, who will remain untouched. They will remain at the purest, highest level. You know, Lucile, no matter how much one shakes up society, the sediment always settles at the bottom, doesn't it? Good night, Lucile. And bless you, darling."

By 1:45 A.M. all guests, except the Tetterleys, had gone. At a time when successful parties are at their zenith, the Boggsens witnessed the nadir of theirs.

(Some of the guests had hastened on to discothèques— though not to Big D's, which was bankrupt and closed, while its once-pursued, popular *disquaire,* Roy Noonan, had jockeyed and danced himself into near oblivion, another victim of overexposure.)

As soon as the bronze elevator door slid shut in the foyer, William Boggsen, boozed and bright-eyed, turned to Bobbsie-Ann. "What happened?"

"Not now."

"Why didn't you fill me in?"

"How could I in the middle of a party?" But Bobbsie-Ann had performed remarkably before her guests, considering the vile and dragsome way Jacqueline de Rocheferron had scuttled her. "Listen, Billy, we've got the Tetterleys in the library and I can't go into this now—"

"Let them wait," a whiskey-fumed William Boggsen said. He laughed. "They're watching TV. It's a new program: the Late Late Church."

"Oh!" Bobbsie-Ann's eyes rolled heavenward.

"Alors," he said, going on then: *"Quelle est l'histoire avec* Jacqueline?"

"For God sakes, do we have to talk French!" Bobbsie-Ann protested.

"I thought you—"

"I detest it! You know that!" Bobbsie-Ann answered.

"What happened? Come on." His arm was around her twenty-two-inch waist as they moved into the vast paneled drawing room, made even more cavernous now by the conspicuous absence of people and the incriminating silence.

Bobbsie-Ann, not having enough stamina left to confront

the Tetterleys, sank onto one of her prized Louis XV sofas; she slumped there heedless of her gossamer Balenciaga sheath. "I didn't care—I mean, I cared, the bitchy way she canceled out but it was *how* she did it! All that hokey soap opera about having to fly right back to Europe, her little boy with a 103 fever and the doctors not knowing what it was—I mean, she hardly sees those children from one year to another—"

"Maybe it is serious, and maybe she—"

"Serious! *Merde!*" Bobbsie-Ann drew faint relief from the vulgarism. "I know what it was. She just decided there were other people she preferred to see—and I know *who*, too, for that matter. She took off for Newport tonight instead of tomorrow. She went on the yacht of her hostess's husband. They've got a big thing going."

"Really?"

"Yes. *She's* the one with the fever," said Bobbsie-Ann. "I mean I just know it's that. It's been all over town. And then she suddenly decided we didn't have enough of her buddies here tonight and why waste her lousy French chic on us! All this started with Firna. She's been putting the bitch's curse on me all over Acapulco. I know it."

William Boggsen took his wife's hand. Glazed but thoughtful, he said, "What did you tell her?"

"Well, at first I believed it. After all, a child that sick. I took it all straight and gave her our best wishes. That's when I said something about: well, if we didn't see her before then, we'd be seeing her in Acapulco next winter. I told her we'd just put down the deposit for that villa in Las Brisas—"

"Good."

"What do you think she said?" Bobbsie-Ann recounted and her indignation soared: "She said: 'Oh, I don't know, *chérie*, I think some of us will not be going back to Acapulco—' "

"What?" William Boggsen, who had that day dispatched to

the realty agent in Acapulco five thousand dollars, jolted forward in the sofa, a sober man.

"That's right. She said—guess what?—" Bobbsie-Ann continued, bitterly mimicking the Comtesse's French: " 'Some of us, *chérie*, are afraid of what is happening to Acapulco. There is too much *publicité*, too many stories and too many people from the cinema buying property there now. Some of us are afraid it will soon no longer be good. There's an island—very primitive, with no regular ship service, no air service—and some of us are looking into this—but Acapulco is now becoming too popular, ordinary. *Quelle domage*, eh, *ma petite* Bobbsie-Ahnn—' "

Sixty seconds passed. William Boggsen stood up. "Are we going to have a drink?"

"Yes."

"Come on. We'll discuss it later, soon as we shake the Tetterleys."

"Oh God—they're still here!" Bobbsie-Ann rose from the sofa. Then: "You go ahead, Billy. Tell them I'll be right in, and fix me a drink—"

She went very slowly to the east wing of the apartment to her bathroom. She attempted to retouch her makeup, but it became a stupid process: her eyes kept wetly blurring. This made her so furious she picked up one of Tony Ammonds' treasures, an exquisite eighteenth-century porcelain apothecary jar, and hurled it across the marble expanse of the bathroom: it struck the imported bidet and was crashed to bits.

Feeling a measure improved, Bobbsie-Ann went to the library to join the last-dog Tetterleys. The TV set, which was kept concealed in the splendid corner armoire, was turned off.

The level of everyone's highball glass was noticeably low, though the spirit of the Tetterleys seemed high—they seemed almost beatific, basking in this raffish late-hour bacchanal.

Billy Boggsen, silver tongs in hand, lifted the cubes out of the silver ice bucket and dropped them into a glass. "Here you are, Bobbsie-Ann."

She sipped the drink, not too slowly, but with all the craving of her now parched life.

"I was just saying to Billy"—Dina Tetterley crossed her legs, and her white gown, which showed a bizarre nakedness of shoulder, made the traditional and refined swishing sound of expensive silk—"I was just telling Billy how often the gang —I mean the Young Women's Auxiliary of St. Matthews—how often we say: oh if we only had someone like Ann Boggsen, our problems would be solved."

Reluctantly, politely, Bobbsie-Ann lowered her glass long enough to say: "Problems?"

"Oh, you've no idea." Dina Tetterley crinkled what *Fig Magazine* liked to call her Blue Willow eyes. "By problems I mean raising funds for St. Matthews' new East Side Center. Oh, it's much too complicated and I mustn't be"—she paused before uttering it—"dragsome."

No, you mustn't, thought Bobbsie-Ann, but it's too late.

"I mean," Dina seemed anxious to add, "when one thinks of all you've done for Heart and Kidney and Cancer—"

"She's had it, she's through. Believe me, Dina." Billy Boggsen attempted as helpfully as he could to get his wife safely out of range.

"Oh, I'm sure you've had it," Dina said, turning back to Bobbsie-Ann with that same sicksome sense of mission. "But I know you'll appreciate what we're up against. As a matter of fact, just two days ago, last Thursday noon, and Gidgie Vanderbilt—she's chairman of the Funds Committee—said what this gang here needs is another Bobbsie-Ann Boggsen—"

But Bobbsie-Ann had been badly singed by the flame of Jacqueline de Rocheferron's snobbery, and she was still too distressed to recognize immediately a tribute like this, even though it came from one of the most sacred of cows.

"Honey, make a small curtsy." It was Billy Boggsen who had to acknowledge the testimonial to his wife.

"What?" Bobbsie-Ann looked up; she shook her head then, as if jolting awake from a violent dream.

"Anyway"—Dina Tetterley stirred, and her body, which *Fig* described as supple as a fencer's foil, was arched forward in a graceful curve of adoration—"anyway—and I promise to snap on the Blab Off—on Thursday when all of us on the committee nipped over to The Colony for lunch and postmortems, Poopsie Rockefeller—she's vice-chairman—said: well why don't we simply clip a leaf from Mrs. Boggsen's book and run up a fund-raising ball but not just only for our own congregation?" Dina paused. "That's what I wanted to talk to you about, Bobbsie-Ann—I mean please don't think I'm trying to hook you into church—but I was thinking if we could have lunch. Whenever you can make it. We could meet at The Colony or Le Trianon, and maybe Gidgie and Poopsie could just sit in and listen—"

Valiantly, on Bobbsie-Ann's behalf, Bill Boggsen tried again. "I doubt it, Dina. My wife will never take on that scene again."

"Lunch?" Bobbsie-Ann said. A haze was beginning to rise between her and the charred ruins of the evening.

When the haze lifted, she saw, however dimly, the splendor of the Romanesque mass of St. Matthews rising on Park Avenue and 67th Street, its four bronze portals and its arch-tiered tower, and she saw that renowned Sunday morning procession and the ushers and Gidgie and Poopsie—

And—

"Well"—Bobbsie-Ann spoke with clear, unmuddied decision in this spontaneous moment of Epiphany—"well, we might do just that, Dina."

"Oh, *goody!*" cried Dina Tetterley and touched what *Fig Magazine* called her tassel of taffy hair.

And now William Boggsen, staring at his wife, had no alternative but to tug off his black tie and loosen the collar of his dress shirt.

"Tell me something, Dina." Bobbsie-Ann's voice came lilting through her spiritual illumination. "What time does the Sunday service start at St. Matthew's?"

Mid-June: a strenuous day for the auctioneer, Phillips Quentin, a gentleman favored by New York aficionados of the "great sell."

$29 million is the record of his sales this past auction season, which he divides between Manhattan and New York.

$29 million: Rembrandt, Gainsborough, Gauguin, Braque, Léger, Cézanne, Picasso—

Today: Waldo Stryker.

Today: there will be chaos.

Yes, the word is out. H. Hartley is unloading his celebrated collection of Pop Art.

Even the knowledgeable Phillips Quentin has been mildly surprised.

Quentin is a well-mannered man who can also be high-handed; he is charming but often patronizing. Tall and long-fingered, his sharp thin aquiline nose is poised like a knife above the chunky meat of his mouth. He is a candid blend of esthete (Bernard Berenson taught him much) and Philistine.

Today's sale—the first major auction of Pop Art—will commence that evening: he suspects it will be an agitating, if not outright tremulous event. Feelings are apt to run high. But will prices?

Now Phillips Quentin is standing at the noble window of his office on the third floor of the gallery. He is looking down on Madison Avenue, looking down to see the familiar Saturday parade: the New York couples, the bachelors, the men-less women, all dressed or costumed to the nines, as if they were models for a peripatetic mural. Up and down, between 57th and 89th streets, they go, nipping in and out of the countless art emporiums.

The official Saturday afternoon therapy of the cultured and the soi-disant cultured of the city. See a collector salivating for a picture, watch the bidders for the bargains: it is gambling time; for when a painter's works are dumped by a collector of Hartley's rank, most of the crowd runs scared; champions of the artist's work become mute as the prices plunge. (Yet sometimes a picture picked up cheaply enough at auction and held long enough might someday miraculously come to life again in Lazarus-like and profitable resurrection.)

This evening will bring a mass of people here. For the Madison Auction Gallery, like the Parke-Bernet, is a natural Saturday wayside stop for strollers and lookers. Here they can browse through the many large exhibition rooms which feature previews of antique furniture, jewelry, rugs and tapestries to be sold during the forthcoming week. Chiefly, however, one expects the serious collectors, the speculators, the dealers and the press.

Soon they will gather in the main auction room to begin their contest with the auctioneer. It is a time when Phillips Quentin, in his elegantly rumpled gray suit, with stickpin gleaming from his cravat, will ascend the paneled rosewood rostrum (flanked inelegantly by assistants and porters and office staff, electric adding machines, telephones, TV cameras and other equipment necessary in this cold and genteel game, and commence his special sorcery: for to Phillips Quentin no experience in life —be it eating a Lucullan dinner or bedding down a smasher of a young widow—can match the thrust of pleasure he feels as he "draws a sale").

Soon he will mount the rostrum, and after a grave smile directed impersonally at the audience filling the fan-shaped auction arena, he will utter his familiar invocation: "Good evening, ladies and gentlemen—"

The Grovenours, en route to the Madison Auction Gallery, paused beneath the white and gold canopy of 1027 Fifth Avenue to exchange greetings with Andrews, the old and palsied doorman. As soon as they started southward, Grove said, "I don't know why in hell we have to go to this bleeding auction."

"I told you before, Grove. We have to. I promised Hank Hartley." Rosemary, rinsed blond, and petite, stepped along briskly in her own creation of pink linen, darkly accented by her own designed mauve-tinted metal earrings and necklace, her death-white stockings and the stumpy pumps with the New England Puritan buckles by Roger Vivier of Paris. "I simply have to be there."

"It wouldn't be because you have to be there with all the rest of the mob, would it?" said Grove. "And I wouldn't think you'd want to run into Waldo Stryker."

"Oh, he won't be around. Hank said he wouldn't."

"Listen, Rosie, I am the very last one to hold a brief for Stryker, but the poor bastard is going to get clobbered on that auction block, and you know it. And so are we. That painting of his you paid two thousand dollars for is going to be worth exactly fifty cents after tonight."

"Can't you think of anything pleasant to say? Do you always have to be so black and gloomsey? How do you know we might not get *three* thousand for it? Anyway, I have to sell it. We need the space. How else can I hang that new Top painting?"

"I think you're losing me," said Grove. "What new Top painting? What is Top, if I may expose my gauche ignorance?"

"Oh, really, Grove. Everyone knows Pop is almost finished and Top is in," stated Rosemary.

"They do?"

"Hank Hartley has already bought up seven pictures by the new group, the best of the Top artists. It's a whole new dimension," Rosemary effused. "They're kind of like sculpture, they bulge or jut from the wall, they're topographical."

"I see," said Grove. "But that's still no excuse for taking your great chum Stryker's picture and throwing it on the pile tonight."

"We just have no room for it. And if Hank Hartley—"

"What you mean," broke in Grove, "is if Hartley dumps his Strykers, everybody else dumps theirs too, is that it?"

"Grove, why do you have to be like this?"

"You mean so square and un-with-it?"

"I just don't know what's happened to you, I truly don't," she declared, and touched her saucerlike sunglasses. "I mean, I just can't figure you out—and that business with the Judge, the way you behaved, and not even consulting me first—"

"City Hall is a nice place to visit," offered Grove rather desperately, "but I'm not sure if I want to work there."

"This is a fine time to take out your Funny Pills," she said. "The Judge was terribly upset, he was terribly gloomsey about it."

Gloomsey. But he could take cheer: in less than two hours, as soon as the auction was over, he'd be ringing that glorious bell on East 83rd Street. Less than two hours: Christine.

"I think it was a mistake, Grove."

"So is going to this auction," he said: two hours more, Christine.

"Oh, we won't be there long, and then you can go on to your meeting," she said. "And I can't be late for that opening of Campville."

"Umm," he murmured hastily. Campville was a new boutique for new mod fashions, and attending this champagne stunt would be Many of the Mods Who Mattered. "Even so," he said, "I don't know why we—"

"Don't change the subject, Grove," she peppered away at him. "I just can't forgive you for the way you acted, deliberately turning your back on an opportunity for us—you. After all, the Judge—"

"Umm." He'd ordered more plants (caladiums, fuchsias, sweet alyssum, English daisies, mirabilis) to supplement Christine's garden. He wondered if they would have been delivered this afternoon.

"Grove, are you listening?"

"I am." He supposed he was one of the most active horticulturist-adulterers in the city.

"Grove."

"What?" Reluctantly he swiveled his attention back to her.

"Will you please tell me what's wrong?" Rosemary demanded. "Sometimes I just don't know what's the matter with you."

He looked at her. "I know what's the matter with *you*, though. You're getting scratchy from all that newspaper coverage the Valencorts have been getting—" Undoubtedly the new golden pair of the year, one poetic journalist had rhapsodized.

"Oh, stop it," she protested too vociferously. "I'm not talking about Minni and Mitch, I'm talking about you. I mean, a man just doesn't ignore the possibility of the Mayoralty of

New York without even discussing it with his wife. You used to discuss everything with me. Honestly, Grove, I truly can't understand how you can be so indifferent to—"

He had cooled down Judge Cunningham's overture finally for many reasons, though, of course, the most obvious was known only to himself and Christine.

From Rosemary now, stubborn, petulant silence. But then her voice took on a more mellifluous tone. "Actually, Grove—it doesn't have to be all that final. The Judge told me you can still—"

"I can still what?"

Rosemary hesitated. "I invited him up for a drink Monday."

"You what?" Incredulously he stared at her. "I thought you were leaving on that trip Monday." Rosemary (and her pop costume jewelry) was scheduled to depart for a two-week publicity junket to department stores in the Midwest, Texas and California.

"I *am* leaving Monday," she said, "but I thought after all his interest in you and all the trouble he's gone to, we ought to have him over for a kind of nice chattsey drink."

Chattsey. "Is that what you thought?" He quelled his rising resentment. "I appreciate that. Thanks so much."

"Grove. You've got to do it."

"I do? Well, I don't seem to have much choice, do I? I'll give him some bourbon, but that's it. The rest is off my shoulders. For now."

Also off his shoulders, for the time being at least, was the real, the big burden. For she was leaving Monday, and he'd decided he wouldn't confront her in view of her imminent trip: only a brute would face his wife with news like that on the eve of her departure.

And he didn't want to be a brute, did he?

He'd wait until she came back two weeks from Monday.

He'd tackle it then: a real red-blooded American man is always ready to take on a tough assignment. He never shirks. Unless given an opening.

"But you will talk to him, you promise?" Rosemary's persistence was admirable.

They had turned into 81st Street, moving now past the town houses and apartment buildings: the buoyant summer evening was redolent with the dry scent of window-box geraniums and the lethal fumes of chrome chariots.

"Listen, Rosie, I am not interested in getting free rent at Gracie Mansion—"

"Honestly, Grove, I don't know what's come over you. Nothing I suggest, nothing I say or do, can please you." Rosemary's voice rose as her grievances multiplied. "I just can't figure you out anymore. You keep putting me down and you keep putting down my work. You complain when I have to go out and then the other night when I was home, perfectly cozy, you were suddenly all jumpy and jingly to take off." A pulsing pause: "And don't think I don't know why. I know why."

"Oh?" A man can live even though his heart ceases beating.

"Yes." Her eyes were bright and bitter upon him now. "I know what's been happening. You want no part of me and you haven't for a long time!"

But if that was the final sum of her knowledge (and it probably wasn't) Grove had his answer ready. "Look, Rosie, with your allergy to the conjugal bed, I wouldn't talk—"

"Grove, if you—" But she halted: she waved to someone—it was Daphne Bernlinsk who, in white leather motorcycle jacket and white Courrèges boots, had just snorted to the curb straddling her Honda—and Rosemary's reproachful eyes began to twinkle and signal, her body lost its rigid combativeness, seeming now to become supple, even eloquent—for people, whole colonies, cults, schools and coveys of people, S and S'ers and

Far-Outers, surely the most advanced social philosophers of our time, were converging on the Madison Auction Gallery, moving into the 81st Street entrance, many of them stirred to an almost sexual hunger to bid in a bargain or witness the toppling of yet another of their beloved icons.

Now Rosemary was transformed: a sixteen cylinder Go-Car, all the energies and neuroses which went into her projects, her work, her effacing of the abortive past, were again in full combustion as she hastened her pace, projecting her personality, driving fiercely to hold onto her rating in the popularity poll, the trophy that confirmed her position as one of the prize tigers running in the annual New York In-ism Sweepstakes.

"I've had enough of this bullfight," Grove murmured to Rosemary after he'd witnessed almost an hour of the auction. He pushed back his chair and made his way out of the main salesroom.

Out he went to mix in the traffic of the exhibition halls, through English Furniture, Chinese Artifacts, Flemish Tapestries. Next week's items on preview.

But there was no escaping the slaughter in the *corrida*, for each of these exhibition rooms had a prominently placed TV set on which, through the closed-circuit system, you could see and hear Mr. Phillips Quentin in pursuit of his quarry:

"—ITEM NUMBER 26: 'TOILET AND SINK.' 1960. WALDO STRYKER. EXHIBITED AT THE MUSEUM OF —MAY I COMMENCE AT A DECIDEDLY LOW THIRTY-FIVE HUNDRED DOLLARS?—COME NOW, LADIES AND GENTLEMEN—"

An hour to go. He'd be gone then, beyond the bull ring, ringing that glorious bell on East 83rd Street.

An hour. The painting Rosemary had up for sale—he consulted the handsomely printed catalogue—would be auctioned within the next hour.

"BUT LADIES AND GENTLEMEN, HOW CAN WE PERMIT THIS? THIS PICTURE 'TOILET AND SINK' IS CONSIDERED BY SCHOLARS OF POP ART—WHAT, SIR? SIXTEEN HUNDRED? FOR THIS REMARKABLE CANVAS? MAY I SUGGEST THAT FIVE THOUSAND DOLLARS WOULD BE MORE COMMENSURATE WITH ITS VALUE—VERY WELL THEN, AS A MERE STARTER, I HAVE SIXTEEN HUNDRED DOLLARS—"

Grove hastened on. A mistake. For he found himself directly in the path of Waldo Stryker who, despite Rosemary's prediction, had been unable to stay away. Stryker, bearded and in tight levis and shiny black vinyl shirt, looked up.

"Hello, Waldo." Out of embarrassment more for Rosemary than himself, Grove greeted the painter.

Another mistake.

Stryker had that narrow, smoldering gaze upon him.

"—'TOILET AND SINK'—SOLD! EIGHTEEN HUNDRED DOLLARS—"

As now Waldo Stryker looked away, and strode past Grove, muttering some dark imprecation.

Not long afterward, Grove heard:

"LADIES AND GENTLEMEN, I AM GOING TO CALL AN INTERMISSION OF FIFTEEN MINUTES SO THAT WE MAY STRETCH OUR LIMBS AND, I TRUST, OUR POCKETBOOKS—"

Olé.

Now: time to go. Beg off from bloodshed.

He'd duck into the reception room, telephone Christine to say he'd be getting there sooner: ah, these minor precautions, these very same furtive maneuvers he and Christine once attributed only to second-rate or shoddy people, but which each of them now had learned to use with such agility, having to shuttle as they did between an innocent wife, a dying father, and the watchful eye of church and state (and now, Judge Cunningham).

"Grove—" Rosemary found him in Flemish Tapestries. "You aren't leaving?"

"Not yet." He retreated. "But as an idea it is not without its temptations, is it?"

"Oh, isn't it awful, the way it's going?" said Rosemary.

He nodded. "I'm sure they'll be presenting Stryker's ear to the crowd. I saw him, incidentally."

"You saw Waldo?"

"Yes."

"Oh—" Rosemary glanced around: a steady platoon of people was passing by now, most of them going into the next hall to French Furniture. "What did he say, Grove?"

"He mumbled something," said Grove. "I don't know what it was but I'd guess he nailed me as a barbarian *cum laude*."

"Oh." Rosemary touched the mauve necklace which hung almost down to her navel. Then she said, "Have you seen Minni and Mitch? Or Daphne?"

"Not yet—" He paused. "But isn't that your friend Bobbsie-Ann over there?" It was. Yes. Bobbsie-Ann Boggsen was coming in from the reception room in the company of another young woman, recognizably S and S. "Dina Tetterley, isn't it?"

"*Shhh!*" Rosemary had already turned her back to the advancing pair.

But Bobbsie-Ann Boggsen, in the uniform of her white Chanel suit, did not, evidently, see them, going through the room with Mrs. Tetterley, moving with eager pace into French Furniture.

"Why do we have to stand here?" said Rosemary, a curiously harsh texture in her tone. Then: "I've been thinking, I haven't the heart to see Waldo now—why don't I try to round up the Valencorts? They can be my guests, come to the Campville opening with me, and you can get on to your meeting."

"Bully," said Grove.

"Or what you *tell* me is a meeting," Rosemary added in a voice constrained and unclear.

"Yes." Grove, who had prematurely peered out to the telephone booths in the adjacent reception room, abruptly turned. "What? What did you say?"

"Didn't you hear me?" Rosemary was watching him rather keenly, though almost at once her gaze was diverted. "Oh, there they are—Minni!" She beckoned to the young Valencorts— Minni, girlish in her boyish haircut, who came over now with Mitch, boyish in his girlish haircut.

Grove was thankful for the intrusion: it gave him a needed interval in which to ask himself if Rosemary's behavior and a few of her innuendos or statements tonight might not just possibly suggest that this rather uncertain paradise in which he'd been living was far more precarious than he'd ever imagined.

No: that was ridiculous, that was the reasoning of a man whose conscience was pressured by the swelling tumor of guilt.

Yet—she had made those statements or innuendos and she had acted oddly indeed, though never actually coming out into the open, showing her hand or asking him to show his.

Grove reached for his handkerchief: a patina of sweat had developed on his brow.

". . . don't you think so, Grove?" Minni Ogden Valencort was looking up at him, lithe in her splendid St. Laurent pantsuit.

"What?"

"This auction," Minni said. "Of all the super-duper disasters! People are saying the whole Pop Art movement is pooping out."

"Minni—" Mitchell Valencort, in flowered shirt and double-breasted blazer, nudged her. "This man here keeps insisting on a picture, we'd better get it over with."

At this juncture, the press photographer stepped forward and swiftly flashed the couple and hurried on.

"Look, Minni—" But Rosemary's forehead was puckered with sudden consternation as she glanced at the retreating figure of the photographer. "Minni, I was thinking, if you two want to leave, why don't you let me scoot you over to Campville, it's a new boutique and they're having a private party. But—"

"Oh, Campville!" Minni Ogden Valencort looked at her husband. "I'd almost forgotten. We were supposed to go, weren't we, Mitch?"

"I guess so," said Mitchell Valencort. "They sent those silly telegrams yesterday and today."

Rosemary was silent.

"Well," said Minni Ogden Valencort, "it's a little early, why don't we twitch around here for a while, and poop out at nine?"

The Valencorts had scarcely departed when Waldo Stryker, who was passing through the exhibition hall, changed his course and strode directly over to the Grovenours.

"Hey"—Stryker was at Rosemary's side—"I just wanted to say thanks, baby."

"Oh, Waldo—"

"Forget it, Rosiepooh." The painter's breath was pungent with bourbon.

Grove would have preferred to leave now, but of course he

couldn't abandon Rosemary to what was certainly an aggressively hostile Stryker.

"Waldo," she was saying to the painter, "I want you to understand something—"

"Why you joined the rest of the rats?" Stryker said.

"Waldo." Grove moved in. "If I may say this for Rosemary and—"

"Forget it, Grove. If your wife wants to run with the rat pack, why should anybody try to apologize for her?"

"In the first place, Waldo"—Grove, with no case, attempted the mediation—"this is almost totally Hank Hartley's collection. And if you want to raise hell about it, aren't you shaking your fists at the wrong people?"

Almost unwittingly Waldo Stryker squinted belligerently around the vast tapestry-hung room as if still hoping for the sight of Hartley: however, that renowned discoverer and collector of art was conveniently absent, being in Venice. Then Stryker said, "What's the difference? One rat smells like another to me."

"Listen, Waldo," Rosemary was saying and her hand was on his black vinyl sleeve. "Waldopooh, darling, please let me finish. What you don't know," she went on improvising, not without some shrewdness, "what you don't know is that I put my picture up just so that I might help raise the prices. There's a minimum price on my picture and if the auction doesn't bring it—"

Stryker was not impressed. "Forget it. You don't owe me anything." Venom seeped into his words. "After all, all I did was make you the most looked-at girl in New York. I made you, baby, in case you've forgotten. That's all I did. You were the end, the cube! But that wasn't enough for you, was it?" Stryker stirred, and walked off, only to halt, turn back: "I'll tell you one thing, baby—I think Bobbsie-Ann was right."

"What?" said Rosemary.

"Maybe if you'd been minding your own store, your husband wouldn't be out doing his shopping someplace else."

Grove, like a prizefighter who has trained for a defensive bout, anticipating his adversary's main strength, keeping his guard up high, prepared for a blow to the head, felt himself reeling, staggering back, stunned by the punch that had come low and treacherously from the wrong direction.

Waldo Stryker had gone. And when Grove could finally bring his gaze to Rosemary, when he saw the way she was regarding him, her upper teeth clamped tight over her lip, he opened his mouth but closed it almost immediately: he was still unable to summon a sound.

Not until Rosemary moved away from him, going now into the reception room, could he generate action. "Rosemary—" He reached her.

She kept moving. She passed through the high room and down the great curve of marble staircase to the circular street foyer.

"Rosie." His hand was hard on her wrist: he drew her back into the marble-cool hollow formed by the lofty stairway's arch.

"How did she know?" Rosemary said.

"What?" He was startled by the comparative irrelevance of her question.

"How did Bobbsie-Ann know?"

Even in Grove's benumbed state he surmised the answer to that: the source was Christine's own tenant, who did business with Tony Ammonds, who of course was a friend of Bobbsie-Ann, Waldo Stryker and undoubtedly of Dexter Knight and—

"How could she possibly have known?" Rosemary said again, as if that were her chief concern, leaving Grove even more confounded. She seemed to have skipped over his entire existence.

And how, Grove was now consumed to know, had Rosemary discovered it?

And how could she know and still go through the auction, conducting herself in public almost as if nothing had happened?

"Rosie—let's get out of here."

"What?"

"I said let's get out of here." When he saw the way she was looking at him, he said, "Rosie, I . . . I'm sorry. It's rotten it had to come this way, from somebody else—" Grove still found himself inarticulate, lacking in this crucial moment the glibness and authority of the practiced adulterer, libertine, wine, deceiver, procrastinator.

He was caught between two almost irreconcilable forces: he wanted to somehow protect her feelings; yet he had to find out how much she really knew, how she'd found it out and how long she'd known it.

"Rosie—"

No answer.

"I've been wanting to tell you, but the—"

His attempt was blocked: she swung away, her back to him, and she was crying, her shoulders were hunched as if she wanted to hide within herself.

It was a shattering sight. It was also the first of her reactions he could understand. He reached out and put his arm around her.

"—AND NOW ITEM NUMBER 44," came the crisp cadence from the nearest TV installation upstairs. "'SPARE TIRE.' 1962. WALDO STRYKER. WHAT AM I BID?"

But as soon as he'd touched her, she shook herself free.

"Rosie—" He tried again to put his arm around her, for he

could no longer bear the sound of her sobs, the convulsive movement of her shoulders.

He should not have succumbed to sentiment. But here he was buckling beneath the wet accusing fingers of her tears; he was unable to stand up to this spectacle of a woman, Rosemary, bent in dismay and weeping.

Oh, Rosie, Rosie, he wanted to communicate some tenderness. Instead, he said, "Rosie, we can't stay here like this, for God sakes, not here—"

He was startled, for she swung around, tearstained, and brushed past him and hurried into the nearby ladies' room.

Leaving him stranded there, in this public place, holding on to the ragged strands of his dignity and remorse. Alone with the woeful ways that had brought suffering to his wife.

"—ITEM NUMBER 45. 'CANS OF CAT FOOD.' 1962—"

Alone with his hateful lot, waiting for her.

Still she hadn't come out. How long had it been? Ten, fifteen minutes? A grim, agonizing prospect: should he get a woman attendant and send her into the ladies' room to see if anything— Oh, no, he was becoming unhinged.

But when abruptly the figure of Rosemary appeared, he could have kissed her now tear-dry face, for here she was, all in one piece. "Rosie—I was worried about you!"

A quivering instant. Tears, he feared, were surely on the brink again. He said, "Are you all right?"

Her answer was a glance, withering and yet somehow resigned.

"I have to talk to you," Grove said.

"What's the point?" Rosemary said hoarsely.

The question seemed to unsettle him.

"What's the point? What do you have to tell me?" Rosemary spoke more rapidly. "What I already know? I've known it for— for two weeks, except that I just wouldn't believe it, I knew it was true but I wouldn't believe it, I refused. You don't have to tell me anything—"

Two weeks.

Involuntarily Grove stepped back.

"—THIS PICTURE 'BATHTUB WITH CAN OF DRAINO'—"

"I kept hoping it would be over," Rosemary was saying. "It has to be, Grove. I know it will. It has to be."

How simple, ah, how simple it would have been if a few weeks or months ago he'd simply gone to her and said he wanted a separation, a divorce. And needing not to mention Christine or anyone else. No reason except that he had become an unhusbandly husband and needed to be free. How simple.

"It has to be over, Grove."

Grove had to say, "That's not what I have to talk to you about, Rosie."

"What is it?"

"It's—" Grove reached deeply, for the words seemed lodged, rusty and inaccessible on the sea-bottom of his conscience. "We've got to talk about a separation."

"Oh—" A trembling look.

But he'd spoken.

"Oh—you can't—we can't." She choked on it and coughed to clear her voice. "Grove—there just can't be any separation."

Her statement confounded him: if she knew about his miserable defection, how could she stand there dry-eyed and not want to push him out the door, hurling after him her curses?

"—ITEM 47—'DINER'S CLUB CREDIT CARD'—LADIES AND GENTLEMEN, THIS PICTURE IS HUGE, A MONUMENTAL STATEMENT FIT FOR MUSEUM WALLS OR A HIGH-CEILINGED DRAWING ROOM—"

But no, in spite of what she knew, she preferred the worst of him to separation. It added up not at all.

"Rosie"—he could ignore it no longer—"who, I mean how did you know?"

"Oh, what does that matter? No one needed to tell me. I wish they hadn't." She swallowed. "Maybe I'd never have believed it if Waldo hadn't said—" She shook her head: "That hideous Dexter Knight. He didn't tell me actually, he's too hideous for that. But he implied he'd heard it from—oh, they're all in that closed little clique—"

He was beset by more confusion. Rosemary, who in years past would flare into a frenzy of jealousy if another woman so much as lowered a lash in his direction, seemed in this crisis to be moved by totally different values.

"They're such a horrible little clique," she continued, "and I hate them all. But everyone knows what they are, how they can make up the worst malicious gossip, but thank heavens poor Judge Cunningham never goes near them—"

He stared at her uncomprehendingly.

"I mean—" her hand was touching his—"Grove, I've been all through this with myself, I've tried to keep it to myself, I've had to. We have to."

Numbly he stared at her.

"I know you," said Rosemary. "I mean, I know this will be over. I expect it to be. I know how it was with Corlis Wilbur. I know it'll be over. Otherwise how could I ever have spent all that time with the Judge? How else could I have asked him up next Monday? I wouldn't have dared. But if he sees for himself that you—"

"—ITEM NUMBER 48. 'ELIZABETH TAYLOR NOSE AND MOUTH'—"

"Grove—"

"What?" he croaked through the fog of his stupefaction.

"Grove, for now, you won't do anything—I mean rash or—"

"I'm not sure I know what you—"

"I mean," she said, "you promised you'd see Judge Cunningham, and you will, won't you? You don't have to make a decision, not even then. If you—if you accept that post as Deputy Commissioner—if you at least accept that. That's all he expects for now."

It was beginning to close in on him. Just as the person he knew as Rosemary was beginning to draw away from him: her nature had expanded, hadn't it? She was now capable of this kind of cool, this kind of resilience. Formidable Rosemary: all roads must lead to Gracie Mansion. She could evidently take the hardest, most dangerous detours if they brought her out in front of the Mayor's manse. Or the Albany State House. Or—there was no telling, was there?

Yes: she was the end, the cube, as Stryker had said, and that wasn't enough for her. She was a designer of jewelry, a fashion consultant. She was assuredly on her way. Yet—

"Rosie—"

"Yes?"

He couldn't say it: he couldn't call her: she had talked about him, about Corlis Wilbur, about herself, but the name Christine had been left unspoken: in its place was Judge Cunningham.

"Nothing," he said.

"What were you going to say?"

"Nothing."

"About my going away?"

"No."

"Because I think that's for the best, Grove. And when I get back I know this will be over." Rosemary made the statement out of what must have been her conviction that a man cannot finally resist the lure of power.

And when you begin to contemplate the Mayoralty, you do not leave your wife.

Unless you're insane.

Insanely, Grove said, "Rosie, you've got everything wrong. I'm sorry, Rosie—"

"Grove, all I ask for now is—" She stopped.

Passing on their way out, two middle-aged men of the S and S brigade were in earnest colloquy:

"You knew, didn't you," one of them was saying, "that Joe's lost his shoeshine concession at the St. Regis? He's had to move over to the Waldorf."

"No. I didn't know that."

"Yes. It's going to mean a whole new way of life for me, going to the Waldorf every morning instead of the St. Regis."

"—'TRAFFIC LIGHT'—"

"—FROM THE COLLECTION OF MR. AND MRS. B. B. GROVENOUR—"

For an instant Rosemary turned, listened, then abruptly faced Grove again. "Grove. Look at me."

He looked at her.

"Do I have your word? About Monday?"

"Yes," he said, but only to placate the stranger.

A bleak interval. Then in a rather arbitrary gesture, she glanced at her watch. It was as if she wanted or hoped to mark the end of the first stage of a difficult campaign.

"Grove—how do I look? I mean my eyes?" Before he could reply, she said she'd have to make up her face again. "I can't go to Campville looking like this." She hastened into the ladies' room once more.

The British incantation of the auctioneer reached him:

"—'TRAFFIC LIGHT' SOLD. THIRTEEN HUNDRED DOLLARS—"

Thirteen hundred. His loss. Stryker's loss. And Rosemary's. He wished it could have been measured only in dollars.

The auction must have been nearing its end, for more people were leaving, more footsteps sounding on the marble staircase.

"I don't care what you say," came the voice of a querulous and S'er passing through the foyer, "it's a disgrace for a club like the Union having dirty windows and those dusty frowzy drapes—"

As soon as Rosemary returned, he saw at once that all her armor had been latched and clicked back into place: she was ready, though perhaps not exuberantly so, to reenter the tournament. "Grove—I forgot about the Valencorts—I'd better go up and see if they—" She hesitated, not leaving yet: she was suggesting he go up with her.

He joined her, but as they turned to go upstairs he saw that the young Valencorts were on their way down—or rather trying to make their way down, for their progress seemed to be impeded by what looked like a mob of friends or disciples.

"Minni—" Rosemary tried to signal her.

But Minni Ogden Valencort could not possibly have seen her above the heads of the cloying gang around her and Mitch.

"Daphne," Rosemary called, "are you going to the—"

"What?" Daphne Bernlinsk, chic in white motorcycle couture, seemed preoccupied.

"Are we all going to the—" Rosemary began again.

"Oh—certainly, Rosemary." Daphne turned hastily to answer a question from Giles Folor, the Boston novelist. "Oh, no, Giles, we're headed for the Campville opening. Oh sure, you can borrow the Honda, I'll be walking over. With the Valencorts." She looked back, the omnivorous poodle-eyes moistly on the *golden pair of the year*. "Oh, Minni, I've decided something: why don't you and Mitch come to my place after Campville? I want my boss at *Hipman* to meet you. I'll get hold of the New Order gang and some old order champagne. Does that sound like your cuppa?"

"Whoops!" Minni Ogden Valencort cried out her endorsement. A party after a party. Could anything be closer to panacea?

"And don't let me forget," Daphne Bernlinsk said, "to show you my three new Top paintings—absolutely *no one's* seen them yet." With the possible exception of *Time, Vogue* and *Hipman*.

"Minni, darling. Mitch—" Hurrying, slithering past Rosemary, Peter "Sonny" Sahn, in suit of wine-striped denim, held his camera high: "Let's just get this one for dear old putrid *Fig!*" He took several more photographs of the Valencorts.

"Oh, hi, Rosemary," called Minni. "Where've you been?"

"Where?" But then Rosemary's smile became very bright: "In the Ladiesmaidies. Where else?"

"Grove—" Mitchell Valencort fingered back the jungle fronds of his hair. "Grove, you coming?"

"Oh, he has a meeting," said Rosemary. Then facing him: "Or have you?"

"Yes," Grove had to say.

The offhand question. Rosemary still holding out for him a last chance. She would be on her way Monday in successful, insatiable pursuit of her own image, still hopeful or convinced that Grove would in the end succumb to the Judge's influence, that he would never dare disturb the status matrimonius.

Ah, Rosie. Despite her right thinking, how wrong she could be.

For his direction was absolutely clear, though it was on more than one level: he would talk to his friend Cunningham on Monday, but he would not yield to the Judge's considerable persuasion.

Not then. That would have to be deferred. Alas? Yes: alas. Grove could not see beyond Christine. And even that had to wait on another man's death. But first Christine. Not until then would he allow himself a political commitment.

"Grove, that meeting—" Rosemary was saying. "Are you going to it?"

"Yes," said Grove.

He stepped back, as another wedge of people came through. More greetings, many kisses resounding, ricocheting in the marble foyer: the young Valencorts were almost suffocated by the pressing attentions of more converts.

And Rosemary, standing now on the periphery, looking rather perplexed, shaken, almost dazed at the indifference, the swiftness with which she was being eclipsed—it might have seemed swift, though in truth it must have been on its way subtly, soundly, for some time, this moment now coming only as a natural outburst or culmination.

Yet it was happening just as it had happened to her predecessor.

"Hey!" someone called.

It was Bobbsie-Ann on her way out, flanked by two other young women, Dina Tetterley and Gidgie Vanderbilt.

"Hi, Rosemary," said her former friend, looking over then at the ebullient golden pair, the newest new personalities of the year, turning back now, her canny stare dilated with comprehension. "Didn't see you at first." The smile Bobbsie-Ann offered was candidly triumphant, yet softened, perhaps involuntarily, by some impulse of sympathy.

Rosemary floundered again. Not long. There was a familiar gesture, that determined jab of her small chin, to power her over the immediate catastrophe, rise beyond it, as if she already must project herself to the world that would begin for her on Monday. So that now, partially recovered, she was able to match Bobbsie-Ann's smile, perhaps even transcend it. "Hi, Bobbsie-Ann. Going to Campville?"

"No. We're due at the Auxiliary—St. Matthew's." And Bobbsie-Ann marched off, leading the way for her two companions.

When Grove emerged, alone, he started for East 83rd Street: it was a short walk, though tonight it would take longer. A languishing twilight was drawing with it the last damson hues.